Delivering Santa

Mikael Carlson

WARRINGTON
PUBLISHING

DANBURY, CONNECTICUT

Delivering Santa
Copyright © 2024 Warrington Publishing

Printed in the United States of America
First Edition
ISBN: 978-1-944972-44-8 (paperback)
         978-1-944972-43-1 (ebook)
         978-1-944972-45-5 (hardcover)

Book cover designed by JD&J
Edited by Mike Waitz at Stick & Stones

Novels by Mikael Carlson:

– The Michael Bennit Series –
The iCandidate
The iCongressman
The iSpeaker
The iAmerican

– Tierra Campos Thrillers –
Justifiable Deceit
Devious Measures
Vital Targets
Revealed Secrets
Decisive Endgame

– Watchtower Thrillers –
The Eyes of Others
The Eyes of Innocents
The Eyes of Victims
The Eyes of Addicts

– America, Inc. Saga–
The Black Swan Event
Bounded Rationality
Boiling the Ocean

– The Dancing Trilogy –
The Dancing Life

– The Santa Trilogy –
Banning Santa
Delivering Santa

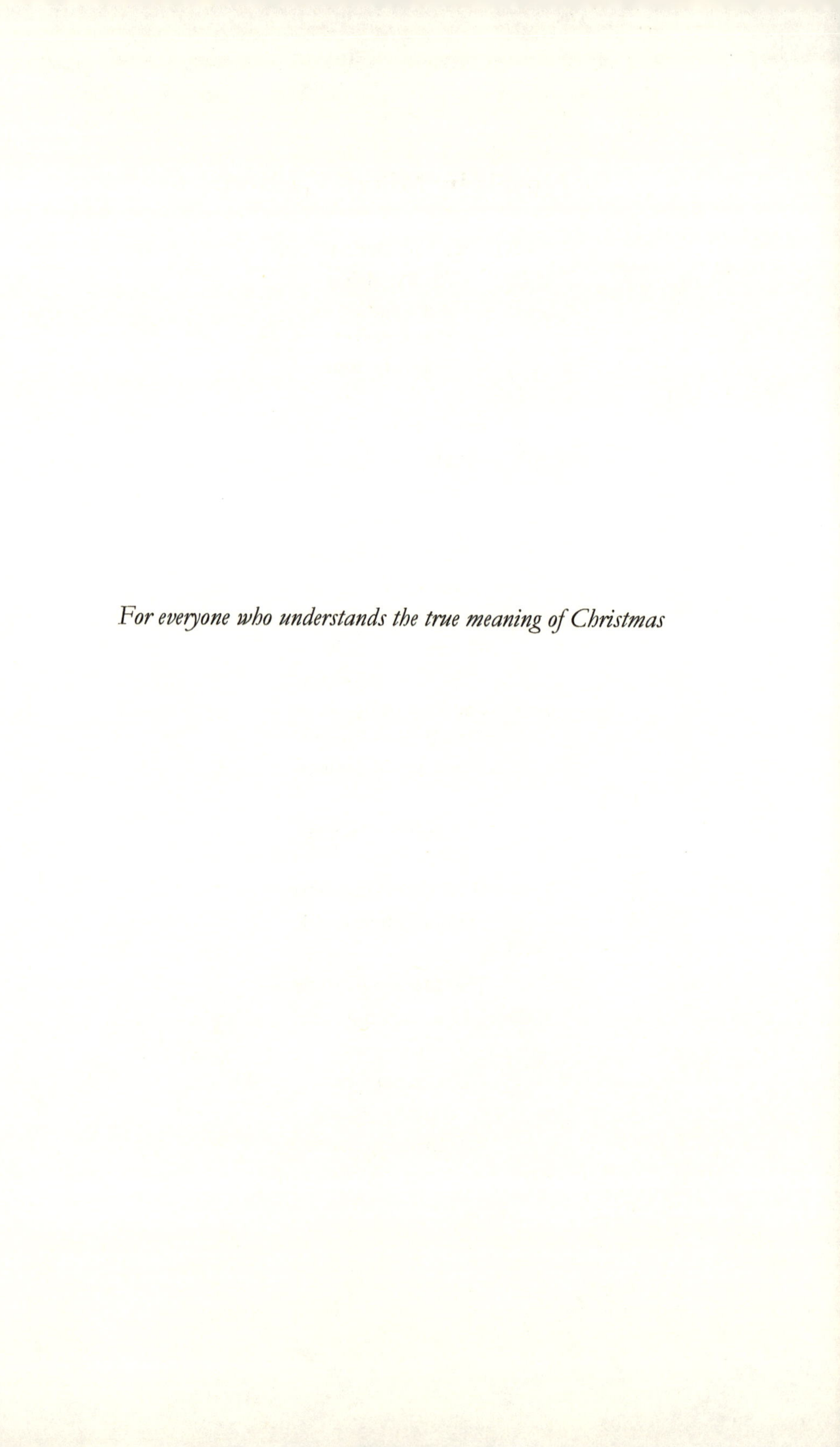

For everyone who understands the true meaning of Christmas

Chapter One

SVP MALCOLM CHAPMAN

The blinds close, the lights dim, and the laptop's screen is simulcast to the huge digital display at the front of the room. Malcolm steps aside and presses play on the small remote control he's holding in his right hand. The video of a boy in a hospital bed with his parents and sister at his side plays on the screen. It's not exactly the start of a feel-good Christmas story.

A woman steps into frame near the foot of the boy's bed. The chyron reads, "Juanita Pérez," and has the St. Louis's Channel 5 News logo on the opposite end. She's wearing a dour look on her face, using her body language to set up the story.

"While many people are out Christmas shopping and enjoying the holiday festivities, the same cannot be said for Antonne Tucker. His twin sister Alaya and his parents, Marvin and Nori, can only watch as the eight-year-old is now confined to a hospital bed after a minor fall on the playground that almost killed him."

The video changes to show B-roll footage of a playground before cutting to an ambulance pulling up to the emergency room of the hospital. It's an effective way to set up the story the reporter wants to tell in her voiceover.

"After Antonne cut his leg open, he was taken to the school nurse for a bandage. It didn't appear to be a serious injury, but after nearly two hours, the bleeding hadn't stopped. School officials called the paramedics, and Antonne was rushed here to the Gateway Children's Wellness Center. Doctors have diagnosed him with a rare condition called hemophilia B, ironically called the Christmas Disease.

"It's a rare, lifelong bleeding disorder caused by a genetic defect that results in insufficient production of a liver protein that helps the blood to clot. People with the condition are particularly vulnerable to unstoppable bleeding in muscles and internal organs.

"Patients diagnosed with the disease require frequent and costly transfusions of the factor IX protein to survive, but there is a promising yet expensive alternative that could help Antonne lead a long, healthy life. The pharmaceutical company Heilung has developed Hemoexgen, a therapy that would drastically reduce or even eliminate the need for factor IX protein transfusions.

"But at the cost of three and a half million dollars for one dose, the family isn't optimistic they'll ever come close to affording it. Marvin's health insurance carrier has already refused to cover the cost, so the family has established a PleaseHelpMe fundraising page to help pay for the treatment. Even at Christmas, they aren't optimistic they will reach their lofty goal. It's a sad situation for the Tucker family, but you may be surprised what Antonne said he wanted for Christmas."

The voiceover ends, and the report cuts to an earlier interview where Juanita is sitting beside Antonne's bed while his family looks on. The kid looks miserable. It's understandable – what eight-year-old would want to be chained to a bed, especially this time of year?

"What do you want from Santa Claus for Christmas this year?" Juanita asks him.

"I want him to come here and meet my sister," Antonne says in a sweet, innocent voice. "I want her to meet Santa Claus."

"You want her to meet Santa Claus? Why?"

"Because she doesn't believe in him anymore. He came to Washington last year. I want him to come see her so she knows he's real."

"Maybe a little holiday magic can help Alayah believe again while her brother fights for his life to beat the Christmas Disease," the reporter says, walking back into the camera's view. "For STL News 5, I'm Juanita Pérez—"

The video clip pauses, and the blinds in the conference room open. The executives sitting around the table don't look impressed or the least bit concerned about what they just saw. They don't understand the storm that is heading in their direction. The VP of North American marketing sees it all too clearly.

"Malcolm, why am I watching a local news report out of some middling American city?"

St. Louis may only be half the size of Frankfurt, but that isn't the reason they are watching this news report. The CEO doesn't understand modern media because he doesn't want or need to. Klaus Eberhardt is an old-school, hard-boiled German businessman. The family who owns this company brought him in fifteen years ago to take Heilung Pharma to the next level. Eberhardt's take-no-prisoners approach has made the company a household name and industry juggernaut. He's never had a need to adapt to changing times.

"Because it's no longer *just* a local news report. Shorter clips of this have become a viral sensation that's racking up millions of views all over social media."

"Along with cat videos and college girls complaining about their last date. Tell me why I'm listening to a sick child ask for Santa to meet his sister?"

"Because I think we should help."

"Well, if you think we should help, let me pick up the phone and call Santa myself."

Snickers at the CEO's sarcasm replace grumbles from the men and women in the room. Malcolm isn't surprised. He's the newest of the executives here and hasn't had the chance to prove himself. Six months may be a long time, but proving you belong at the big table in the headquarters of a massive multi-billion-dollar pharmaceutical company takes much longer.

"Santa visiting a sick child isn't the problem. It's what happens with the story before that. As this video continues to circle the globe, the conversation will eventually turn to the price tag we put on Hemoexgen. People will begin to howl at a price they think is outrageous, and we'll be made to look like the Grinch who stole young Antonne's Christmas."

"How so?" the CEO asks, leaning back in his chair.

"This story is meant to pull on heartstrings. The reporter did a masterful job portraying it that way. It will cause people to think we should give him the treatment at no cost."

"Wouldn't that be great!" Eberhardt exclaims, stretching his arms out to his sides for effect. He brings them in and wags a finger at the people seated at the table. "In fact, I think we should give all our ground-breaking drugs away for free. It doesn't matter that we've spent hundreds of millions of dollars and countless years getting regulatory approvals for them. We'd be doing our part for society. Who cares if we're bankrupt in six months?"

"I wasn't suggesting that—"

"People are under the mistaken impression that we run a charity here," the CEO continues. "They don't realize how much drug development costs. If we give it away, that's less money available for researching the next breakthrough drug. Or am I wrong, Malcolm?"

"Sir, you know that, and I know that, and everyone in this room knows that. Try explaining it to the American public at Christmas. Or the world, for that matter."

The smile disappears from Klaus Eberhardt's face as every pair of eyes in the room shifts to him. He remains locked on his vice president of communications, his face frozen and emotionless.

"Give me the room."

All the executives quickly file out, including the chief marketing officer, Franz Brunner. Malcolm isn't among them. It doesn't take a genius to figure out that when the big boss asked for the room, it was for a private conversation with one of his VPs. Malcolm remains standing in the front of the conference room as the CEO stands to look out the floor-to-ceiling window.

"Do you know why I brought you here from the United States? It's because I recognize your potential. Everyone you worked with in America spoke very highly of you. That's the kind of talent I want working here."

"Thank you, sir."

"Don't thank me yet. I demand a lot from my executives. It takes a lot to reach the inner circle here in Frankfurt and even more to keep the job. Just because you're considered an up-and-coming corporate leader doesn't mean you are one. Relocation to headquarters doesn't guarantee the promotion you covet. Do you understand?"

"Yes, sir, I do."

"Then it's time for you to begin proving you belong here. Your instructions are simple – make this story go away, and do it without giving that kid the drug."

"Uh…" Malcolm says, looking like he got hit with a brick. "How am I supposed to do that?"

"That's what I'm paying you to figure out. Solving complex problems is a part of the job. If you want to join the executive ranks here, you'll solve this one for me. You're an expert in marketing, and I'm counting on you. Don't let me down."

Eberhardt places a reassuring hand on Malcolm's shoulder and nods before leaving the room. It's just another example of modern corporate leadership – give an underling an impossible task and demand results with no guidance as to how to accomplish it. Malcolm tried to be proactive, and in doing so, just made this his problem.

And that isn't the biggest one. Malcolm needs to go home and explain this to his wife. His marriage is already feeling the strain after relocating to Germany. The transition has been tough on them, but the demands of his new headquarters job allow for precious little family time. His seven-year-old son Braylen is feeling the effects, and his wife Janelle is growing more vocal about his constant absence. She's been teetering on the edge of a meltdown since he missed Thanksgiving dinner for a series of staff meetings. News of this assignment at Christmas is likely to send her into one.

Chapter Two

COMMUNICATIONS DIRECTOR
MACKENZIE WALSH

MacKenzie enters the West Wing foyer and is greeted by the Marine standing at his post. She looks around at the garland, white twinkle lights, gold ornaments, and the gorgeous trees that adorn the room. It's a lot of effort to decorate like this for one month. She thinks it's pretty, but Christmas hasn't been her thing for a while now. Even if it was, it's hard to argue that the first lady didn't go overboard with this year's White House holiday décor.

As the president's communications director, it fell to MacKenzie to help coordinate the Christmas messaging with the first lady's staff. That's how she knows that volunteers from across the country helped decorate the White House for the season in anticipation of over a hundred thousand visitors lining up to see their work. And it was a lot of work.

This year's decorations include fifteen thousand feet of ribbon, forty-five thousand ornaments, twenty thousand bells, and a small forest of one hundred ten Christmas trees scattered around the White House complex.

The kitchen staff created their annual gingerbread White House using fifty sheets of sugar cookie dough, forty sheets of gingerbread dough, forty pounds of chocolate, and fifty pounds of royal icing. There are more than one hundred fifty thousand lights on the trees, garlands, wreaths, and displays in the White House. MacKenzie is thankful she isn't paying the utility bill even if her tax dollars are.

After arriving at her West Wing office, she drops her purse on the chair and sheds her coat. Congress is still in session, but not much will happen between now and recess. The holiday messaging is done. It's the time of year she can kick back and relax until the engine of government fires back up in the new year. At least, that's the hope.

"Mac?" Elaine asks, poking her head into the office. "The boss wants to see you before the morning gaggle."

"I'll be right there."

MacKenzie takes a deep breath, wondering what's going on. The White House chief of staff wouldn't have sent his administrative assistant to fetch her unless it was important. The president likes to meet with the senior staff for five minutes before he starts his intelligence briefings. The informal meeting is colloquially called the "gaggle," and that's usually where high-priority tasks for the day are doled out. There's only one way to find out what this is about.

Unlike on the television show *The West Wing*, the White House chief of staff's office isn't situated adjacent to the Oval Office. The set designers for that show took a great number of liberties with the layout for production reasons. In real life, the chief of staff's office is on the opposite side of the wing from the president's and about as far away from the communications office as you can get.

MacKenzie reaches the corridor and makes her way past the Oval Office and Roosevelt Room. She passes the advisors' offices and dining room before entering the chief of staff's reception area, where Elaine is already seated.

"You can go right in."

"Good morning," Marco Ramirez says from his desk after she opens the door and begins to close it behind her.

Marco has been the president's best friend since college and has worked with him since he began his political career in the House of Representatives. When he was elected, the one position that nobody had to speculate about filling was White House chief of staff. Marco has been training for this position for years.

"Good morning. Elaine said you wanted to see me. What's up?"

MacKenzie joined the campaign staff early. Marco had a list of people he wanted in the months leading up to the first primaries and caucuses, and she was near the top. After graduating from GWU, she worked for several successful senators and governors before entering the national scene. It was a big jump and corresponded with an even bigger life change. Now, she's an integral part of the senior staff, and even though Marco is her boss, there's no need for any formality in private. They all play for the same team.

"Did you see the video from St. Louis?"

"The sick kid who wants Santa to visit his sister to prove to her that he's real? Yeah, I saw it. It's been tough to miss."

"It's a hell of a human interest story."

"Santa isn't *real*, Marco."

He smirks, and MacKenzie already knows where this conversation is heading. "Tell that to the people watching last year's hearing. Or did you forget?"

How could she forget? Not only was his testimony before the congressional subcommittee magical, but the after-party lasted four days. It's the merriest she has ever seen this country, and the media obsession only grew when they couldn't find flight or customs records of Santa entering or leaving the country. The conspiracy theories born from that news have eclipsed the moon landing hoax and second shooter on the grassy knoll in popularity.

"I once watched a magician saw a woman in half on stage. It was amazing. I'm also pretty sure she lived."

Marco nods, conceding the point. "You think it was all smoke and mirrors?"

"I don't believe he is *really* Santa Claus if that's what you're asking."

"Do you think Alaya Tucker would?" Marco asks, leaning over his desk.

"You can't be serious about this."

"The American people are making me get serious about it. The family started a PleaseHelpMe fundraiser. Do you want to guess what it's up to in the last twenty hours after that report aired?"

"A lot, I'm sure."

"Over three hundred thousand and climbing."

"Then maybe Antonne will get the money he needs for the treatment in the end."

MacKenzie is growing increasingly nervous. It's a private matter and not something that the federal government should be getting involved in. Tell that to Marco and, by extension, the president.

"I hope so, too, but that wasn't young Antonne's Christmas wish. I was thinking, wouldn't it be great if we could end the year by delivering Santa to his sister for him?"

This is how every one of her nightmares starts. "Marco, this is a feel-good story, but it doesn't have legs. It will be gone from the news cycle by the time the eggnog is."

"I agree. That's more reason to capitalize on it now."

"If we take this on and *can't* deliver Santa, we'll look like idiots."

"Ah. Did you get this from your crystal ball?"

MacKenzie frowns. Just because she can see the consequences of things doesn't mean she knows the future, regardless of what the staff sometimes thinks. She has always maintained a simple mantra – if you are going to run through a minefield, do it for water to survive, not to buy a third car you don't need.

"No, from my fifteen years of doing this for a living."

"And I became the president's chief of staff because I'm an affirmative action project," he sarcastically counters. "If we deliver Santa, it's worth a five-point bump in the polls. That's a great way to start off the next Congress."

"Fine. Who do you want me to send to Finland?"

"Funny you should ask," Marco says, steepling his hands and grinning.

"Wait. Me? Are you kidding? It's almost Christmas!"

Marco stops and looks around his decorated office. "I hadn't noticed."

"You know what I mean."

"I also know that it's a holiday that you don't care much about. Sherlock Holmes couldn't find your Christmas spirit. You don't decorate, don't carol, don't like holiday parties, and you have no family to tell you that you're a Grinch. So, there's no reason for you not to go."

"Except that I have no Christmas spirit, and you're sending me to the North Pole to visit friggin' Santa Claus!"

"His village is on the Arctic Circle, not at the North Pole," the chief of staff corrects.

"Whatever."

"Give it a chance, Mac. Maybe Santa will have the same effect on you as he did Camilla Guzman."

The representative from California was nicknamed "Guzman the Grinch" for her antics of bringing legislation to ban public displays of Santa Claus to her subcommittee.

Americans tuned in, mainly because, for the first time in recent memory, it wasn't a political battle between the left and right. It was a showdown between people who love Christmas and people who were indifferent to it. It made for great television.

"Her transformation into a Christmas lover was political spin for losing on that ridiculous bill," MacKenzie counters.

Marco raises an eyebrow. "Was it?"

After Santa Claus testified, she had a serious change of heart. Skeptics, including MacKenzie, chalked it up as a brilliant way to save face. Others believe that he had a significant impact on her during his testimony, yielding a fundamental change of heart. Whatever the reason, she won her reelection bid last November in a walk.

MacKenzie shakes her head vehemently. "I'm not the right person for this assignment, and you know it."

"You're the White House communications director, Mac. I'm sure you can handle traveling to Scandinavia and asking Santa for a favor. You craft messages for a living, for crying out loud."

"Exactly. That's what I should be doing here, along with running my staff."

"Really? That's what you're going with as a defense? It's three weeks until Christmas. The lame-duck session on the Hill ends in a few days, and nothing is going to happen anyway until the next Congress is sworn in. I think we can manage for a few days without you."

"Marco—"

"Book a flight to Finland. Ask Santa Claus to make a sick child's Christmas wish come true by paying a visit to him and his sister in St. Louis. That's what the president wants."

"And if he says no?" MacKenzie asks, rising from her chair, opening the door, and stopping.

The chief of staff smiles. "Tell him it's *your* Christmas wish."

Chapter Three

STOWE BESSETTE

Stowe stares blankly at her computer screen. She isn't looking at a draft of pending legislation or policy measure that Congresswoman Pratt is looking to introduce on the House floor. That would be too productive for December in the nation's capital. It's an online shopping site because she still hasn't found gifts for Nana and PopPop.

Work on Capitol Hill has ground to a halt. Congress is in a lame-duck session, meaning this is the period when elected leaders continue to meet following the November election but before the newly elected legislators take office. Because bitter outgoing members lack the motivation to vote on significant legislation before leaving office, it's a period of significantly reduced productivity. That may be an understatement. Except under special circumstances, absolutely nothing happens.

Normally, she would be excited about using the time to find the perfect gift for her grandparents. In fact, in most years, she would already have her Christmas shopping done. Not this year. If she could close her eyes and wake up in the new year, she would. It's been like that since the summer.

"Hey!" Mandy exclaims, rushing over to Stowe's desk and breaking her uninspired gaze at the monitor. "A bunch of us are heading out for some drinks. You wanna come?"

"Nah, I'm not really up for it."

She folds her arms across her chest and taps her foot. "Stowe, it's Christmas."

"I know what the calendar says."

"Then you know that you're two months behind in singing Christmas carols and only at about a third of your usual consumption of hot cocoa."

Stowe doesn't respond. The observation doesn't require a response. This isn't a year for caroling or hot chocolate. The holidays are a time for merriment, and she doesn't feel very merry.

Mandy sits on the corner of her desk as she's prone to do. "Does your epic mopiness have anything to do with what you were doing around this time last year?"

"I haven't put much thought into it," Stowe says, plastering a fake smile on her face.

"You're a horrible liar."

"I'm fine, Mandy. Go enjoy your night out."

Her roommate looks like she wants to argue but decides against it. They made a pact long ago not to wade too deep into each other's business. Mandy crosses that line far more than Stowe but likely doesn't want to push her luck. Not this year. Stowe knows that her friend can sense that she's hurting, and she's right, not that she'll ever admit it.

"Okay, I'll see you at home."

After five minutes, the office clears out. Stowe leans back and raises her eyes to the ceiling. She stares at it for a while, not hearing or noticing the congresswoman creep over and stand beside her desk.

"You're not fine."

Stowe immediately stands, startled. "Congresswoman. I'm sorry, I…can I help you with something?"

"Yeah, you can admit that it's unhealthy to mope around the office instead of going out with the rest of the staff. Stowe, you should enjoy the holiday season before we head back to Vermont."

"I'm fine, Congresswoman."

"I heard you say that to Amanda. She didn't believe it either. Take a seat."

She does as instructed. This isn't a conversation Stowe wants to have with her boss, but Angela has always been hands-on when it comes to her staff. The office is professional, but she's the type of person who takes an active interest in the well-being of the people who work for her. Sometimes, it can even be too intrusive.

"I like you, Stowe. You have a good head on your shoulders, and you're a worker. You are also the most Christmas-loving staffer in this office. At least until this year. That's how I know that you're anything but 'fine.'"

"I…I'm just not in a festive mood this year. I don't know why," Stowe says, lowering her eyes.

"Yeah, I'm sure it has absolutely nothing to do with Wyatt Huffman," the congresswoman deadpans.

"It doesn't."

"Mmhmm. Classic denial. It must be a letdown."

Stowe feels herself getting angry and fights to keep her tone even. "Wyatt and I were never going to work. Our relationship…we don't believe the same things."

"I wasn't talking about your relationship with Wyatt, but since you went there, I have a confession to make. Did you know that John Knutson and I were good friends even before the subcommittee hearing to ban Santa Claus?"

Stowe is surprised at that revelation but doesn't say anything. In this political era, consorting with a member of the opposite party is considered treasonous. Things have gotten that bad in politics. The people on the other side of the aisle are the enemy and should be treated as such. That's what made her working with Wyatt so awkward in the beginning. It's what made their relationship even more so.

"It's true," the congresswoman continues. "We didn't advertise our friendship because we work in a hyperpartisan Congress that legislates in a divided country. He's supposed to be the enemy, and we were expected to treat each other as such."

"I didn't know you were friends. How do you guys not fight like cats and dogs?"

Angela laughs. "Sometimes we do. Politically, we don't agree on much. But he's a good man. Even our spouses get along well. Politics doesn't define who we are, Stowe. Values do. And for all of John Knutson's misguided political beliefs, our family values align perfectly."

Stowe remains silent. She wishes she could agree but can't.

"Look, it's none of my business what happened between you and Wyatt. It's not affecting your work, so I shouldn't even be bringing it up. But I hate to see what it's done to your Christmas spirit. The fact is, you two shared a Christmas fairy tale last year. That's what I meant about this year being a letdown. The experience of bringing Santa to testify in Washington is tough to match, let alone beat."

"I'm not trying to."

"Clearly," the congresswoman says with a smile as she places her hand on Stowe's shoulder. "But just because you can't replicate old memories doesn't mean you can't make new ones. Christmas is about celebrating with those around you. If you didn't get that from Santa last year, you missed the point entirely."

The congresswoman isn't wrong, and Stowe didn't miss the point. She didn't need it to be made in the first place. She isn't in the mood to celebrate this year. It's that simple.

Angela cocks a thumb over her shoulder. "I'm heading home. You should do the same. I'll see you in the morning."

Stowe takes her recommendation, packing her things and donning her coat. Maybe she can find something on television that isn't Christmasy, like an action movie. With her luck, they'll be playing *Die Hard*, which Wyatt maintains is the best Christmas movie ever made. She angrily shakes the thought from her head as she steps out of the office.

Chapter Four

WYATT HUFFMAN

Montana is "big sky" country. It got that moniker from an early 1900s advertising campaign and was popularized later on by a book. It is catchy, but that's not why Wyatt loves it here. It's the land under that big sky that draws him in.

There isn't much of anything in Central Montana. That's the point. There is nothing but rolling hills and raw natural beauty for as far as the eye can see. Completely absent is the hustle and bustle of urban Washington and the scheming and shenanigans that come with working in the nation's capital. Montana is a simple place with hardworking, honest people.

Most of all, Wyatt likes it here because it's quiet. With only the sounds of nature around him, he has time to think and be present in himself. That's not something he could do back east. It was too distracting.

Of course, the tranquility can also be short-lived. Everything is serene and quiet until the moment it isn't. That time is now as Wyatt hears the footfalls of the approaching horse long before bothering to turn to see who it is.

"I can see why you like these early-morning rides," his sister says as she walks her steed up beside him. "They're peaceful."

"They are until your younger sister arrives uninvited to spoil the solitude. What are you doing out here, Ellie?"

She shakes her head, her silhouetted hat moving against the vibrant dawn colors in the east. "Nobody sent me to find you if that's what you're wondering. I thought it was time we had a talk."

"I come out here so I don't have to talk to anyone," Wyatt argues.

"You don't say much at the ranch either, so what's the difference?"

"I talk plenty."

"Yeah, sure, but not about the things that matter."

Talk is overrated. If there is anything that Wyatt learned during his time in D.C., it's that. All people do in Washington is talk. He's had enough of it. He certainly doesn't want to discuss what brought him back to Montana.

"Like?"

"Like how you're doing."

Wyatt frowns. It feels like his mother asks that every fifteen minutes. It's only appropriate that his sister gets the same answer the family matriarch does.

"I'm fine."

"Oh, Wyatt. You're my brother, and I love you, but you are most definitely *not* fine. You're mopey, depressed, and it's starting to piss me off."

"Are you putting your shrink hat on again for me?" Wyatt says, scoffing.

"I'm a rancher from Montana. I fill whatever role I need to. Right now, it's getting up before dawn to ride out here to have an early morning intervention with my stubborn brother. I heard your date with Missy went well."

Wyatt turns at the sudden change of subject. "Who did you hear that from?"

"Missy. You forget that this is a small town, unlike Washington."

"People talk about each other all the time there, for the record. Yeah, we had a nice time, I guess. She's sweet, but she isn't—"

"Stowe?"

Wyatt noticeably winces. It's been five months since their fight that caused him to leave her and the nation's capital for good. He isn't sure he's said her name once in the time since. In fact, he'd bet that he hasn't. The wound is open, raw, and still bleeding.

"She isn't Voldemort, Wyatt. You don't have to go around calling her 'she who shall not be named.'"

He ignores the cheesy Harry Potter reference. "I know."

"Wow," Ellie says, leaning over her horse to try to look him in the eyes. "That woman did a number on your heart."

"Don't start. I didn't leave my job because of her."

"Oh, yeah, it's because you were *dying* to come back and work for Dad at the ranch. Who the hell do you think you're kidding? I may be younger than you, but I wasn't born yesterday. You're not a rancher, Wyatt. It isn't in your blood like it is in mine and Colt's. You're here because Stowe ripped your heart out and stomped on it. There's no shame in it. We've all been there."

"All? Ellie, you've been smitten with Billy Olson since you passed him that note in first grade."

Ellie chuckles. "You have a short memory, big brother. We had our fair share of ups and downs along the way before we got married. Billy and I got through it, but it wasn't always easy."

She's right. Things between them weren't all roses and champagne, especially in high school. He remembers coming home from college one weekend to find her bawling on the couch. He was about to get into the truck to beat her future husband to a pulp for being stupid. Their brother was set to ride shotgun on the odyssey. That's the Huffman way.

"So, is this the point where you're going to tell me I need to move on with Missy?"

"No, because I know you won't. You still love Stowe. That much is clear. I'm only asking you if this is the life you *really* want. And you don't have to answer the question for me. You need to answer it for yourself before you get trapped here and become a miserable old man screaming for kids to get off the lawn."

Wyatt frowns but doesn't counter his sister's proclamation. She's right. He does need to figure out what his future holds and if this is where he wants to be. He came home because it was a familiar refuge, but he's slowly remembering all the reasons he left in the first place.

"Are you coming?"

Wyatt fills his lungs with cold Montana air. "No, I'm going to stay here for a while longer."

"Okay," Ellie says, starting to walk her horse back toward the ranch before stopping. "Wyatt? Do me one favor: If you're going to stay, please don't turn into the town heartbreaker. I don't want to hear the complaints from the eligible bachelorettes that my brother is an asshole."

Wyatt smirks and nods, and Ellie urges her horse into a canter in the direction of the ranch. After a minute, the sound of the hooves disappears into the quiet stillness of the Montana morning. Silence has returned, and with it, the loud barking of the questions she planted in his head.

What does he want? It's a good question. He could return to working for Knutson, maybe at his district office, so he doesn't have to return to D.C. The congressman told Wyatt when he left that he'd be welcome back at any time. But is politics really what he wants to do? Was he happy doing the job?

Those are all questions he'll need to answer as soon as he can make it through this Christmas season. Once the gifts are opened and the new year starts, choices will be made. Until then, he has to take things a day at a time. It's the only way to survive the holiday this time around.

Chapter Five

COMMUNICATIONS DIRECTOR
MACKENZIE WALSH

MacKenzie crosses the open area filled with young families and couples posing for pictures. She wonders if this is really where the Arctic Circle passes. It must be. That kind of fraud would have been uncovered long ago. It does make for a fun photo opportunity. Not a lot of people can say they've ever been here.

With the possible exception of the official post office, Santa Claus's office is the focal point of this village. Despite its obvious draw, the exterior is very unassuming. There are no velvet ropes outside for a line to form. Girls dressed like elves aren't there marshaling a crowd and handing out candy canes like they do at center court in a shopping mall. This may be a tourist destination, but it doesn't have the feel of a tourist trap.

A pair of families pour out the door behind energized kids bouncing around like they were intravenously administered a solution of Red Bull and Pixy Stix. She supposes that any child who meets a man who delivers their gifts on Christmas would be awed and excited. Hell, a year ago, he did that to half the adults in America.

MacKenzie enters the office, not sure what to expect. There is nothing ornate about this place. It has the look and feel of an old workshop splashed with copious amounts of Christmas décor. The front area is small and only has a counter for greeting guests. The main attraction is likely behind the far wall.

"Hello," a small woman dressed like an elf says. She must be wearing contacts to give her rainbow eyes that trippy sparkling effect. "Please, go on in. Santa is waiting for you."

MacKenzie cocks her head. Is he waiting for *her*, or is that rhetorical?

"Do I need to pay?"

The elf with the golden blonde hair laughs. "Santa doesn't charge to pay him a visit. Go on back. I'll bring you two some hot cocoa."

MacKenzie thanks the elf and cautiously approaches the opening. She sticks her head in to find a man sitting on a plain wooden bench, looking much like he did at the hearing. His red jacket isn't bright red under the white apron, his pants are green, and his boots are brown. He isn't wearing a hat, either, exposing his white hair. Santa's beard is still long and wavy, reaching almost down to his stomach. The media speculated for weeks over the differences between the Santa at the hearing and the one usually depicted in the United States. Somehow, it gave him more legitimacy.

She wasn't at the Guzman hearing, but like much of America, MacKenzie was watching his testimony on the news. It was great television, but she couldn't understand why the people in that hearing room were so captivated. Now, she gets it. There is something about him that's…magical.

"Please, have a seat, MacKenzie."

She apprehensively takes a seat next to the man. "How did…? I didn't tell you my name."

"Oh, Santa knows. I can see you are burdened, but first, let me ask you, do you celebrate Christmas?"

She averts her eyes, not expecting such a direct question. "Of course."

"No, MacKenzie, I don't mean putting lights on a small tree in your apartment and watching *Miracle on 34th Street*. Do you *celebrate* Christmas?"

"I…uh…." She can't make herself answer the question.

"Everyone does it differently. Did you know the Swedish have something called the Yule Goat? It dates back to ancient pagan festivals, but the tradition got a new life seventy years ago when someone made a giant straw one. Now, they build the forty-two-foot-high goat in the same spot every year.

"Families in Poland share an unleavened religious wafer called an *oplatek* on Christmas Eve. Each person breaks off a piece as they wish each other a Merry Christmas. They don't sit for dinner until the first star appears, and an extra setting is left at the table for uninvited guests.

"And Christmas isn't even a national holiday in Japan, but they still celebrate it. Instead of gathering around the table for a meal, families head out to their local Kentucky Fried Chicken. Seriously, I'm not making that up. Traditions are important, even if they are recent ones. Do you do anything to celebrate the Christmas season, MacKenzie?"

"No, I don't suppose I do anything special."

"You go through the motions," Santa observes.

"Yes."

"And that's part of the reason you didn't want to come here. You struggle to experience the magic of Christmas and didn't think you should be the one to ask what you came here to ask."

The conversation pauses when the elf from the front brings in a pair of hot cocoas on an antique tray. Each of the steaming drinks is in a hand-crafted mug topped with whipped cream and completed with a candy cane stick for stirring.

"Oh, thank you, Aurielle," Santa says.

MacKenzie takes a sip. If Heaven had a taste, this would be it. The richness and flavor instantly conjure up her happiest memories.

"The elves make the best cocoa."

"No argument here. Santa, do you know what I'm here to ask?"

He smiles. "Was I right about your not wanting to come here?"

MacKenzie wraps her hands around the mug. "Yes, you were right…about all of it. I haven't had any real Christmas spirit in…well, a while now. I'm sorry."

"For what? There's no reason to apologize. Do you think you are the first person to ever forget the magic of the holiday?"

"You must think I'm the Grinch."

"No, you're not green, and I don't believe your heart is three sizes too small. You're here to ask me about Antonne Tucker and his sister, Alaya."

MacKenzie can't stop her mouth from hanging open. Here we go again. "How did you know that?"

Santa Claus's smile grows even broader. "YouTube."

"Of course," she says, not certain whether to believe him. "I was wondering if you would be willing to grant his Christmas wish."

"His or yours? That was how you were told to sell it to me, correct?"

"Seriously, how could you know that?" MacKenzie asks, her brow scrunching in disbelief.

Santa laughs, not using the deep ho-ho-ho seen in commercials and suburban shopping malls. It's more of an amused chuckle.

"MacKenzie, I keep a ledger of who's naughty and who's nice. How do you think I manage that?"

"Microsoft Excel?" she asks, offering a cheeky answer that is instantly regretted. Fortunately, her host doesn't seem the least bit offended.

"You have always had a marvelous wit. It got you in plenty of trouble as a child, if I remember correctly. Tell me, do you think I should go?"

Smoke and mirrors. That's how she answered anyone who asked her about Santa's testimony before the congressional subcommittee. He did his research and used it magnificently. But if that was true, how could he have known she was coming? Even someone scouring the Internet could never know how much time her sass landed her in the principal's office growing up. She shakes off the thought.

"It would be a nice gesture for a boy who's dying."

"But?"

"No buts."

"Yes, there is. Please, MacKenzie, this isn't Washington, D.C. I am not a politician. You're free to tell me how you really feel about it. It will stay between us."

"What's happened to the Tucker family…I don't have children. I can't imagine what they must be going through. My heart aches for them. I think…I think that my boss is trying to exploit the situation for political gain."

"Do you agree with that?"

MacKenzie forces a smile. "I'm in politics. It's what we do."

"In your heart, do you agree?" Santa asks, leaning toward her slightly.

"No, I think it's wrong. Antonne should get his wish for his sister but for the right reasons."

"I agree," Santa Claus says with a nod.

"So, you'll come to St. Louis with me?"

"No," he says, placing his hand on her knee. "I will agree to let you arrange a meeting with Antonne, but someone else has to ask me."

MacKenzie knows that Santa turned down the first request to testify. Now she knows how those staffers must have felt. It's deflating to hear that her request isn't good enough for him.

"I'm sorry, Santa, but they only sent me."

"I understand. And I'm asking you to have your bosses send someone else with you when you return. If Marco Ramirez truly wants to bring some Christmas magic to the world, he will have to trust me. So will you."

MacKenzie swallows hard. "Who do you want us to have ask you?"

Santa smiles and sips his cocoa. She wouldn't testify to it under oath, but for a brief second, she swears she sees a twinkle in his eye.

Chapter Six

SVP MALCOLM CHAPMAN

Relocating is stressful under the best of circumstances. It's hard to move away from friends, family, and the familiarity of an area you lived in for years. It is even more stressful when the destination is a foreign country. There are a natural language barrier, cultural differences, tax considerations, and logistical challenges to overcome.

Fortunately, Heilung contracted a third party to make all the necessary arrangements for the Chapman family, which made things somewhat easier. Personal items were packed and shipped, and the remaining furniture and unused home items were placed in storage. Work visas were procured, schooling for Braylen arranged, and a fully furnished apartment was reserved for them in Frankfurt. All things considered, it went smoothly.

The residence the company procured is an apartment in a nice building not overly far from their corporate headquarters. It's spacious, even by American standards, and well-appointed. There is a gym and even a pool available for use. It is designed for ex-pats, so the amenities are meant to match would you would get in most U.S. cities.

Malcolm slides the key into the lock and opens the door. The floorplan is an open layout, with the dining area, kitchen, and living area all combined into one large space. The three bedrooms are located down a short corridor, as are the three bathrooms.

The apartment is eerily quiet. Malcolm misses the days when his wife greeted him at the door when the workday was done. Of course, his hours were far more predictable back then. Now, it's anyone's guess when he can break free from the chains of the office, and she got tired of waiting for a text letting her know his ETA.

Long hours make for long days. When Malcolm accepted this assignment, he never realized how demanding it would be. In fairness, he was warned by some executives who work at headquarters, but he wasn't listening. He was fixated on the lucrative promotion that promised more money and more opportunity. He never considered the toll it would take on his family.

He and Janelle made the decision to come to Germany together. She viewed it as a new chapter filled with new possibilities. They could spend weekends traveling the continent, exposing their son to the wonders of cultures and historical cities he would rarely get to experience while living in the U.S.

Malcolm looked at it as a promising job opportunity for someone whose career is on an upward trajectory. It was a win-win until it wasn't. Now, six months after arriving in Germany, they are nearing the breaking point.

"You're back," Janelle says, closing her robe as she appears in the living room.

"Yeah. Long day," Malcolm says, pulling off his shoes. He sighs, feeling good to have them off his feet. "Where's Braylen?"

"It's after ten, Malcolm. I put him to bed two hours ago."

He checks his watch, not realizing it was that late. He was gone before his son was up this morning. That's another day that he hasn't seen him. He doesn't know how many that makes, but he's betting Janelle knows the precise answer.

"I'm surprised you waited up." It was an innocent observation but came out as more of an accusation.

"I may have had you texted or called to let me know when you'd be home," she says in retaliation. "But since you didn't, I decided to do some reading."

Janelle has always been a voracious reader. She had two novels jammed into her pocketbook on their first date. When he saw them and questioned her, she simply stated that it was her backup plan if she didn't like him and the date ended early. From that day on, he has never seen her without a book within arm's reach.

"Another romance novel?"

"I have to get it from somewhere. At least the characters in the book see and talk to each other."

Malcolm crashes into the couch and rubs his eyes, knowing where this is going. "Janelle, do you really want to have this conversation right now?"

She folds her arms. It's the universal sign of defiance and disapproval. When his wife is concerned, it's a severe storm warning. Hurricane Janelle is blowing in.

"Why not?"

"Because I'm already worn out and don't want to go twelve rounds with you over something I can't control."

"Fine," she says, her tone indicating something other than acceptance. "We'll have it tomorrow when you get home after ten. Or the next day. Or the next. Lord knows that we haven't had much of a chance to have it before now."

"I'm sorry. I have a lot going on at work. How many times do I need to apologize?"

"You always have a lot going on at work. It's worse since we've been here. I don't want your apologies. I want my husband back from his corporate overlords."

"We've already discussed this. You told me that you supported me, Janelle. You know how important this assignment is for my career. I'm trying to provide for our family."

"Not being present for your family is not providing for them," his wife fires back. "I know you work hard. It's one of the reasons I fell in love with you. But this is different. Since we've come to Germany, you've become someone else."

"What? Who? All I'm trying to do is earn this promotion!"

"And sacrificing our marriage and our family in the process of getting it!"

"That's not fair, Janelle," Malcolm says, scoffing and shaking his head.

"Nothing about this is fair. Not for you, not for me, and definitely not for our son, who only wants to spend time with his father."

Malcolm catapults off the sofa like he was shot out of a cannon. "I spend time with Braylen!"

"Oh, yeah? When?"

"Whenever I can."

"Which is rarely, fast approaching never. You promised to take Braylen to the Christmas markets. When do you plan on doing that?"

Malcolm looks down. She isn't going to like this. "I have something big going on at work, and—"

"It's *Christmas*, Malcolm."

"Believe me, I know, and I'm sorry. But this came directly from the CEO. It's important. Klaus is relying on me to get the company out of a jam."

"Tell that to your son, assuming he's even awake the next time you're home. Maybe he'll see through the disappointment to accept your apologies. I'm done hearing them."

Janelle moves into the bedroom and closes the door without another word. That was the end of the conversation, at least for tonight. Malcolm sits back on the sofa and loosens his tie. This is supposed to be the big step he needed in his career, but it isn't working out like he thought it would. He guesses that the old adage is true: If you want to make God laugh, tell him your plans.

Chapter Seven

STOWE BESSETTE

Despite the Christmas decorations, Washington is still bleak in the winter. At least the spring has the cherry blossoms to brighten up the city, and the summer comes with the excitement of tourists. Fall is pretty everywhere. But winter? She'd take Vermont over this any day.

Stowe arrives at the office early. The staff party went late into the night, so she doesn't expect to see any of her peers anytime soon. Mandy was hammered when she stumbled into their apartment and passed out in her clothes on the couch. Thank God none of them drive in this city.

She follows the morning routine of placing her bag down and hanging her coat. Before she powers on her computer, Stowe spots the note on her desk asking her to report to the congresswoman immediately after arriving in the office. That's odd to her. None of the elected representatives come to work this early during a lame-duck Congress unless they're sleeping in the building, which some of them do. This can't be good.

Knowing there is no point in delaying the inevitable, she heads through the outer office and knocks on Angela's door jamb. "You wanted to see me, Congresswoman?"

The representative from Vermont lifts her eyes from her computer screen. "Stowe…yes, come in and take a seat."

"Is this about our conversation last night?" Stowe asks, smoothing her coat as she sits in the visitor's chair across the desk.

It's probably wishful thinking. The congresswoman may have delved a little too deeply into Stowe's private life, but not to the point where an apology is warranted. Even if one were, she's still a politician, and the words "I'm sorry" rarely escape their lips. There are two reasons for that. The first is that those words can be used against them, and the second is that they are never sorry.

"Not at all. I have a special assignment for you to work on. You've seen the Antonne Tucker video by now, I'm sure."

"Along with half the world," Stowe muses.

"I figured. What you probably don't know is the president sent the White House communications director to Finland to ask Santa to pay the young boy and his sister a visit."

Stowe sits a little straighter in the chair. The memories of her visit there with Wyatt come flooding back. Some of them are good…others, not so much. Their fight after Santa said no that morning was brutal and not something she likes reflecting on.

"MacKenzie Walsh went to Rovaniemi? Let me guess – Santa said 'no' because it's his busiest time of year."

The congresswoman holds her hand flat out and rocks it side to side. "Eh, you're half correct. He said 'no' because of who was doing the asking."

Stowe's jaw tightens. "I don't think I like where this is going."

"Well, my dear, you're going to like this part even less. Santa said he would only consider the request if you and Wyatt Huffman did the asking."

Stowe closes her eyes for a moment. It's worse than she feared. "Wyatt…he doesn't work for the congressman anymore."

"I'm aware. John Knutson is still upset about that."

"So, it's a non-starter."

The congresswoman folds her hands on the desk. "I don't think we should give up that easily."

"Well, that man is as stubborn as a mule. I can promise you that Wyatt won't even pick up the phone if the caller ID says 'Washington, D.C.'"

Angela chuckles. "John said the same thing. That's why I'm sending you to Montana today to convince him to join you."

Stowe's jaw drops. After Wyatt packed his things and left, she swore never to travel west of the Mississippi to ensure she would never run into him. Some of that is out of anger. Some of it is out of embarrassment. Only in her worst nightmares has she imagined seeing Wyatt Huffman again.

"Sending me to…? You can't be serious!"

"I am. You've been to the Huffman Ranch, right?"

"Once, but that's not the point."

"I'm making it the point. Stowe, this was a direct request from the president of the United States. He asked for you by name, but that's not why I'm asking you to go."

Tears form in the corners of Stowe's eyes. This is the worst possible way for a day to start. It's the most awful thing her boss could ask her to do. She would rather travel to Gaza and negotiate with Hamas than to Wyatt's home and face him on his turf.

"Then why are you? Do you think it will be therapeutic or something?"

The congresswoman ignores the sass and waits a few beats for her staffer's emotions to simmer down. "Because you get results, Stowe. You have always gotten results. It's why I was so comfortable sending you out with Wyatt to find Santa Claus last year. Look how that turned out."

It worked beyond their wildest expectations, but they returned to the States thinking they had failed. It wasn't until Santa appeared at the doors to the committee room that they knew they had succeeded. It still feels more like luck than any convincing argument they offered.

That was then, and this is now. Too much has happened since that day. Way too much. Stowe fights through her emotions to form a logical defense.

"Ma'am, I am the very last person on this planet that Wyatt wants to see, much less listen to."

"Maybe. But I'm also betting that he eventually will."

"Why?"

"Because you're you, and he's that kind of man. Call it a hunch. Take the trip and make your pitch, Stowe. Pour your heart into it, not because I asked, but because it's a young boy's Christmas wish. If Wyatt still says no, then it is what it is. I won't hold it against you. But this is a shot worth taking."

There is no getting out of this one. Angela has made up her mind, and God himself won't change it. The best thing she can do is get it over with as soon as possible…or hope the plane crashes on the way there to put her out of her misery.

"Okay. When do you want me to leave?"

"You have a flight this afternoon. Go home and pack. You can be at the Huffman ranch in central Montana by tonight."

Stowe rises. "I'll let you know how it turns out."

"Stowe?" the congresswoman calls out as she reaches the door. "I want you to do me a personal favor while you're there. Keep an open mind, and maybe even an open heart."

Stowe nods and retreats to her desk to collect her purse and coat. An open mind. That's easy for the congresswoman to say. A lot of damage was done last summer. This is not going to be a pleasant reunion.

Chapter Eight

WYATT HUFFMAN

Wyatt looks up from his laptop when he hears a commotion downstairs. He thought he heard the doorbell but didn't give it much thought. He can hear the voices echoing up the stairs and through his door. The greeting is…different. This isn't the neighbors stopping by or friends stopping in for a visit. Curiosity gets the best of him.

He climbs off his bed and pulls his bedroom door open to head downstairs to see what the fuss is about. As he descends the stairs, he sees that everyone in the living room is seated in their usual spots except his mother, who is standing next to….

"Stowe?" he asks, freezing in place.

"Hello, Wyatt."

Wyatt has to close and open his eyes to ensure this isn't a dream. Or, more appropriately, a nightmare. One question dominates his every thought.

"Wh-What are you doing here?"

"You didn't invite her?" his mother innocently asks.

He stares incredulously at his mother. "That depends – did hell suddenly freeze over?"

"Manners!" she chides.

The room drops into an eerie silence. Only the sound of the crackling logs in the fireplace punctuates the silence. The Huffmans all take turns looking at Stowe, Wyatt, and each other. If tension were a visible fog, the room would be pea soup with zero visibility. Everyone is waiting to see whether the gunslinger or the sheriff draws first in this modern-day Western. Wyatt isn't sure which role he's playing in that scenario.

"Awkward," Ellie says from her chair after the silence drags on too long.

"I…uh…I'm sorry to drop in like this. I was wondering if we can talk, Wyatt."

He folds his arms across his chest and welds them in place. It's a defensive posture, or so his therapist-in-waiting sister would say. Maybe she's right. But he's not about to lower them so long as Stowe is standing in the living room.

"We have nothing left to say to each other. You made that very clear."

"Wyatt! Stowe came all this way—"

"Uninvited, Mama! And unwelcome. I'm sure she knows the way back to Washington."

Wyatt is hoping for a little support. This is his father's ranch, and he wasn't warm and fuzzy to Stowe when she visited in April. Instead, the family patriarch remains in his chair, looking like Lincoln carved in marble at the west end of the National Mall. He doesn't say a word, and Ellie's husband knows not to get involved.

"Fine," his mother says. "You may not want to talk to Stowe, but I do. We just finished supper. Can I fix you a plate, dear? You must be famished."

Wyatt scoffs and storms out of the living room and into the kitchen. He jams his feet into his boots and dons a coat before walking out to the horse barn and flipping on the light. His mother may be making his ex-girlfriend feel welcome, but he doesn't need to.

He grabs the grooming kit and slides open the stall door. Wyatt's steed is wondering what the hell is going on. His horse senses that he's boiling in his emotions. Still, an unexpected brushing is a treat, so he eagerly eats the apple Wyatt gives him before enjoying the long strokes from the stiff brush gliding along his back.

"I forgot how pretty she was. Stowe is much better-looking than Missy Petersen."

"Don't start, Ellie."

His sister leans against the wall that separates the stalls. "If it makes you feel any better, Pops is pissed she's here, too."

"It might be the only thing we have in common," Wyatt grumbles.

"Good. Now, get past it."

"Oh, yeah? Why should I?"

"Seriously, Wyatt, you used to be smart before you worked in Washington. Is everyone there that dense?"

"It's the seat of the federal government, so yeah, pretty much."

Ellie grabs his hand mid-brushstroke. Her grip is like a vise. Wyatt forgot how strong she is and how strong-willed she can be.

"Look me in the eyes and tell me you aren't the least bit curious about why your ex-girlfriend suddenly showed up on our front porch unannounced a couple of weeks before Christmas."

Wyatt leans closer to his little sister's face. "I'm not the least bit curious as to why she's here."

"You are so much like our father sometimes," she says, releasing his hand.

"What the hell are you talking about?" he asks, resuming the brushing.

"You're still in love with her. I know you are, so don't deny it. But you can't see past your anger, just like Pops."

"You're damn right that I'm angry!" Wyatt says, throwing the brush to the ground and startling his horse.

"Good! That's the first time you've admitted it since you've been home. Now, man up and go find out what the girl wants."

"No! I'm not doing that. A conversation with Stowe Bessette isn't worth wasting a molecule of oxygen on."

"Why not?"

Wyatt has an old Rolodex filled with reasons. There are hundreds of them. He mentally selects one that his sister is most likely to recognize as legitimate.

"You weren't there last summer, Ellie. You don't know how things went down between us at the end. She—"

"Broke your heart?"

Wyatt bends down and picks up the brush. Even his horse is into this conversation. He looks back at his owner, waiting for a witty response. One isn't coming. Arguing with Ellie is the worst. He can't recall ever winning a single back-and-forth with her. She might as well be the love child of George Carlin and Dave Chappelle because she didn't get her razor-sharp and lightning-quick wit from either of their parents.

"Wyatt, you should find out why Stowe traveled all the way to Montana. There has to be a reason. If nothing else, it will give you the closure you need. I wouldn't have ever told you to go back to D.C. to get it, and I really never thought it was a possibility until ten minutes ago when there was a knock at the door. But you desperately need it."

Wyatt shakes his head. "Not gonna happen."

"Fine. I tried to be reasonable, but hardball it is. Agree to see Stowe, or I will tell every girl in this town that you have herpes. Missy will be devastated."

Wyatt scowls before suppressing a smile as his sister struggles to stifle her laughter. He finally breaks. It's the first time in weeks that he's found a reason to laugh. It's not a threat – it's a declarative statement of intention. Spreading that rumor is something Ellie is more than capable of.

"You know I'll do it."

"You're impossible."

"That's what little sisters are for. Two things before I go – turn on the heat in the tack room so the poor girl doesn't freeze to death out here."

"Yeah, because that's too much to hope for," Wyatt growls.

"Second, and more importantly, go easy on her. I saw the look on her face when Mama answered the door. She's terrified to be here. There's something to be said for that."

Chapter Nine

STOWE BESSETTE

The Huffmans know how to do Christmas. There are almost as many decorations adorning this ranch as there are back in Vermont at Nana's and PopPop's. She would be content looking at them all if Wyatt's father would give her a moment of peace. He started in on the abysmal state of American politics and hasn't let up.

"All those charlatans in Washington know how to do is take our money and waste it. The more we give them, the more they want."

"Bill, leave the poor girl alone," Wyatt's mother pleads.

"She's part of the problem, isn't she? She works there."

"It's okay, Ms. Huffman," Stowe says, summoning what courage she can.

"No, you call me Bridgit, dear."

Stowe smiles and nods at her. "I happen to agree with him. Ronald Reagan was right when he said, 'The nine most terrifying words in the English language are I'm from the government, and I'm here to help.'"

Bill chuckles. "What party are you with? Because—"

"Does it really matter which? Can you honestly argue that either of them knows the meaning of fiscal responsibility?"

"I see Wild Bill Huffman is holding court," Ellie interrupts, appearing at the entrance to the kitchen and removing her hat before Wyatt's father has the chance to unload on Stowe.

He waves a dismissive hand. "I'm just telling it like it is."

"Oh, like you're the arbiter of absolute truth," Bridgit mumbles.

"Well, Stowe, let me save you from more of his Montanan rancher ranting. The doctor will see you now."

Stowe sets down her tea and tentatively rises from the chair. Her legs feel like lead as she crosses the living room. Wyatt is willing to talk. There's no way of knowing whether that's a good or bad thing without actually finding out.

"You'll need your coat. It's December, and the only thing the damn Canadians give us is timber and their cold air."

Stowe stops in the middle of the living room and grins as she turns to face the family patriarch. "My grandparents live on a mountain in Vermont. I can handle the cold."

He nods. "Suit yourself."

"Come on," Ellie says, redonning her hat. "I'll show you the way."

Stowe follows Wyatt's sister out the door and turns with her toward the stables. She wraps her arms around her chest, paying the price for wanting to sound tough in front of the grizzled old rancher. It's absolutely freezing out here.

"Thank you for talking to him, Ellie."

"You're welcome, but you should know that he's not at all happy to see you, and I'm not exactly on your side in all this."

"I didn't think you would be. I'm sure Wyatt has said some pretty horrible things about me since he's been home."

Ellie kicks a lump of frozen snow as they walk. "Actually, he hasn't mentioned your name even once since he's been home."

Stowe lowers her eyes. That's a revelation. Out of sight, out of mind, or so the old adage goes. Wyatt is a strong man, so she shouldn't be surprised that he could move on that quickly. If only it were that easy for her.

"He forgot about me pretty fast."

"Nah. You hurt him that badly. Don't tell him I said that. He'll get revenge by slipping a diuretic into my morning coffee."

Stowe turns her head in surprise at the admission. "That wasn't my intention."

"It doesn't matter what your intention was. You did. My big brother is a gigantic pain in the ass on his best day, and the last five months have not been his best days. I don't care what happened between the two of you, but if you break his heart again, I swear I will snap your neck and make it look like a skiing accident."

Stowe's not sure if Ellie is kidding. Probably not. She's the future matriarch of the Huffman clan when her mother passes, and she's just as protective of the family. It doesn't matter. The odds of her and Wyatt ever ending up together at this point are long. Very long.

"Understood."

"What's it like seeing him again?" Ellie asks as they reach the stable. "For you, I mean."

"It hurts. A lot."

That must have been what Ellie wanted to hear. That doesn't matter, either. Stowe didn't say it to appease her. She was being honest.

For all the anger and bitterness that led to last summer's fight, Wyatt's leaving left a massive hole in her life…and in her heart. She thought she would get over it. They weren't dating *that* long, after all. It took seeing him for the first time in months to prove that she hadn't even begun that journey of healing.

"He's in the tack room - first door on the left near the middle of the barn. Good luck, Stowe."

Stowe steels herself, feeling like she is going to need a lot more than luck. The walk through the stables has all the characteristics of a perp walk to the electric chair. The stalls look like jail cells, the passage is straight and wide, and overhead lights are dangling from the roof every ten feet or so. All that's missing is a man shouting, "Dead man walking." Or dead woman, in her case.

"If you're expecting an apology about my reaction to seeing you, you won't get one," Wyatt says without looking at her as she enters the small room.

"I wasn't. I would have reacted the same way. Actually, I would have thrown something heavy and hard at your head if our roles were reversed."

She hoped the playful banter would break the ice, even a little. It doesn't.

"What are you doing here, Stowe?"

She stares at the ground and rocks back and forth on the balls of her feet. "You know, I rehearsed on the entire flight here from Washington what I was going to say when I saw you. None of it sounded right."

"Just…don't play games. Just spit it out."

"I was sent here," she confesses, looking him in the eyes for the first time. It's best to get that out of the way early.

"I figured. No way you would come voluntarily. By who? Knutson? Pratt?"

"The president of the United States."

Wyatt sits on a tack trunk and folds his arms across his chest. "All right, I didn't see that coming. Why?"

The opening gives Stowe something to talk about other than their failed relationship and the hard feelings it caused. She tells him the story of Antonne Tucker and how the White House approached Santa to pay him a visit. She stops after she gets through St. Nick's instructions to the communications director.

"You've got to be kidding me."

"Oh, I wish I was, believe me."

"I don't work for…even with Santa asking, you know that there's no way I'll say yes to this, right?"

Stowe presses her lips together and nods a few times slowly. "I told Angela Pratt as much. She sent me here to ask anyway."

"Then, you wasted your time. I'm not doing the bidding for anyone in Washington, and I'm sure as hell not going anywhere with you. Ever."

Stowe hangs her head. There is anger in his eyes. The last time she saw them like that was last August, right before the summer recess…right after she said things she has regretted ever since. It was also right before he left Washington, never to return.

"I understand. It's settled," Stowe whispers, unsure how to address this next part. "Uh…your mother asked me to spend the night in the guestroom."

Wyatt exhales sharply and snickers as he stares at his hands. "Of course. She likes you. She's probably taking a page out of your nana's book and covering the ceiling in mistletoe as we speak."

Stowe is warmed by the memory. Nana's mistletoe antics are well known in her part of Vermont, and she actually got it to work. Wyatt and Stowe technically shared their first kiss under a sprig near the kitchen door. It simultaneously feels like yesterday and a lifetime ago.

"I'm going to make you the same offer you extended to me at Nana and PopPop's a year ago…if you don't want me to stay, I won't."

Time is relative. It can fly by, or it can crawl. How it moves is often a matter of perspective. Wyatt mulls over her offer, and seconds feel like minutes. What is probably only a handful of ticks on a clock feels like the length of time it takes Congress to do anything useful.

"No, I don't want you out on icy, unfamiliar roads at night. Your driving sucks, and you're likely to hit a bison standing in the middle of your lane."

"Okay," Stowe says, stifling a smile as she shuffles to the tack room door. She stops without looking back. "For what it's worth, I am sorry about what happened last summer. I know it doesn't change anything between us, but I thought you should know."

Stowe practically whispered the apology. She expected him to yell and scream and go off on an unhinged rant about words that should have been uttered long ago. Instead, she gets nothing in response. A thought pops into her mind that he didn't hear her.

"Have a good night's sleep, Stowe."

She heads out of the tack room and the stables toward her car to retrieve her suitcase. Have a good night's sleep. There isn't much chance of that happening. It's more likely going to be her lying in bed, staring at the ceiling, contemplating the uncomfortable thought of, "What if?" Ronald Reagan was wrong. Those are the most dangerous words in the English language. Ask anyone who has ever been forced to lie awake at night and think about them.

Chapter Ten

COMMUNICATIONS DIRECTOR
MACKENZIE WALSH

Washington is a city defined by its battles. Not the ones between armed combatants like in the War of 1812 but the political ones that shape the business of the day. Some of those fights are ideological, others are partisan. The one that is least talked about today is the ongoing battle between the legislative and executive branches. They are in a relentless tug of war over power, and most Americans can't be bothered to tune in.

That's why MacKenzie spends precious little time at this end of the National Mall. Capitol Hill is deep inside enemy territory when you work at the White House, even when meeting with party faithful. There are staunch allies and even convenient friends here, but meetings with them take place at 1600 Pennsylvania Avenue. The president only comes here for the State of the Union address, and MacKenzie has no reason to be here unless the president is. Wrangling Congress is the job of the legislative affairs office, not communications.

Regardless of her reservations on the matter, a visit to the Cannon House Office Building was in order. This could have been done with a phone call, but John Knutson is from Montana. She thought her chances of this tactic succeeding were better in a face-to-face meeting. As luck would have it, she sees him walking up the sidewalk as she turns the corner.

"Congressman Knutson! Congressman Knutson!" MacKenzie shouts, rushing over to him as he stops and turns.

"Miss Walsh. What are you doing on the Hill?"

"Looking for you, Congressman. You look surprised to see me."

Representative Knutson looks around, probably searching for hidden cameras. "Well, let's be objective here…it's not every day I get ambushed by the White House communications director on the way to work."

"This isn't an ambush," MacKenzie argues.

"This is Capitol Hill, and we are in opposing parties. There's no doubt that it's an ambush."

"Fine, call it what you will. I'm here to talk about Wyatt Huffman."

He presses his lips together and nods. "Ah. And as I already explained to your boss, Wyatt Huffman doesn't work for me anymore."

"No, but Marco knows that Wyatt has a great deal of respect for you and will probably hear you out."

John Knutson isn't that much older than MacKenzie, but he rewards her with the same look her father used to give her as a child when she was caught in a lie.

"Miss Walsh, let's do something novel in this town and be honest with each other. The White House chief of staff barely knows who I am, let alone my relationship with a former staffer who he also barely knows. Stop playing games with me. It's Christmas."

"Sorry. Old habits die hard. And please, call me MacKenzie," she says with a smile. "Have you spoken with Angela Pratt?"

It's a dangerous question to ask around here. Partisan politics demands strict adherence to the rule that the other side is the enemy, and no fraternization is ever permitted. The hearings last Christmas were the closest thing to a bipartisan love-fest that the country has seen in decades. She knows from some inside information that Pratt and Knutson are close and doesn't have a problem with that.

"She called me late last night after Stowe told her Wyatt said no to her request."

"You're not surprised?"

The congressman shakes his head. "After what happened between those two last summer, not at all."

His tone makes the little hairs on the back of her neck stand up. "You sound a little bitter about it."

"A little. Wyatt's a good man and a hard worker. It was tough losing him from my staff when the dust settled."

"And you blame Stowe Bessette?"

Her tone was more accusatory than she meant it to be. She doesn't mean to imply that the congressman is incorrectly assigning blame. Maybe it was her fault, and maybe it wasn't. MacKenzie has enough drama in her life without inserting herself in a lover's quarrel between two staffers that led one to resign.

"No, I blame this place. I blame a leadership that refuses to let us collaborate and a public that demands we hate each other. Stowe and Wyatt's relationship didn't break down because they didn't love each other. It broke down because it's what politics demanded."

"Wouldn't this be a great opportunity for them to reconnect?"

"Probably, but I'm not going to interfere. That's a hard and fast rule from lessons learned."

"Look, Congressman, if your apprehension is because you want to make this a partisan thing—"

"It isn't, MacKenzie, especially when Christmas is involved. After what happened at the hearing last year, you should know that."

She does, but working every day at the White House trying to craft a message has made her weary, jaded, and constantly on guard. Knutson may not try to make this political, but he'll be the exception to the rule. If this goes south, his party will pile on. It's the law of the political jungle.

"Members of your party are going to try to turn this into a circus."

"Yeah, probably. If the roles were reversed, your party would do the same. It's not right, but unfortunately, it's the way it is right now. I happen to think Antonne Tucker should get his Christmas wish. If the White House wants to help make that a reality, then you won't hear any objections from me."

"But you won't help?"

Knutson presses his lips together. "There is nothing I can say to Wyatt that will get him to reconsider. If Stowe can't convince him to join this quest, nobody will. Trust me on that."

"He already said no, so that isn't going to happen," she says in a defeated tone that she hopes will help secure his cooperation.

"MacKenzie, if I learned anything from what happened last year, it's the power of Christmas magic, especially when Santa Claus is involved. Don't lose hope just yet. I need to get to the office. Have a good day."

"You too, sir."

That didn't go as she had hoped. It also didn't go as badly as it could have. John Knutson is a reasonable man in a job where being unreasonable is rewarded with donations and media air time. She didn't think picking up the phone and making a call to a former staffer was a big ask, but MacKenzie sees his point in refusing even if she doesn't agree with the refusal.

She checks her watch. It's time to get back to her office. Plan B is shot, so she needs to come up with Plans C through Q. One way or another, she needs to compel Santa Claus to pay a visit to St. Louis before Christmas Eve.

Chapter Eleven

SVP MALCOLM CHAPMAN

The sip of water soothes Malcolm's throat. He has done a lot of talking today, and the continued grilling from the media is driving up his word count. This will be the third and last major interview with an international news outlet for the day after a slew of smaller talks with local or regional outlets. It's also a testament to the wonders of modern technology. Instead of traveling to studios or having them dispatch a team to set up a remote here, it's all being done via videoconferences.

Like most mega corporations, Heilung has invested in high-end video and teleconferencing equipment. This room has multiple high-definition cameras run by software that will switch angles depending on the speaker and even zoom in and out. None of that is necessary for these interviews, but Malcolm thought the setup was neat the first time seeing it in action.

The first two major interviews were a little contentious, but nothing Malcolm couldn't handle. This isn't his first rodeo. Nobody spends time in a corporate communications or public relations department without knowing how to handle themselves during an interview. Journalists all use the same tactics – a high-stakes game of "gotcha" designed to make their interviews go viral and garner more attention.

This last one is with a major American cable news organization, while the first two were smaller outfits. Malcolm originally thought that he drew this assignment because he is from the States, and the sound of a German defending their obscene drug prices after losing two world wars wouldn't play well. It's more than that. The CEO handed him the assignment to squash the bad press from this Antonne Tucker story, so this is his baby.

Fortunately, this should be the easiest of the three. This particular outlet is an ally, so these will be softball questions lobbed right over the plate. Malcolm is looking to ace this, have a quick meeting with his staff, and then head home at a decent hour for once. That will make Janelle happy.

"We're coming to you in thirty seconds," a producer's voice announces over the videoconferencing unit. "Can you give me a final audio check?"

"Testing, one…two…three. How do I sound?"

"Perfect, and the video is great," she confirms. "We're patching studio sound to you now. The anchor just finished the lead-in."

"Joining us from Heilung's corporate headquarters in Frankfurt, Germany, is Malcolm Chapman, senior vice president of corporate communications. Thank you for joining us, Malcolm."

"Thank you for having me," he says with a smile, cognizant that there is a several-second transmission delay between here and the States.

The anchor is smiley and pleasant as they discuss Antonne Tucker and his sister, Alaya. Malcolm offers perfunctory sympathy for his plight, relating that he has a son of his own about that age. He ends with expressing hope that the boy gets his Christmas wish and that Santa visits his sister. Easy-peasy stuff.

"The Christmas wish for everyone who has heard that story is that he gets the medication he needs to live."

"That's not entirely true," Malcolm corrects. "There are treatments—"

"But not a cure," she interrupts. It throws him a little.

"Hemoexgen isn't a cure, either."

"Of course, but it will give him a much higher standard of living. How can your company justify such a lofty cost for this drug?"

Malcolms sits a little straighter in his chair. This is getting a little testier than he expected. "I understand it may seem that way—"

"Seem? The cost per dose is three and a half million dollars!"

"Yes. Extensive research and development went into this. We need to recoup those costs—"

"By gauging anguished parents? By bilking insurance companies so you can pad your profit margins?"

There are few things more disrespectful than interrupting someone mid-sentence. It expresses the notion that their words have no value and aren't worth listening to. This anchor doesn't mean it that way, although he doubts that she does care. She's using the technique to get under Malcolm's skin. It's working. The constant interruptions are making his blood boil.

"That's not what's happening."

"Oh, because everyone has three and a half million dollars in a piggy bank on their bedroom shelf."

"This drug cost is necessary."

"I doubt that, as I'm certain most of our viewers do. What were your company's profits last year?"

"We are a private company and do not need to disclose those."

"So, we can assume they are substantial."

Malcolm fights to remain impassive. His warm smile is gone. She's coming at him and is goading him into disclosing sensitive financial information, which he won't do. That's the fastest way to get himself fired. He tries to bring the conversation back to the benefits of their products.

"Much of Heilung's revenue covers production costs or is reinvested into research for other life-saving drugs."

"In the process, those who need it most can't get it. Tell me, Malcolm, what good is a drug that people can't afford? Should they simply shrug and accept their fates?"

"If they can't afford it…yes, that's the way the world works."

The adrenaline dump is hard to hide. His whole body is racked with nervous energy, and the journalist cocks her head, silently wondering if he really said that out loud. He's a trained communications executive – there is no way she expected Malcolm to misstep that badly. The unforced error is going to be replayed on televisions and podcasts around the world over the next twelve hours. That's the curse of the Information Age.

"I'm sure that is very comforting to Antonne's parents," the anchor says before he has an opportunity to correct the error. "Malcolm Chapman of Heilung Pharma, thank you for being here."

The feed cuts out, and the camera switches off. Malcolm leans back and closes his eyes. That will easily top the list of worst interviews he's ever done, and the timing couldn't be more dreadful. The fallout from this will be a thousand times worse than the interview itself. It doesn't look like he will be home early today after all.

Chapter Twelve

WYATT HUFFMAN

This isn't a typical morning ride. The sunrise is the same, the temperature has dipped but is still close to what it was yesterday, and the scenery is just as majestic. What's changed is the circumstances. Yesterday, Wyatt was contemplating his future, knowing in his heart that he needed to pick a post-Stowe direction. Today, his ex-girlfriend is sleeping in the family's guest bedroom. What a difference twenty-four hours makes.

Until last night, Wyatt would have expected a comet crashing in their yard or even Taylor Swift breaking down on the road and staying the night before the thought of Stowe Bessette showing up. Some things cannot be predicted under reasonable circumstances. That's one of them.

But she's here. She apologized for what happened, for what that's worth. And she made an offer – one that Wyatt isn't about to entertain. He hopes she'll be gone by the time he returns to the ranch. He got the closure Ellie said he needed…or as much as he should ever expect to get.

The sound of hooves clapping the ground echoes behind him. He was listening for them this time, knowing there was no way his sister was done pleading her case. He's not surprised that she followed him out here, but he's not inclined to listen to her arguments this time. What's done is done.

He doesn't turn as the horse slows to a walk behind him. "I don't need any more of your armchair psychology sessions, Ellie. I'm not in the mood."

"I'm never in the mood for your sister's psychobabble," a deep masculine voice responds. "That woman should have been a shrink instead of a rancher. Glad I'm not the only one she bothers with that crap."

Wyatt jerks around in his saddle and watches his father walk his horse up beside him. "Pops? What are you doing here?"

"There's too much damn estrogen in the house. I needed to get the hell out of there while I still have some sanity."

"Billy's there, isn't he?"

Bill Huffman smirks as he joins his son in gazing at the rolling hills. "Like I said."

Wyatt grins. Billy Olson isn't a girly man, but he isn't nearly as macho as his father would have liked for his only daughter. The family patriarch gave his blessing because the guy loves Ellie, and she adores him. He treats her right, and she's happy. If not for those things, his father would have driven her future husband off the property with a shotgun long before he popped the question.

"You look like you have the weight of the world on your shoulders. You make a decision yet?"

"About what?"

"Stowe's offer."

"You know about that?"

"Wyatt, you've been gone for a while, so let me remind you how things work around here. Your mother drags information out of people and then spills it to Ellie, who then blabs it to…well, everyone. Yeah, I know about it."

Ellie takes after their mother. She hasn't achieved the elite level of town gossip queen, but she's in line for the throne. She knows about everyone's business in this small part of Montana, and her information network is extensive and well-developed. It made her herpes threat that much more realistic.

"Glad to see the Huffman family gossip train is still chugging down the tracks."

"At full speed. Well?"

"I made my decision last night. I told her no."

Wyatt's father scoffs and shakes his head. "Then you're dumber than the morons we elect as leaders in this country."

The admonishment takes Wyatt by surprise. "I thought you'd be happy I wasn't leaving."

"A part of me is, but a bigger part knows you won't be. Ranching's in my blood, Wyatt. It always has been. You wanna know why we've had friction since you were in diapers? Ranching ain't in yours. I resented that for a long time."

"That's a bold admission."

"Courtesy of Ellie's psychobabble," his father concludes.

"I like the ranch just fine, Pops."

"That's my point. You *like* the ranch, you don't *love* it. I'm married to this land like I am to your mother. You appreciate it, but you'll never understand the bond I've formed with it…the same bond that your older brother has."

The eldest of the Huffman children is just like their father, only slightly less jaded. He loves everything about Montana, Abel, and this ranch. He got married young to a girl who had no interest in ever leaving this area. He is the heir apparent to the ranch when Wyatt's father retires, and the old man would have preferred to leave the land to all three kids. Wyatt knows he's not included in that part of the will.

"One of my many failings, I'm sure."

His father scoffs. "You don't get it. I want grandkids, Wyatt. Your brother is too busy raising and selling our cattle to get your sister-in-law knocked up, and I'm pretty sure that limp Willy back at the house is shooting blanks. Ellie will have to sleep with the UPS guy or something if they want kids. You may be my last hope."

"I'm not getting back together with Stowe," Wyatt declares, not sounding as sure as he should.

"Why not? She's a beautiful woman and a hell of a lot smarter than you are. If you think you'll ever do better than her, you need to spend more time with your sister, the shrink."

Wyatt turns in his saddle. "I didn't think you liked Stowe."

"I didn't. I thought she was a hippie tart who drank too much maple syrup growing up. But then she flew across the country to confront her ex-boyfriend in front of his entire family to ask for help delivering a Christmas wish to a dying boy she doesn't even know. That takes big stones, son. And a heart of gold. Her stock went up a few points."

That's the most praise anyone will get from Wild Bill Huffman.

"She was ordered to come," Wyatt says, trying to douse his rising opinion of her with some ice-cold water.

"Meh," his father says, waving his hand away from him. "We both know that she wouldn't have unless part of her wanted to. I may be an old cattle rancher in flyover country, but a blind man could see that she still loves you, and you still love her."

"So, you think I should help her?"

"You're a grown-ass man. Make your own damn decision. Just know that I won't abide your whining or brooding about it later."

"Of course not," Wyatt mutters. Touchy-feely is not the Bill Huffman way.

"Look, I've never been much for giving you advice, and most of what I say you ignore anyway, but hear me now, son. The good Lord doesn't give us many second chances in life. Maybe you and Stowe are meant to be together. Maybe you ain't. But if you don't take this opportunity, you'll never know…and a young boy in a hospital might die without his sister believing in Santa Claus."

"He's not really Santa Claus, Pops."

"Would you have said that a year ago when you were playing kissy-face with Stowe at the bottom of a Finnish hill?"

That's a fair point. For the second time in ten seconds, Wyatt is reeling. Since when would his father really care about some sick kid in Missouri? A neighbor, sure, but someone he doesn't know? And how the hell does he remember that story when Stowe and Wyatt told it last spring? He wasn't paying a lick of attention.

"How do you remember that story?"

"Wyatt, just because I pretend to ignore you and your siblings doesn't mean I'm not actually listening. The way I see it, the trail in front of you is clear. The only question is whether you're strong enough to follow it."

That was a challenge…and a blessing. Wyatt's father has always criticized him for his life choices. He didn't agree with his attending college and hated that he was working in Helena after graduation. To top it off, his father despised Wyatt's moving to D.C. to work on Capitol Hill. Now, he's practically encouraging him. This may rank as the strangest father-son conversation in Huffman family history.

"Thank you, Pops."

"Uh-huh. Good luck, Wyatt. Tell Santa I said hi."

He tips his hat as Wyatt steers his horse for the ranch, breaking into a gallop.

Chapter Thirteen

STOWE BESSETTE

Ellie was insistent on her staying put. Stowe doesn't know what is going on other than Bridgit and her tag-teaming to ensure any plan of leaving before Wyatt returns from his morning ride isn't executed. The carry-on suitcase Stowe brought with her is by the door, and she could make a break for it. Unfortunately, Ellie Huffman Olson isn't the kind of woman you mess with. It's better than even odds that she will get tackled before making it off the front porch.

The conversation is polite and lacks any hostility or snarkiness about what happened last summer. Stowe might even call it warm. It stops when the kitchen door opens, and Wyatt appears in the living room.

"How was your ride, dear?" his mother asks.

"It was nice," he says, turning to Stowe. "You're still here?"

Stowe lowers her eyes. It wasn't an accusatory tone or even one of annoyance. But it isn't the sound of a man pleasantly surprised to see that she isn't already hurtling up the state road toward the airport.

"Well, we should let you two talk," Wyatt's mother says, rising from her chair. "Come on, Ellie."

His sister walks over and gives Stowe a hug. "Take care of yourself."

She shoots a look at Wyatt before heading to the kitchen with her mother. He spots the suitcase near the door but doesn't say anything. The first move is hers to make.

"I…uh…I was going to leave while you were out on your ride. Your sister and mom wouldn't let me."

"I didn't realize you and Ellie had grown so close."

"We, uh…I think she's trying to get under your skin."

"Yeah, that's what little sisters tend to do," Wyatt concludes, knowing that Stowe is an only child raised by her grandparents. "Why did you come here?"

"You know why."

"I know what you told me," he says, sitting down on the sofa while gesturing at the chair across from it. "I want to know the real reason."

Honesty was never a problem in their relationship. The truth was never buried to avoid hurt feelings. If Wyatt didn't like an outfit she was wearing, he would tell her when asked. It was refreshing to know that everything he said was from his heart. That's what made the first time he told her he loved her so emotional and special. She has always reciprocated.

"This isn't a conspiracy, Wyatt. That is the real reason."

He rubs his chin. "I was willing to accept that. Then, I thought back to when we were first ordered to work together. We agreed to meet at a coffee shop. Do you remember what happened?"

She grins. "I did all the work so that I would only need to spend as little time as possible with you."

"That's right. You breezed in, told me the plan, and said you had it handled. Then, you breezed out just as fast. So, I can't help but think that you could have flown to Montana, maybe even driven to Abel, chilled at a coffee shop or diner for a few hours, and then reported to Angela that I said no."

"I didn't want to get caught lying," Stowe argues.

"Who would know? John Knutson won't call me, and you know I wouldn't have picked up for anyone else."

Stowe blows the air out of her lungs and looks away. "I...I don't know."

"Did you want to see me?"

Tears appear in the corners of her eyes. She wipes them away quickly. "No. I was terrified to see you."

"Why?"

"Because I didn't want to have this conversation. I didn't want to relive...."

Her voice trails off. Wyatt stares at her until it's clear that she has no intention of finishing the sentence.

"Then why did you come?"

She looks him in the eyes. "Because Santa Claus asked for us."

"He doesn't know we aren't together," Wyatt counters.

She half-smiles. "Are you willing to bet on that? He knew our names before we told him, remember?"

Wyatt nods.

"Look, I can't undo the past, nor do I want to relive it. You're right, I could have lied about seeing you, but I thought it was important for you to have the choice. Santa asked for both of us. I understand if you don't want to go, but I didn't want to make the decision for you."

He forces a smile. "Okay."

"Okay, what?"

"Okay, I'll go with you to Finland. Just give me fifteen minutes to pack," he says, standing.

Stowe's mouth hangs open a little. Wyatt is probably the stubbornest man she has ever met. Once he declined the offer in the stables last night, she figured there was nothing that could change his mind. She still can't believe what she's hearing.

"Are you serious?"

"Are you trying to talk me out of it now?"

"No, I just—"

"I'm not doing this for the president, Angela Pratt, or even you. I'm doing this for Antonne Tucker and his sister. If the two of us visiting Santa is what it takes to make that happen, then so be it. I don't have any real reason not to go."

Wyatt doesn't offer further explanation. He heads upstairs to pack and presumably change clothes for the trip. Ellie comes into the living room, leaving her mother in the kitchen. She joins Stowe, who is gazing up the stairs in disbelief.

"That man is full of surprises."

"That's my big brother. He may take the scenic route, but he always ends up on the right path. Just remember what I told you last night," Ellie says, putting her two fists together and making a snapping sound. "Skiing accident."

"I don't think you need to worry about that," Stowe concedes. "That ship has sailed."

Ellie looks at her and then glances up the stairs before smiling. "Sure, it has."

Chapter Fourteen

SVP MALCOLM CHAPMAN

Six o'clock. At this time of year in Frankfurt, only a digital clock can tell you if it's a.m. or p.m. It's still dark out, and only Malcolm's fatigue alerts him that it's early morning…very early morning.

He didn't get home when he wanted to. Not by a long shot. The damage control from his disastrous interview with the American media began mere minutes after the anchor unceremoniously ended the grilling. The staff was quick to point out that a statement would need to be released, and the social media teams would need to respond to the online hate that was quick to pour in.

Nine o'clock became eleven, which then became one, then three. Malcolm only managed to break free from the office because of the need for a shower and a change of clothes. Today won't be any easier. He's tired, his ego is bruised, and he hasn't even begun hearing about it from his bosses. It's like the movie *Office Space*. He may not come in late using the side door so Lumbergh doesn't see him, but Malcolm does have eight unofficial bosses and one likely very upset chief marketing officer to deal with.

They will all have their say while he and his team try to coax people into forgetting his disastrous answer to a simple question. This is the calm before that storm resumes. At least he can see Janelle and Braylen, if only briefly.

He's exhausted. It takes three times to get the key into the lock of his apartment door. He half thought his wife would open it for him after the second aborted try. No such luck. When he finally unlocks it and steps into the small foyer, he expects to see Braylen at the table, feasting on a bowl of sugary cereal. Janelle will be fussing in the kitchen, probably regretting feeding him Froot Loops. Neither is the case.

"Hello?"

There is no answer. Malcolm drops his keys in the dish and moves into the living area. All the toys are put away, and the throw blankets are folded neatly on one of the sofa's cushions.

"Janelle? Are you awake?" Malcolm calls out, heading for their bedroom.

It's not inconceivable that she and her son both slept in, but it'd be rare. He opens the door and pokes his head in. The bed is made. Curious. He does the same in Braylen's room, and his bed is also made. The only noise in the apartment is coming from the ticking of dozens of clocks of all shapes and sizes in his son's room. Neither of them is here. Malcolm scratches his head, wondering where they could be at this time of morning.

The answer comes quickly enough. The note on the kitchen counter is folded in half like a table tent.

Took Braylen to the Christmas market. We'll see you when we see you.

- J

Malcolms snatches up the note and collapses on the sofa with it. He studies it like it's a missing part of the Dead Sea Scrolls. It's short and to the point. Janelle didn't sign it with "love." That's where their relationship is right now.

It's their first Christmas overseas. One of the things they were looking forward to doing as a family was exploring the wonders of European Christmas markets. Most major cities have them, and the Frankfurt Christmas Market is one of the oldest and most celebrated in Germany. It's primarily located in Römerberg Square, right in the heart of Frankfurt's old town. It's not that far from here, so why did they leave so early?

The sink is empty. There were no bowls or plates in it. Maybe Janelle took Braylen out to get breakfast before checking it out. That makes sense. A family adventure has turned into a mother-son outing. Malcolm knows he is missing out on so much. This sacrifice needs to be worth it.

He sighs heavily. Braylen's eyes lit up when his father told him about the large Christmas tree adorned with lights and ornaments that stands in a place of honor at the market. He explained that there are performances, including choirs and brass bands, adding to the festive atmosphere. There is even a historic carousel that's popular with children and adults alike. Braylen couldn't wait to go.

Typically, the market starts in late November and runs until just before Christmas. That's probably why Janelle took him now. When Malcolm couldn't commit to taking them because of his work obligations, she didn't want Braylen to miss out. Today, they will be meandering between all the beautifully decorated wooden stalls that are selling everything from traditional crafts to Christmas decorations to toys.

Malcolm shakes off the thought and forces himself off the sofa. He treks to the bedroom, eyeing the bed and fighting the temptation to lie down. It's a bad idea. If he hits that pillow, he may not wake up until noon. That will be three hours of the CEO looking for him. He may even send some underling here to retrieve him.

No, sleep is not a possibility right now. The tasks for the next couple of hours include a shower, a change of clothes, and then waiting at his office desk for the inevitable call from Klaus Eberhardt's administrative assistant. Malcolm fumbled yesterday, and now he needs to play defense. His job may depend on it.

Chapter Fifteen

COMMUNICATIONS DIRECTOR
MACKENZIE WALSH

Working in the West Wing of the White House is never boring. Sure, it doesn't have the urgent pacing that most Americans see depicted on television, but there is always more work to be done than there are hours in a day. Large amounts of coffee and a high degree of efficiency are required to plow through even the top of the pile.

The pace quickens when travel is involved. MacKenzie doesn't accompany the president on most trips. When she does, the amount of time to do the required work condenses significantly. That's what she's facing now, only she isn't going someplace with the commander-in-chief. This is a solo mission.

"Knock, knock," Marco says, speaking out loud as he bangs on the door jamb.

"I don't have time for you right now," she says without looking up. It's a hell of a way to speak to her boss, but they have been like that with each other for a while.

He ignores MacKenzie's warning and makes himself comfortable on the couch opposite her desk. "And as White House chief of staff, I don't really care. Congratulations. From what I hear, Stowe Bessette came through."

"Apparently."

"Was there a quid pro quo?"

"I don't know," MacKenzie says, still not looking up.

Marco smirks and reaches forward, grabbing the HDMI cable running to the back of her monitor and yanking it out.

"Seriously?"

"You have a staff, Mac. They can handle whatever you don't get to. I want details. The president is asking questions I don't have the answers to. That's not a great spot for me to be in. I don't want to ruin my reputation with him for knowing everything."

"I haven't met the woman, let alone talked to her. I don't know how she convinced Wyatt to tag along. It could be anything ranging from crocodile tears to sexual favors. Is that what you want to hear?"

"No, that will only get the president to call me from the residence and ask more questions. What did Angela Pratt say?"

"That they caught a flight connecting through Chicago," MacKenzie says, looking at her watch, "meaning they're probably somewhere over Ohio by now."

"Out of curiosity, did you have a backup plan in case Stowe Bessette failed?"

MacKenzie leans back in her chair, resigned to the fact that her boss is in a chatty mood today. "Not a functional one. I was thinking about flying back to Finland, drugging Santa, and kidnapping him."

"That'll earn you coal in your stocking…for life."

"Not to mention breaking who knows how many international laws. Now, plug my monitor back in. My flight leaves soon."

"No, it leaves when you say it does. You're not flying commercially back to Scandinavia. The president has offered you the VC-25B."

"Wait…I'm traveling to Finland on Air Force One?"

Marco frowns. "Technically, it's only called that when he's on board. You'll have to come up with something slicker for St. Nick. I'm thinking Santa Force One."

"Sure, let's make it sound like he's invading the country. The media will have a field day with that."

She can hear it now. The right will scream that it's a misallocation of government funds. The far left will shout about the militarization of Santa Claus. This needs to be handled right in the messaging and optics, or the goodwill gesture will backfire spectacularly, leading to public mockery that will haunt them until the next election.

"Am I really getting public relations tips from the woman who just admitted to thinking about drugging and kidnapping Father Christmas?"

"Santa Sleigh One."

It was quick and off the top of her head, but anything to move this conversation along. The chief of staff mumbles it a few times before wearing a satisfied grin.

"That…that actually has a nice ring to it."

"You don't keep me around only for my stunning good looks."

Marco stands and adjusts his jacket. "Stowe Bessette and Wyatt Huffman should be landing in a couple of hours. I've arranged transportation for them from Dulles to Andrews Air Force Base. Your car will be outside the West Wing entrance in ninety minutes."

MacKenzie shrugs. "Well, at least the flight will be roomy. Plug my monitor back in." Marco grimaces. There's something he doesn't want to tell her. "What?"

"About the roomy thing…the president is giving you his plane so you can make a big splash. That means you'll have a press pool on board."

"What? Seriously? On board? Not just at the hospital?"

"I'm surprised you didn't insist on it. Your staff is putting the group together now. The media have latched onto this story and want a front-row seat. If it makes you feel any better, they promised me they would be on their best behavior."

"Since when have those vultures ever kept that promise?"

It doesn't matter which party occupies the White House – a love-hate relationship exists here with the press. Some administrations are better than others, but there is always antagonism and gotcha reporting at play. Promises made are promises broken in that business. Most reporters would sell their own mothers for a scoop.

"Never," the chief of staff says with a laugh. "But then again, nobody wants to upset Santa right before Christmas."

"Oh, really? What are the odds that any of them are on the nice list?"

"Remote, but the reporters don't know that, and you probably shouldn't tell them."

It's sage advice. "You realize that if something goes wrong or Santa says no, the world will hear about it before I can pick up my phone to call you. There will be no spinning it, and we'll look like—"

"Idiots? Let's hope that Santa doesn't say no. No pressure, though," he says with a smile. "Have a good trip, Mac."

Marco disappears from her office.

"Hey! Plug my monitor in!"

"Do I look like I'm in the IT department to you?" he shouts after a laugh. "Get one of the interns to do it."

MacKenzie groans and fumbles for the cable. She tries inserting it upside down and in the wrong slot a few times before finally getting it inserted in the proper port. Marco is in too good of a mood. She almost likes it better when he's stressed out. Unfortunately, she's going to have to wait for the new year for that pressure to return.

Chapter Sixteen

STOWE BESSETTE

They sat in different parts of the aircraft during takeoff and the climb up to cruising altitude. Air Force One is the official callsign of the aircraft when the president of the United States is on board. The modified Boeing 747 widebody is configured with several different areas, including a suite for the president and first lady, a conference room, a dining area, and seating for the White House staff, Secret Service agents, and, unfortunately, journalists assigned to the press pool.

The first family's private area includes a bedroom, bathroom, and office space. That's what Santa will enjoy on the trip back to the United States. That's not to say that the rest of the plane isn't spacious and extremely comfortable. It's also afforded a degree of privacy.

Wyatt is in one of the White House staff seats, staring out the window at nothing but an expanse of the North Atlantic. Stowe takes a deep breath. This probably isn't a good idea, but it's better to get it out of the way before meeting Santa Claus. He eyes her as she sits in the seat across from him.

"Are you sure that's a good idea?"

"Why wouldn't it be?"

"The last time we traveled in this direction together, the plane lost an engine, and we ended up in Iceland."

Stowe hasn't forgotten about that, but she doesn't want to think about it right now. The unfortunate diversion led to an interesting couple of days on the volcanic mid-Atlantic island – days when she began to develop feelings for Wyatt.

"I don't think there's much of a chance of that happening this time. This is the best-maintained plane in the world. The Air Force sees to that."

She knows that's true. A lot of care is placed in the maintenance of the aircraft, given its role in ferrying around the leader of the free world. The Air Force has a specialized team dedicated to performing that work under a high degree of scrutiny and unwavering adherence to strict safety standards.

"Are you sure you want to tempt fate?"

"Is this your way of saying you don't want to sit next to me?"

Wyatt doesn't respond as he returns to looking out the window. That's a passive-aggressive yes. She learned to read his body language long ago.

"Look, I'm trying to make this…a little less awkward for both of us."

"I think there are better odds of us having an engine failure."

Stowe is beginning to wish she had a stiff drink in her hand to get through this. Taking on his stubbornness head-on isn't going to have the desired effect, so she opts for a softer approach.

"I meant what I said in the stables when I apologized."

"I know."

Stowe stares at her hands as she wrings them. "I thought maybe you were thinking that I said it to get you to agree to come."

"I didn't think that at all."

"But you aren't accepting my apology."

He shakes his head. "It's not that simple."

Sometimes, there are misunderstandings in a relationship. Hurtful things are said, but a sincere apology is enough to get things back on the right track. Then there are the transgressions that border on the unforgivable. Infidelity is one of them, although that wasn't the case here. This is something far different.

"I know I said a lot of horrible things to you that night," Stowe continues. "I was angry, and I took it out on you. I was completely wrong to do that."

Wyatt turns to look at her. "You still don't get it, even after all this time."

"Get what?"

"It wasn't what you said to me that ended us, Stowe. It's how you *felt* about me while you were saying it."

"What do you mean?"

"You didn't just hate the fact that the bill got passed – you hated *me* for my role in it. You hated that I believed in it."

"That's not true!" Stowe screeches.

"It is. You *needed* to win. You lost the battle at work, but you were determined not to lose the war in our relationship. You were determined to change my mind…show me the error of my ways. My opinion didn't matter to you. You wanted me to adopt your point of view or face the consequences if I didn't."

"I thought I was right. I still do."

"Okay, *Jessie*."

Stowe recoils. That wasn't a low blow – it was a dagger to the chest. Jessie Stills was Wyatt's high school sweetheart. They broke up in college after she became more political. Wyatt still professes that he loved her because of who she was, not what her political beliefs were. To him, that's all that mattered.

She had a different opinion. According to Wyatt, she would spend hours trying to change his mind on even mundane issues. It took a toll on their relationship before it finally reached its breaking point and could go no further. Jessie was his first love, and Stowe thinks he still hasn't completely gotten over her.

"That may be the worst thing you've ever said to me," Stowe concludes, fighting to tamp down emotions ranging from a deep hurt to raging anger.

"Am I wrong?"

"Yes, you are!" she practically shouts.

"No, I'm not," Wyatt says, breaking eye contact for a long moment before staring at his hands as he rubs them together. "Look, I agreed to come and make the pitch to Santa. That's as far as this is going to go. Once he agrees and we return to the States, we go our separate ways. I will be civil until then, but that's all you're getting."

"Fine."

There is nothing more for Stowe to say, even if she wanted to. Wyatt has dug in, and if that's what he believes, she isn't going to change his mind. That's why she thinks the comparison is ridiculous – she has never tried to change him like Jessie did. They had one fight over one bill their bosses were sparring over. That's it.

She storms off, only getting as far as the next cabin before breaking down and collapsing in a seat. She never *hated* Wyatt. How could he possibly think that?

Through her tears, she makes an even more unsettling realization. Wyatt may be right about part of his conclusion. After the bill passed, she was angry. Stowe was desperate to convince him that she was right and he was wrong. Even if it only happened once, it must have been an echo from his dark and painful past with Jessie. No wonder he left Washington. At this point, she doesn't blame him.

Chapter Seventeen

WYATT HUFFMAN

It doesn't take long for MacKenzie Walsh to take the seat Stowe vacated. Wyatt has seen the White House communications director on a few occasions, mostly on television. As a lowly congressional staffer, he didn't hobnob with the bigwigs in the West Wing. Not to mention that his boss and the president are in different parties. There are precious few conversations with the opposition these days.

When he did see MacKenzie, she was always dressed very professionally – a suit jacket and skirt, blouse, sensible heels, and her blonde hair in an updo. It's down now, framing her face and making it appear softer. She's also in jeans and a sweater that hugs her body. She looks good.

"You were a little hard on her, don't you think?"

"I don't need you or anyone else judging me," Wyatt snaps.

MacKenzie holds her hands up. "I'm not. It's just an observation."

"I agreed to come here and make the pitch to Santa. The president will get his feel-good story, and a boy will get his Christmas wish. I'm doing what you asked, so please keep your observations to yourself."

The words are harsh because they're meant to be. Wyatt gets enough unsolicited advice from his little sister to fill three lifetimes. He doesn't need a political operative from the White House judging him, especially on a personal interaction.

"I've been in Washington for a while now. That's the politest way I've ever heard anyone make a demand. Fair enough. I'm actually jealous of you two, in a way."

"Why's that?"

MacKenzie tucks a strand of her blonde hair behind her ear. "Because I haven't had a reason to fight with a man like that in…well, a long time."

"Is there a celibacy requirement in the West Wing?" Wyatt asks, turning to stare out the window again.

She lets out a laugh. "Not officially, no. But the demands of the job…the time…it makes romantic relationships difficult."

That got his attention. "And the politics?"

MacKenzie nods. "That too, sometimes, but it's usually a first-date conversation. I have plenty of those and precious few second ones."

"Conversations or second dates?"

"Both."

Wyatt adjusts his seat in the chair. "Tell me, Miss Walsh, have—"

"MacKenzie. Or Mac. Please. Calling me Miss Walsh is what my mother does to remind me that I'm still unmarried with a ticking biological clock."

"All right. MacKenzie, have you *ever* seriously dated someone from the opposite party?"

She cocks her head playfully. "Are you offering?"

Wyatt scoffs. "Please tell me you aren't flirting with me three minutes after witnessing a fight with my ex-girlfriend."

"In my experience, that's typically the best time to flirt with a man," she says with a grin. "In this case, I'm not. If that were the case, I'd make you an offer to join the mile-high club right now."

Wyatt grins. That's a lie. He might be nursing a broken heart, but he's not dead. She is absolutely flirting with him. It's in her eyes and the way she keeps teasing her hair. Normally, as a guy, he's not tuned into things like that. For some reason, he is this time.

"Who says I'm not already a card-carrying member?"

"All right. Good point, I don't know that for sure, but I'm betting it's not on Air Force One. To answer your question, yes, I have been serious with someone who wasn't a member of my party. I've had two great loves in my life. Cliff Sutton was the second one. I lost my first love because I didn't immediately want to settle down and have five kids."

"Did he?"

"He and his wife have four and counting," MacKenzie confirms. "Cliff was my shot at living happily ever after, and it lasted three years."

"What broke you up?"

"That's kind of personal, isn't it?"

"No more so than your eavesdropping on a quarrel between exes."

"Touché. No, my split with Cliff had nothing to do with politics. It had everything to do with my career, though. He worked for the State Department, and I had just started consulting with a national campaign. When things got serious, he wanted to get married. It was important to him."

Wyatt nods. "Did he propose?"

MacKenzie's face tightens, and she noticeably winces. That brought back a painful memory. Wyatt has had his own fair share of those in the past twenty-four hours.

"He did. I had to tell him no in front of all our friends and family, and…he didn't take it well."

"Do you regret it?"

MacKenzie lowers her eyes. "Sometimes."

"Where is he now?"

"I don't know. We lost touch. Cliff doesn't have any social media profiles. He probably met someone else, had a couple of kids, and settled in Albany or something. I didn't sit here to rub salt in your wound or flirt with you…okay, maybe flirt with you a little. I wanted to…." MacKenzie presses her lips together. "I could have saved the relationship after I told him no and chose not to. I was scared of what he would say and let the idea of reconciling rest on his shoulders. That's one of those once-in-a-lifetime decisions that change someone's future. It certainly changed the trajectory of my life."

"You think I should give Stowe a second chance?"

She shrugs. "That's up to you. You're a handsome man, Wyatt. You won't have a problem finding someone else. The problem is, whoever you end up with *won't* be her. By the time you realize that for yourself, it will be far too late."

"Why are you telling me this?"

MacKenzie looks around and edges forward in her seat. He's beginning to wonder if she's about to share a state secret, but it's likely something more personal that she doesn't want overheard.

"Because Stowe did something yesterday that I wasn't willing to six years ago. She chose the path I didn't take when she traveled to Montana to see you. And you chose a path she probably didn't expect you to when you agreed to come to Finland."

"I'm doing it for Antonne Tucker," he argues.

MacKenzie nods before cocking her head. "Are you?"

She places her hand on his shoulder and lets it slide off as she walks away. Wyatt returns his gaze to the vast nothingness out the window. This was a bad idea. He should have stuck to his original plan of waiting until Stowe left the house before he returned from his ride. So what if his father had to deal with his brooding? At least it would have spared him this agony.

Chapter Eighteen

SVP MALCOLM CHAPMAN

Inevitability. The dictionary describes it as "the fact of being certain to happen and unable to be avoided or prevented." Malcolm actually opened a browser on his computer and looked up the definition online as he sat at his desk, pondering his fate. It's what one does while waiting for the other shoe to drop.

The Treaty of Versailles made World War II inevitable. Hitler's nationalism sped up the process, but the German people weren't forever going to tolerate the reparations the Allies imposed on them. The same applies to Hollywood marriages between A-list celebrities. For most, divorce is inevitable, and most people see the splits coming from ten miles away.

Inevitability is what led him back to his desk so early this morning. His wife and son weren't home, so there was no reason to mill around his apartment. While he feels like he's losing them, he doesn't want to add unemployment to the family's stress. It may be okay with Janelle. A pink slip would also mean a likely return home to the United States.

It's not if the CEO calls him on the carpet for a tongue-lashing. It's when. He expected the phone to ring first thing. Klaus Eberhardt is not a patient man, and there is no doubt that he heard about the flubbed interview minutes after it aired. So, why hasn't he called?

It's a question that has popped into his head every five minutes for the past seven hours. Malcolm restricted himself to working at his desk and taking only short breaks, knowing that a summons would come. Lunchtime came and went. The early afternoon turned into the late afternoon. Nothing. Not a peep from the chief executive's office or from Franz, the chief marketing officer. When his assistant finally does call, the request is clear and curt: Report to his office immediately.

The journey feels like a condemned man walking to the gallows. There is no telling what Klaus is going to say or do. Malcolm has been wargaming scenarios all day in preparation. When he arrives at the CEO's office, his assistant tells Malcolm to go right in. That's not a good sign, but maybe it's better to rip off the Band-Aid and get this over with.

Klaus isn't sitting behind his desk. Instead, he's standing in front of the window, staring out with his hands clasped behind his back. He doesn't bother acknowledging Malcolm when he walks into the office. The communications vice president stops just behind the visitor's chair and waits.

"Was it a mistake?"

"Sir?"

The CEO turns at the waist to look at him. "Bringing you on assignment to Frankfurt. Was it a mistake?"

That's a challenge he didn't expect. Maybe he should have anticipated it. So much for his preparations.

"I don't think it was, no," Malcolm says.

"I'm beginning to question your judgment if you believe that's true."

"I did three interviews back-to-back. There was only an issue with the last one."

Klaus nods. "It only takes one."

"I can—"

"Recover? Spin it? Make it go away?" The CEO finally turns to face Malcolm and shakes his head. "You're talented, but you're not that good. There is no putting the genie back in the bottle. You provided the media with a clip they can use to beat us over the head whenever they want. And because of this whole St. Louis kid situation, that's all they want to do. That is your fault."

Malcolm nods. "It is."

"You admit it?"

"I was the one being interviewed. There's no denying it's my fault."

The CEO turns to look out the window again. "The board has been lighting up my phone all day. I've heard from more than half of them. They want someone's head on a pike."

"Offer them mine."

"You sound like you don't want your job anymore, Malcolm."

He hangs his head and looks at the ground. His father was a Marine. Growing up in a house with a veteran for a father means enduring hard life lessons and countless stories about military life. The education didn't propel him to wear the uniform, but it did instill some valuable lessons. Chief among them is the meaning of leadership. His father always preached, "Take charge and then take responsibility."

"I do, sir. But the reality is that I made the mistake that landed us in this predicament. I can't undo it, so I am responsible for the consequences. If that's the cost, it must be exacted."

Klaus turns and nods. He returns to his seat behind the desk and sits.

"Are you offering your resignation?"

"I'm prepared to if asked," Malcolm admits.

It's classic deflection. He isn't going to take it that far unless the CEO demands it. He's willing to sacrifice his future prospects at Heilung. That doesn't mean he's going to commit career suicide.

"Very well. I was prepared to ask for it. Then I learned that you were here all night with the team working on damage control. Security has you badging out at five-thirty before returning three hours later."

"I needed a shower," Malcolm says.

"That's the kind of dedication I demand from our executives. It's also your stay of execution. You're getting a second chance at fixing this, Malcolm. I strongly advise you to make the most of it."

"Yes, sir."

"Go home and get some rest. You're going to need it. This will require long days until Christmas when we expect this story to finally die."

"Thank you, sir."

That's the last thing Janelle is going to want to hear. He may have been better off getting fired so far as she is concerned. That's a problem for later. Until then, he needs to huddle with the staff to find a way to push the barbarians from the gate.

Everyone is coming for them. The media, governments, patient advocacy groups, and even lawyers smell blood in the water and are circling like the sharks they are. It's going to fall on Malcolm to stop the bleeding. All he needs to figure out is how.

Chapter Nineteen

COMMUNICATIONS DIRECTOR
MACKENZIE WALSH

The wheels squeal as the rubber makes contact with the asphalt runway. MacKenzie can feel the lumbering plane decelerate as it rolls to the end of the strip located about ten kilometers north of Rovaniemi's city center. She wonders if they crossed the Arctic Circle, knowing that it bisects the northern end of the airport.

Sixty-six degrees, thirty-three minutes, thirty-nine seconds is the farthest north of the Equator she has ever been. The Arctic Circle is an imaginary line above which the sun stays continuously above or below the horizon for twenty-four hours during the summer and winter solstices, respectively. It's not a true landmark in the traditional sense. The only way to know you are at it is from a readout on a GPS or a sign that someone built to attract tourists.

The plane taxis to a spot on the tarmac, and the engines shut down. Arrangements have already been made for their arrival. A small fleet of vehicles has been procured to convoy them from the "Gateway to Lapland" to Santa Claus's Village. With a little luck, the round-trip journey to collect Santa shouldn't take more than a few hours. They could be in St. Louis tomorrow morning.

She patiently waits in her seat as a stairway is rolled into place for disembarkment. Her phone vibrates, and she checks the caller ID before sighing. That didn't take long.

"Keeping tabs on me?"

"Every step of the way," Marco admits. "How was your flight?"

"It was fine. We're disembarking now and will head straight to Santa's Village."

"Good. The sooner you get Santa to St. Louis, the better."

MacKenzie repositions the phone against her ear as she cocks her head. That's a sudden change in direction.

"I would have thought you wanted to milk this."

"I did, but then the narrative changed. You have access to a multiple million-dollar communications system on that aircraft. You haven't been keeping up with current events?"

"I was busy handling a domestic dispute. What did I miss?"

"An exec from Heilung Pharm did an interview with one of the cable news outlets last night that went sideways. Instead of fading into the background today, it went viral and picked up steam instead."

She exhales. That explains it. Interviews are tricky, especially in the era of the twenty-four-hour news cycle, where journalists are only interested in playing gotcha to get more clicks and views. It's not easy to avoid their traps, and this executive clearly didn't.

"Let me guess – he tried to justify the cost of their drug."

"It was a full-throated defense for the most expensive drug in America. Needless to say, it didn't play well. That quickly shifted the narrative from wanting a boy to get his Christmas wish for his sister to why a life-saving drug is so unaffordable."

"And Heilung is a campaign contributor."

"Of course."

MacKenzie nods. Major contributors fund campaigns for a variety of reasons. Money provides access to policymakers, allowing them to express their viewpoints and concerns to the men and women in a position to affect legislation they care about. How much that influences a candidate or politician varies, but all of them look after the top contributors to a certain degree. The president is no different.

"Look, I happen to agree that the price is too high," the chief of staff continues, "but we can't exactly say that in the press room."

"Have we gotten the question?"

"No, but we will."

There's no doubt about that. The administration has a very capable press secretary, but it won't be an easy needle to thread. People in medical need are at odds with drug providers. It's hard to support one without ostracizing the other, and nobody wants to upset a major contributor.

"And you think Santa visiting the kid will make this story go away?" MacKenzie asks, knowing that likely won't be the end of it.

"I think it swings it back into something we want at Christmas. Santa has to say yes, and you need to get him on that plane heading back here tonight."

MacKenzie rolls her eyes. "That's the plan, but are you saying I should have brought the chloroform just in case?"

"No, I'm telling you to be compelling."

She likes Marco, but sometimes the White House chief of staff thinks things are easier than they are. It's easy for him to say from behind his desk in the West Wing. MacKenzie can't even do the asking, let alone be compelling. That's why she's here for a second time to fulfill Santa's request.

"That's Stowe's and Wyatt's department, in case you forgot."

"Then convince them of the urgency. I'm counting on you, Mac. Make this happen."

The aircraft door is opened, and cold air rushes into the cabin to welcome them to the Great White North. Air Force personnel begin marshaling people off the plane. Make this happen. Yeah, sure. At this point, kidnapping Santa might be an easier option.

Chapter Twenty

STOWE BESSETTE

Gone is the giddy excitement of last time. Some of that is because of repetition. The first time doing anything is far more exciting than a repeat performance. A year ago, Wyatt and Stowe had the added benefit of getting to know each other during this trip. They were still buzzing after their shared time in Iceland, and they were on the precipice of completing their assignment. Or so they thought.

The circumstances are far different this time. They've already met Santa and have been to his office on the Arctic Circle. They had a relationship that ended badly, and the reunion has done nothing but dredge up old feelings and bitter memories. After the altercation on the plane, Stowe just wants to finish this little mission and go home.

The pair leads the gaggle through the square. Stowe looks around as the reporters gawk at the Arctic Circle pillars, knowing they need to get pictures straddling the line like most tourists who visit here do. This place hasn't changed at all since the last time she was here.

"You guys understand the time pressures, right?" MacKenzie asks from behind them.

"You've made them crystal-clear on the way here," Wyatt moans.

"Multiple times," Stowe adds without turning.

"I'm sorry. I don't mean to belabor the point, but I really need you to come through on this."

"We'll do what we can," Stowe assures her, sounding anything but confident.

MacKenzie turns to issue instructions to the press pool. She's confident and in control. Wyatt watches her intently before looking at the ground.

"You think she's hot, don't you?"

Stowe wants to kick herself for asking that question. It's not because she doesn't want to know, because part of her does. It's just that her bitter tone made her sound like a jealous ex-girlfriend. Which she supposes she partly is.

"MacKenzie's not my type."

"Blonde?"

Wyatt looks her dead in the eyes. "Political."

Stowe presses her lips together. That hurt. Wyatt doesn't say anything more before he spins and shows himself into Santa's office. He holds the door for Stowe, who follows him in. The area behind the wood counter is vacant. There is no chipper blonde elf with rainbow eyes to greet them this time.

MacKenzie joins them, and the trio slowly moves through the opening in the wall. Santa is standing instead of seated, looking much as he did on their first encounter. This time, he is holding a tray with three cups of steaming hot cocoa.

"I almost didn't think you would come," Santa says, carefully placing the tray down on his wooden bench.

"It's good to see you again, Santa."

"And you, Stowe. How are you, Wyatt?"

"Never better."

He made it sound like the response someone would give after walking out of the dentist's office.

"You remember MacKenzie Walsh," Stowe interjects before Wyatt says something stupid.

"How could I forget? I hate to be rude, MacKenzie, but I have something I would like to discuss with Stowe and Wyatt in private. Would you mind excusing us for a little while?"

The request catches her off guard. "Uh…sure. I'll be outside with the legion of press pining to see you, Santa."

Wyatt smirks. Stowe knows what he is thinking – the statement smacked of desperation. Santa nods graciously at MacKenzie before the White House communications director shows herself out.

"Come and sit with me for a while," Santa says, handing them each a mug before gingerly sitting on the bench.

Stowe takes a sip and instantly relaxes. She isn't sure if it's the warmth or one of Kris Kringle's secret ingredients, but she isn't about to question the warmth that washes over her. She would ask Santa what his elves lace this cocoa with, but the only answer she'd get is joy and happiness, or something to that effect.

"You have a lot of questions, including the one you came here for. But that's not the one that's at the top of either of your minds. So, go ahead, don't be shy. Ask me."

"Why did you request us to ask you to visit Antonne Tucker?"

"Ah, direct and to the point. I can always count on you to come through, Wyatt. The short answer is that I wanted to see you. I wanted to see the both of you."

"Why?" Stowe meekly asks.

Santa leans forward as if ready to share a secret. "You know why."

"It didn't work between us, Santa," Wyatt interjects after sharing a quick look with Stowe. "That's the end of the story."

"Is it? When stories end, there is nothing more. *'Twas the Night Before Christmas* finishes with my wishing everyone a Merry Christmas and a good night. It doesn't explain what happens next. There is no 'next' in that poem. You are both here. Your story is still being written."

"We had a fight…do I need to tell you this?"

He smiles at Stowe. "No, I will not make you rehash it. Santa already knows. What concerns me is that you two have lost your Christmas spirit."

Neither Stowe nor Wyatt argues against the observation.

"Christmas should bring a feeling of joy and warmth. Most people call that the spirit of the holiday or Christmas magic. It's generated when people gather to decorate the tree, sing carols, or share meals with friends and family. The feeling is heightened through acts of kindness and generosity or simply by spreading goodwill to those around you. Ultimately, Christmas magic is about embracing the spirit of the season.

"Unfortunately, it has a downside. Christmas, like all holidays, ends. The lights and the decorations come down. The joy…well, for too many, it gets put in storage with them. Life returns to normal. That shouldn't be the case, should it?"

"No," Wyatt and Stowe say together.

"Yet it does. Every year."

"If Christmas magic were present every day, then it wouldn't be special," Wyatt argues.

"That's true. But the feeling of wonder and joy should be. Your relationship was filled with it…until, of course, it wasn't."

"Santa—"

"No, Wyatt, I did not bring you and Stowe here so you could find love with each other again. Life doesn't work that way, and neither do I."

"Then why are we here?" Stowe asks.

"I need your help working on something special that I have planned."

"Our help?" Wyatt asks.

"What do you mean by special?" Stowe piles on.

Santa doesn't answer. He stares at them with a twinkle in his eye.

"Does that include coming to the United States with us to meet Antonne and Alaya Tucker?"

"Yes."

Stowe looks at Wyatt, who is just as surprised as she is. That was easy. Almost too easy. Maybe it's foolish to think St. Nick would have the same response he did a year ago. Or maybe whatever special thing Father Christmas has cooked up for them is the surprise. There is only one way to find out.

"The president of the United States sent his plane for you," Wyatt informs him. "We can leave…well, right now."

Santa smiles and lets out a short laugh before he sips his cocoa.

"No, we can't."

Chapter Twenty-One

WYATT HUFFMAN

Wyatt stares blankly at Santa Claus. He wishes he could say the response was completely unexpected, but after their experiences in this office the last time they were here, he ruled nothing out. The key is to get to the heart of the problem. Santa already agreed in principle to meet the young boy and his twin sister. The mystery that needs to be unlocked is why he can't depart tonight.

"I don't understand," Stowe quickly says.

"I have a great many things to attend to before leaving. The two of you understand the demands on me this close to Christmas better than anyone."

"We do," Wyatt croaks.

"But there are—"

"When do you want to leave, Santa?" Wyatt asks, cutting Stowe off.

She shoots him a fiery glare. Nobody likes being interrupted. Stowe was more receptive to listening to MacKenzie's warning about time pressure. She still works on Capitol Hill. Wyatt isn't on anyone's timetable. He may want to get this over with, but if Santa wants to wait a week, it's not a big deal to him. He was asked to make the pitch and secure the visit to St. Louis. So long as that happens, it doesn't matter to him when.

Santa strokes his long beard. "In the morning. I know MacKenzie won't like the delay, but one evening will not make much of a difference for her. It *will* make all the difference for my plan. In the meantime, I need the two of you to do something for me tonight. There is someone I need you to grant a very special Christmas wish for…someone I think you will both find deserving of it."

He stands and retrieves a red envelope from a nearby table. He hands it to Stowe with the reverence of a Japanese executive presenting a business card. Wyatt cranes his neck so he can see it. The deep red envelope has their names written on it in the prettiest gold cursive lettering he has ever seen.

"Who is the Christmas wish for?"

"You'll see, my dear. Please follow the instructions on the card. Then, meet me here first thing in the morning, and we'll begin our journey."

Wyatt and Stowe finish their cocoa and say their goodbyes to Santa before leaving his office. Now comes the hard part – they have to tell MacKenzie and the reporters in the press pool that they need to find lodging tonight. That may be easier said than done, considering this is one of the most popular times of year for tourists visiting Lapland.

"What do you mean, 'tomorrow?'" a furious MacKenzie asks. "I thought I explained how important this was."

"You did, but Santa adheres to his own schedule," Stowe argues. "We learned that the hard way. At least he agreed to meet the Tuckers."

"Unacceptable."

Wyatt gestures at the office door. "Then you are free to express your displeasure to Santa, Mac. I wish you luck with that."

Stowe looks at him. He said 'Mac." It was familiar. Too familiar. Despite his denials to the contrary, he likes her, and it's causing Stowe to burn up inside. Yes, she knew he would move on after their breakup, but she never thought she'd be around to witness it. It's almost as bad as if he started dating Mandy, although that would never happen for multiple reasons.

"Fine. What am I supposed to tell the media?"

"You could do something novel and start with the truth," Wyatt says, grinning.

"They're at the Arctic Circle, and there is a lot to do here," Stowe adds. "Reindeer sleigh rides, dog sledding…."

"I recommend the northern lights tour. I'm sure that will keep them preoccupied for a night."

"What about lodging?"

Wyatt shrugs. "Worst-case scenario, they can stay on the plane. I know of worse places to sleep."

MacKenzie sighs and makes her way over to the media, who have taken an active interest in their conversation. Stowe runs her finger below the flap and opens the envelope Santa gave her.

"We should find a place to stay the night in Rovaniemi before they get gobbled up. He's sending us to a restaurant. Do you know where it is?" she asks, showing him the address.

He sighs. "We both do. You'll see."

The pair starts walking back to the convoy parked in the lot outside the main entrance. She can't understand why Santa would need help granting a Christmas wish. Well, there is one unnerving reason she can think of.

"Do you get the feeling that we're being set up?

Wyatt cracks the first smile Stowe has seen since that fateful night in Washington.

"Santa Claus is involved. I'd almost guarantee it."

Chapter Twenty-Two

SVP MALCOLM CHAPMAN

There is still no answer at the apartment or on Janelle's cell. Malcolm doesn't leave a message on either this time. If she hasn't listened to his previous messages, there is no reason to believe that she will listen to this one. In all the time they have been together, they have never been out of communication for this long. If one of them was running late or a change of plans was needed, it warranted a call.

Most of the time, it is Malcolm who placed it. Janelle is a stay-at-home mom. It was an arrangement they decided on even before they got married. He said it wasn't necessary – she's highly intelligent and was on an upward trajectory in her career when they met. It didn't seem fair that she would sacrifice that to start a family. But Janelle was adamant that she didn't want a stranger raising their children and was comfortable with the decision. She expected to have a second child years ago, but life has gotten in the way.

Malcolm's career continued to result in promotions, and with each one, the demands on his time grew. In the corporate world, more responsibility means more income but also more time away from home. The move to Germany only made the growing problem worse. Now, her reaction has reached critical mass. Since she isn't picking up her phone, Janelle may be far angrier than he thought she was.

He sets his phone down and turns his attention back to his computer. Worldwide media interest in Santa's upcoming trip to St. Louis is picking up. The Americans visiting his office in the Arctic Circle is being covered by many outlets. Everyone is getting caught up in this story. It's the perfect thing for the media to cover during the holiday season.

It's not hard to figure out why this has become so sensationalized. Most adults know there is no Santa Claus, but Malcolm watched the congressional hearing in Washington last year along with millions of others. He watched a man flown in from Finland relay personal facts about politicians that he couldn't possibly have known. It clearly jarred the members of the subcommittee while leaving the viewing audience in awe.

Some people dismissed the testimony as a parlor trick – the same twisting of online research or educated guessing that allows mediums to pretend to talk to the dead. At least, that's the rationale that is given. Others believe wholeheartedly that the man, even if he isn't actually Santa, is special. The balance of the world is content to revel in the magic he brings to the world. That's what makes this story so dangerous.

Malcolm isn't sure what to believe. All he knows is that life won't begin to return to normal for him until this is over, assuming he still has a job by the time Santa meets that boy in Missouri. The CEO has handed him a near-impossible task. He can't help but feel like he's being set up for failure. The stress is taking a physical toll on his health. And then there's his marriage.

He kills the live feed on the computer and tries Janelle's cell again. She clearly isn't at the apartment, so where is she? He was starting to get worried hours ago. It's beginning to turn into panic. Something bad could have happened to her and Jaylen. What other reason is there? The mere thought of that causes him to break into a cold sweat.

There is still no answer at home or on her cell. Malcolm types out a text:

I'm worried sick now. Please call me.

He looks to see if the status changes. His phone indicates whether a message has been read, and this one hasn't. Neither have the previous ones. Despite closing his eyes and willing it, the text doesn't change to "read," nor do the ones he sent before it. Janelle isn't paying attention to her phone. Or something is very wrong. Or she could be ignoring him.

Another, almost equally disturbing thought pops into his head – could she be leaving him? It's a thought he wouldn't have conceived of before coming to Germany. He wouldn't have even had the thought a week ago. But Christmas, the time of joy and spending time with family, has brought a level of strain to the marriage they've never had to endure.

He stares at his phone, willing it to ring. It doesn't. Janelle isn't home. She isn't responding to texts or calls. And she has their son with her. The work stress is bad enough, but Malcolm feels himself descending to the bottom of a bubbling emotional cauldron. He wishes he had never taken this infernal assignment. The price is turning out to be too high.

Chapter Twenty-Three

STOWE BESSETTE

They are only days away from the winter solstice when the city of Rovaniemi won't see the sun. That's the wonder of the Arctic Circle. That means it's not pitch-black outside the windows but dark enough that Stowe has completely lost her sense of direction. So has Wyatt because he doesn't react to anything until their rideshare pulls up in front of the Arctic Sky Hotel.

"You've got to be kidding me," Wyatt moans when he sees the building's façade.

Stowe shrugs. "They had a vacancy."

She made the arrangements in the car ride over here. It was one shot, one kill. Accommodations were secured during her first call, and they spent the remaining ten minutes of the drive in complete silence. He shouldn't be surprised that this hotel was the one she chose. Some would call it fate, but it's more because of familiarity. The number was stored in her phone from last year.

"Only one?" Wyatt asks. "We're not sharing a room again."

That wasn't her intention. The first time they were here, there was an issue with one of the rooms they reserved, and the hotel was booked up. So were the rest of them in the small Nordic city. Wyatt offered to find another lodging solution after offering her the available room. She insisted that he stay with her after getting to know him in Iceland. It was eye-opening. Despite the awkwardness, he was a perfect gentleman.

"Would you rather freeze to death outside?"

"Yes."

The answer was firm and decisive. Stowe lowers her eyes. She is trying to be playful, but Wyatt still isn't up for that. She's not trying to win him back, at least intentionally. What's done is done, but it's not too much to hope for a little less awkwardness between them for the remainder of this journey. It may be futile.

"They had two rooms," Stowe says, trying to hide her hurt. "It won't come to that unless you sleepwalk."

They check in and drag their small suitcases up to their rooms. Fifteen minutes later, Stowe and Wyatt meet in the lobby to head out to their Santa-directed dinner. Neither of them is looking forward to this, even if it's for different reasons.

"All right," Stowe says, adjusting her gloves. "Where is this restaurant?"

"It's not far. Follow me," Wyatt says, turning and heading east down the sidewalk.

"We don't need to call for a ride?"

"It's a nice night for a walk."

Stowe purses her lips as they cross the street. They are both from cold weather states, so the temperatures aren't going to bother them. It's actually warmer here than it is back in Montana or at Stowe's grandparents' mountain cabin. She didn't think he would want to walk anywhere with her. After a crossing, she decides to seize the opportunity it provides.

"You know—"

"We're here," Wyatt says, cutting her off.

Stowe looks up at the restaurant's sign. She shakes her head. Of all the dumb luck....

"This place?"

"I told you that you knew where it was."

He got her again. It explains why he was okay walking. The pair enters the restaurant. There aren't many patrons. The three or four tables of diners are all tuned in to a man along the windows who is searching for something on the floor. Apparently, it's dinner and a show in Rovaniemi tonight.

"Table for two," Wyatt says after the hostess greets them.

"Certainly. Please follow me," she responds in perfect English. That's the fascinating part of this place – everyone here speaks the language, likely learning it right alongside Finnish while they were in school.

The hostess grabs a pair of menus and leads the couple to a table. Wyatt is watching the man under the table intently before stopping. He starts chuckling, unable to hide his amusement. She can't see what's so funny.

"What?"

"You'll see," he says between laughs. "You're not going to believe this."

He veers right, walking over to their table. The hostess gives Stowe a bewildered look, and she can only shrug. The man is still on the floor, growing increasingly frustrated and desperate. It isn't until his companion, who's seated at the table, looks up that Stowe realizes what Wyatt finds so amusing. Of all the gin joints in all the towns in all the world....

"Tell me you didn't lose her ring again, Johan."

Hanna looks up and covers her mouth. "Oh, my God!"

"What?" Johan says, quickly trying to stand and banging his head hard on the table. He rubs it as he turns and looks up at the two people standing behind him.

"Wyatt? Stowe?"

Hanna jumps out of her seat, and Johan stands. The couples share hugs. They may have only met once, but they share a bond that will last a lifetime. It's the warmest of greetings, and for one fleeting moment, the awkwardness between Stowe and Wyatt melts away.

"What are you looking for?" Wyatt asks, watching Johan's eyes return to the ground.

"My wedding band."

Stowe smiles and nudges Hanna. "We warned you he would be dropping things for the rest of his life."

"I'm no expert, but shouldn't that be on your finger?"

"We aren't married yet," Hanna says in a tone that is more matter-of-fact than annoyed.

"What?" Stowe asks. "What are you waiting for?"

"That's a long story. Do you guys want to join us?"

She doesn't need his permission, but Stowe feels compelled to glance at Wyatt to check his reaction. He does the same thing. For two people who are no longer together, old habits die hard. His head bobs up and down.

"Absolutely," Stowe answers.

"I'm still missing the ring. I heard it hit the floor, so it should be right here."

That's true for a diamond engagement ring. The wedding bands most men wear don't have stones and are round as a wheel. Wheels roll, so Wyatt walks to his left, scanning between the tables. He stops and excuses himself to a couple eating nearby, bending and picking up a tungsten ring with Nordic engravings.

"Is this it?"

"To the rescue again," Johan muses, his voice dripping with appreciation.

"You really need to stop making a habit of this," Wyatt advises him with a smile.

The four of them sit, guys on one side, girls on the other. A waitress comes and takes their dinner orders before departing to get the kitchen working on them.

"What brings you guys to Finland?"

Johan gestures at his fiancée. "It was Hanna's idea."

"We lost your number. I've spent months trying to track you down…are you guys together yet?"

It was the most awkward question she could ask, but Stowe knew it was eventually coming. Johan and Hanna thought they were an item back at the lava cave and said as much. Naturally, they would be curious to see if the relationship developed, which it did. Then it fell apart.

"That's a long story," Stowe deflects.

"I knew it. I told you they would be."

Stowe hazards a look at Wyatt. She expects him to say something snide or sarcastic or, at a minimum, correct her. He doesn't bother setting the record straight. At least, not right now.

"Yes, dear."

"Oh, you're learning fast," Wyatt says with a smile.

"To get back to the story, we set the wedding date in April and were about to give up looking for you," Hanna continues.

"You see, Hanna and I really want the two of you there."

"That's so sweet," Stowe says, her hands covering her heart. "We only met that once in Iceland. You didn't need to invite us."

"Are you kidding? Hanna tells that engagement story every chance she gets. Both of our families are dying to meet the crazy Americans who risked their lives in the cave to retrieve the ring."

"And all our friends, too," Hanna adds. "It's their favorite story."

It is an epic tale. After Johan dropped the ring trying to put it on Hanna's finger, it ended up bouncing off the footbridge and onto a lava rock. Wyatt climbed over the railing and extended himself in a plank position to retrieve it. When he couldn't reach, Stowe used him as a bridge, sliding down his back to his shoulders to cover the remaining difference. It took incredible trust between two people who despised each other a week earlier to pull off. The tour guide wasn't at all amused by the rescue, at least initially.

"None of that explains why you are in Rovaniemi."

Wyatt is reading Stowe's mind. She was wondering the same thing and about to ask that herself.

"We visited Santa up at the village earlier today," Hanna informs them, her voice a little higher from excitement. "We told him the story of what you did for us and said the only thing we wanted for Christmas was to be able to contact you."

"And here you are," Johan says, his hands outstretched to the two of them.

"It was your Christmas wish," Stowe says, her voice low as she stares at Wyatt.

"Exactly!"

Wyatt and Stowe share a knowing look. A cynic could easily pass this off as a coincidence. They were on their way to Finland before Hanna even made her Christmas wish. While that's true, how could Santa have known they would be at this restaurant at this particular time?

Those are questions that will likely forever go unanswered. Not that it matters. They get to enjoy dinner with long-lost acquaintances they thought they would never meet again. That's the magic of Christmas, courtesy of Santa Claus, who most people profess doesn't really exist.

Chapter Twenty-Four

COMMUNICATIONS DIRECTOR
MACKENZIE WALSH

MacKenzie spent the entire night tossing and turning. It wasn't the accommodations or the mattress, which was insanely comfortable. No, it was the inability to shut her brain off. Once her mind begins racing, it doesn't want to stop until it reaches the finish line. That happens on occasion, especially when something is bothering her. Even the fresh, cold, arctic air couldn't make her tired enough to drift off into sleep. The weight of this assignment saw to that.

Every conceivable thing that could go wrong today ran through her mind. Santa could change his mind. He could have an emergency arise, like the elves unionizing and going out on strike. He could die of a heart attack. The scenarios got even more ridiculous from there.

Fortunately, none of it happened. She showered, dressed, repacked, and had an early breakfast. Everyone gathered at the village and Santa was waiting by the time they reached his office. He made a good show in talking briefly to the reporters. He even took a few pictures with them on the line that marks the Arctic Circle. MacKenzie is fairly certain that even Wyatt and Stowe don't have that snapshot.

A cart was brought over to bring Santa's steamer trunk to the convoy. The man doesn't pack light, but nobody was rude enough to point that out. The only real surprise is that his elf is joining them for the trip. MacKenzie didn't expect the blonde-haired, rainbow-eyed girl to come along. Not that it matters. There is more than enough seating on the plane.

She feels herself relax during the drive to Rovaniemi International Airport. Everything is coming together. MacKenzie phoned Marco to give him the news and called the flight crew to prepare for their imminent arrival. Everything is going to plan, and that's almost unsettling.

The convoy pulls up next to the aircraft. The media embarks first, as is the tradition. Santa patiently waits his turn and stares up at the sleek, yet massive blue and white plane. The VC-25B is a Boeing 747-8i that recently replaced the aging VC-25A models. The aircraft has numerous modern upgrades ranging from improved electrical power and communications systems to autonomous ground operations capabilities. All of that pales in comparison to its majesty.

Despite the desire to change the livery to red, white, and blue, which makes sense, the airframe maintained the classic Air Force One design. The light blue is slightly deeper, and the engine housings are a darker blue compared to the old robin's egg blue. Other than that, the scheme is largely the same as it was decades ago.

"Impressive, isn't it?"

"It's certainly bigger and roomier than my sleigh. Much slower, though," Santa says with a wink.

"It's capable of in-flight refueling. Can your reindeer do the same?" MacKenzie asks playfully.

"No, they graze on carrots the kids leave for them as I go rooftop to rooftop. It's a more environmentally friendly mode of transport than one that requires fossil fuels."

MacKenzie fights back the urge to launch into a diatribe about the president's green energy initiatives. Somehow, she doesn't think Santa really cares. He may even know about them. A man who maintains a naughty and nice list of every kid on the planet is undoubtedly well-informed. Then again, he really isn't *Santa Claus*. No jolly old St. Nick is circumnavigating the globe as he delivers presents to deserving boys and girls on Christmas Eve.

"What do you say, Santa? Ready to go to St. Louis?"

"Yeah, about that," he says as MacKenzie takes a step toward the stairs. "I'm afraid I must insist on a change in destination."

Her heart sinks. The shoe has finally dropped.

"I'm sorry? What do you mean?"

MacKenzie looks at Stowe and Wyatt. They both shrug. If Santa is changing the itinerary, they don't seem to have been let in on it.

"I mean that there is somewhere we need to go first."

"Santa, I'm sorry, but we're expected in St. Louis."

"I understand, MacKenzie, and we will go there. I promise. There is someplace we need to go first."

A circuit breaker in MacKenzie's mind pops. Everything was going so well. She was so close to making this a reality. Now, he wants to change the itinerary? That's not going to work.

"I'm…I'm afraid that's not possible."

"Why? Does this plane only go back and forth to America?"

"No, we can take it…there is a flight plan."

MacKenzie closes her eyes. That was a dumb thing to say, but it's all she could come up with under pressure.

"I understand. I have to deal with that every Christmas. We should really talk about the inherent bureaucracy of your FAA on this journey. The red tape is becoming unmanageable. It's almost worse than flying over Russia these days."

Stowe tries to stifle a smile. Wyatt does the same. They are both failing miserably. The comment is clever, but this isn't funny. She has a mission to accomplish, and that doesn't include taking Air Force One on a tour of Europe, or wherever Santa wants to go.

"People are counting on us," MacKenzie continues to protest. "They are counting on *you*."

"As they do every Christmas. Have I ever let them down? Have I ever let *you* down? And, no, you can't count the one year you didn't get Water Lily Barbie under the tree. You got the pink bike you wanted instead."

MacKenzie's mouth hangs open. It is a rare moment when the White House communications director is rendered speechless. But she is.

"Shall we go?" St. Nick asks.

That's the end of the conversation. Santa is doing them a favor by visiting St. Louis, and a brief diversion isn't a completely unreasonable demand. He walks toward the plane, his elf beside him. MacKenzie could try something underhanded, like telling the Air Force pilots to ignore him, but that is likely to end in disaster once they land. Santa is a man who theoretically travels the world in a sleigh and would quickly figure out that his instructions aren't being followed.

"Where does Santa want to go?"

Stowe and Wyatt glance at each other. "We have no idea," she admits. "The only way to find out is to climb aboard and see what he tells the pilot."

That's not likely the whole story. MacKenzie was dismissed from Santa's office. There was a reason for that, and she's willing to bet this is it. But there is no point in calling that out, and she catches up to Stowe and Wyatt, who are heading for the stairs.

"How did this Santa know about Water Lily Barbie?"

"You're going to be asking questions like that a lot by the end of this trip, Mac," Wyatt says, grinning. "Trust us on that."

Chapter Twenty-Five

WYATT HUFFMAN

Wyatt is getting restless. There are a lot of questions floating around his head. They are the same ones MacKenzie has, and Stowe likely also shares them. He decides to press for some information and leaves his seat to head to the front of the aircraft. The door to the president's office is closed, as Wyatt expected it would be. He only has the chance to rap on it once before it swings open.

"Santa will see you," Aurielle says.

"Thank you. And cocoa? You make the best I've ever tasted."

Her already trippy eyes glimmer in delight and appreciation. "Thank you. It's already waiting for you."

"Wyatt!" Santa bellows from the desk. "Come in, come in."

He does as instructed, accepting the mug the elf prepared for him. He only made the decision to walk in here thirty seconds ago. He's not even going to try to figure out why there is a steaming hot cocoa waiting for him.

"Are you comfortable, Santa?"

"Are you kidding? Look at this place," St. Nick says, gesturing around him. "How was it seeing Johan and Hanna last night? You must have been surprised."

"How did you…? No," Wyatt says, shaking his head. "I'm not going to ask. Seeing us was her Christmas wish?"

Santa wears an amused smile. "One of the easier ones I get to grant. You and Stowe are going to their wedding, yes?"

"We couldn't say no."

"Couldn't?" Santa asks, leaning over the desk. "Or wouldn't?"

Wyatt grins. "The latter."

"Good. I would have been disappointed if you did, although not as disappointed as Hanna. What you did for them in Iceland…that was special."

Wyatt's mind races. He never told Santa that story. Then he remembers that Hanna did, although there is just no knowing whether he was already aware. He has a long history of insights into things he should know nothing about. Just ask the members of the subcommittee who are still trying to figure it out a year later.

"Santa, why aren't we going directly to St. Louis?"

"Ah. You've been talking to MacKenzie. I think she's sore at me over the last-minute change of plans."

"No, she's…concerned, but I'm asking for myself. The pilots wouldn't tell her the destination. I'm beginning to think you promised them an F-22 for Christmas in return for their silence."

Santa laughs. "The elves haven't perfected stealth technology. There isn't much use for it in teddy bears and bikes."

"A stealth bike would make someone the coolest kid on the block. I know I would have wanted one growing up. Is this trip part of the plan you were telling Stowe and me about?"

Santa takes a sip of his cocoa, prompting Wyatt to do the same. He's thankful that Aurielle brought it with her. One sip transports him to a place of happiness and joy. Maybe it's the sugar or the chocolate she uses. It could be something else entirely.

"Wyatt, we live in a marvelous age. A lot of people don't look at it that way, but there was a time when travel wasn't as easy as it is today. Crossing an ocean or mountain range was a dangerous journey that would take months. Now, you can find yourself on the other side of the world very safely in the span of a day.

"That ability has made the world smaller. Cozier. But it also has taught people to concentrate more on arriving at the destination than the journey to get there. Everyone focuses on results and doesn't take time to appreciate how they achieved them. They don't live in the present."

"Are you talking about people…or me?"

Santa shrugs. "I know you aren't comfortable being with Stowe right now. In case you are curious, she isn't comfortable either. But for a fleeting moment last night at dinner, it felt like old times again, didn't it?"

He'd be lying if he disagreed. A quick dinner turned into more than four hours. The conversation was anything but strained or forced. Fortunately, there was little talk of his relationship with Stowe. There were a few mentions of better times, but a lot of the talk was about Hanna and Johan or the hearing with Santa Claus in Washington last Christmas.

"We're not getting back together, Santa."

"I understand. All I ask is that you continue this important journey with me."

"You still haven't explained what we're doing."

Santa smiles. "We're creating some Christmas magic."

"Isn't it enough to give a dying child his Christmas wish?"

The question was more argumentative than Wyatt intended. The last thing he wants to do is annoy Santa.

"I'm sure you know that the legend of Santa Claus can be traced back hundreds of years to a monk named St. Nicholas. It's believed that Nicholas was born sometime around 280 A.D. near Myra, in modern-day Turkey."

"Aren't you St. Nicholas?"

Santa looks at himself as he presses his hands against his torso and strokes his long white beard. "How old do you think I am?"

Wyatt presses his lips together. That's a fair point. Despite the mounting evidence that this man is special, he has to remind himself that he isn't really Santa. Everyone knows he doesn't exist.

"St. Nicholas was admired for his piety and kindness. Out of that grew countless legends. It's said that he gave away all of his inherited wealth and traveled the countryside helping those who were poor and sick. One of the best-known stories is the time he saved three poor sisters from being sold into slavery by their father by providing them a dowry so that they could be married."

Wyatt gives him a look. That's a tradition relegated to the dustbin of history, probably for good reason. Most people can't imagine marrying for a dowry now, although personal wealth and financial means are still used as substitutes.

"It was a much different time than it is now."

"Clearly."

"There are many ways to bring joy and happiness to the world, Wyatt. The easiest among them is buying a gift. Harder is finding the right one. The hardest is causing people to *feel* without providing them something of material value to elicit that response. Acts of kindness are the most enduring gifts people can give each other."

"What does that have to do with wherever we're going?"

The twinkle returns to Santa's eye. That's all the answer he's going to get. For whatever reason, their guest of honor on this flight wants to keep that a secret. Wyatt drains the rest of his cocoa and stands. One more try won't hurt anything.

"Santa, are you ever going to tell us what your plan is?"

He smiles and spreads his arms out. "What would be the magic in that?"

Chapter Twenty-Six

SVP MALCOLM CHAPMAN

The hasty call went unanswered, and the desperate text took agonizingly long to receive a response. For a moment, he thought maybe his phone was broken. It would explain why Janelle is out of communication. When the terse response did come, the suggested meeting place was surprisingly close. It's the perfect opportunity for Malcolm to go for a walk and stretch his legs. He could use the physical activity.

Frankfurt is a major city with almost 800,000 inhabitants. Despite its population, everything is comparatively close together and within walking distance. As the locals would say, it's a city of short distances. The city center is densely built-up and shops are within easy walking distance in almost every part of the city. This is no exception.

The bakery smells amazing, but Malcolm didn't come here for the Franzbrötchen or Berliners. He's here to meet an ambitious media contact who owes him a favor or two for past services rendered. He only hopes she sees it that way. Favors have a bad habit of not being returned in this line of work.

"Thank you for coming," Malcolm says, sliding into the chair across the small table from Aera.

"I'd be lying if I said your call didn't appeal to my journalistic curiosity. The timing is a bit suspect. I would have thought you were hiding in shame in some God-forsaken bunker in the middle of nowhere."

"It was a tempting thought, but the CMO would have sent me right back to the front lines. I'm not here to talk about my disastrous interview."

"I didn't think you were. Unfortunately, people are going to talk if they spot you meeting a beautiful Asian seductress instead of Christmas shopping with your wife. It will make her jealous."

Aera has a point. In her mid-thirties, the Korean-born, naturalized American citizen stands out in Germany. In truth, she would stand out anywhere. The petite woman is physically fit and armed with feminine wiles that entrance men like sailors listening to the siren song in *The Odyssey*. Being married, Malcolm is immune to her charms, but only barely.

They became fast friends when he first arrived in Frankfurt. To her, he's a trusted source high in the ranks of Heilung. She is a fairly trustworthy member of an otherwise vicious media. Their relationship has proven to be symbiotic, even if she gets more out of the arrangement than he does.

"Janelle already isn't my biggest fan right now."

"Uh-oh," Aera says, leaning back and taking a sip of her coffee. "Why not? No, wait, let me guess. The demands of work are taking you away from her."

Malcolm presses his lips together to suppress a scowl. "You know your stuff."

"It's not an original story. I know women, and I definitely know Heilung Pharma."

"It's not that bad there."

"It absolutely is! Since you're not here to talk about your train wreck of an interview, are you going to give me some fluffy statement to print?"

"No. We're off the record."

"How off the record?" Aera presses.

"All the way off it."

Aera puts her notebook away and packs up her laptop. Malcolm thinks she's about to cut this conversation very short.

"Was it something I said?"

"No. Sorry, I'm just avoiding temptation. I don't want you suing me."

"Are you writing a Santa story, too?"

"Along with pretty much every other journalist on the planet. That's why I'm fishing for a statement from you. But since I'm not going to get one, what's on your mind?"

That's a loaded question. What isn't on his mind? Malcolm's failing marriage and the inescapable demands of a tyrannical CEO are first and foremost. Those are just the first two items on a long list that is only growing longer with time.

"How I get people to stop writing negative stories about Heilung."

She laughs like she's sitting in the front row at a comedy act. "I thought this was going to be hard. Malcolm, just give Antonne Tucker the drug he needs, and poof! Like magic, all your problems disappear."

He hangs his head in frustration. "I can't. It was my first recommendation, but the CEO explicitly shot that idea down."

"That's not surprising. There isn't a generous bone in Klaus Eberhardt's body."

"That's not true," Malcolm argues.

He doesn't know why he's defending the cantankerous head of Heilung Pharma. He doesn't deserve that level of loyalty, especially since the denial rings hollow. Aera put her statement as politely as she could. Eberhardt is the Grinch in this story, plain and simple.

"I've been reporting from Frankfurt for five years now. How many dozens of stories do you think I've done on Heilung? They're one of the city's largest employers and the world's most influential companies. I've researched Klaus. I've talked to him. I've even had one regrettable dinner with him. I *know* him. Trust me, it's true."

"Okay, but put yourself in his shoes," Malcolm argues, more out of interest in how she would handle this. "Would you hand over a three-and-a-half million-dollar-per-dose medication if you were Heilung's CEO?"

"Absolutely not. I'd put it in a small box and gift wrap it first. Wake up, Malcolm. You already know that the positive publicity and free advertising that would be generated alone are worth twice the cost."

"Well, he's not going to do it. Call it a lack of generosity or because Eberhardt is a ruthless businessman. The reason doesn't matter, only that it's a route he won't take. So, how do I fix this knowing that?"

She takes another slow sip of her coffee. "You don't."

"Come on, Aera. You're a genius at this stuff. You'd make mid-six-figures a year running a marketing shop if you weren't a journalist."

She holds her hands out to her sides after setting the cup down.

"What do you want me to say? The story has gone full-blown viral, and it cannot be killed. You can batten down the hatches and hope for the best as you ride out the storm, but if you think the stories are bad now, just wait. The narrative will shift once Santa meets young Antonne and his sister. Everyone will be talking about the cost of the medicine because that's the only part of the story left to tell."

"You're full of good news."

"I'm just breaking it down for you, real world. There is a bright side you could consider."

"What's that?"

"Well, let's see…Santa's elves could be making the drug in their workshop. I don't think even Klaus would risk suing Santa for patent infringement."

Malcolm scoffs. "Sure, he would."

"Good luck, my friend. I don't envy the position you're in. But when you find yourself canned and moving back to the States, be sure to keep in touch. See ya around."

See him around. That's not likely with the way things are going. Suddenly, Malcolm isn't in the mood for coffee. He needs a much stronger drink.

Chapter Twenty-Seven

STOWE BESSETTE

The convoy pulls up, and the passengers open the doors of the Suburbans and climb out. Stowe looks around. She's never been to Austria and has spent the trip glued to the car window. Across the seat from her, Wyatt was doing the same thing. The visit to the heart of the old Austro-Hungarian Empire is an unexpected treat, at least for them. MacKenzie Walsh would vehemently disagree.

She was confused about how Santa managed to arrange transportation for when they arrived at their destination. That's her job, and she was kept in the dark about the destination until an hour before they landed. Stowe doesn't know if annoying her is part of Santa's plan, but she spent a chunk of the flight pleading with Stowe to get things back on schedule. As if she, or anyone, holds sway over Father Christmas. So, instead, they are here.

Karlsplatz is one of Vienna's major transportation hubs and most significant squares. While it isn't as iconic as Washington's National Mall, it has similar architectural beauty and cultural significance. Karlskirche, near the park's southeast corner, is one of Vienna's most impressive baroque churches. The Otto Wagner Pavilion was the former entrance to the city's rail network and now serves as a small museum. The Wien Museum offers a comprehensive look at the history of Vienna from its earliest days to the present.

All of this surrounds a magnificent green space that hosts the Art Advent Market in front of the church. This market is known for its focus on arts and crafts. The booths have a variety of handmade items, and vendors keep the crowds well-fed with organic food and Christmas treats. Santa is definitely in his element here.

"Stowe, Wyatt…I have something I need you to do for me," Santa says, clearly enjoying the beauty of the square before turning to them.

"Of course you do," Wyatt says with a smile that Santa returns.

Aurielle produces two red envelopes with gold lettering, much like the one Santa handed them at his office.

"In this first envelope are your instructions. Please follow them carefully. When you meet Stefan, give him the second envelope."

"Another Christmas wish?" Stowe asks.

"An important one."

"We won't let you down, Santa."

"I know you won't."

People are beginning to gather in large numbers. Reporters are already eagerly snapping pictures and recording videos. Everyone is looking forward to seeing him in action. He starts walking toward the market but doesn't get far before the first child greets him. Whatever Santa's mission is here, it's going to take a while to accomplish.

"Where do you think he finds the energy?" Stowe asks, opening the envelope and scanning the contents that contain their instructions. She pulls out her phone and begins typing.

Wyatt is watching as pure glee erupts on the faces of the children and their parents. "You've had Aurielle's hot cocoa. I think I figured out what the secret ingredients are."

"Caffeine and love?" she posits.

Wyatt shakes his head. "Cocaine and meth."

"Are you up for a walk?" Stowe asks after a laugh. "Where we're going is only fifteen minutes away, and it might take us longer if we go by metro."

"Do you know where you're going?" Stowe holds her phone up, showing the route displayed on the app to Wyatt. "All right. Lead the way."

The walk begins to warm them up under their goose-down jackets. Vienna is chilly, but Stowe and Wyatt are northerners who packed for Finland. This chill in the air is nothing.

Vienna is strikingly clean, with well-maintained sidewalks, clear signage, and very little vehicular traffic in this area. It's not as enchanting as a walk through a temperate Vermont forest, but it makes for a nice urban walking experience. The city streets are beautifully decorated for Christmas. Lights and ornaments are doing their part to create a festive atmosphere. The people are taking care of the rest.

With some time to kill before their appointed rendezvous per the instructions, they wander into the Stephansplatz Christmas Market in front of St. Stephen's Cathedral. It has a mix of traditional Austrian products, live music, and vendors serving mulled wine and roasted chestnuts. From the feeling to the atmosphere, this, simply put, is a physical manifestation of Christmas spirit.

"I wish we had something like this in the States," Stowe says, closing her eyes and breathing in the aromas wafting from the various food stalls.

"Right? Your Nana would love this place," Wyatt says, picking up a handmade wreath and admiring the workmanship.

"Yeah, she would. And your mom would need a cargo plane to get these decorations back to Montana."

"Or two."

Stowe taps Wyatt on the arm as they meander down Bondergasse to where it meets Am Hof. "Is that the carriage we're supposed to meet?"

Fiakers, or traditional horse-drawn carriages, are an iconic part of Viennese society. Carriages offer a cozy way to explore the city's famous landmarks, making these rides highly popular with tourists. From what Stowe has seen, fiaker stands are located throughout the city. Most of the trips they offer are short, twenty-minute and longer, forty-minute rides that cost over a hundred euros. This particular carriage is larger, very ornate, well-maintained, and absolutely beautiful.

"There's only one way to find out," Wyatt says, striding over to an anxious man pacing back and forth as he cranes his neck to check the river of people walking past him. "Excuse me? By any chance, are you Stefan Leitner?"

"I am! Are you the Wrights?"

That must have been who he was expecting. Stowe frowns. "I'm afraid not."

He rewards them with a disappointed look as his stress returns. "They didn't show up."

"Does that happen often?" Wyatt asks.

"We cater to tourists, so it isn't unheard of. But our services aren't inexpensive, and our tours are non-refundable. I don't like to see people lose their money, especially at Christmas. Thankfully, our riders are here before we are most of the time. Unfortunately for the Wrights, we are too far past the start time to conduct the tour. Can I help you with something?"

"Yes," Stowe says, retrieving the second red envelope from her coat. "We were asked to give this to you."

He eyes it suspiciously. "Who's it from?"

Stowe winces. This is going to sound weird coming out of her mouth. "Santa Claus."

Stefan's eyes light up. "I saw on the television that he arrived in Vienna. It's all over the news. You're both traveling with him?"

"We've been enlisted as honorary elves on this trip," Wyatt admits, causing Stowe to smirk at his embracing the role.

Stefan cautiously opens it and begins reading a lengthy letter. He leans back against the carriage, fighting tears. It's a losing battle. Emotion overcomes him as he finishes. Grasping the letter in his right hand, he wraps his arms around Stowe and hugs her.

"*Herzlichen Dank*," Stefan says before walking over to Wyatt and hugging him just as hard. "Thank you so much. You have no idea what this means to me. You've made my Christmas."

"You're very welcome."

Whatever was in that letter must have been profound, but Stefan isn't offering insight, and Stowe isn't brazen enough to ask. She thinks maybe Wyatt will, but he looks content at the thought of making the man's holiday a touch more special. That, and that's the kind of gossip he couldn't care less about.

One of the horses begins nuzzling Wyatt as it scratches the bridge of his nose down its long face. Wyatt doesn't budge as the horse begins rubbing its head up and down his chest. Stowe is pretty certain the force would have knocked her over.

"She likes you. Do you own horses?"

"I grew up on a ranch in Montana in the United States," Wyatt states proudly.

"That explains it. Horses are very intuitive. They have the gift of seeing people for who they really are."

"We are happy we could deliver that envelope to you. Have a very Merry Christmas, Stefan."

"And you, as well. You two make a beautiful couple."

It's going to be a long trip if people keep saying that. It was bad enough that Johan and Hanna made the assumption, but at least they had reason to. Stefan is a perfect stranger, yet he picked up on their vibe. Too bad it's no longer true.

"We're...we're actually not together," Stowe informs him.

"Really? I would have sworn differently. Since my tour didn't come, I have an open slot. Would you two care for a slightly abbreviated carriage ride?"

"We couldn't impose," Wyatt says.

"It's no imposition at all," Stefan counters, excitement dripping from the tone in his voice. "I already have the food and wine ready to go. Even the horses already like you. All you have to do is say yes."

Stowe looks at Wyatt with pleading eyes. A carriage ride in Vienna is too amazing to pass up. She knows that a romantic ride with her is near the bottom of Wyatt's to-do list right now, but she hopes it's not the *last* thing.

"It's one of those once-in-a-lifetime opportunities," Stowe says, trying to make a logical point without sounding as enthusiastic as she feels.

"Agreed," Wyatt says with a nod. "Let's do it."

Chapter Twenty-Eight

COMMUNICATIONS DIRECTOR
MACKENZIE WALSH

This would be a magical and charming place if MacKenzie still enjoyed Christmas at all. For her, it's a liability — one that conjures up bad memories. She may be the least-festive person in this square, and it probably shows.

Santa sure is having a good time greeting children and posing for pictures with them and their parents. She doesn't know where he finds the energy. He looks like he's a million years old, yet he grows even more energetic and enthusiastic with each passing moment. He feeds off the energy of the people here, much like the best politicians do at rallies with their constituents.

Stowe and Wyatt have disappeared to who knows where. So long as they are at the plane when it's time to leave, it isn't her problem. At least the press pool hasn't wandered off. Still, with the Bobbsey Twins absent, there's nobody left to help advocate with her, so MacKenzie is flying solo when she pulls St. Nick aside.

"Santa, I know you want to spend time with the people, but we really need to get back on the plane."

"I understand your time pressures, MacKenzie, but you really need to learn to relax and enjoy the moment."

"I will enjoy the moment you meet Alaya Tucker, causing her eyes to light up," MacKenzie confesses in a passive-aggressive appeal to move this along.

"Soon enough."

"Okay. What are we doing here, Santa?"

He spreads his arms and gestures around him. "Spreading Christmas cheer."

Santa clearly doesn't care that this is an American taxpayer-funded junket. She wants to say that spreading cheer isn't what the government does, but there are too many reporters around, and a comment like that would go viral in nanoseconds. MacKenzie isn't keen on becoming an Internet meme. She already has enough drama this holiday.

Her phone rings, and she sees it's from her boss's cell phone. Speaking of drama. She punches accept and holds the device to her ear.

"Don't say it."

"Say what? I stopped paying attention to your travels after Santa Sleigh One took off from Finland. I figured you were over the Atlantic and I had no idea that you landed in Austria until I saw it on CNN. Was the plane's compass broken or something?"

"Santa insisted on a last-minute change of destination."

"That's funny. I thought you worked in the White House for the Executive Branch, which means you work for me. When did you agree to start taking orders from Santa Claus?"

"Around the time you told me to do what it takes to get him on that plane. That's the mission, right? We are heading for St. Louis, but Santa insisted we come here first. So, here we are."

Marco sighs. "And you couldn't call?"

"There's no cell phone coverage at thirty-six thousand feet."

It's a lame excuse, but the only one she could fabricate. MacKenzie didn't want to call Marco because she didn't want to have this conversation. Who could blame her?

"No, but there is a multi-million-dollar communications system on that plane designed to be used in the event of *nuclear* war. You could have tried using that."

"I didn't know where we were heading until an hour before we landed in Vienna."

"Fine. Whatever. How long will you be in the Austrian capital?"

"That's a good question. I don't know. Santa isn't saying. I'm going to tell the press pool to make accommodations—"

"I don't care about them. I do care about what I'm going to say to the president, who just learned that Santa Claus hijacked his plane and is taking it for a global joy ride."

"It's not like that."

"Well, there is a press room full of reporters who are growing more curious by the hour. They want to know what Santa is up to, and I don't have any answers for the press secretary to offer them."

"Neither do I. Tell her to stall."

"MacKenzie, I can't possibly be clearer about this: Find out why you are in Austria and then get Santa to St. Louis. The agreement was to transport him to Middle America, not to The Alpine Republic for some light Christmas shopping and wiener schnitzel."

"I'll do what I can."

"No, you need to do what the president asks. Get it done, Mac."

Marco hangs up. MacKenzie checks to see that the call disconnected before stuffing the phone back in her pocket. She sighs heavily. Get it done. Yeah, right. If he thinks it's so easy to argue with Father Christmas, he should come here and do it himself.

"That sounded tense," Keith Meadows says from behind her.

Of the members of the press pool she would have wanted overhearing any part of that conversation, he'd be at the bottom of the list. Keith is a long-time denizen of the White House press briefing room. Now covering his third president, he's a senior correspondent and is usually one of the most inquisitive members of the media. And the most aggressive one. To say that he doesn't like this administration is an exercise in understatement.

"Eavesdropping on my call?"

"Just the end of it."

That's probably a lie, but she decides not to challenge him on it. "I work at the White House. Everything is tense there. You know that."

"Better than most," he admits. "I've also been there long enough to know when something isn't going as planned. This trip wasn't sanctioned by the president, was it?"

"Why would you ask that?"

"Answer the question."

"That wasn't a question, Keith. It was an accusation. You're fishing for a story that doesn't include Santa Claus flying from Finland to a beautiful Christmas market in Austria to spread goodwill. What's the matter? Too optimistic and cheerful for you?"

"Fine. Deep background only. Was this diversion sanctioned by the president?"

Deep background is a journalism term used in political reporting. It's considered more restrictive than "off the record," meaning the information provided by a source, MacKenzie, in this case, cannot be directly quoted or attributed in any way. It was a tactic devised by the media to maintain complete confidentiality. This type of "deep background" information is shared with journalists to provide context and understanding, not that they always play by the rules. Most of the reporters she knows would sell their souls for a scoop, and some of them already have.

"Same answer."

"You know, I'm hearing chatter in my newsroom back home."

"It's good to know that the Washington gossip mill that masquerades as the press corps is working like a well-oiled machine in my absence."

"They're starting to wonder what the point of this trip is," Keith says, ignoring the slight.

"To deliver Santa to a young—"

"Yeah, yeah, yeah, only we aren't in St. Louis, are we?"

"Wow, those four years of J-school at GW are really paying off. Your powers of observation are uncanny," MacKenzie says with a sneer, mocking his credentials as a journalism major at George Washington University. "I have to get back to Santa."

"Hoping the problem is going to go away isn't an effective tactic, MacKenzie," he calls out to her as she walks away.

"Enjoy your time in Vienna, Keith!"

MacKenzie's stomach is turning. It isn't the aromas of the market or the jet lag. This is becoming a growing problem. Her boss is impatient, the president is anxious, and the press is beginning to sniff around. She really needs to end this now before Keith finds something to write about that paints the president in a negative light during the holidays.

Chapter Twenty-Nine

WYATT HUFFMAN

This is a unique and luxurious way to explore Vienna's historic city center. Whoever conceived of the idea of combining a traditional horse-drawn carriage ride with a gourmet dining experience was a genius. It pairs two favorite tourist activities – eating and sightseeing, and does it in a beautiful horse-drawn carriage.

Whoever the Wrights are splurged for this tour. When Stefan mentioned the food, he didn't tell them it was a three-course meal prepared by a renowned Viennese restaurant. Along with a bottle of wine, the meal is served in the carriage on a table designed for dining comfortably during the ride. Wyatt thought about saying no to this. He's glad he didn't.

Stefan turns from the driver's seat. "I can close the carriage if you two are getting cold."

Wyatt looks at Stowe, who shakes her head. "I'm from Montana, and she grew up on a mountain in Vermont."

"And we came here from the Arctic Circle," Stowe adds. "We'll be okay."

"Please let me know if that changes."

Stefan launches into a monologue about the city and some of its sights. They listen intently, and Wyatt asks a few questions out of genuine curiosity. When Stefan falls silent, Wyatt and Stowe lean back to literally enjoy the ride.

"I'm sorry," Stowe almost whispers.

"For what?"

"I may have guilted you a little into doing this."

"You mean you didn't intend on us getting offered an almost ninety-minute romantic carriage ride through the magical streets of Vienna at Christmas while huddled under a blanket?"

"No," Stowe says with a half-hearted laugh.

Wyatt smiles. "Santa did."

"He said he wasn't trying to get us back together."

"Stowe, please tell me you've noticed that there is a big difference between what Santa says and what Santa does. He's creating the circumstances for it. Dinner with old friends we met in Iceland. A letter to a carriage driver who offers us…this. Really?"

"Fair point. You didn't have to agree. I know that you hate me. I would have understood if you said no."

Wyatt stares at the magnificent old-world facades of the buildings the carriage passes. It's not that simple. She should know that.

"I don't hate you, Stowe."

"You have every right to."

"Yeah, I do. You made it very clear what you thought of me in August."

Stowe hangs her head. "No. I don't think I made it clear at all."

Wyatt waits for further explanation but none is coming. He doesn't know what she means but he refuses to ask. If Stowe wants to explain what she said during that argument, that's on her. Unfortunately, it doesn't look like she wants to. The result is an awkward silence.

"Have you noticed all the dirty looks we're getting? What's that about?" she asks, giving in to the burning desire to shatter the silence between them.

"Jealousy."

"Stop it! You're not *that* good-looking."

Wyatt laughs. "I didn't mean it that way. We're drinking wine in a beautiful carriage while everyone's feet are getting sore and callused from walking on cobblestones. Who wouldn't be jealous?"

"True. It's easy to get lost in the moment."

"Yeah, well, that wouldn't be the first time that's happened to us."

Stowe doesn't argue that point. She can't. They always seem to find themselves in romantic situations. It started when they got to know each other at the Blue Lagoon. Then, it was the serenity and closeness of their reindeer ride in Rovaniemi, sledding down a mountain under a moonlit sky, and seeing the majestic northern lights. Wyatt can add a carriage ride in Vienna to the list.

"You sound like you regret it."

"I sound like I regret the way it turned out."

Stowe nods. Both of them return to enjoying the scenery and the ride. Neither of them wants to spoil the moment or let the bottle of wine they are splitting affect their judgment. Both of them know that rehashing what happened in the summer is likely to lead to another argument that will spoil this moment. Wyatt isn't about to let that happen.

Chapter Thirty

SVP MALCOLM CHAPMAN

Malcolm meets every couple of hours with his senior staff. Karoline and Luisa are capable directors with equally skilled teams. The former is a marketer with fifteen years of experience. The latter is younger, as social media experts usually are. They do very good work, not that any of it is being appreciated, especially by Malcolm's boss.

Franz Brunner decided to drop in and get a briefing on their progress. As Heilung's chief marketing officer, he has spent his prime years answering to Klaus Eberhardt. Malcolm may want a promotion, but he doesn't want that job. Franz is difficult enough to deal with. He couldn't imagine rising to the C-suite in this company and having to deal with their belligerent CEO.

The four people watch footage of Santa boarding the plane in Finland and then his arrival in Vienna, Austria. It became global news when the American president's jet headed south instead of west across the Atlantic. Everyone is caught up in the speculation as to why he went there.

"They're calling it Santa Sleigh One instead of Air Force One," Karoline narrates from the far side of the table.

"Clever."

"I thought so. I'm half surprised someone didn't paint a red nose on the front of the plane. It's only a matter of time before it gets photoshopped in."

"Who's covering it?" Malcolm asks, leaning back in his chair. "How far is the reach on this?"

Karoline nods at Luisa, who works the television remote. She switches to a Japanese news station that is still covering the arrival in Vienna and the trip to a Christmas market. Then, the television changes to an Indian station where the anchors are talking over a slide show of still images of the American president's plane. The last channel is the most surprising. An Arab man is covering it for the Middle East's most prestigious network. None of those networks broadcast to large Christian populations. She mutes it after a few seconds.

"Does that answer your question?" Luisa asks, earning a grimace from Malcolm.

"Fortunately, news of the trip has overtaken discussions about our drug and its price. Replays of your interview have been pushed off the screen by Santa Sleigh One's landing in Vienna instead of crossing the Atlantic. Everyone has gone into speculation mode."

"Including us. Does anyone have any idea why Santa is there?"

"Who cares?" the CMO barks. "Klaus wants to know how you're going to handle this, and frankly, so do I."

"We are handling it," Malcolm assures him.

The words that came out of his mouth didn't sound like much of an assurance. The tone was one of desperation and annoyance. That wasn't the intent, but the last few days have left Malcolm frazzled. As a result, he seems more aggressive.

"Really? It doesn't show."

"We've done everything we can to tamp things down," Malcolm says after taking a breath.

"What about social media?"

"We've made a dozen posts on our main and secondary accounts," Luisa chimes in. "All of them have been ratio'd."

The term "ratio'd" may have originated on Twitter before it became X, but it applies to situations where a post on any platform receives more replies than likes or shares. When people engage with a post to criticize or mock it rather than to support or share it with their friends and followers, it's a strong indication that they are upset at the poster because they disagree with a decision or comment. As of now, they aren't happy with Heilung.

"Do we have any friendly members of the media we can lean on?" Franz asks.

"We have friendly reporters," Karoline offers, "but they are slaves to editors, and editors are slaves to bosses who relish clicks and views. This is the story of the year. They aren't going to alienate their audiences by coming out and defending a three-and-a-half-million-dollar-per-dose drug."

"Then it's your job to explain why it costs that much."

"This is the season of giving, Franz. Even if most people accept our reasoning, which they don't, nobody wants to hear a profit-driven justification this close to Christmas."

"You were tasked with getting out of this mess, Malcolm," the CMO says, pointing a finger at him. "I asked how you plan on doing that, and all you come back with are insinuations that we should give it away. We're not doing that, so what else do you have? How are you going to fix this?"

It's the moment of truth. Malcolm has one more idea up his sleeve. His boss isn't going to like this either, but if he can convince him, then maybe he has a fighting chance to keep his job. If this doesn't work, he's out of options.

"By enlisting Santa's help."

A look of confusion grips Franz's face. "Okay…what does that mean?"

"Heilung doesn't want to hand over the drug for free. I get it. It sets a dangerous precedent. If we do it once, there is fear that we'll have to do it again. To get around that, we'll give it to Santa to give to Antonne Tucker for Christmas."

"Give it to Santa?"

It wasn't a question so much as a statement of disbelief.

"Yes. Santa hands it to Antonne in a gift-wrapped box, and he opens it live in front of cameras and millions of people. The boy gets the medication he needs, and hugs and tears ensue. Everyone will know we provided it, and it makes a great story for the press to run with. It's a win-win."

"Except we are handing over a profitable medicine and getting nothing in return."

"That's not true – we'll get goodwill and a lot of free advertising from the world's favorite feel-good story."

"That doesn't pay the bills, Malcolm," Franz says, smacking the table with the palm of his hand.

That is an old way of thinking. Social media has changed the game because it provides everyone a megaphone and platform to organize. Companies can no longer prioritize earnings and profit over perception and interest. It is far too easy for people to retaliate, and they absolutely will in this case.

Right or wrong, people want modern companies to be good corporate citizens. When they run afoul of those expectations, boycotts ensue. The loss of revenue from an organized effort like that is often measured in a number with six zeroes following it. It could be a rough couple of quarters or even years for Heilung if they don't make this one sacrifice. It amazes Malcolm that the executives here don't see that.

"You asked for the way out of this. That's the way out."

"And Klaus has already told you, in unmistakable terms, no."

Malcolm shakes his head. "He's wrong."

Franz stares at his SVP for a long moment before standing. "I don't think you want me to tell him you said that. We are a multi-billion-dollar pharmaceutical company, not a charity. We can weather the storm if we must, but it will be without you if that's the best you can come up with."

The CMO spins and marches out of the conference room. So much for him being on their side. He's protecting his job and nothing more.

"It was actually a really good idea," Karoline assures him. Luisa nods.

"Well, I'm open to new ones."

The two women lower their eyes. There aren't any other ones. People following this story want a happy ending that doesn't only include Antonne getting his Christmas wish for his sister. They want him to be okay. They want Heilung to hand him the drug. Nothing else is going to suffice.

If Klaus remains stubborn about this, then the game is over. No marketing team on the planet can force someone to think or believe a certain thing. All they can do is influence, but the executives here don't seem to understand that. They are willing to take one on the cheek, making Malcolm a sacrificial lamb in the process.

Chapter Thirty-One

COMMUNICATIONS DIRECTOR
MACKENZIE WALSH

Christmas markets may be a long-standing European holiday tradition that's gaining popularity worldwide, but nothing like this has arrived in the United States. Maybe small towns and villages in the heartland do something similar, but none of the big cities have anything that approaches this. The closest thing is what New York City hosts in Bryant Park during the holidays, but that has a completely different vibe.

This is only one of several markets in Vienna from what she was told. MacKenzie wonders how busy the others are. Are people flocking here because it's one of the best markets to visit, or is the crowd larger because word has spread through the masses that Santa is here? There's no way to know the answer to that question.

The atmosphere is certainly festive. There are thousands of twinkle lights strung up, the aromas of various foods waft to her nostrils as they ride the cool breeze, and the live music and carolers enhance the merriment. A dance troupe is even performing not far from the crowd that has gathered to see St. Nick.

MacKenzie wishes she could enjoy this, but she can't. It's bad enough that Santa is seeing fit to delay their arrival in St. Louis, but it's also too much Christmas for her. It isn't her favorite holiday by a long shot, and for a very good reason.

But here she is, powerless to move things along and practically freezing to death. She's more of a warm-weather girl, preferring Caribbean beaches and Mai Tais over frigid, snowy wastelands and hot chocolate. Why Santa would choose to live at the North Pole or Arctic Circle is beyond her grasp to comprehend.

"What's wrong, MacKenzie?" Santa asks, taking a moment away from the sugar-addled children. "You look miserable."

She starts to answer before looking around to ensure nobody from the media is eavesdropping. Keith can't be trusted not to report any conversation he overhears. He can barely be trusted to respect someone being off the record.

"I don't understand why we're here."

Santa spreads his arms and gestures around him. "Is this place not magical?"

MacKenzie presses her lips together. "It is. I guess."

"Oh, come now. These markets are the embodiment of the holiday season. Town squares and city centers are transformed into festive winter wonderlands. Did you know that the first instance of a Christmas market can be traced back right here to

Vienna? Technically, it wasn't Christmas-specific at the time. That title goes to the one held in Bautzen, Germany, in 1384."

"How do you know this stuff?" MacKenzie asks.

"I'm Santa Claus," he says with a laugh. "Those first markets were more generally winter markets where locals could stock up on goods and supplies to last through the cold months. Over time, they began focusing selling on products and goods associated with Christmas."

"Santa, please, why are we here?"

"How much do you know about me, MacKenzie?"

"You, or the myth of Santa Claus?"

"It's the same question. For example, I'm known as *Judge Judy* for children. I keep a list of who's naughty or nice and dole out rewards or punishments for their behavior accordingly. That wasn't always the case. In your country, the myth of Santa Claus was created to keep adults, not children, off the naughty list."

"What?"

MacKenzie has never heard that before. He has to be making it up. In all the stories she's heard about Santa as a child and even as a grown-up, not one ever described him aiming to keep adults in line. He must be fabricating this for her benefit.

"It's true. In the early 1800s, Christian leaders banned Christmas celebrations, calling them unscriptural and paganish. I can't entirely agree with the decision, but I understand their perspective. Unfortunately, they had a bigger problem – the townspeople wanted to party. By December, the crops were harvested, and sailors were less than enthusiastic about braving winter gales on the high seas. They had time on their hands.

"So, on December 25, men would get drunk and stumble around cities looking for stuff to loot. It was colonial Black Friday, spring break, and New Year's Eve all in one. A good time, I'm sure, but something that the clergy would be remiss to ignore. So, they decided to make Christmas more family-friendly, and the Saint Nicholas Society offered their namesake as the perfect frontman for the cause."

"Saint Nick," MacKenzie whispers.

"Drawing on the Dutch legend of Sinterklaas, sketches were created featuring St. Nicholas soaring high above New York houses as he delivered presents to well-behaved children. The reputation was already there. All they had to do was foster it.

"A decade later, an anonymous poem called 'The Children's Friend' was penned. It featured a magical figure named Santeclaus, who drove a reindeer-led sleigh full of rewards and filled obedient children's stockings with little presents. It was a genius move if the goal was to get drunks off the streets. Christmas became a family event with children as the focus."

"I've never heard of that poem," MacKenzie admits.

"No, probably not, but you have heard of the one from an Episcopalian scholar named Clement Clarke Moore. He wrote the work 'A Visit From St. Nicholas.' You might know it better as 'The Night Before Christmas.' That's where modern depictions of me are derived from."

"Santa—"

"None of those poems offer a *reason* I do what I do. Do I exist for the kids…or for their parents? Am I a means of parental control of children as the subcommittee eluded to, or do I also influence the actions and behavior of adults as well?"

"Santa, with all due respect, none of that explains why we're here at a Christmas market in Austria."

She sees it for sure this time. There is a noticeable twinkle in Santa's eye, and it isn't from the strings of lights or the flashes of cameras behind her. He offers her a warm, gracious, and knowing smile.

"It will."

Chapter Thirty-Two

STOWE BESSETTE

The carriage ride was nice. Okay, it was way better than nice – it almost felt like old times. Well, not that old, but after what happened in August…. It was something Stowe never thought would happen again, at least not with Wyatt Huffman.

The last five months have been hard. Stowe wanted to be strong and convince herself that she didn't need him, but everything she told herself was a lie. Sure, she can survive without a man – any man. But that isn't the point. She was *happier* with him in her life. They had grown accustomed to being with each other, even after such a short period.

But Wyatt left, and she was convinced he had moved on. He didn't, but his reception at the ranch wasn't warm and fuzzy. He made it clear that his being here only has to do with delivering on Antonne Tucker's Christmas wish. Wyatt is a straight shooter, so there is no doubt that is his intention. So, after the carriage ride, Stowe was surprised her ex asked if she wanted to get a cup of coffee. She couldn't say no.

Stefan gushed over Café Frauenhuber, the oldest continuously operating and perhaps most famous coffeehouse in the city. It is even asserted that both Wolfgang Amadeus Mozart and Ludwig van Beethoven performed at this venue. Vienna is renowned for its coffeehouse culture, where people gather to read, write, and converse over a virtual cornucopia of pastries and snacks. Even UNESCO recognizes the importance of these shops in the city's social and cultural life. So, it wouldn't be surprising if two of the world's preeminent composers did.

Wyatt sits back, puts his hands on his stomach, and groans. "Between Aurielle's cocoa and this *Apfelstrudel*, I have enough sugar in my system to flap my arms and fly back to Montana."

"That feat would give the news something more to talk about," Stowe says with a smile. She knows what he means. This trip is doing nothing good for her waistline.

Wyatt doesn't return her sympathetic grin. Instead, he leans forward over the table. "What did you mean in the carriage when you said you didn't make it clear?"

Stowe presses her lips together. She should have known that's why he wanted to come to the coffee shop, other than its being a landmark. He wants the conversation she initially wanted on the plane.

"You're not going to want to hear this."

"Probably not, but Ellie said I need closure to move on."

Stowe's jaw tightens, and she swallows hard. "And you want it now?"

"Yeah."

"Okay," Stowe says, folding up the paper napkin and placing it on her plate. "I pushed you away."

"That much was pretty clear."

"It wasn't because of the reasons you think. It has nothing to do with who you are as a person or even our political differences. Sure, I was mad about losing on the bill, but that was an excuse."

"Then why?"

There was a point during the fall when the leaves were changing in Vermont that Stowe went outside her grandparents' cabin with a cup of coffee and reflected on how this conversation would go if she ever spoke to Wyatt again. She felt the cool air on her face and admired the leaves changing on the trees, thinking that she should be honest with him. She dismissed those thoughts as the weeks flew by, thinking the time for that talk would never come. Now, it's here. Unlike on the trip to Finland, he's ready to listen.

"Because I completely fell in love with you."

"Weird way to show it," Wyatt concludes.

"I know. I felt the same way about Bobby in the beginning. That moment at the lake opened my eyes to him, just like the Blue Lagoon opened mine to you. Once upon a time, I couldn't imagine myself without Bobby. I thought that man was perfect for me."

The story of Bobby Sinclair is a tragic one. He snuck a kiss under her nana's mistletoe, and Stowe hated him for that. Then he saved her from harassment from a trio of boys that summer at the lake, and she had a change of heart. She fell in love with him, but after taking the job in Washington, they drifted apart. Before long, it became clear that they wanted different things out of life. The relationship met its sudden and permanent end when she caught him red-handed cheating on her.

"Then, I was without him. He changed…or I changed. Either way, I was alone. Fast-forward to this past summer, and I found myself feeling the same way about you. Everything was great, and I was so happy. Then the bill came up, and I thought you were changing. I felt myself changing. I got scared."

"So, you decided to end it?"

She shakes her head. "That wasn't my intent. I wanted to create some space between us. I needed room to put walls up to protect myself."

"By doing the same thing to me that Jessie did?"

Stowe lowers her eyes. "This is going to sound horrible, but that thought never crossed my mind. I know that she was a big part of your life, but in our time together, you rarely mentioned her."

Jessie Stills and Wyatt were high school sweethearts. They were inseparable, even into college. They shared all the same interests, common values, and a culture that comes with a rural upbringing. Then Jessie got political. Whenever they didn't agree, she made it her mission to change his mind. It ultimately broke them up. That's why Wyatt is so angry with Stowe. He accused her of doing the same thing, which she did.

"I moved on."

"And that's why I didn't even consider it. Do you know what my biggest fear was when we started dating? That seeing the world from different sides of the political aisle would drive a wedge between us. Winter and spring came and went, but that never happened. You never let our work get in the way of what we had, even though I was terrified that it eventually would. Fighting over that stupid bill gave me a chance to make this a self-fulfilling prophecy."

Wyatt doesn't say anything. It's a lot for him to process. He no doubt had his own ideas about what happened, some of which he shared. The reality is jarring. It's time for her to take the responsibility everyone close to her has begged her to take. Mandy would be doing cartwheels in this coffee shop if she were here for this.

"That fight had nothing to do with you. It was all me. My demons got the best of me. That's the only way I can explain it."

"You figured this out on your own?" Wyatt finally asks, almost sounding impressed.

"I talked to a therapist," Stowe confesses, causing him to raise an eyebrow. "Her name is Amanda, and she isn't shy about pointing out my failings after a bottle of wine."

Mandy is the debutante daughter of wealthy parents. She isn't in Washington because she needs the money. With her trust fund, she could spend her years partying on Miami Beach in the summers and skiing in Aspen in the winters. She just isn't wired that way. Working on Capitol Hill is something that she wants to do. Because she's free of the financial constraints that burden the rest of us, she's open to expressing her opinions however she sees fit. That's true at work and is especially true with her friends outside of it.

"She is direct."

"You have no idea," Stowe moans. "Mandy really likes you. She liked who I was when we were together. Every day, she would remind me that you brought out the very best in me and that I was an idiot for pushing you away."

"That couldn't have been easy to hear."

"It wasn't, at least at first. I was so pissed at Mandy's constant barbs that we barely spoke for most of September. But the more I thought about it, the more I knew she was right. I never should have acted like that. I should have explained how I was feeling instead of lashing out like I did. And that's why I'm sorry."

Wyatt stares at his empty espresso cup, turning it slowly in its saucer. "Is that why you really came to Montana? To win me back?"

Stowe shakes her head. "No, because I know I won't win you back. I've spent the last few months living through the five stages of grief. I'm now on acceptance. You told me that Ellie said you needed closure. I suppose I needed it, too. And I wanted to apologize to you because you deserved better than what happened in August."

Wyatt begins to say something and stops. Stowe doesn't know what he's thinking. She shifts in her chair, bracing herself for whatever comes out of his mouth next. Instead of something profound or even angry, he glances at his watch.

"We should go meet Santa before he decides to leave without us."

Chapter Thirty-Three

WYATT HUFFMAN

The pair walks back to Karlsplatz roughly the way they came. The return trip takes them down the same streets and past the same buildings, but it still looks different. It's the change of perspective, Wyatt supposes. That's an interesting metaphor for his life right now. It's amazing how one conversation can completely upend things. Truths he had either divined or convinced himself of weren't really truths at all. They were misconceptions. Or so he's being led to believe.

But Wyatt knows in his heart that Stowe wasn't lying in the coffee shop. As angry at her as he was, and still to a degree is, the woman he fell in love with isn't capable of that level of deceit. She admitted mistakes in a way no one he's met ever has. She admitted them to him in a way that he never could if the roles were reversed.

Then, the bomb dropped. Stowe admitted that she was in love with him. The "L" word was never used in their time together. It has a special meaning for both of them. Even though he felt it, the time and place he was going to utter it had to be special. It never arrived before that fateful summer day.

Admitting that she was scared was another revelation. That's the opposite of what Wyatt spent five months convincing himself of. With his world turned completely upside-down, he's at a loss for what to do next.

"How will we find Santa?" Stowe asks, interrupting his train of thought when they reach the park.

"Easy. Follow the crowd."

That tactic bears fruit within minutes. A horde of children is gathered around him while their parents and the media take pictures. The word of Santa's arrival has definitely gotten out. There are easily ten or fifteen times the number of people in the Christmas market as there were before they left.

MacKenzie is standing off to the side with Aurielle. Unlike the elf, who is enjoying the moment, the White House communications director looks constipated. He almost feels bad for her. They were in her position once, armed with a decree to accomplish a mission and unable to fulfill it because St. Nick had other plans. She needs to understand that it will all work out in the end. Wyatt doesn't think MacKenzie wants to hear that right now.

There is one notable exception to the mob gathered around the jolly elf. A mother and child are waiting off at a distance to the side. She seems hesitant over what to do. Wyatt walks over, and he can hear Stowe following him a couple of paces behind.

"Hi. I don't think there's a line to meet Santa. You can walk right up to him."

"Thank you. I think my son is a little intimidated," the woman explains in perfect English with a hint of a Southern accent.

"You're American?"

"Born and raised. We're recent ex-pats to Europe. And honestly, I understand why my son is apprehensive – I find Santa a little intimidating, too."

"We know the feeling," Stowe reassures her. "We were starstruck when we first met him."

"You've met Santa?" the boy asks, his eyes filled with awe and wonder.

"We have," Wyatt says with a smile. "We're even traveling with him. He's very nice, if a little devious sometimes."

Stowe offers him a knowing smirk before turning her attention to the boy. "Would you like to meet him?"

"What do you think?" his mother asks.

The boy stares for a long moment and shakes his head. He turns and walks away, heading for a set of vendor booths ten yards away. His mother apologizes for his abrupt departure and gives chase.

The energy around Wyatt changes as a crowd forms around him and Stowe. He turns to see Santa standing behind him.

"How was your ride, Wyatt?"

"I'll talk to you later about that, Santa," he says with a grin. "Do you see that little boy over at the booth with the vendor selling clocks? He wants to meet you, but he's a little scared."

There's a glimmer in Santa's eye. "Well! We can't have that, can we?"

He walks over to the booth and takes a knee next to the boy. The reporters in the press pool jump into action, all jockeying for position to get a shot worthy of whatever headline this excursion earns. The boy stares at him with eyes the size of dinner plates, but he doesn't retreat behind his mother's legs like Wyatt thought he would. Maybe it's not fear but something else driving his apprehension.

"Hello there, young man. I'm Santa Claus."

"Hi."

"Do you like the clocks?"

The boy nods.

"He has a thing for clocks," his mother says, placing her hands on her son's shoulders. "I have no idea where he got that from."

"Oh, my dear, few things in life perfectly encapsulate form and function like a clock. They can be beautiful or plain. They can be as large as Big Ben or small enough to fit on your wrist. But what they do best is not only measure time but remind us that every second we have on this Earth is precious. Which one do you like?"

The boy points at an ornate mantel clock, stained in Christmas colors, with a gold face. The man in the booth gently pulls it off the shelf so the boy can have a better look. His eyes absolutely light up.

"Oh, that is a beautiful one. Would you like it for Christmas?"

He eagerly nods.

"We'll take it," Santa says as cameras click away behind them. The woman starts to protest, but Stowe whispers something in her ear, and she falls silent.

The man tries to hand it to Santa, but he points at the boy. "How much?"

"I can't charge you, Santa," the man says in heavily accented English.

"Nonsense. Your daughter, Brenna, is an equestrian who asked for additional lessons this year because she wants to ride the Lipizzaner stallions at the Spanish Riding School here in Vienna someday. And your son, Matthias, wants to be a scientist and asked for a special chemistry set. You are working here to earn extra money for both. You must take the money we offer for the sake of your children."

The man is completely stunned. The crowd of people around them look at each other in amazement. The only two people who aren't surprised are Wyatt and Stowe. They've experienced this firsthand on a few occasions. The critics and naysayers can try to rationalize it away, but they know differently. This man may not whip around the world on a flying sleigh while delivering presents as the legend says, but he is special.

"I got this, Santa," Wyatt says, pulling out his wallet and handing the man a few hundred euros.

"How did…how did…?"

"He's Santa Claus," Stowe says as Wyatt nods at the man. "That's all that needs to be said about it. Have a Merry Christmas."

The man thanks them profusely, and Wyatt and Stowe join Santa, who is talking to the boy's mother. Her son is completely oblivious. He hasn't taken his eyes off the amazing clock he got for Christmas from Santa.

"You look upset," Santa says. "Is there anything I can help with?"

The woman forces a weak smile. "No. It's just been a rough week. I'm thinking about going home."

"And where is home?"

"The U.S. We're from Virginia."

"It just so happens that we are heading in that direction. Would you like to come with us?"

Wyatt glances to his left in time to see MacKenzie's jaw drop. Her face crinkles in a mix of confusion and annoyance. She looks like she's about to lose it as she pushes through the crowd gathered around Santa. Thank God looks don't really kill. They'd be attending Santa's funeral next week.

Chapter Thirty-Four

COMMUNICATIONS DIRECTOR
MACKENZIE WALSH

MacKenzie wants to scream, but shouting at Santa Claus before Christmas won't be a good look with so many people around. Nevertheless, something needs to be said. This absurd diversion to the foothills of the Alps needs to end. Air Force One isn't public transit. It's not a bus you can hop on, pay a fare, and ride to your next destination.

"Santa, I'm sorry, but they can't go with us."

"Why not?"

She didn't think this through before jumping into the fray with that declaration. MacKenzie didn't expect him to question her on it, but here they are. She needs to quickly come up with something plausible.

"We aren't authorized to take on additional passengers."

"It's okay," the woman says, clutching her son. "I don't want to cause trouble."

"It's no trouble at all," Santa assures her. "You're an American citizen, correct?"

"Yes, we are."

Santa turns to MacKenzie. For a fleeting moment, it looks like he has another twinkle in his eye. "Is it the position of your president that he won't help American citizens in need when it is of no inconvenience or additional cost to your taxpayers?"

MacKenzie freezes. Damn, that was a good rebuttal. Almost anything she says will sound crass and uncaring. She's aware that cameras are rolling and that the press pool is itching for an angle on the story. She needs to be very careful.

"We don't allow unauthorized personnel aboard Air Force One, Santa."

"Of course. That's a reasonable restriction when the president is on board," he says, allowing her to relax slightly. "But it's not Air Force One right now. It's Santa Sleigh One, or so the pilots told me. Isn't that true?"

MacKenzie catches a glimpse of Keith out of the corner of her eye. He is writing this entire conversation down in shorthand. That's all she needs. If the vulture writes a story and the editor comes up with a catchy enough headline, Marco will have her sitting in the corner during the White House Christmas party.

"This woman is from Virginia, and we aren't going there. We're going to St. Louis."

Santa nods and bends down to address the child. "We are going to a hospital to see a very sick boy who's almost your age. Would you like to accompany us? You can even bring your new clock."

The young boy who was too scared to approach Santa minutes ago nods enthusiastically.

"Is it okay with you?" Santa asks his mother.

She smiles, fighting back her emotions. "Yes. I can't think of a finer way to spend the days before Christmas."

"They aren't going to Virginia anymore, MacKenzie. I would like them to accompany me to St. Louis. I'm sure there is space on a modified 747 for two more."

MacKenzie appeals to Wyatt and Stowe, who are standing only a few feet away. They stare at her blankly. Neither is the least bit interested in coming to her aid. That figures.

"Fine. I will get the necessary approvals."

"Excellent," Santa says, clapping his gloved hands. "Can you return to your hotel and get your things? We'll meet you at the airport in, say, ninety minutes. We'll leave tonight."

"Absolutely!" the mother says.

"We're leaving for St. Louis tonight?" MacKenzie asks, confirming that she heard him correctly. It's the best news she's received all day.

"No, we're leaving Vienna tonight. We need to make another stop."

The excitement that gripped her mere seconds ago turns to dread. "Santa—"

"I will tell you where on the plane so you can make the proper arrangements. I know you don't like me doing your job for you."

"It's not that. It's…we have people traveling with us who want to get back home to their families."

"I understand," Santa says, nodding before he turns to the press pool. "I have a very special gift to deliver, and I would love you all to be present for it if you're willing to travel with me for just a little longer. Is that okay with you?"

There is a chorus of agreement from the group of reporters. It may be the first and last time they agree on anything. Another diversion is a price each is willing to pay for more stories.

"It's settled, then. But in the interest of fairness, I will let the final decision lie with Stowe and Wyatt. They are only here because of my request, so I will understand if they want to return home to *their* families."

Wyatt and Stowe look at each other. He nods at her.

"We go where you go, Santa."

There is another twinkle in his eye. "Then let's get moving."

MacKenzie is struggling to control her emotions. It will be another harsh chat with Marco and more questions from the president. The media is going to have a field day, and the president's critics will start making noise. Worst of all, Wyatt and Stowe could have ended this and didn't. MacKenzie feels somewhat betrayed. They know how important this is.

"You want to tell me again how this is all going according to your plan?" Keith asks with a grin before walking to chase down Santa.

Chapter Thirty-Five

SVP MALCOLM CHAPMAN

Focus is a critical skill. It impacts many aspects of life and is a considerable contributor to personal growth and professional success. It has helped Malcolm climb the ranks to become a senior vice president in a huge multinational pharmaceutical corporation.

He has always been able to concentrate on tasks, even with considerable distractions. As an adolescent, he never needed any of the drugs that mitigated the effects of attention deficit disorder like many of his peers. The ability to keep his mind solidly working on a task made him productive and efficient and resulted in higher quality work because he was able to reduce errors and pay closer attention to details.

That's on a normal day. Janelle and Braylen are missing, and if that isn't bad enough, out of communication. Worrying about them is taking a toll. Malcolm is anxious, can't concentrate, and is even having problems remembering things. Worst of all, he's taking it out on his colleagues. He's impatient and has caught himself snapping at them over trivial things.

Malcolm's phone finally rings, and for once, it isn't work-related. The picture of his beautiful wife posing in a flower garden fills the screen. He snatches it up and scrambles out of his chair and through the door of the small conference room to avoid his colleagues' prying ears before he answers.

"Janelle? Thank God! Are you okay? I've been worried sick."

"I know. I'm sorry. I should have at least sent you a text to let you know that we're okay. It wasn't fair to make you worry."

It isn't fair at all, but Malcolm wisely keeps his mouth shut. He knows that Janelle would never have put up with him doing that, but now isn't the time to point out her hypocrisy. He's just glad she called and relieved that his family is okay.

"I saw your note on the kitchen counter. I thought you were only going to the Christmas market."

"We did. Then I got on the Autobahn and went to another in Stuttgart and another in Munich. We've just kept driving. Braylen is having a great time. He can't get enough of them."

"That's good. I'm sorry I missed out."

"Are you?"

That question cuts deep. He absolutely is sorry. Malcolm would much rather be spending evenings with his family than trying to manage a PR disaster that he has no hope of controlling.

"Why didn't you come home?"

Janelle scoffs. "What was the point? You aren't there."

"That's not fair."

"There is nothing fair about this, Malcolm!" He might need to keep his voice low in an office environment, but that doesn't apply to his irate wife, who can still be heard even though the phone isn't on speaker. "Not for you, not for me, and definitely not for Braylen."

"I don't want to fight about this now, Janelle," Malcolm says, taking a cleansing breath to maintain his calm.

She doesn't understand. How could she? As successful as she was in her career before Bray was born, she's been out of work for a while now. Janelle can't fathom the demands and stress that being an executive at Heilung generates. Worse, Malcolm has no idea how to make her understand.

"Me neither," his wife quietly replies.

"When are you coming home?"

"I'm not," Janelle declares. "I'm going to take Braylen home to spend Christmas with my parents."

"What? You can't do that! You can't take my son away from me at Christmas."

"Why not? Your job has no problem taking my husband and his father away from us." Malcolm audibly sighs into the microphone. "What? That's not what you want to hear? Do you want us to wait around that dismal apartment in the hopes you'll actually spend time with us? That you will be there when Bray opens his gifts?"

"I'll be there on Christmas day!"

"Are you sure? Because I'm not. You are giving everything you have to gain this promotion, and there is nothing left for your family."

"Janelle, please don't do this," Malcolm pleads.

"I am doing this. You are making this choice, and these are the consequences. You are placing your job over your family. That's your decision because your career is important to you. But I'm not about to spoil Bray's Christmas because his father has different priorities. He needs to be around family, and if you can't accommodate that, I have to make other arrangements. I'm sorry."

"Janelle—"

"If you want to spend Christmas with us, get on a plane and come to my parents' house. I'll let you know when we get there. Don't worry about us traveling. We'll catch a flight from here and be fine. You have bigger things to concern yourself with."

Janelle hangs up without waiting for a response or saying goodbye. Not that there is anything Malcolm could say that would get her to change her mind. Once she makes a decision, she's completely immovable. Her weighing the decision over the past day or two is the only reason she's still in Germany. This call is nothing more than a warning that his wife is taking action.

Malcolm feels like he was kicked in the gut. If there wasn't enough heat coming from the CEO and CMO, he just added another impossible situation to the list. Something has to give, and it has to be soon.

Chapter Thirty-Six

WYATT HUFFMAN

Wyatt takes a deep breath. It's not about what this call is going to cost in terms of money. The federal government is paying the tab for this conversation. It's what the cost will be when he gets home. He's never going to hear the end of it.

"Hello?"

"Hey, sis."

"Wyatt?" she asks, likely confused about the caller ID. "Why does my phone say you're at the White House?"

"Uh…the signal from the plane is probably being bounced off a military satellite and routed through the defense network to the White House switchboard before being sent across the United States to Montana."

Ellie laughs. "You don't do anything halfway, do you, Big Brother? You're on the plane now?"

"Cruising at thirty thousand feet or so."

"Nice. How was Austria?"

"Beautiful. Very Christmas-y."

"Mmhmm," his sister says, no doubt loading the guns for the salvo Wyatt knows she's about to unleash. "And how is *Stowe*?"

And there it is. "Do you really need to bring that up?"

"Seriously? Did you think there was a chance in hell of calling me and not getting that question? No, you didn't because you're smart. That means you called because you wanted to talk to me about her. So, go ahead and spill. The doctor is in."

Wyatt shakes his head. His sister is a piece of work.

"You know, Papa said you drive him nuts with your armchair psychology."

"Good. Stop changing the subject. Did Stowe apologize again for what happened between you two?"

"Yes."

Wyatt launches into a brief recap of what transpired since they left Montana, constantly looking around the cabin to ensure Stowe isn't in earshot. He doesn't go into gory detail. There is no time, and the particulars aren't that important. Ellie can use her imagination to glean what was said. She's good at that.

"It sounds like someone did some serious soul-searching after you left."

"Her roommate helped. Mandy is as persistent as she is blunt. She's a version of you, now that I think of it."

"I like her already. So, you're conflicted."

"Why would you say that?" Wyatt asks.

"Because you're my brother, and I know you as well as anybody. You *never* would have called me if you had everything figured out. You wanted to take the trip to get closure and say goodbye. Now, Stowe has opened up and you realize the truth wasn't what you thought it was. You're second-guessing yourself. How am I doing so far?"

It's uncanny. Wyatt wants to argue or at least punch holes in her amateur shrink skills. But he can't because she's spot-on.

"Your silence speaks volumes," Ellie concludes.

"What should I do?"

"I can't answer that, you moron. You're a big boy. Man up and make your own choices. Otherwise, I'll buy you a package of diapers and a bottle when you get home."

Wyatt ignores the dig. "What would you do in my situation?"

"I would never have landed in your situation in the first place," Ellie says with a laugh.

"Fair enough," Wyatt says, closing his eyes. "I'm asking for your advice, sis, maybe for the first time in my life. Please don't make me beg for it."

"Okay, okay, okay…I'll enjoy the moment later. Let me ask you this: Are you having fun?"

Wyatt snickers. "We went on a carriage ride around the center of Vienna and had espresso in its oldest coffeehouse before leaving."

"Oh. That sounds romantic."

"It…it was."

"Then you're having fun?"

She's going to make him say it. His sister is persistent. The words will need to come out of his mouth to move on with this conversation.

"I am."

"Then, continue the journey, dummy. Take the pressure off yourself. If you reconnect with Stowe, then it happens. If it doesn't, then at least you can move on while knowing that it wasn't meant to be. If you're curious, Missy is mourning the fact that you're out of town on an epic adventure with your ex."

"Missy…I had forgotten about her."

"Yeah. That should tell you everything you need to know about where your heart is. But you're a man, and that makes you good at navigating streets and terrible at navigating affairs of the heart. And you still love her, Wyatt. Stowe even admitted to loving you. That's really all that matters. The rest is noise."

"It's not that simple."

"Really? Nobody is holding a gun to your head. The fate of the world doesn't rest on you and Stowe getting back together. You're traveling around the world on the *president's* plane with *Santa Claus*. That's the stuff that fairy tales are made of. Stop being you by overthinking this. Kick back and enjoy the journey."

A contented look settles on Wyatt's face. He may rue the day he asked his little sister for advice, but right now, it's worth it. Her words were exactly what he needed to hear.

"Maybe you should have been a shrink."

"Nah. People are easy. I like horses and cows better because they don't talk. Now, I need you to do something for me."

Wyatt smirks. "I'm not telling you that you're the best sister ever."

"You will when this is over, and it should go without saying anyway. Until then, please, please, please don't make Stowe suffer. She opened up to you, so I'm guessing she's feeling pretty vulnerable right now. Don't do anything moronic, like punishing her for that."

"Okay, I won't."

"Really? Good."

The sound of surprise in her voice is amusing. "You expected me to argue?"

"Duh. Our herd of cows is less stubborn than you are."

"Thanks for the talk, Ellie," Wyatt says, his voice as sincere as he can make it.

"You're welcome. Now, don't screw it up. And steal me a pen or something with a logo from Air Force One. I want a souvenir from the president's plane as payment for this session."

Chapter Thirty-Seven

STOWE BESSETTE

The arrival at Aeroporto di Firenze-Peretola, formally known as Amerigo Vespucci Airport, was anything but uneventful. Word quickly spread of Santa Claus's next destination. The result was thousands of onlookers and a small army of media there to document the landing and disembarkment.

Santa handed Wyatt another red envelope before they descended the stairs from Santa Sleigh One. Instead of keeping the destination a secret, he told Stowe and Wyatt to tell the driver to take them straight to L'Albergaccio. The name didn't ring a bell for Stowe until they got fifteen minutes from Florence's city center and saw the signs. It wasn't hard for the driver to find, although it's likely he already knew where it was.

Niccolò Machiavelli is a big name here. The famous Italian Renaissance political philosopher was exiled to his familial Tuscan home after his political downfall and subsequent removal from Florence. Hundreds of years after his death, the estate has been preserved and converted into a public museum that offers insights into Machiavelli's life and works. Stowe and Wyatt don't need much by way of introduction. Every political science student in America knows Machiavelli.

"Honestly, this is the last place I expected Santa to send us," Wyatt says, staring out the window.

"Why's that?"

"You studied Machiavelli in college. He is the father of political realism and was the first to officially suggest that the ends often justify the means. Is there a political philosopher with a more cynical view of human nature than this guy? He was all about convincing others that we are all motivated by self-interest and are thus easily manipulated. It may be true, but does that sound like something Santa advocates?"

"Not at all. You don't think that Santa believes we're the same way because we were both in politics?"

"Nah. I highly doubt it."

"Why?"

Wyatt winks. "Because Santa *knows*."

Stowe laughs at the line they hear all too often. "Shall we open the card and see if that sheds light on why we're here?"

Wyatt gets the honors this time. He slides his finger under the flap and opens the red envelope with the gold lettering. His face changes to one of amusement, and he laughs when he finishes scanning the card inside.

"Santa has a sense of humor," he says, showing it to Stowe.

"Find your common ground, be yourselves, and, most of all, have fun," she reads. "Oh, yeah, sure, Santa isn't trying to bring us back together at all."

Wyatt doesn't argue. They head for the reception area to buy tickets to the museum. Visitors can take guided tours for a fascinating look at Machiavelli's time at the estate, his writing process as one of history's most influential political thinkers, and the historical context of his works. At least, that's what the brochure states. They decide to take a tour that includes the villa where Machiavelli lived, the wine cellar, and the garden.

After a fifteen-minute wait, the tour begins with their guide, Giovanna, explaining that her first name was popular during Machiavelli's time. She's gracious as she describes each room and takes questions from the other people with them. The house is furnished with the simple yet functional tables, chairs, and desks of the Renaissance period. It's not an estate like Versailles in France or Neuschwanstein Castle in Bavaria. In America, it would be considered a middle-class home.

But this is Tuscany. There is a reason tourists flock to this region of the Italian peninsula – the scenery is marvelous, the wine is superb, the people are friendly, and the food is out-of-this-world good.

"I could live comfortably here."

"It's not Montana," Stowe chides.

"Nothing is Montana, but there is a reason I left Big Sky Country in the first place. There's much more to the world, and all of it is worth visiting. My father never understood that. It's one of the many reasons we don't see eye-to-eye."

Stowe bites her lower lip and grasps her hands behind her back. She shouldn't say this. It could turn a nice day into something more dramatic…and hurtful. But her curiosity is burning, and she needs to know where she stands with Wyatt after their talk in the coffeehouse. This is an opening to find out.

"You know, when we were together, we never had that conversation."

"What conversation?" Wyatt asks, checking out a painting on the wall.

"Where we would settle down if we had stayed together. I always thought you would insist on Montana."

"I would have insisted on *visiting*. Honestly, I always thought we would end up in Vermont near your grandparents."

Stowe stops. That was unexpected. Not just his responding to the comment without anger but the choice of location.

"Really?"

"You're right. We never did talk about this and probably should have," Wyatt says, not shutting down the conversation like she thought he would. "Nana and PopPop are older. I figured you would have wanted to spend as much time with them as possible."

"What about your family?"

"My parents have Ellie and Bill and Colt and Maddy. My brother and sister and their spouses are already enough for them to handle."

The tour moves on, and they fall in at the rear of the group. Stowe opened her mouth, and now she's kicking herself because she did. It's not because it started an argument like she feared but because it opened the door to a far more dangerous visitor – regret. He was willing to put *her* family first. Wyatt was willing to move two thousand miles from his ranch and live in a part of the country he barely knows. How many other men would be willing to do that? More importantly, how was she so stupid to push this man away?

Chapter Thirty-Eight

COMMUNICATIONS DIRECTOR
MACKENZIE WALSH

Piazza di Santa Croce is a historic square prominently located in the heart of Florence, Italy. It's not the place surrounding the famous red-domed Duomo. MacKenzie learned that the hard way when a proud Florentine schooled her on the significance of this iconic piazza.

The square is named after the Basilica di Santa Croce, or Basilica of the Holy Cross in English. It's one of the largest Franciscan churches in the world and is renowned for housing the tombs of famous Italians such as Michelangelo, Galileo Galilei, and Machiavelli. In front of the church is a statue of Dante Alighieri, the famed Italian poet who authored *The Divine Comedy*. Ironically, that was MacKenzie's favorite work of literature when she was an undergrad. She has a hardcover copy sitting on her bookshelf and still reads it from time to time.

The piazza has been a central hub of public life in Florence since the Middle Ages, hosting significant events, public gatherings, celebrations, and markets like this one. This Christmas market is held every year from the end of November to mid-December. Like the ones in Vienna and inspired by the markets in Germany, wooden stands are filled with both Florentine and German gifts and dishes, from the spiced fruitcake called *panforte* to bratwurst.

Scarfing down a sausage is out, even if it smells amazing. If MacKenzie is going to get dragged to Italy, she's going to eat Italian cuisine. Santa is entertaining the children and their parents in the piazza, so she breaks away to get something to eat. Some of the members of the press pool join her in surveying the cute restaurants along Largo Piero Bargellini. She orders a dish and a carafe of wine and savors the meal when it arrives. It's one of those "put your fork down after every bite" dishes.

"If you're here to ruin my enjoyment of this lasagna, keep your mouth shut and find another table," MacKenzie admonishes as Keith takes a seat.

"Nope. Wouldn't dream of it. That looks amazing."

"It tastes even better. Is Santa staying out of trouble?"

"He's still doing his thing. Half the world media was waiting in that plaza for him. He has managed to wow all of them with what he knows. I would normally say it was staged, but that isn't true, is it?"

"I warned you not to ruin this for me. It would be a shame to waste this wine by dumping it over your head."

Keith holds his hands up in surrender. She would have done it, too. He may be a respected journalist, but some lines are not to be crossed. People back home would understand that if he were audacious enough to report the incident. You don't mess with a woman enjoying a meal as delicious as this.

"Why did you agree for Santa to continue?" MacKenzie asks. "If even one member of the press pool said no, we would be on our way to St. Louis. I figured it might be you."

"Why?" Keith asks with a chuckle. "Because I'm Scrooge?"

"Something like that."

He rubs his chin. "Call it journalistic curiosity. I want to see what happens next. You really don't know why he's doing this, do you? Either you're lying, and this is the greatest scheme ever devised by the White House, or Babbo Natale really is Santa Claus."

"Why do you say that?"

"Have you read the news? For the second time in two years, St. Nick is dominating the headlines. There has never been this large a collection of feel-good stories. There is no political intrigue."

MacKenzie makes a face.

"Okay, there's a little political intrigue in the news cycle, but there's no talk of wars or divisive social issues. Front pages are devoid of the crap we're fed on a daily basis. It's all about one man's journey to deliver joy, and he's single-handedly making the world a happier place because of it. Everyone back home is saying that the mood of the country has changed."

"Tell that to Heilung Pharma," MacKenzie mumbles.

She's keenly aware of the toll this is taking on that company. Marco finds ways to remind her that they are big donors with a lot at stake in the outcome of this. Part of her is surprised Keith hasn't hit her with that question yet. His newsroom absolutely has access to the donor rolls published by the Federal Elections Commission.

"Well, charging three-point-five mil for a drug is stupid, but that's on the back burner for now. Everyone is enjoying watching Santa Claus enchant the crap out of people. What happened at the booth in Vienna...well, it's making believers out of our readers."

"Keith, do you honestly think it's a good thing that people believe in a mythical elf who owns flying reindeer?"

"At least they have something to believe in. There isn't much of that going around these days. These stories have generated more readership than anything we've printed since the hearings last year."

"Somehow, I don't think you're content with that," MacKenzie says, savoring the last of her lasagna. "You feed on scandal, and that's why you keep asking about whether this was planned. You are itching to ambush me."

"It's not an ambush, but it does feel to me like something bigger is going on. I'm just wondering if you have a hand in it."

"What do you mean?"

"This can't just be about Santa traveling to meet little kids. It's too small. There must be a larger motive behind this. Go ahead, you can tell me. Deep background."

MacKenzie sighs. There's the deep background thing again. If there was any reporter she trusted less than Keith Meadows to go on deep background with, she hasn't met him or her. And that's saying something when you're the White House communications director.

"This is about delivering Santa to grant a Christmas wish. The sooner that happens, the better. I wish there was some grand plan to unveil, but there isn't one. I want to deliver Santa to a St. Louis hospital, go home, and sleep until the calendar turns to January."

"Oh, MacKenzie, where is your Christmas spirit?"

"I lost it long ago. Let's leave it at that."

"Do we have to? I think there's a story there," Keith pushes.

"Not one that I plan on telling you," MacKenzie says, finishing her wine and dropping a bunch of euros on the table. She doesn't know if they tip here, but it's best to be safe when you're traveling with Babbo Natale. "I need to get back to Santa and try to convince him not to take us to Japan next. Enjoy your meal."

Chapter Thirty-Nine

WYATT HUFFMAN

Giovanna takes her position next to the gold stanchions and red velvet rope designed to keep tourists from sitting at the relic for pictures. Niccolò Machiavelli's desk has significant symbolic and historical value. Even if it is a replica, which nobody is certain of, it represents the space where he wrote his seminal works — some of which are still quoted and drawn upon today. Whenever a politician or leader does something underhanded or devious, it's always labeled as Machiavellian. There is a reason for that.

"Machiavelli wrote *The Prince* around 1513 while exiled at the Albergaccio estate. This is more than a piece of furniture — it's emblematic of his forced withdrawal from public life and his subsequent transition to literary and intellectual pursuits. It would have accommodated his writing materials—quills, ink, and parchment.

"The desk is more than just a writing surface. It represents the space where Niccolò could reflect on his political experiences and then channel those insights into his writings. Many have called his works the foundation of modern political science. They laid the groundwork for discussions on power, statecraft, and human nature that influence political thought even today."

People take pictures at the desk but move on quickly. It has more than a passing interest for Wyatt and Stowe. They were both political science majors who worked or are still working for members of the U.S. House of Representatives. They have a healthy respect for the impact of Machiavelli's works. There are politicians in Washington who look at *The Prince* as a bible.

"Wow."

"'Wow' is right. I never thought I'd be staring at the space where one of the most influential works of political theory was written."

"Too bad Machiavelli never knew its impact," Wyatt muses. "He dedicated it to Lorenzo de' Medici, the ruler of Florence at the time, to gain his favor and maybe an official appointment. Unfortunately, it wasn't published until five years after Machiavelli's death."

Stowe weighs that in her head. "That doesn't mean de' Medici didn't see it. Our government leaks like a sieve. Was it that different back then? Machiavelli could have shared a copy pre-publication."

"Maybe," Wyatt concedes. "Do you think *The Prince* has modern relevance?"

"It addresses timeless challenges politicians grapple with — leadership, power dynamics, human behavior…. Machiavelli was spot-on about the ways most people acquire power."

"Inheritance, fortune, and personal prowess," Wyatt finishes.

"Bingo. He famously argued that a prince should be feared more than loved if he's incapable of both. That's something your party knows a lot about."

Stowe winces. She didn't mean for Wyatt to see that, but he did. If her intent is to start a fight, that's a way to do it. He decides to give her the benefit of the doubt that old habits die hard, and she didn't mean anything personal with the barb.

"Ouch. Keep the gloves up," Wyatt cautions but accompanies the warning with a wry smile. "Machiavelli is known for his stance that rulers shouldn't be bound by ethics if they conflict with political necessity. Which party does that sound like?"

"Both, actually," Stowe says with a grin.

Times have changed. During the summer, that conversation would have plummeted into an argument. Wyatt cares a little less because he isn't in Washington anymore, but maybe they've both learned to relax a little and have fun with their political differences. The more he thinks about life in that city, the more he realizes how toxic it is. Who they are matters far more than who they vote for.

The tour continues into the garden and the wine cellar. When it finishes, Stowe and Wyatt enjoy a quick meal, complete with a table wine that is to die for. The conversation was lively and fun. It almost felt like how it was during the spring when their relationship was new and unfamiliar.

With lunch over, they decide that there isn't much left to do at L'Albergaccio. They retreat to the SUV, where their driver is patiently waiting. This is all in a day's work for him, evidenced by the paperback on the passenger seat.

Stowe sighs after they climb into the vehicle. "Are you feeling as unfulfilled from this mission as I am?"

"Yeah. I mean, I had fun, but…did we miss something?"

"I don't know. Santa's instructions were vaguer than usual. I guess we'll find out when we see him."

Wyatt instructs the driver to head for the Christmas market in Florence. There has been no news from MacKenzie, so they assume he is still there. The driver pulls the Suburban off the curb and drives slowly down the narrow street.

"Stop the car!" Wyatt barks as he stares intently out the window. His eyes are riveted on something.

"What? What is it?"

"Isn't that our tour guide?"

Stowe cranes her head around Wyatt to get a better look. "Yeah, I think…what is she doing?"

"Nothing that's going to work."

She is struggling to strap a collapsed wheelchair to a motor scooter that's not much bigger. These mopeds are a prevalent mode of transportation, at least in this area of Italy. Wyatt has seen hundreds of them here. He imagines they're favored for their good gas mileage and convenience in navigating the narrow and congested streets of the region. That explains why the Italian brand Vespa has become a cultural icon.

"Giovanna?"

The sound of her name startles the woman, but she relaxes once she looks up. "Oh, hi! Did you enjoy the tour?"

"Very much. You did an excellent job, thank you. Do you need some help?"

"No, I'm okay," she says, looking at the wheelchair and twine in dismay. "I'm trying to get this home to my father, and it's…."

"Cumbersome. You're going to have a hard time driving that thing if you can even manage to secure the wheelchair to it at all. Would you like us to take it to your house for you?"

"No, I can't ask you to do that."

"You're not asking," Stowe says, flashing her dazzling smile. "We're offering."

"It's no problem, really. We have the space," Wyatt adds, cocking his thumb over his shoulder at the Suburban.

She looks at the large black vehicle and then back at the wheelchair that's leaning against the back of her moped. "You don't mind?"

"Not at all," Stowe reassures her.

Giovanna points down the road. "It's not far. We live in Spedaletto. It's just a minute or two drive down Via Scopeti."

"We can follow you."

"Thank you so much for this! I really appreciate it."

Wyatt takes the wheelchair over to the Suburban and loads it up after the driver pops the back. He must have been watching the interaction. Stowe climbs in and instructs the driver to follow the woman on the motor scooter. He immediately complies once Wyatt closes his door.

"Do you think this is what Santa meant?" Stowe asks.

Wyatt shrugs. "He couldn't have known that she needed help. He can see who's naughty and nice, but he doesn't have a crystal ball. I think this is just a one-off. Giovanna needed help, so we're helping. I wouldn't read too much more into it. Once we drop this off, we can head back to the city. Mac hasn't called, has she?"

Stowe checks her phone for texts or missed calls. "Radio silence."

It's odd that she hasn't checked in, but it doesn't matter. They will do their good deed for the day and see her and Santa soon enough. Wyatt only hopes jolly old St. Nick isn't disappointed in them.

Chapter Forty

STOWE BESSETTE

The drive was as short as Giovanna promised. The ninety-second trek down the road was followed by Wyatt unloading the wheelchair and bringing it into the house for her. In gratitude, she offers the two of them glasses of wine and a board with cheese and cured meats. Stowe tries to respectfully decline, but their tour guide won't hear anything about it. Italian hospitality is a thing, and one glass won't delay them long. Not that Stowe is adamant about turning it down – the wine in this region is amazing.

Giovanna is the perfect host, but she's also troubled. After some prodding by Wyatt, she finally opens up. Her mother passed away a year ago after a long illness. Her father, Jacopo, has barely left his room since the funeral and has been bedridden for months. She's convinced he's just waiting to die so he can join her mother in Heaven, and the thought of losing him, too, breaks her heart.

Stowe wishes she had any advice to give. Her grandparents are full of life, and she hasn't had to worry about that kind of ordeal. All she and Wyatt can do is comfort Giovanna, and neither feels like they are up to the task. A knock at the door interrupts the conversation. After checking to see if her two heroes are expecting anyone, she rises and answers.

"Babbo Natale?"

"Hello, Giovanna. Please forgive the intrusion. May I come in?"

"Yes, of course," she says, staring at him like a teenage girl would if she met one of the Jonas brothers back in the day. "Please."

MacKenzie follows him in and introduces herself as Giovanna gawks at the long convoy of SUVs now lining the road. It requires an explanation, and the White House communications director apologizes for dragging a horde of media to her doorstep. Most of them are out of their vehicles and are milling around, capturing a lot of attention from the neighbors.

Stowe and Wyatt look at each other with a mix of awe and bewilderment. How did Santa find them here? They weren't in communication, so it should have been impossible. Maybe they tracked the GPS in the Suburban. That's as plausible as any other guess, other than the standard "Santa knows" excuse.

"Babbo Natale, it's an honor to see you, but why are you here?" Giovanna asks.

Stowe swears she sees a twinkle in his eye again. "To grant your Christmas wish."

The woman covers her mouth with both hands. "You're going to heal Papa's heart?"

Santa frowns. It may be the first time Stowe has ever seen that. "There are some things that are outside my power. I cannot mend a broken heart any more than I can force two hearts together."

Stowe and Wyatt share a look. Maybe not, but he sure likes to try.

"But I can give Jacopo something that you both want, with your permission." The woman nods, and Santa turns to MacKenzie. "Can you please bring the boy and his mother in?"

Several members of the press pool follow the mother and son into the humble kitchen. He's still clutching the clock Santa gave him like it's a teddy bear. Giovanna stares at it hard and cocks her head.

"Possiamo vedere tuo padre?" Santa asks her.

"Sì, sì, certo."

"Where does an old man who lives in Lapland, Finland, learn to speak perfect Italian?" Keith Meadows leans over and asks Stowe.

"Wait until you hear his Swahili," Stowe says, grinning. She doesn't know if Santa can speak it, but the reporter doesn't know that.

Giovanna opens the door, and nobody expects the sight before them. A feeble old man is curled up in bed, but that's not what draws everyone's immediate attention. The room is full of clocks. Most of them are ornate mantel and table clocks on shelves, but some fancy wall clocks are hanging around the room on nails. Each of them looks like a masterpiece.

"Papa, some people are here to see you."

"Non voglio vedere nessuno! Vattene!"

The media filters into the room, their cameras out and recording. The old man raises his head off the pillow. He sees the reporters lining the wall and Babbo Natale standing in the doorway. He's unmoved at the sight. In fact, he's even more annoyed at the intrusion.

"Chi sono queste persone? Dite loro di andarsene. Ora!"

Jacopo's face softens when he sees the boy. It's not the presence of a child that warms him, but the expression on his face. He is looking around like he just entered the main gate at Disney World. His eyes are wide-open, and his mouth is agape. This room is practically a shrine to clock lovers.

"What? What are you...? That's a German Christmas mantel clock. It's beautiful," the old man says in a soft voice. "Is it yours?"

"Santa gave it to me in Vienna. I want you to have it," he says, holding it out to the man. "It should be with its friends."

The boy's mother covers her mouth, her eyes filled with pride. The man sits up in his bed and gently accepts the clock. He studies it carefully, slowly running a finger over its edges. Stowe's heart melts. It is a beautiful clock, but she doesn't appreciate it an iota as much as Jacopo does. He looks around the room at all the other mantel clocks adorning the shelves.

"This is a strange gift for a young boy. Do you like clocks?"

The kid nods vigorously. There is wonder in his eyes, and his excitement is palpable. Everyone in the room can feel it, including Jacopo. Suddenly, the listless, angry man gets new energy and takes on a much different demeanor.

"Do you see that one over there? It's very special. Come, let me show you."

Jacopo climbs out of bed and steadies himself on the headboard. The boy looks like it's Christmas morning. His smile is radiant and lights up the bedroom.

"Papa?"

"Not now, *figlia*," he says, waving a dismissive hand. Jacopo takes the boy's hand and walks him over to one of the dozens of clocks on the far side of the room.

"Every clock here has a story. This one is the first one I ever bought with my beloved wife, Rosetta. This was her favorite, but she also liked cuckoo clocks. Do you like those?"

Giovanna is overcome with emotion and flees the room in tears. Alarmed, Stowe and Wyatt chase her back into the kitchen. Surprisingly, Santa seems content to watch the interaction in the bedroom.

"We're sorry if we upset you," Stowe consoles as their host sits at the table. "We can ask Santa and the media to leave if—"

"No, it's not that," Giovanna says, closing her eyes tightly for a moment as she waves off the comment. "It's...Papa hasn't mentioned my mother's name since she died. And that's the first time he's moved around in months. That's why I brought him the wheelchair...I hoped it would...You don't understand...you couldn't. His getting out of that bed was my Christmas wish."

Chapter Forty-One

SVP MALCOLM CHAPMAN

For the first time in days, Malcolm has stopped watching the news. Part of the reason is that the constant stream of stories about Santa reminds him of his failures to quell the media narrative about the cost of their drug. But that's not the entire reason.

The executives are exacting their pound of flesh. He has been reading angry emails from major shareholders and board members forwarded to him from the CEO, CFO, and countless others. An optimist would say that they are being helpful by keeping him up to speed on the sentiments of Heilung's stakeholders. Malcolm isn't that much of an optimist. He has an exposed wound, and they are rubbing salt in it until the pain is too much to bear. Whether it's to save face or preserve their standing in the company, executives are eager to hang that albatross around his neck.

Public relations is a crucial arm for any corporation. Malcolm and his team help maintain Heilung's public image, burnish its reputation, and deepen relationships with stakeholders. This is done through consistent messaging and strategic communication targeted at achieving a specific end. When they are in crisis, like now, it means managing the situation publicly and privately by communicating important information to mitigate damage and restore trust.

After his botched interview, Karoline and Luisa managed the public outcry by distributing press releases, answering reporters' questions, and being proactive on social media. None of those efforts are having the desired effect. The relationships with journalists and media outlets he's fostered through favors and inside information aren't bearing fruit, and everyone has lined up against them on social media. That's not Malcolm's biggest problem, though.

Shareholders play a massive role in influencing any company's actions and strategies. Their influence is heavier during a crisis. There is little doubt that they are pressuring the board of directors, who in turn are turning up the heat on Klaus Eberhardt. These emails prove that. The board isn't just demanding information – they want accountability. That means they want someone's head for the misstep, and the other execs aren't being shy about letting him know that it will be his.

"Wow, that is so touching," Karoline says from the other side of the room.

The two women are huddled around Luisa's laptop. Karoline, not the warmest or fuzziest person he has ever worked with, has her hand over her heart and looks like she wants to cry. Malcolm can imagine very few things that would move her to the brink of tears.

"What is?"

"Santa is in Florence," Luisa informs him.

"I know. That's not breaking news anymore."

"Out of the blue, he's visiting some lady's house on the outskirts of the city. Her father was sick or something. Apparently, the old man has a thing for antique clocks. A boy traveling with them was brought into the man's bedroom and was looking around in awe."

Malcolm perks up. "Clocks?"

"Yeah. The room is full of them…really beautiful ones. Anyway, the kid was carrying one that he got as a gift, and he gave it to the old man because he wanted his clock to be with its friends. Isn't that the cutest thing? The whole Internet is going nuts over it."

"Can you put it up on the television?" Malcolm asks.

"Sure."

Luisa punches a few keys on her laptop and screencasts the picture to the large television on the wall. She scrolls the red bar at the bottom of the news story to the beginning and clicks the play icon.

Malcolm doesn't hear what the reporter is saying in the voice-over. He is focused on the shot of the kid, and when he finally turns to face the camera, his mouth drops.

"Look at the old man. His eyes light up," Karoline points out.

"That kid is so adorable!" Luisa almost shrieks.

"That's my son," Malcolm manages to say despite his mouth going completely dry. "That's Braylen."

The women look at Malcolm and then at each other. When their eyes return to their boss, he looks like he just saw a ghost.

"What's your son doing in Italy?"

"My wife…it's a really long story."

"Are you sure that's him?"

Malcolm offers Karoline the "seriously?" look. "Braylen has had a thing for clocks since he was a baby. He didn't sleep through the night until we put one in his room that had a loud ticking sound. That did the trick. He's loved them ever since. His room in our apartment is full of them and sounds like an old episode of *Twenty-Four* with all the ticking in there."

"What's *Twenty-Four*?" Luisa asks.

Malcolm shakes his head. The show ended its nine-season run in 2010, meaning she was probably only eight or nine when it ended and too young to appreciate how great it was. Still, it's iconic television, and she should at least check it out on a streaming channel.

"Never mind, you're making me feel old."

"Malcolm," Karoline says, folding her hands in front of her. "Are you saying that your wife and son are traveling with Santa Claus, and you didn't tell us?"

He leans back in his chair and steeples his hands to match her body language. "I didn't tell you because she didn't tell me. She told me she was going home for the holidays. Nothing was mentioned about *how* she was getting there. I assumed she would book a commercial flight like everyone else, not hitch a ride with St. Nick."

"Well, this could be a massive problem for us. Santa is heading to St. Louis to visit Antonne and Alaya Tucker. If news gets out that the wife and son of the SVP for North American marketing for Heilung are with him—"

"I know, I know," he says, shutting down the line of thought. Nobody needs to tell him what a disaster that would be.

Malcolm stands abruptly and yanks his computer's power cord from the socket built into the conference room table. He slams the lid down and snatches it up.

"Hold down the fort."

"Where are you going?" Luisa asks.

"To get some answers," he says without looking back as he flees the conference room and heads for the elevator.

Chapter Forty-Two

WYATT HUFFMAN

This visit is lasting much longer than he thought it would. Santa doesn't seem to be in any rush to leave the woman's house. It almost feels like he's killing time on purpose. There is no way for Wyatt to know what that reason could be, nor is there any point in speculating. He needs to wait it out like everyone else.

Not that there is a lack of people to talk to. Italian families generally have close-knit relationships. Generations of fostering deep-rooted cultural values means that even extended families play a significant role in daily life. Elders are still highly respected and are prominent in the decision-making and child-rearing of their closest relatives.

One of Wyatt's favorite parts of Italian culture is their closeness. Families frequently gather for large meals. Holidays like Christmas, Easter, and Ferragosto in mid-August are significant family events they mark with special feasts and traditions. It's even not uncommon for multiple generations to live together or near each other, which is why Giovanna is staying with her father.

Even when not residing under the same roof, extended families often settle in the same neighborhood or city. It's not surprising that many of Giovanna's siblings, nephews, and nieces have stopped in. Many of them brought dishes of food to share with members of the press. Before long, it feels more like a family reunion than a visit from Babbo Natale.

Alessio Bartolini is among the last to show up. He's Jacopo's youngest son, and it looks like he's coming fresh from work. His mouth hangs open after he makes his way through the small kitchen and peeks into the bedroom. The sight of his father up and moving around moves him to tears.

Wyatt can't believe the old man is still at it. Santa retreated from the small house over an hour ago to meet the neighbors and their children. He's a big hit, as he is everywhere he goes. Braylen hasn't lost any interest in the clocks. The pair are now in their third hour of the stories behind the clocks on the shelves.

"I cannot express how grateful I am for this," Alessio says in heavily accented English.

"It wasn't my doing," Wyatt admits. "This is all Santa Claus."

"Yes, but my sister tells me that he wouldn't be here had you not offered to help her with the wheelchair. I appreciate your kindness…and what it resulted in. I have something for you. Hold on."

Alessio leaves, covering the short walk from the front door to his small vehicle parked along the curb outside the house.

"Be yourselves," Stowe whispers into Wyatt's ear. "Santa knew we would offer to help her."

"How? How could Santa know that Giovanna would need help and that we would be in the exact spot to offer it?"

Stowe shrugs and shakes her head. "I'm done trying to figure that out."

Alessio returns with a large burlap sack slung over his shoulder. "Please, take these as a token of my appreciation."

"That's not necessary," Wyatt argues.

"No, please. It's not much, but it's the least I can do to show my appreciation. I run a sporting goods shop in Florence. I want you to have these."

"Really, we can't—"

"Thank you, Alessio. You are very generous," Santa says after appearing in the doorway.

"Babbo Natale. It is so good to meet you."

Wyatt and Stowe slip outside while Santa spends a few minutes talking with the Bartolini family. The crowd along the street is starting to thin out. Santa emerges behind them, his eyes twinkling and his face wearing a joyous smile.

"I trust that you two had an enjoyable day."

Stowe places her hand on his shoulder and stares at him through serious eyes. "Santa knows."

He laughs heartily, throwing his head back. "Yes, he does."

"It's almost time to leave here, Santa," Aurielle says, appearing out of nowhere.

"I almost wish you were going to say we are staying a few days," Wyatt confesses.

"One of the great joys of traveling the world is finding places you want to return to someday. I'm quite certain you both can find your way back here."

"Santa, I have to ask…what's in the sack that Alessio gave you?"

Santa gestures at the bulging white cloth bag cinched with a drawstring at the top. It looks like the one he is pictured carrying in most of the imagery of him.

"Look inside, Wyatt."

He does as instructed. "They're soccer balls. Why accept them?"

"Oh, I don't know…they may come in handy. Aureielle, let's go tell MacKenzie we are ready to leave. I'm certain she will be thrilled to hear the news."

Santa and his chief elf walk back out in the direction of the convoy.

"We should say our goodbyes as well," Wyatt says.

"You know, I thought you were going to ask what the point of this visit was."

"Honestly, that's what I was about to ask."

"What stopped you?"

Wyatt smiles at Stowe and shrugs. "I don't think I want to know at this point. I'm just going to enjoy the journey. We'll reach the destination soon enough."

Chapter Forty-Three

COMMUNICATIONS DIRECTOR
MACKENZIE WALSH

The December temperatures reach the high sixties in Florence. The weather is much better here than in Vienna, so MacKenzie excused herself from the house and went outside to enjoy it. The reporters left the boy and the old man to obsess over the clocks a while ago. Videos were uploaded, and context was provided to their newsrooms back home. Some even did remotes for audiences live from the street.

Every major network covered it live or with a short delay. With their work complete, the reporters in the press pool are getting a little antsy. Santa has spent more time at the house than she thought he would. Now, everyone is wondering what is next, and that includes MacKenzie.

She placated them as much as possible. Part of her wants to turn her phone on to check the news to see how the stories are being received, but that's a bad idea. She turned it off for a reason.

Her driver walks over to her with a satellite phone in his hand. "Ms. Walsh? I have the White House chief of staff on the phone for you."

That figures. In the Digital Age, it's almost impossible to hide. That's doubly so when you work for the U.S. government. One cannot simply power off a phone and hope nobody can reach you.

"Yes?" she asks, placing the phone against her ear.

"Seriously? You turned your phone off? I've been trying to reach you for an hour."

"The battery was low," MacKenzie says, lying through her teeth. It's at eighty percent charge.

She didn't want to deal with yet another call from her testy boss. The pressure back in the capital is getting to him, and it's bringing out his colorful side. He's usually relaxed or even gleeful while playing the political game in Washington. Not this time.

"I'm a little busy here. What do you need, Marco?"

"Need? I need you to deliver Santa. The president is growing increasingly upset — this trip was supposed to be an easy win for us. Instead, he's starting to catch flak from everywhere. Even members of our own party are starting to reach out to ask for an explanation as to why this is taking so long."

"I don't understand. Who could possibly be upset about this? The media is eating it up. The whole world is following this like it's the Olympics."

"That's mostly true. The majority of news outlets are completely on board with Santa's brand of spreading Christmas cheer. Others are taking a different approach.

The less-friendly members of our press corps are starting to discuss the cost of your trip. Do you have any idea how expensive it is to operate Air Force One?"

MacKenzie's jaw tightens. "About $180,000 an hour if you include fuel, maintenance costs, and crew salaries. Since a modified 747 burns about five gallons of jet fuel per mile, I imagine the price tag for gas alone is tens of thousands of dollars per hour of flight."

"That's right. And none of that factors in the costs of your logistical support from the State Department with each city you visit. We're going to have an increasingly hard time justifying that."

MacKenzie frowns. It's not that hard. Government waste is a real thing, and she has seen stacks of money spent on things far less beneficial. Budgets are bloated, and it's nice to see the government spending a few dollars on something positive for once. If the reaction of most of her fellow Americans is any indication, this is one instance where they don't mind the expenditure.

"Marco, have you ever thought that certain members of the media are complaining because this act of humanitarianism is making the president look good?"

"I don't see how your trips to Vienna and Florence are doing anything."

"They're not *my* trips, they're Santa's. And if you can't see the positive impact, then you aren't paying attention."

All things considered, the stories coming out of the press pool have been positive. Even Keith Meadows hasn't filed anything that would ruffle feathers back home. At least, not yet. MacKenzie is still wary about his confirming that this isn't part of any master plan and what he will say about it when he does.

"Mac, I'm going to state it plainly. This needs to end now," Marco decrees.

"Fine. I'll hand Santa Claus the phone, and you can tell him that yourself."

"You're the White House communications director. You convince people every day of things that they may not want to hear. Convince him."

"It's not that easy."

MacKenzie hears a hand slam on a desk. It was loud enough to force her to move the phone away from her ear.

"Then make it easy! You're in charge, MacKenzie. Tell him that the plane is going to St. Louis. If he wants a ride, those are the terms. Otherwise, he's on his own."

"Wait a second! Are you seriously telling me that you want the optics of the president abandoning Santa in Italy if he says no?"

Marco sighs loudly enough to make it sound like he's holding the microphone next to a leaf blower. "There *is* no Santa, Mac. He's an old man from Finland who's using this situation to get free travel around the world."

"Around the...? We've only been to two cities on one continent, Marco."

"And again, you've accomplished nothing by visiting either."

"The press would disagree, and so would I. You should have seen with your own eyes what happened here in Tuscany."

"I don't need to see it with my own eyes. That's why you're there."

She would rather be anywhere than here. MacKenzie didn't volunteer for this. It was an assigned task despite her desperately trying to find a way out of it. There is no reason for her to be compelled to defend this, but she is anyway.

"I told you not to send me on this trip."

"Well, I did send you. And you went. Now, it's your responsibility."

"And I accept that, so let me do it my way."

"We're going around in circles. You serve at the pleasure of the president, and he wants this over. We're done talking about this, Mac. I am going to advise the president to demand that the Air Force return his plane to the U.S. He's the commander-in-chief, so they'll follow the order even if that means the pilots get coal in their stockings this year."

MacKenzie shakes her head. The aircraft is operated by a crew of Air Force personnel, including pilots, navigators, communication specialists, and security personnel. He's right – they are going to follow whatever orders they're given.

"I need you to explain to everyone there that the next stop for Santa Sleigh One is St. Louis, Missouri. St. Nick will either be on board, or he can take his own sleigh home."

Chapter Forty-Four

SVP MALCOLM CHAPMAN

It's an eleven-hour drive from Frankfurt to Florence, Italy, without breaks. There would need to be at least a couple for fuel, food, and a bathroom stop. Some of that time could have been made up thanks to the unlimited speeds on much of the Autobahn, but that's under ideal conditions. It's December, and the weather is far less than ideal for driving in the Alps.

That's the reason winter tires are either mandatory or strongly recommended in this region during the winter months. An accident caused by the driver of a vehicle without appropriate tires may result in fines or liability issues. Malcolm has winter tires on his car, but driving to Italy is out of the question for another reason – it will take too long.

That means flying. Fortunately, there are departures from Frankfurt to Florence throughout the day that will deposit him right at the airport. Malcolm doesn't know how long Santa plans to remain in Italy, but the clock is ticking, and he's racing against it.

The flight is ninety minutes long. If Malcolm factors in another ninety at the airport to check in and clear security, and the half hour it will take him to get there from the office, that's three and a half hours. It should be fast enough to intercept Santa, his wife, and his son. It needs to be.

It takes Malcolm a little longer than thirty minutes to get to Frankfurt Airport, thanks to traffic on the B43. He parks, checks in, and makes it to the gate with precious little time to spare. The initial boarding has already begun when his phone rings. It's the office, so this can't be good.

"Hello?"

"You're a hard man to track down, Malcolm," Klaus Eberhardt says. "You aren't in your office, so I checked the conference room, where two lovely women said you rushed out of here without any explanation as to where you were going or when you would be back. Is this how you ran your team in the United States?"

"I'm at the airport," Malcolm says, eyeing the boarding process intently.

"Why are you at the airport when you should be here managing this crisis?"

"I am managing it."

The CEO scoffs. "All evidence to the contrary. Do you think we're off the hook simply because the world media is all caught up in the latest episode of Adventures with Santa?"

"No, all the attention is going to make things worse when he arrives in the U.S. and meets Antonne Tucker and his sister."

"I agree. So, why aren't you chained to your desk preparing for that eventuality?"

"Because all the preparation and spin in the world isn't going to help us when Santa meets a sick child. We need a different approach."

"Like?"

"A direct conversation with the man himself."

Malcolm winces. That sounded a lot crazier coming out of his mouth than it did in his head. Still, it's better than telling his heartless CEO that he is off to try to save his marriage. The "two birds with one stone" argument isn't going to work on a man who is practically married to the corporation and thinks everyone else should be, too.

"That isn't going to do any good. If you think it will, I really have to question why you were hired in the first place."

"Sir, this is the best option we have left."

"And I disagree."

There is no chance of Malcolm escaping this disaster with his job if he plays by the CEO's rules. It almost feels like the deck is being stacked against him on purpose. They are more interested in a sacrificial lamb than doing the right thing, or at least trying to. Since that's the case, there is nothing left to lose.

"With due respect, sir, I think you're wrong."

"Is that so? Then, you must think I'm not running the company and should become an executive somewhere else."

"Are you firing me?"

There is a long silence on the other end of the call. Malcolm waits to hear his fate, forcing himself not to pipe up and push for an answer. It will come soon enough, one way or the other.

The line at the gate has all but disappeared. The airport staff hasn't closed the doors yet, but that can be only moments away. There is no way this flight can leave without him on it. The next one isn't until later tonight. The odds of catching Santa Sleigh One before it departs will be remote if he doesn't board now.

"Not yet," Klaus finally says, his voice even but decisive. "Do what you need to do, but if you aren't back at your desk tomorrow morning, this will be a very different conversation. We won't be talking about a promotion or better opportunity within the company – we'll be discussing your future at Heilung altogether. This is a very big moment for you, Malcolm. I suggest you make wise decisions."

Klaus ends the call before waiting for a response. The timing is perfect as the gate attendant announces the final boarding call for Flight 9498 to Florence. Malcolm walks over and scans his boarding pass. The clock isn't only running for him to catch up to his wife and son, but also for his career. He can do this. He has to.

Chapter Forty-Five

STOWE BESSETTE

Getting the press pool loaded up in vehicles for the drive back to Florence is an adventure in cat herding. Reporters have their own agendas, and that doesn't usually mean doing what they're told. MacKenzie is the White House communications director, so she has some experience with it. Her job entails more crafting messages than delivering them to the hungry piranhas in the press briefing room, but Stowe doubts those activities involve babysitting. Still, she thinks she's doing an admirable job playing cruise director on Santa's European tour.

Washington is ground zero for the political media apparatus in the United States. The countless newspapers, magazines, dedicated television networks like CSPAN, online platforms and blogs, and radio and podcasts located there play a crucial role in shaping public opinion and policy. These major media once had a monopoly on setting the national agenda for political discourse. That is beginning to change.

The perceived partisanship of media outlets has become actual biases, coloring their reporting red or blue and eroding the public's trust in the process. Corporate ownership calls the shots, and their editorial decisions are often lambasted by individual voices on social media. Instead of disseminating news to the masses, the result has been to cater to specific political audiences, creating a polarized media landscape filled with misinformation, manipulated data, spin, and opinion inserted as fact.

The result in the nation's capital is an aggressive style of "cutthroat journalism" where reporters compete to break stories. The emphasis is often on speed and sensationalism over accuracy and ethics, leading to gross exaggerations and abysmal factual errors. There are no lengths that journalists won't go to for a story, including using intrusive or ethically questionable methods like deception, exploiting vulnerable sources, and ambushing individuals using "gotcha" questions.

MacKenzie is a high-ranking government official, so nobody will weep at her getting grilled by the press. There are few people in the country more adept at handling questions posed by the likes of Keith Meadows than she is. But Stowe has listened as he is taking things too far.

"Face it, MacKenzie. You have lost control of this. Santa is taking you for a ride."

"If that's what you think, run with it," she says, waving a dismissive hand.

"I plan to. You can give me a quote now, or I can say that the White House declines to comment."

"Careful, Keith," Stowe interjects, commanding his attention. "You may end up with coal in your stocking if you keep making threats like that."

The journalist grins. "Miss Bessette…I feel it's my responsibility to tell you something your parents should have told you years ago – there is no Santa Claus."

The arrogance of this man is astounding. He even leaned in and whispered that to her like she was a toddler.

"Well, thank you, Mr. Meadows," Stowe says, nodding. "I'm glad you feel free to fill the knowledge void they left after they were tragically *killed* when I was a child."

That wiped the smug grin off his face.

"I'm…sorry, I—"

"Secondly, are you *sure* there's no Santa Claus?"

"Quite. What I'm not sure of is why the United States government is indulging in this little foray around Europe."

Stowe shrugs. "Does it matter?"

"To me, no. To the American taxpayer…."

Stowe narrows her eyes. Keith Meadows doesn't care an iota about the American taxpayer. He's not a financial watchdog or interested in combating government waste. His intentions aren't that pure.

"Ah. You see the makings of a scandal and want to be the first to get the scoop. Got it."

"I report the news, Miss Bessette, as unpleasant as it often is."

"Injected with speculation, innuendo, and sometimes outright gossip. But, hey, whatever works to get those clicks and social media likes, right?"

The 24/7 news cycle introduced by cable news networks back in the 1980s and '90s has paired with online platforms to perpetuate a lust for constant content. Instead of accurate, in-depth reporting, the focus shifted to covering breaking news and sensational stories in the never-ending war for public attention. Being right was sacrificed on the altar to the god of being first. The more juicy the story, the more media outlets climb over each other to cover it, so long as it's convenient to their political agendas.

It's not a new development. Newspapers owned by media titans like William Randolph Hearst and Joseph Pulitzer engaged in "yellow journalism" in the late 19th and early 20th centuries by printing sensational and often fabricated stories to boost sales. Modern tabloids and some online news sites continued that tradition, forcing mainstream outlets to do the same. It's why so many Americans from both sides of the political aisle despise journalism, making it one of the least-respected career choices.

Keith didn't like Stowe's insinuation one bit. "You work for Representative Angela Pratt, don't you?"

"You know I do, which means you're threatening me quietly."

"No, I'm just asking a question to confirm information."

"Ah, yes, deflection. Another of your talents. You want me to be afraid that you'll put the congresswoman in your crosshairs because I'm speaking out. It won't work. I don't care, and I don't think she will either."

The journalist smirks but remains silent.

"How do you bake a cake, Keith?"

"What?"

"How…do…you…bake…a…cake?" Stowe asks, using the most condescending voice she can muster.

"I don't. I buy one at the store."

"That explains a lot about you. First, you preheat your oven and grease and flour the pans. Then, you whisk together the flour, baking powder, and salt in a medium bowl before setting it aside. In a separate bowl, the butter, sugar, eggs, and vanilla get mixed before combining the wet and dry ingredients. You pour the batter—"

"Who are you, Julia Child?" Keith interrupts. "Or are you auditioning for a reality television baking show?"

Stowe can't suppress her smile. There are few things more rewarding than getting under the skin of someone this pompous.

"My point is baking a cake is a process, not just the end result. Christmas is more than a day – it's a season. It's what makes both of them so rewarding."

"I get it. You think this is all leading to something…what? Frosted and delicious?"

Stowe smiles. "I was going to go for heartwarming and magical, but you're the journalist. Use whatever synonyms will get you the most clicks. That's what you do."

Keith scoffs before looking around and realizing that the entire convoy is waiting on him. Reluctantly, he pulls on the door handle and climbs into the back of one of the Suburbans, allowing MacKenzie and Stowe to walk back to the lead vehicles.

The boy and his mother emerge from the house, waving back at their hosts as they depart. The kid is carrying a clock, but it isn't the one he arrived with. This one is gold in color and shimmers even in the fading sunlight. It makes Stowe smile. The old man must have given it to him as a replacement for the Christmas clock.

"It wasn't necessary, but thank you for the rescue," MacKenzie says as they make their way to the front of the convoy. "The way you ran out the clock on him was expert-level stuff."

"I've learned a few things during my time in Washington," Stowe confesses. "I'm sure it's only a temporary reprieve."

"I'll take it. Where did you learn to bake a cake?"

"It was one of my favorite things to do with my grandmother when I was growing up. Keith is lucky I went with that instead of the Christmas cookie recipes. I have some really good ones memorized."

Chapter Forty-Six

SVP MALCOLM CHAPMAN

Time. His son has a better understanding of it than Malcolm does. For adults, it's wasted, kept, spent, invested, or bided. To Braylen, it's treasured and appreciated. That's why he likes clocks. He has learned its value at a tender young age. It's one of the many lessons Malcolm has learned from his son. Too bad he isn't paying better attention to some of Braylen's other insights.

Time has been an enemy for much of the trip down from Germany, not an ally. Malcolm doesn't know if Santa Sleigh One will still be parked on the tarmac as the wheels of his Airbus A321 touch down. He cranes his head to try to find it out the window. It would have helped had he been scanning out the other side of the aircraft.

Fortunately, he learns as soon as he exits the jetway that the aircraft hasn't departed. Santa is still in Italy, so Malcolm has that much going for him. The news on the television is carrying the feed of his convoy live. Now, it's going to be an adventure to figure out how to get out to the aircraft. It's not like the Italians, or police at another airport for that matter, will let him traipse across the tarmac and walk right up to it. That means he might need to do something slightly more drastic.

Fortunately, making a break for it through a security door and sprinting in a mad dash over the asphalt expanse before getting tackled isn't going to be necessary. Santa's visit here garnered enough media coverage to ensure that a large crowd was ready to send him off. The airport authorities roped off a sizable area near the aircraft to control the crowd while still keeping people a safe distance away. The challenge has become getting close enough to the front for Janelle and Braylen to spot him.

The convoy pulls into the airport just after sunset and drives to within fifty meters of the waiting 747. Malcolm curses under his breath. He's still too far away, and they are packed into this area like sardines.

Determined to get closer, he muscles his way through the crowd, earning more than a few nasty looks and some shouting of words in Italian that likely aren't complimentary. The last three rows of people are the hardest to breach because of the kids with them, but he manages to make his way to the metal barrier.

"Janelle! Janelle!" he shouts, waving like a deranged fan at a Taylor Swift concert.

She stops and looks around as Malcolm tries to swing his leg over the steel divider. It's a bad idea. A pair of policemen descends on him and knocks his leg back over, shouting at him in Italian. The commotion has the desired effect. Janelle spots him and scurries over.

"Malcolm? Wait, it's okay!" she exclaims, pleading with the officers. "That's my husband."

The men still have a hold of him and pause only long enough for his wife to cover the distance between him and the group escorting Santa. Braylen is on her tail, and his eyes light up when he sees Malcolm.

"Daddy!"

Braylen rushes over and tries to hug his father's leg through the barrier. The police officers look at each other in confusion. At least they have started to relax. Italian prisons may not compare to Russian gulags, but he'd rather not find that out firsthand.

"What are you doing here?" Janelle asks.

"I'm looking for you."

"How did you know we were in Florence?"

"I saw Bray on television. The news has been running footage of what happened with the old man and the clock on a continuous loop. I caught the first flight down here that I could get."

"What about your job?"

Malcolm shakes his head. "I'll worry about that later."

By now, the pair has the attention of the entire crowd around them. The oohing and ahhing reaches a crescendo as Malcolm looks up to see Santa Claus only a few steps away. The shouts of glee coming from the airport crowd are almost deafening.

"Is everything okay?" Santa asks, flanked by a young man and woman.

Santa may be a mythological figure, but Malcolm's mouth still goes dry, and his eyes go wide at his presence. "Everything is fine."

"Santa, this is my husband, Malcolm."

"It's very nice to meet you. You have a wonderful family," Santa says.

"Thank you."

"Does this mean your journey with me is ending, Janelle, or would you like to invite your husband along on the rest of the trip?"

"Are you heading to St. Louis, Santa?"

"Eventually," the jolly old elf says.

"Faster if MacKenzie Walsh gets her way," the woman next to him adds.

"You'll have to forgive Stowe and Wyatt. They are still learning to embrace the journey instead of the destination."

Janelle looks at her husband, and he shrugs. "I'm happy to tag along, but only if it's okay with you."

She nods at Santa, who gives some instructions to the officers. They separate the metal barricades just far enough to let Malcolm squeeze through. He thinks about holding his wife's hand as they walk toward the aircraft but decides against it. They still aren't in a good place. At least a long flight across the Atlantic will give them the chance to sort some things out. Or so he hopes.

Chapter Forty-Seven

COMMUNICATIONS DIRECTOR
MACKENZIE WALSH

It's been a long day, and MacKenzie is hoping to get some sleep on the trip across the ocean. One of the many mysteries surrounding Santa Claus is where he gets his energy. It must be the hot cocoa and candy canes that Aurielle serves him on a near-hourly basis. Whatever it is, the man has seemingly boundless energy. MacKenzie is about half his age and is completely wiped. She certainly isn't anxious for the conversation that's coming.

There was little reason to tell Santa what instructions the pilots were given. Too many things could go wrong. It's shady and maybe even devious, but MacKenzie has a mission to accomplish. Marco made the call, so she's going to let the pilots break the bad news to St. Nicholas. When they reach the top of the stairs, the flight crew is waiting for him with sullen looks on their faces.

"Well, this can't be good," Santa says.

"Good evening, Santa. I'm afraid it isn't. We have some bad news for you."

"You're going to tell me that you were instructed to bring me directly to St. Louis."

The man and woman, dressed in their Air Force service uniforms adorned with more than a dozen ribbons and silver pilot wings with stars and wreaths over them, look at each other. They may be of different ranks, but they are trusted colleagues more than superior and junior officers. The colonel will get the final say, but it doesn't mean he won't solicit his co-pilot's opinion.

"Ordered is a better word, sir," the woman finally answers.

"What's the problem?" Stowe asks, coming up alongside Santa.

"Apparently, someone wants me to go directly to St. Louis."

"I can't imagine who might have arranged that," Wyatt says, joining the gaggle while looking at MacKenzie through accusatory eyes.

"It wasn't me. I swear," the White House communications director argues.

"It was Marco Ramirez," Santa says. "He's a decent man, but he doesn't have much faith in people. He had trust issues as a child, too. That's probably handy in his line of work, but it does suck some of the joy out of life."

"Is there anything you can do?" Wyatt asks the pilots.

"I'm sorry," the colonel says. "Orders are orders. We could both get court-martialed for disobeying them. At a minimum, we'll never be allowed to fly Air Force One again if we don't comply."

"I can't ask them to give that up," Santa says to Wyatt and Stowe. "Colonel Robinson has dreamed about being in the Air Force since he was old enough to walk. His father was a member of the ground crew for a B-1B Lancer at Dyess Air Force Base in Texas. They would spend their evenings near the end of the runway watching the bombers take off. He died in a tragic training accident when the colonel was a teenager. I know you miss your father very much, and I know he would be very proud of the man you've become."

The colonel's face softens. He closes his eyes and nods.

"After the funeral, he pledged to his father that he would follow in his footsteps and join the Air Force. Except, he wanted to fly planes, not work on them. He applied to the academy, but it's a very competitive school. There was very little chance he was going to earn the congressional recommendation he needed for entry. So, in his sophomore year of high school, he made a wish – a Christmas wish."

"How do you know that?" Colonel Robinson asks.

"Because, sir, I granted it. You had just lost your father. If there was ever someone who deserved a Christmas wish, it was you. That's why you got to meet one of your state's U.S. senators at a high school function."

"You got me into the Air Force Academy?"

"It doesn't work that way, Colonel," Santa says, waving his hands defensively. "I granted a wish for you to meet him. The rest you did yourself. The same is true for Lieutenant Colonel Hwang. Your parents were immigrants to the United States. They moved to a small town, and you felt very isolated and alone. To help you integrate with the other children, they began taking you to a Christian church. Do you remember what you asked me as a child that Christmas?"

"I do," she says, fighting back her tears.

"And was it granted?"

"It was. Santa, this can't be real. How did you…?"

Santa shrugs. "Granting Christmas wishes is the best part of the job."

"But there is no Santa Claus," the colonel argues.

A twinkle appears in Santa's eye. "Do you really believe that, or is it what you are conditioned to say? The world is a magical place, filled with mystery and governed by forces that we don't fully understand. But just because I may not circumnavigate the globe in a flying sleigh, does that mean I don't exist?"

MacKenzie can't argue that point. The thought of flying higher than the birds was unthinkable two hundred years ago. For most of human history, men and women looked up at the moon with no way to touch it. That changed in the 1960s. For as far as humanity has come, there is still so much that isn't understood about what governs the world we live in.

"Santa, we can't disobey the president," the colonel finally says.

"I understand, DD."

The man freezes. Statues are more animated than he is for a full ten seconds before his jaw finally quivers. "You can't know that nickname."

Santa closes his eyes and nods. "Santa knows."

"What is DD?" MacKenzie asks, beating Stowe and Wyatt to the punch.

"It…it's a nickname I haven't heard for decades. 'DD' stands for Daredevil…my father used to call me that because of all the stupid things I would do as a kid."

MacKenzie has no idea how Santa could possibly know that. She glances at Wyatt and Stowe, who don't look remotely surprised. Santa hasn't spent any time with their flight crew on this trip. Even if he did know their names, no amount of research would have unearthed that nickname. Hearing it again clearly shocked the pilot.

"I feel bad about putting you in a predicament, Colonel. I understand that orders are orders, but there is one last special place I would like to stop before we visit Antonne Tucker. It's important…it's *my* Christmas wish."

That could easily be construed as a master class in manipulation. MacKenzie doesn't think that was Santa's intent. There is too much sincerity in his voice. The others seem to notice it, too. Everyone grows quiet.

The colonel turns to his co-pilot. "I'm willing to take him there, but I won't do it if you aren't in agreement. It could cost us our jobs."

"Something tells me it won't. If Santa thinks it's important to make one final stop, then I'm in."

Everyone looks at MacKenzie. She could probably put an end to this right now, but she'd be the bad guy. Everyone else wants to follow Santa's lead, and he is the one doing them a favor. Screw what Marco Ramirez has to say about it.

"I'm going to catch hell for this, but what's one more stop going to cost us at this point?"

Santa claps his hands. "Excellent! Thanks to both of you and you, MacKenzie. Will you be willing to join me for a cup of cocoa once we are airborne? Some arrangements need to be made."

"Of course."

Aurielle hands the pilots a red card. "Our next stop for your flight plan."

They thank her, and everyone retreats inside the aircraft to find their seats. MacKenzie stops the colonel before he climbs the stairs to the cockpit.

"DD? How did you earn that name?"

"It all started when I built a ramp and tried to jump my tricycle over a stream on the base in Texas," the colonel says, grinning from ear to ear. "I was three or four at the time. My father thought it was hilarious. Mom, on the other hand, wasn't amused."

Chapter Forty-Eight

WYATT HUFFMAN

For whatever reason, Wyatt and Stowe don't spend much time together on the plane during these flights. Maybe they need time apart to think. Maybe they're afraid that too much conversation will lead to another argument. Whatever the true reason is, it gives him a chance to tend to some other business.

He likes MacKenzie. Not in a romantic way, despite her attractiveness. There is something about her. She may be from the opposing party, but he could see being friends with her. Or, at least, friendly.

She's also suffering. It's more than just the stress of performing this task for the president. She's miserable, and worse, she has nobody to talk to about it. Wyatt knows how that feels. He's spent the last five months in the same predicament.

He sits down next to MacKenzie without so much as a word. If she noticed him, she didn't react, much less say anything. She is lost in thought, her face close to the window as her eyes stare at the night sky above the Mediterranean Sea.

"I see Aurielle brought you some cocoa."

"Uh, yeah…it's my second cup. It's the only thing making me feel better."

"What's bothering you?"

"Are you my shrink now?" she turns and snaps as Wyatt holds his hands up in surrender and gets up to leave. "I got chewed out by the president and the White House chief of staff for not following orders."

"What did they say?" he says, easing back into the seat.

MacKenzie sighs and stares out the window. "The usual. I'm not in the mood to talk about it or anything else."

"Yeah, I wasn't either when you dropped by my seat and did it to me not long ago."

"This is different."

"Not really. You offered an opportunity for me to join the mile-high club."

"I was joking, Wyatt."

He smirks. "You were half-joking."

"I thought things between you and Stowe were improving."

"They are. I didn't come here to take you up on the offer. I want to know why you hate Christmas."

Wyatt learned a few things during his time in Washington. Maybe it was all the committee hearings that Knutson forced him to attend. But the lesson is that when you want an answer from someone, soften them up first. That works on most people, with the exception of his sister, who sees right through the tactic. Fortunately, MacKenzie doesn't, despite her likely knowing how to do it even more effectively.

"I don't hate Christmas."

"You don't celebrate the season, either."

"It's personal," MacKenzie declares.

"Most stories are."

She shifts uncomfortably in her seat. This isn't the conversation she expected to have. For a moment, Wyatt thinks she's about to shut it down. Then, her eyes soften into something more…remorseful.

"I'm surprised Santa didn't tell you mine. I'm sure he knows."

There is no doubt in Wyatt's mind that Santa knows. If St. Nick has proven anything to the world these past two years, it's that he's practically clairvoyant. His knowledge of people's pasts is almost shocking. With that knowledge comes a measure of discretion. Santa rarely offers up insights that could portray anyone negatively. In that way, he's like the reverse of a tabloid magazine.

"That's not how he operates."

"All right. Since you seem to really want to hear this…do you remember when I told you about Cliff?"

"Yeah, I think so. He was your second great love whose proposal you declined in front of your friends and family."

MacKenzie nods. "What I didn't tell you is that our families and friends were there because it was Christmas Day."

"Oh. Ouch. And now you associate Christmas with your decision."

MacKenzie taps her nose and points at Wyatt. She turns to stare out the window at the inky nothingness as a long silence grows longer. Wyatt doesn't press for details. She will speak when she's ready. It just takes a while.

"Nothing sucks the joy out of the season like bad memories."

"Or regrets?"

"I love my job," MacKenzie says, almost sounding like it was a reflex.

"Do you?"

"Okay, maybe not right now. I don't expect you to understand."

"I understand better than you think I do. I felt the stress last year. I was a low-level staffer for Congressman Knutson. He and Angela Pratt entrusted Stowe and me to find a Santa Claus for those hearings on the Hill. We thought we miserably failed right up to the point when Santa walked into the committee room."

"What's your point?"

Wyatt doesn't know what compelled him to have this conversation. He certainly doesn't need to defend Santa. Maybe it's because he feels bad for MacKenzie. She's in a tough situation, and her confession about Christmas more than explains why she wants this to end as quickly as possible.

"Like you, we were intent on getting Santa where we wanted him. In our case, it was a hearing room on Capitol Hill. Santa slow-rolled us and forced us to enjoy the journey instead of only focusing on the end goal. We saw the northern lights, went for a reindeer ride, and even went to elf school. Stowe and I ended up together because of those adventures."

MacKenzie leans forward. "Okay, it's my turn to ask you a question. What split the two of you apart?"

"Short answer? We forgot the lesson Santa taught us."

"You're saying I should ignore the White House chief of staff and president of the United States and just go along for the ride?"

"No, I'm not saying that. I won't tell you what to do. What I'm saying is that Santa isn't going to let you down, Mac. He's going to travel to St. Louis and meet the Tuckers, just as you want him to. But he'll do it on his schedule, and I promise you, whatever he's cooking up with these side quests is going to result in something epic."

"What makes you say that?"

"Past experience. And because he's Santa Claus, whether you believe that or not."

It's Wyatt's turn to put his hand on her shoulder before moving to another cabin to enjoy the rest of the flight. Hopefully, he gave her something to think about other than Cliff and the consequences of a decision made years ago.

Chapter Forty-Nine

COMMUNICATIONS DIRECTOR
MACKENZIE WALSH

This wasn't the last place MacKenzie expected Santa to want to go, but it was near the bottom of the list. Morocco is a constitutional monarchy in Northwest Africa, bordered by the Atlantic Ocean and the Mediterranean Sea. The area has been inhabited since prehistoric times, with significant influences coming from the Roman and Phoenician civilizations, along with the indigenous Berbers.

Arab Muslims conquered the region in the 7th century, leading to the widespread adoption of Arabic as a language and Islam as the predominant religion. That's part of what makes this particular stop so confusing.

Santa Claus may not be a religious symbol, but he is the quintessential icon when it comes to celebrating the birth of Jesus Christ. Why would he want to come to an Islamic country? That's the question on everyone's mind as the plane touches down at Marrakech Menara Airport.

Fortunately, the press pool dressed for the cold weather of Finland. The temperatures are much warmer here, but the clothing selection means that everyone is wearing conservative attire. Travelers to Morocco are expected to dress and act in ways that are in accordance with prevailing tradition. Most of the body should be covered, especially for women, because of the value placed on modesty. That won't be an issue. The women all left their sundresses in their closets.

An official greeting party moves into position at the bottom of the stairs after they are rolled up and secured beside the hulking 747. The press departs first, followed by everyone else. Santa has changed into much more utilitarian clothing for this visit. Gone is the flowing red robe with white trim that he donned in Italy. Despite the toned-down look, it's still very Scandinavian and not dissimilar to what he was wearing when MacKenzie met him at his Arctic Circle office.

She takes a position near the media, who are waiting off to the side of the stairs. Wyatt, Stowe, and the Chapmans move across from them. There isn't much other media here, at least not nearly in the numbers they saw in Italy.

"Are you going to tell me what we're doing here?"

"You'll find out along with everyone else, Keith."

The answer doesn't seem to satisfy him. "Santa does know that this country is ninety-nine percent Sunni Muslim, right?"

"He knows whether you're awake or sleeping or naughty or nice. So, yeah, I'm guessing he's got that figured out."

She doesn't know that at all. Santa is an old man from Finland, not the real Santa. He could be confused or even have dementia. He wouldn't be the first public figure to be afflicted by that.

"Well…this ought to be interesting, then," Keith muses.

He's not entirely wrong. This is a diplomatic minefield. MacKenzie has no idea how a Muslim country, even one as moderate as Morocco, will receive such a prolific Christian figure. As Santa descends the stairs and walks up to the government representative, they are about to find out.

"*As-salaamu 'alaykum,*" the dignitary greets his white-bearded guest.

Santa places his hand over his heart and bows slightly. *"Wa 'alaykum as-salaam."*

"Since when does Santa Claus speak Arabic?" Keith whispers in MacKenzie's ear.

"Weren't you paying attention at the hearing last year? He may be Christian, but he's a man of the world."

"Apparently."

MacKenzie moves closer to Santa. She isn't interested in getting peppered with questions from Keith, especially since she can't answer any of them. Who would know where he learned to speak Arabic? Or why? All she's interested in is getting this latest visit over with in the hope that the next stop is St. Louis.

"*Merhaba.* On behalf of King Mohammed and the royal family, it is my honor to welcome you to the Kingdom of Morocco."

"*Shukran,*" Santa says. "I appreciate your hospitality, and please relay my deep appreciation to the king for accommodating our visit on such short notice."

The official smiles warmly. The monarchy is revered and nearly all-powerful in Morocco. He is the head of the armed forces and named himself the Commander of the Faithful in Islam. King Mohammed IV oversees a constitutional monarchy, but the real power is exercised by advisers and ministers. Those roles are largely dominated by his closest friends.

Whether one thinks that's appropriate or cronyism, it's an opinion best kept to oneself here. It is against Moroccan law to mock, criticize, or speak ill of the king. The same applies to Islam. They are criminal offenses that can land an offender in prison.

"Regrettably, the king is in Paris and unable to greet you himself."

"That is perfectly understandable. I had no expectation that Amir al-Mu'minin would be available to greet us."

The official's eyes light up at the use of a title few Westerners understand, much less would use. "My understanding is that you are heading into the mountains. Despite the criticism from some in the Western media, you should know that the government is doing everything it can to help the people there."

"Of course. My intent is not to embarrass the king or his ministers in any way during this visit."

"Then, if I may ask, what is the purpose?"

"In my religion, this is a time of generosity and a desire to spread joy. I can think of no better place to do that than among people who have faced such enormous hardship."

"And you think this will help?" the official presses.

Santa smiles. "*Inshallah.*"

Mackenzie smiles. She knows that one. It means "God willing."

The man nods. "Here is the document you requested. Please consider it a token of our friendship."

"*Shukran bizzaf,*" Santa says, respectfully handing it to Aurielle, who gently places it in a green envelope.

"Please enjoy your trip. Your vehicles are over there. A representative from your consulate here in Marrakech is waiting to escort you."

Content with Santa's answers, the official moves off, and MacKenzie directs the press pool over to the waiting motorcade. It would be an easier task if she had a lasso and cattle prod. Finally, she gets them all flowing in that direction, and they begin loading up the vehicles in the rear. She moves to one of the lead SUVs and watches to ensure they aren't accidentally leaving anyone behind.

"Hello, MacKenzie."

She recognizes the voice instantly and freezes in place. Her mind does the mental gymnastics of determining whether it's real. MacKenzie turns to confirm she isn't imagining things. She isn't. The man in front of her looks just like he did the last time she saw him – except maybe a little more tan. Her mouth instantly goes dry.

"Cliff? What are you doing here?"

"I work here. The State Department posted me in Marrakech two years ago."

"I…I didn't know that."

"Well, we've been out of touch for a long time."

That's an understatement. MacKenzie and Cliff haven't spoken even once since she declined his marriage proposal. There was no apology issued or awkward explanation provided in the aftermath…only radio silence. Now, he's here to lead her and Santa Claus into the mountains of a desert country. This is too surreal to believe.

MacKenzie turns her head and catches Santa handing Stowe and Wyatt a pair of envelopes. It looks like they won't be accompanying the rest of the group on this trip, either. She's dying to know what they've been up to but hasn't asked.

"I won't make you suffer through this awkward visit from a ghost of Christmas past any longer. Your vehicles are waiting," he says, snapping MacKenzie out of her thoughts while gesturing at the small convoy, "and it's about a four-hour drive to the village. Shall we?"

Chapter Fifty

SVP MALCOLM CHAPMAN

Tizi n'Tichka means "difficult mountain pasture" in Berber. It's not hard to see how this winding mountain pass got its name. The road is fairly good and has been upgraded in some segments, so they have alternated between the old and new for parts of the journey. That doesn't mean the trip is easy. Malcolm has found that it's better not to look around too much. The ride is nauseating enough.

The driver informed him that this is one of Morocco's most dramatic and hair-raising drives. Tichka literally means "difficult," and the many switchbacks attest to that moniker. There are few crash barriers, countless precipitous drops, and lots of wind. And then there is the catastrophic damage Malcolm has seen along the way.

The earthquake that struck central Morocco a week ago was headline news for a day or two. It's the second to rock this mountain range in the last decade, killing thousands of people. This quake measured 5.1 and had an aftershock of 4.3 fifteen minutes later, with the epicenter fifty miles southwest of Marrakesh, not far from the previous one. There is no official death toll yet, but it must be high. There is no way these houses can withstand that kind of force.

The convoy pulls off to the side of the road alongside one of the devastated villages. It's cold up here, and people have been sleeping outside in this weather. These villagers are tough as nails. There is no way that Malcolm would stay here under these conditions.

Several adult men walk over to the lead vehicle in the caravan. The embassy official who met them at the airport walks over to greet them. They look suspiciously at the dust-covered column of black Suburbans. Malcolm can understand why. The convoy would raise eyebrows even back home in the United States if it pulled up to a neighborhood this way.

The driver talks to the villagers, and the conversation grows more animated. The villagers aren't upset or angry, but there is a sense of urgency to the discussion. Santa doesn't intervene. He watches from afar, looking unconcerned. The same can't be said for the woman running this show.

"What's going on?" MacKenzie asks.

"These people are Berbers," Malcolm explains.

"Actually, the official name of Berber tribes in Morocco is Amazigh, meaning 'free people.' The name 'Berber' derives from 'barbarian,' which comes from the Latin word "barbari," meaning foreigner during the time of the Roman Empire. It wasn't intended in an insulting way, but the Amazigh still don't like the term."

"Santa, do you read encyclopedias in your free time?"

The jolly old man laughs before turning to Malcolm with a broad smile. "There isn't much else to do at the North Pole."

"I don't understand," Janelle says. "Why don't they look happy to see us?"

"Because they are very proud people who take hospitality to a new level. They are ashamed that they have nothing left to share with us."

Though most Amazigh live in very modest clay houses with few comforts, with time, some have managed to build bigger homes with modern touches. Electricity made it to this part of Morocco no more than ten years ago, and running water at times is not a thing.

The villagers walk over. They look worn and tired but far from defeated. Santa is wearing multiple layers and is dressed for the mountains. His shirt and pants are muted red and green colors, with brown boots and suspenders. The garb he would wear in his workshop fits in well in the Moroccan mountains.

"*Salam,*" Santa says, bowing slightly.

"*Salam.* You are the Christian Santa Claus?" one of the men asks.

"I am."

"Welcome. What brings you to our village? We do not require charity after the ground shook. We are survivors. We will rebuild ourselves."

"I know you will," Santa assures him. "The Amazigh have lived in these mountains for centuries and will continue to live here for centuries more. Of this, there is no doubt."

Malcolm looks at the growing crowd. More villagers have come to greet their guests, as have a swarm of kids. Amazigh people clearly have lots of children, and these are absolutely adorable. Despite their current hardships, they are still all bundles of smiles and energy. American children would be miserable under these conditions. They throw temper tantrums when the Wi-Fi isn't working. These kids…they are filled with happiness and joy.

"If you will permit me, I do have something for your children."

The man nods graciously, and Santa squats to look at the youngest member of their caravan. "Braylen, would you be so kind as to retrieve the big sack in the back of that vehicle?"

He nods eagerly. "Okay, Santa."

"I'll help him," the convoy leader says.

A couple of minutes later, Braylen lugs it over. It was his task, and he wanted to do it himself. When he drops it, the tie holding the top tight slips off, and several soccer balls spill out. The kids go nuts before looking back at their fathers. The men nod, and the balls are all scooped up by the children before they run toward a flat area.

"Can I join them, Dad?" Braylen asks.

"Of course," Malcolm says, nodding.

He watches his son join the other kids on their makeshift soccer pitch. Janelle wraps her arm around her husband's waist as they watch their little boy play with kids who live an ocean away. They have almost nothing in common – they come from different cultures with different histories and speak different languages. Adults should take notes because none of that matters to innocent children. Playtime is universal, and when one of the village kids scores a quick goal, so is celebrating. It's the most heart-warming thing that Malcolm has ever seen. Fortunately, the media's cameras caught it, too. It'd be a shame for the world not to see this.

"I am not here for charity," Santa says to the villagers as they watch the kids play. "There is little I can do to restore your village that you cannot do yourselves. I want to show the world your strength. You have lost so much, yet your determination is an inspiration to us all."

"Shukran," the man says, bowing in thanks.

Santa turns to face the cameras pointed at him.

"For Christians, Christmas is a time to reflect on the significance of Jesus's birth. The etymology of the word Christmas is literally the shortened form of Christ's Mass. It is a time when we should emphasize love, peace, and goodwill toward all. That includes those who do not share that faith. It's why the holiday has evolved into a festive cultural occasion as well as a religious one.

"Christmas involves exchanging gifts, spending time with family and friends, decorating homes with festive ornaments, and other traditions. But what is its true meaning? Is it the gifts and decorations? Is it the annual economic boost? As I said before the American subcommittee last year, it is much more than that. The true meaning of Christmas has been lost for many years. In the midst of upheaval, crisis, difficulty, problems, and fear comes the true message of Christmas with its hope and goodwill."

Santa turns to watch the children eagerly play. Aurielle brings a large tea set and some Moroccan mint tea. The villagers eagerly accept the small gifts and the women go to work building a fire to boil water. Santa came prepared to bring the hospitality to them.

"Did Santa have these soccer balls with him when he left Finland?" Malcolm asks his wife.

"No. They were given to him by the son of the man Braylen was talking to in Italy."

"So, he had no idea he would have a gift for these children when he got here?"

Janelle smiles. "Of course he did. He's Santa Claus."

Chapter Fifty-One

STOWE BESSETTE

Another city in another country and another card with a mission for Wyatt and Stowe to accomplish. In this case, they were handed two cards, actually. Santa produced one red one while Aurielle gave them another in a green envelope. The first contained a specific set of instructions on how to deliver the second. Of course, it requires a long drive…and, in hindsight, some Dramamine.

The Atlas Mountains are a stunning range of peaks that stretches across Morocco from the southwest to the northeast, dividing the country roughly in half. The heights offer breathtaking views and a unique driving experience that can best be called thrilling and nausea-inducing. The driver takes Wyatt and Stowe through the two-hundred-kilometer Tizi n'Tichka pass, the highest mountain pass in North Africa, which connects Marrakech with Ouarzazate.

The nearly five-hour trek along a narrow and winding road with countless hairpin turns takes them through rugged terrain, past traditional Berber villages, and several places where stopping for a picture was almost a requirement. After reaching Ouarzazate, it's another five hours to Merzouga, a small town not far from the Algerian border.

It's getting close to sunset when Stowe and Wyatt are dropped off alongside a road with huge sand dunes looming in the distance. Their driver walks them over to a shady area where five camels are resting. Three other tourists are waiting for them to start…whatever this is.

"You can't be serious," Stowe says. "I thought we were going to a desert camp?"

"You are," the driver confirms. He holds up a red envelope of his own. "According to my instructions, this is how you are getting to it. I'll meet you there with your bags. I have to take the scenic route."

Stowe isn't amused. She is more comfortable with two planks of wood on her feet than she is riding on an animal. That's Wyatt's domain, and he looks like he's looking forward to this. That's not surprising since his idea of relaxing is getting on a horse's back and galloping at ridiculous speed across the Montana countryside.

They walk over to their guide and follow his instructions carefully. Their camels are already on the ground and ready to mount. The others on this trek are quickly shown how to mount their camels since the sun is getting low on the horizon, and everyone will want a sunset picture. There is no getting out of this now.

Wyatt goes first, moving to his camel's left side, and climbs on. He holds onto the saddle and leans forward slightly when the camel stands. He made it look so easy. Then, it's Stowe's turn.

Everything starts well enough. Stowe manages to climb onto the saddle. It's more comfortable than she thought riding on a camel's hump would be. Maybe this won't be so bad. Then, the camel stands.

Stowe throws her arms around the camel's neck and holds on with a death grip as the camel gets its legs underneath it. Her face is pressed against the steel handle that she should be hanging on to. The animal even looks back at her with a look on its face that can only be described as, "What the hell?" After a moment, she releases his neck, grabs the saddle handle, and straightens while Wyatt chuckles in front of her.

"It's not funny!" she barks.

"You have no idea how adorable you look."

Stowe purchased a scarf to protect her head and face from the sun and sand on one of their brief stops after passing through the mountains. Wyatt opted to get a *cheich*, which is a traditional head covering widely used in the desert regions of North Africa. The garment is made from a long piece of cotton or linen fabric, and he opted for a colored one instead of the more common indigo. The wrapping technique they taught him can be adjusted to ensure ventilation. He looks even more rugged and manly than usual.

The guide begins leading them on foot. Stowe is only seven or eight feet off the ground, but it feels much higher. Wyatt looks back to check on her. At least he isn't laughing.

"You look like you're going to have a stroke."

"I think I am having one," Stowe admits, staring at the ground and wondering how soft the landing on the sand will be if she falls off this beast.

"Okay, sit back in the saddle and relax your legs."

"I can't relax them. I'll fall off."

"You won't fall off. You have a death grip on the saddle handle. Now, feel the camel's swaying motion and move with its gait. Just go with it."

She relaxes. As the tension leaves her body, the ride actually becomes enjoyable, even as they climb the first dune. Erg Chebbi is one of the most famous and breathtaking dune fields in the entire Sahara Desert. Stowe can see why. It offers an incredible desert experience with towering sand dunes, stunning sunsets, and a glimpse into the nomadic culture. She's a mountain girl and could never live here, but it is an amazing place to experience.

The guide stops the caravan to take pictures at the top of a large dune with the sun setting. She has a few taken with just her, but she insists on getting some with Wyatt. Even though they are not together anymore, she has shared carriage rides, a Tuscan estate, and now a camel ride with him. Those are memories she wants to cherish, along with their previous adventures.

They begin moving again, and she can feel the temperature dropping. It's still an hour's ride to the camp, and she's finally starting to enjoy it. Stowe closes her eyes. She never thought she would be riding a camel over sand dunes in a desert an ocean away from home. She also never thought she would share another experience like this with Wyatt after what happened. For the first time in months, she feels at peace. This is what life is all about.

Chapter Fifty-Two

COMMUNICATIONS DIRECTOR
MACKENZIE WALSH

Santa finishes talking to the media. That interview is going to rock the planet. There is nothing like a message of peace at Christmas, and it is going to resonate with everyone. The world is watching them, and Santa is delivering.

MacKenzie's phone rings, and she is half wondering how she is getting service deep in a North African mountain range. There is no doubt who this is. Santa may be delivering, but she isn't. At least not in the eyes of the man running the White House.

"Hello, Marco. I know what you're going to say. Trust me, it'll be worth it when you hear Santa's interview."

"I don't care about an interview. I don't care about Santa giving gifts in foreign countries. I care about what people here are saying. I thought my directions were clear, MacKenzie. I *know* the orders issued to the flight crew were."

"It's one last stop. Not a big deal."

"Not a big deal," Marco says after scoffing. "Oh, how wrong you are. It's a *very* big deal."

"How so?"

"Well, let me see…I'm pretty sure you've met the president. Yes, I recall you standing in the Oval Office for our morning staff gaggles. You've worked with him since he was a candidate. Tell me how much he loves his orders being undermined."

"I didn't undermine anything," MacKenzie argues. "Santa did."

"Oh," Marco sarcastically chuckles, "he'll be thrilled to hear that the U.S. Air Force is taking orders from a fat guy in a red suit."

"Santa isn't that fat, actually. He's pretty spry for an—"

"You think this is funny, Mac? Do I sound like I'm in the mood for your cheeky responses?"

His tone answers the question, or at the very least, makes that question rhetorical. Marco's playfulness is gone. He probably talked the president into this goodwill mission to fetch Santa with a pledge that this would help with their approval ratings. MacKenzie has to believe it is, but Marco might not be seeing the results he was looking for. Either way, she's done with his taking it out on her.

"Have some spiked eggnog and settle down, Marco."

In hindsight, that probably wasn't the best thing to say to her boss.

"Are you serious right now?"

"I absolutely am."

"Mac, I told you to get Santa to the United States. Millions of people—"

"Are caught up in this journey!" MacKenzie practically shouts into her phone. "Pay attention to what's going on, Marco. What's the Tucker family's PleaseHelpMe fundraiser up to now? Two million? Two and a half?"

"Close to three," he admits.

"Then you can't argue some good isn't coming from this."

"Is that what the plan is? Parade Santa around the globe until they hit the magic number? Because, for what this trip is costing, the U.S. government could have covered the price of the drug by now."

MacKenzie decides to leave that comment alone. As for what the plan is, she wishes she could answer that question. It would be great to speak from a position of power. If she knew the plan, she could confidently state that everything is going to work out fine. But she can't say that because she doesn't know what Santa is up to. She has to trust that things are going to work out, and that isn't easy for her to do.

"I have no idea. Santa is calling the shots."

"Including getting two senior Air Force officers to ignore their orders. There are going to be consequences to that."

"Yeah, the American people will love hearing that."

There is a laundry list of things politicians hate and implore their staff to avoid at all costs. The first item on that list is surprises. Elected leaders hate them. Everything must be controlled to the extent possible to avoid embarrassment. Leaks are a close second. Nothing ruins a day faster than having to face the media when information not meant for public consumption makes it into the wild. That's likely why Marco is taking a beat to get his blood pressure under control.

"Are you threatening me?"

"I didn't say that I was going to leak it. But unless you plan on getting a judge to issue a gag order for Santa…no, I don't think that will work, either. Americans would demand the president be impeached over that."

Marco groans. "Why did I send you on this assignment?"

"I've been asking that since you gave it to me, if memory serves. But you did."

"And you've failed to do what I asked."

"Fine. I failed. Whatever. I'm the one on the ground here, not you! If you don't like the way I'm doing my job, get your fat ass on a plane and come here yourself. Otherwise, we're going to do this my way, and by that, I mean Santa's way. That's the end of this conversation. We'll get to St. Louis when we get there. Until then, stay off my back!"

She ends the call and closes her eyes. She's never done that before. Even in a crisis, she's never yelled at anyone on her team, much less the White House chief of staff. It's a career-limiting move.

"Crap," she mumbles.

Marco may be insufferable at times, but he is the man in charge of the West Wing. That makes him her boss, and she just told him off. Careers have ended for less in Washington. He won't fire her, but there is no way she's going to avoid having an uncomfortable conversation about this when she gets back to the capital. She catches Cliff eyeing her from ten feet away.

"What?" MacKenzie snaps.

"Nothing," Cliff says. "I was wondering where the fiery and passionate woman I once fell in love with was, but I think I just found her. I'm betting that was long overdue. Do you feel better?"

Ironically, she does. MacKenzie hates being micromanaged.

"Other than the prospect of being unemployed at the end of this, yes."

"Mac, you're an incredibly capable woman with a pretty impressive resume. You'd get another job offer in fifteen seconds if it comes to that. I'd give you one at the company I'm helping to start if there was a chance in hell that you'd accept the idea of working for me."

"I appreciate the offer, but we both know that won't…what company?"

"It's a —"

"MacKenzie, I'm sorry to interrupt," Aurielle sweetly says, "but Santa would like to head back to Marrakech. We will spend the night in the city and leave first thing in the morning. That should get us to St. Louis by mid-afternoon, assuming you order the pilots to put their foot on the gas."

MacKenzie is about to say that jet aircraft don't have gas pedals before she recognizes the metaphor for what it is. A flying sleigh doesn't have wings, either.

"What about Wyatt and Stowe? I heard they're at least a day's drive from Marrakech."

Aurielle winks at her. "Santa has arranged something special for them. Don't worry. They'll be there before we leave."

MacKenzie has no idea how, but maybe it's time to put her money where her mouth is. She wants Marco to trust her, so she should be willing to do the same for Santa. He hasn't let her down yet. With that thought, she goes to round up the press corps for the journey back to civilization.

Chapter Fifty-Three

WYATT HUFFMAN

The walk from where the guide stopped the camels and they climbed off isn't a far one to the camp. Of course, it's also over loose sand, so it's like walking on a beach. That makes the short trek more tiring than it should be. That doesn't matter. Wyatt is already impressed by what he sees. This is going to be an unforgettable experience.

The camp feels like it's in the middle of nowhere. It isn't, but the perception is what matters. It is the perfect amalgamation of the raw desert beauty and the comfort of a high-end accommodation. Wyatt is used to sleeping under the stars in Montana. This will be a nice change of pace.

The tents here look spacious and well-appointed. According to their driver, they have comfortable beds, en-suite bathrooms with hot showers, and traditional Moroccan decor. He also said the food is a highlight, with most camps serving gourmet Moroccan cuisine in tagines, along with fresh salads, pastries, and other local specialties. It's a good thing, too, because he's famished.

"I can't believe you took a selfie with a camel," Stowe says as they walk down the dune toward the welcoming red carpet running the length of the camp.

"I can't believe he was mugging for the camera. My horses don't even do that."

They are greeted by a man who hands them a warm, wet terrycloth towel to wash their hands and faces and offers them a seat on cushioned furniture. This camp has a number of seats set up like a lounge for relaxing while enjoying the desert landscape. They both accept Moroccan mint tea, or "Maghrebi mint tea," as the man calls it. It's a traditional cultural beverage brewed in a "berrad," which is a small ornate silver teapot. The tea itself is a simple concoction of Chinese gunpowder green tea, fresh mint leaves, sugar, and water. It's also delicious.

"Hello, and welcome! My name is Ali. I own this camp."

"Thank you, Ali. I'm Stowe, and this is Wyatt. This place is really amazing."

"*Shukran*. We try hard to make it as inviting as we can. The camps used to be located in the dunes, but the government relocated us for environmental reasons years ago," their host says, looking around. "This will be my last year here."

"What do you mean?" Stowe asks.

"Our government has a very strict permit system to run these camps. Everything needs to meet a specific code. Well, I was slow to make some required changes, and the window to renew my permit closed. It expires on January first, and then I will have to dismantle all of this."

"Can you rebuild in another location?"

He shakes his head. "No. The slots are all taken. I will have to wait for someone else to have an unfortunate bout of bad luck or when new sites are opened, which rarely happens."

Wyatt grins and nods at Stowe, pointing at her purse. She had completely forgotten about the second card that Aurielle gave her.

"We can't be sure, but maybe this will help."

"What is this?" Ali asks, accepting the green envelope.

"We actually aren't sure," Wyatt explains. "It's a gift for you. Open it, and let's find out."

"Who's it from?"

Stowe looks at Wyatt before answering. "Santa Claus."

"Santa Claus? I'm not Christian. Why would he give me a gift?"

It's a good question. It'd be another to add to the list that Stowe is mentally keeping, but at least this one has a plausible answer.

"Santa has this thing about delivering joy. Sure, he does it to celebrate the birth of Jesus Christ, but he believes that joy is a universal feeling."

"You know this?"

"We've had some experience with it," Wyatt says.

Ali opens the envelope and immediately places his hand over his mouth. He sits in the chair across from Wyatt and Stowe as tears form in the corners of his eyes. He looks at the paper like Charlie eyed the golden ticket to Wonka's chocolate factory.

"I...I can't believe it."

"What is it?" Wyatt asks, likely knowing the answer to that question, just as Stowe does.

"It's a five-year permit. How did he get this?"

"We don't know how he does what he does. We only know why," Stowe says.

"Thank you. Thank you so much," Ali says, placing the permit back in the envelope. "You have no idea how much this means to me."

"I think we do," Stowe says with a smile.

"If you would please excuse me. I need to share this news with my staff. They are all looking for new jobs and will be thrilled to hear that's no longer necessary."

"By all means," Wyatt says.

Ali starts up the red carpet toward the large tent before stopping and turning to them. "Dinner will be served soon. We are going to have a lot to celebrate tonight!"

Chapter Fifty-Four

COMMUNICATIONS DIRECTOR
MACKENZIE WALSH

The media has loaded up in their vehicles, and Santa and Aurielle are safely buckled up in the back of their SUV. MacKenzie gets her driver's attention and points at the vehicle in front. He nods, understanding the message.

She moves to the passenger side and yanks the door open. She climbs in next to Cliff and closes the door before buckling her seatbelt. Cliff doesn't immediately say anything. Instead, he stares at her until she settles in for the long drive back to Marrakech.

"Are you lost?"

"Are you asking the question literally or metaphorically?" MacKenzie asks in return.

"The real meaning of 'literally' is to describe something that actually happened or is true in a real sense. If I say, 'I literally ran five miles,' it's because I ran five miles. In modern usage, it's used to emphasize the intensity of an expression, even if it's not true. We love bastardizing our own language, which is why English sucks. If you say, 'I literally jumped out of my skin,' it's to emphasize fear, not because you had an actual out-of-body experience."

Mackenzie looks at Cliff with a raised eyebrow. "You know I'm the director of *communications* for the White House, right?"

"I'm just saying that I know you aren't *literally* lost. You're in the High Atlas Mountains in the Kingdom of Morocco. What I *am* wondering is if you know which car you're supposed to be in."

She misses him. Most women would find that need for specific information from a man annoying. Not MacKenzie. Communication is all about transmitting a message that is received and understood by another. The more precise the message, the better the chance of acknowledgment and comprehension. She prides herself in being exact with her speech, and Cliff is the only man she has ever met who equals her in that way.

"You haven't changed a bit," she says, meaning it as a compliment. "You're right — I am not lost. Yes, I know I'm supposed to be in the vehicle behind us. No, I'm not getting out of this SUV because, yes, I am riding with you back to Marrakech. If you have a problem with that, you can switch vehicles."

Cliff smiles and shakes his head. "I'm not the only one who hasn't changed."

The vehicle turns and pulls onto the road back the way they came, heading north slowly while the rest of the convoy falls in behind them. She isn't looking forward to the trip back. The winding road and constant changes in elevation mess with her stomach. From what she was told, the south slope of the mountain range is far worse than this is. Thank God they didn't travel any farther than they did.

"I just got word from the State Department that you're flying back to the U.S. with us. Is that true?"

Cliff winces. "I was supposed to be on a commercial flight tomorrow. My bags are already packed and any household goods are being shipped next week. I guess the State Department wanted to save money knowing Air Force One is sitting on the tarmac."

"It's Santa Sleigh One, but…why are you coming home?"

"My assignment is here is over. It's time to move on. Mac, you're not in this car because you want to talk about my travel plans. How much longer am I going to need to wait for you to tell me why you're really sitting next to me?"

"I'm drumming up the nerve."

"That doesn't sound like the fearless woman I once knew."

"Fair enough. Were you mad that the State Department sent you here?"

Cliff stares out the window. That's probably not the question he expected her to ask. In fairness, it isn't the one she wants to ask. Since he's already uncomfortable with this conversation, it's best to ease into it.

"Morocco is a beautiful country filled with great people. There are far worse places to go. I'm actually going to miss it."

"I'm sure, but you didn't answer the question. I don't remember you wanting to leave the U.S."

"A lot changed after…after us. So, when the posting came down, I didn't fight it. I didn't think I would like North Africa, but it turns out that I love it here. Besides, they're Muslims and don't celebrate Christmas. It was nice not having to deal with the constant reminder of what happened."

She knows how he feels. "I'm sorry, Cliff. I never meant to hurt you."

"I know," he says, continuing to stare out his window.

"We never talked about marriage. I wasn't ready."

"I know."

"You never called me after the proposal."

"I know."

This is like pulling teeth. It's time to cut to the chase, so to speak. MacKenzie takes a deep breath and steels herself for what could be a harsh response.

"Okay, I'll ask the question. Why not?"

He takes a cleansing breath before looking at her. "I was embarrassed. I never imagined that day you would say no. That's why I didn't mind proposing in front of our friends and families. Afterward, I went home and waited to see what happened. I wanted to know if you still wanted to be with me. So, I waited almost a full week for the phone to ring, and it never did. I assumed that was my answer."

That's…not what she expected. She should have known better. Cliff isn't a softy, but he isn't harsh or aggressive, either. Lashing out isn't in his makeup. What he likes and cherishes is honesty – something impossible to come by in politics and difficult in a relationship. MacKenzie has dated men who have lied to her over far more trivial things.

"Oh, you have no idea how wrong you are. I wanted to call. I should have. It's just...I thought you were so mad at me."

"I was."

"The proposal...I wanted to say yes, but it wasn't a good time. My career—"

"Has always been the most important thing for you, even over me. And with good reason. You work in the West Wing now."

"Yes, but that doesn't mean I didn't love you."

Cliff forces a fake smile. "Just not enough."

MacKenzie winces. That hurt. It isn't because he meant it to, but because that's what he actually believes. Too bad it's patently untrue, but refuting that conclusion isn't going to get her anywhere. She tries a different approach.

"I'm sure you found someone else."

"Sure, I dated. One relationship actually started to get serious before I ended it. I knew it wouldn't have worked out."

"Why not?"

He looks her directly in the eyes. "Because she wasn't you, and that was never going to be fair to her. It turns out that I'm still not ready to get into a serious relationship."

"Still?" MacKenzie croaks. "It's been years."

"Yeah. I got down on a knee and proposed because I wanted to spend the rest of my life with you, MacKenzie. Maybe some people can get past that quickly, but I'm not one of them."

"Cliff—"

"We need to stop here for pictures," Cliff orders the drivers before turning to MacKenzie. "The press will love it. You'll never see a more beautiful sunset."

He doesn't offer any further explanation as tires crunch on the gravel when the vehicle pulls to the side of the road. Cliff swings open his door and climbs out. This conversation is over for now. But it left MacKenzie with a valuable piece of information – he is still carrying a torch for her. It's only now that she's realizing the feeling may be mutual.

Chapter Fifty-Five

STOWE BESSETTE

Stowe wants to remember this forever. She moves around the camp slowly, soaking in the atmosphere and committing every detail to memory. Long ago, Nana told her that we all exist for a short moment in time. To get the most out of our lives, people need to make the memories they create count. Stowe took the lesson to heart. This is one of those special memories.

She has found peace at this camp outside the big golden dunes of Erg Chebbi and the bigger African sky. Peace both with herself and with Wyatt. Santa knows what he was doing sending them here.

The long car ride over the mountains and to Merzouga allowed them to talk the way they used to. There was no discussion about their relationship or what happened last summer. It was light and breezy banter about almost everything else. Funny stories from college were punctuated with sober lessons learned in life. Both admired the scenery while wondering if they could ever adapt to desert living, considering the climate and topography of where they are from.

They have both been caught up in the moment since their arrival. It's hard to believe they are on the edge of the world's largest desert, an ocean away from home. It's almost surreal. Stowe never would have had Morocco on her travel list. Now, she is already searching for ways to return. It's another destination on a growing list.

The staff at the camp is beyond friendly. Berber hospitality ranks right up there with that of the American South, and the good news in the second card she and Wyatt delivered has only added some zeal to the excellent service. Looking around, it would have been a shame to lose this spot because of a permitting issue. This camp is positioned far enough away from the others to create a feeling of seclusion. When Stowe closes her eyes, she is almost transported to a time of the nomads wandering the desert.

After they got settled into their tent, the first item on the itinerary was dinner. Stowe hadn't realized how hungry she was after an adventurous day traveling to Merzouga and a ninety-minute camel ride over sand dunes nestled under a setting sun. She and Wyatt washed up and made their way to the dining tent after Ali left them.

Dinner is served buffet-style and includes bread, soup, vegetables, and a traditional chicken tagine dish. Stowe doubts the chef will ever earn a Michelin star, but after a long day of travel, it is a welcome and tasty meal that they eat with gusto. Thankfully, there is no lack of food, either. Both of them make several trips back to the buffet to refill their plates.

The conversation shifts to whether her nana or his mother could make such a dish back home. The consensus is they could, but neither ever would. PopPop is a traditional Vermonter and likes the same fare he's been eating all his life. Wyatt's father is a die-hard Montana rancher – his diet has consisted of steak and potatoes since his teeth first came in. Neither would appreciate cooking in a clay tagine.

After dinner ends, Wyatt and Stowe join the rest of the people staying at the camp around the fire pit. They crash on stuffed fabric cushions slightly larger than the beanbags found in a kid's playroom. With no other light except the stars and the lanterns placed outside each tent, the dancing fire is all that illuminates people's faces. It only takes her a few minutes to get completely lost in the moment.

Stowe has always found peace near a fire. Whether it is camping or sitting beside the raging inferno her PopPop likes to build in the fireplace of their Vermont cabin, nothing relaxes her like a crackling fire. She closes her eyes as their hosts break into an artful piece of nomad music.

Ritual Berber music features drums and rhythmic handclapping. After the first song finishes, Ali explains that troupes of musicians called *imdyazn* travel the Atlas Mountains during summer and perform in village squares and at souks. It's a distinct style of music, with songs telling folk stories and historic events through the lyrics. With the explanation out of the way, the five musicians launch into their second piece.

She may have her differences with Wyatt, but this isn't one of them. He is equally at home next to a fire and is enjoying the music their hosts are playing. They may never win a talent show, but it's exotic, entertaining, and the perfect end to the day. Stowe watches as he closes his eyes. Caught up in the moment, she rests her head on his shoulder.

It's a bold move. The slow reconciliation with Wyatt hasn't meant a return to where they were in their relationship in the early summer. It doesn't matter right now. Obsessing over what will happen next between them can wait. Right now, Stowe is in her happy place and not eager to leave it.

Chapter Fifty-Six

WYATT HUFFMAN

Wyatt wanders halfway up a dune and plops on the ground. The fire has burned down, the musicians have put away their instruments, and the other visitors to the camp have found their way back to their tents. It's getting late, and the fresh desert air is inducing drowsiness. He is feeling it, too, but wants to take one more moment to enjoy this before closing his eyes and drifting off to sleep for the night.

The Moroccan night sky is breathtaking. Montana has its own celestial beauty, especially since his ranch is far enough away from the light pollution to see many of the faintest stars in the heavens. But this is an almost unparalleled view of the night sky. The Milky Way is visible as a dense band of stars stretching across the inky expanse overhead. It's a reminder of how small Earth really is when compared to the vastness of the universe.

Stowe joins him without saying anything. She collapses on the ground beside him, her head only a foot or two from his. They lie together on the sand that's still warm from getting beat on by the blazing sun all day. Together, they admire the constellations Orion, the Big Dipper, and the Southern Cross and can see Mars, Jupiter, and Saturn with their naked eyes.

Words would only spoil the tranquility. Any words, not just ones about their past or present or the status of their relationship. The view is magnificent, and that doesn't need to be pointed out. They both stare at the heavens in absolute silence until a bright white streak screams across the sky.

"Oh! A shooting star," Stowe says, catching a glimpse of the meteor shooting through the atmosphere. "Make a wish."

Stowe and Wyatt close their eyes. When they open them, they turn their heads and look at each other. In another time and place, they may very well argue who moved in first. In reality, it's a tie. They roll onto their sides and kiss. It's not like the one they shared while standing in a frigid Finnish forest under the dazzling northern lights. They're lying on the sands of the Sahara under bright stars instead. The scenery has changed, but the kiss is just as perfect.

Both of them roll onto their backs. Neither says anything. Wyatt isn't sure what to say. In more ways than one, it's been a journey to get to this point. Neither of them wants to spoil the moment by saying something stupid. Wyatt sure doesn't.

Stowe must be thinking the same thing. She stands, brushes herself off, and retreats to their tent. Wyatt spends another fifteen minutes admiring the sky. He's more confused now than ever. This feels like a tug-of-war between his heart and his head.

He isn't sure which side he's rooting for. But that kiss was really nice – foreign because of absence, but still familiar because of history.

Content with his stargazing, he makes his way to their tent and pulls open the door. He wants to know whether Santa arranged to put them in the same tent on purpose. Probably. Sharing a room in Finland was a fluke. This trip was planned, evidenced by the red envelopes Father Christmas has been handing out like they're candy canes.

"Am I sleeping outside tonight?" Wyatt asks, pointing at the couch as she emerges from the bathroom dressed in a t-shirt and cotton shorts. She and Wyatt had decided when they moved their suitcases in after arriving that Stowe would get the bed, and he would sleep here. The pillows and blanket have been removed.

"No, we're sharing the bed."

"Uh…okay?"

"Wyatt," she says, shaking her head, "we dated for more than seven months. I'm not letting you sleep on a couch that's three sizes too small. I think you can handle it."

"It's not that…."

"Don't worry," Stowe says with a devilish smile. "I promise not to take advantage of you while you're sleeping."

That isn't his concern, but he doesn't correct her. Wyatt washes up in the bathroom, strips down, dons sleep shorts of his own, and climbs into bed. The mattress is very firm but oddly comfortable. He has no idea what it's made of, but it's not coiled springs. They lie facing each other for a while.

"We should probably talk about that kiss," Wyatt says, unable to restrain himself any longer from bringing it up.

"Are you going to say we were caught up in the moment?"

That was what was said at the bottom of the hill in Rovaniemi. They took a toboggan down the ski slope in the darkness, and she ended up on top of him when they crashed at the bottom. A kiss was called for in the moment. It was the second one they shared, but neither of them really counts the mistletoe mishap at her grandparents' house. So, it was really their first since it wasn't done under duress.

"We lied to ourselves in Finland."

"If you mean that we were looking for excuses not to be together, I agree. Are we lying to ourselves now?"

"It's not that simple, Stowe. We're on another Santa-fueled Christmas adventure. When the holiday ends and life returns to normal, what makes you think it will end differently for us this time?"

It's an honest question and a legitimate concern. Their relationship may not have fallen apart immediately after the holidays, but it still fell apart. It's not a path Wyatt wants to travel down twice. His heart may be screaming "yes," but his head is not on board with that decision.

"What makes you think it *won't* end differently?"

"Okay. I can't be the only one conflicted about this," Wyatt argues.

"Are you kidding? I've been conflicted since I stood on your porch and knocked on the door. That feeling hasn't changed."

"Then why not say it was fun while it lasted and move on? We buried the hatchet. We got the closure we both needed. Do you really want to go down this path again?"

Stowe closes her eyes and rolls onto her back. She opens them and stares at the top of the tent. "Did you move on this fall?"

"What?"

"After we broke up. Did you go on any dates you were looking forward to or even think about having a serious relationship since August?"

Wyatt thinks back to his date with Missy and the conversation with his sister that she is eagerly awaiting his return. She is a pretty woman and someone Wyatt could normally picture himself with. Except for all the reasons he can't. Well, not all the reasons – just one in particular.

"No."

"Neither did I."

That doesn't mean anything, or so Wyatt keeps telling himself. He was so hurt after their split. Why would he want to dive into another romantic relationship so quickly? He needed to get past what happened with Stowe first. Or, at least, that is what he has been telling himself for months. But there is something about this woman that he can't get past. He thought his breakup with Jessie was bad, but this is far worse.

"We can talk about this tomorrow when we're both not about to fall asleep."

"Okay. Good night, Wyatt."

"Good night."

The conversation should be over. Wyatt shut it down, and Stowe didn't want to press. But there won't be any sleeping tonight without one question getting answered. It's been nagging at him, and there is no better time than the present to find out for sure.

"Stowe, I'm going to ask you one last question, and you need to be one hundred percent honest with the answer. Do you still love me?"

She turns onto her side and rests her head on his shoulder, curling into a fetal position as she closes her eyes and exhales. It's not a breath taken out of frustration or annoyance. It sounded like resignation.

"It took all of ten seconds after seeing you come down the stairs at the ranch to realize that I never stopped loving you."

Chapter Fifty-Seven

SVP MALCOLM CHAPMAN

Malcolm could get used to this. Nobody likes the hassle of flying. Long lines at security checkpoints and immigration, crowded gates, impatience during deplaning, and the nervous pacing at baggage claim to see if your belongings made the trip with you suck all the fun out of traveling. This is different. Not only are they experiencing an enhanced version of private flying, but they are lounging on a modified 747 jumbo jet.

It makes this wait more than bearable. Santa Sleigh One is waiting to depart until the two remaining two passengers arrive, as the pilot tells everyone over the intercom system. They should be taking off in the next hour or two. That's good news. The next leg of this journey is an important one.

Malcolm is about to shut off his cell phone when it rings in his hand. He smiles and connects the call. He has relied on his team to hold things together back at the office while he's been gone. This must be another of their check-ins.

"What's up, Karoline?"

"I'm really sorry about this," she says on speaker. "Somebody here wants to talk to you."

"You're a hard man to track down, Malcolm," Franz Brunner says. "Since you weren't taking any of the calls we placed from the office phones, we had to resort to this."

"We?" Malcolm asks.

The question was reflexive. Franz could only mean one person joined him in the conference room. Malcolm made a decision to be here, and now it's time to pay the piper for it.

"Yes, we," the CEO interjects. "I thought I ordered you to return to the office."

"You did, sir. My duties have taken me here instead."

"I see," Klaus says, sounding more dispassionate than expected. "I have to say, I'm very disappointed in you, Malcolm."

That's something his father would have told Malcolm after he did something stupid. The loss of confidence that the head of Heilung just conveyed would have had a profound effect on Malcolm under other circumstances. Even a few days ago, the words would have sent him scrambling to make amends. There is no doubt that is what Klaus is aiming for, but it's not going to happen this time.

"The feeling is mutual, sir."

"Excuse me?" Klaus asks, replacing his calm tone with one that could only be described as indignant.

"You heard me. I have never been so disappointed in a company I've worked for. Tell me, Herr Eberhardt, what does Heilung stand for? What does this company *value* other than money?"

"Watch your mouth, Malcolm!"

"Why? It's brutally clear how this is going to end for me, so why shouldn't I speak my mind? You're the CEO. Franz, you're the chief marketing officer. You are two of the highest-ranking executives in Frankfurt. Can either of you tell me what Heilung does?"

"We research cutting-edge therapeutics and manufacture and distribute those medicines to heal people," Franz says, reciting the marketing propaganda he was charged to put together.

"So long as those people can afford them, right? What about everyone else?"

"Malcolm, this is a business," Klaus interjects. "Without revenue, we can't provide the medications that save thousands every year."

It's a factual argument. Pharmaceutical companies aren't charitable not-for-profit organizations. They need revenue to operate, and that revenue comes from drug sales. But that is far from the whole story, and these men are fools if they think that Malcolm and the rest of the world don't understand that.

"I agree, but there is also a disconnect there. What was the company's profit last year?"

Malcolm braces himself for the verbal assault he's sure is coming. He scrunches his face and moves the phone away from his ear to prepare for the onslaught. It never comes. Instead, he is rewarded with stone-cold silence. It's almost as if he can hear the metaphorical chirping of crickets in the background.

"That's privileged information," the CEO finally utters.

"I'm well aware. I'm the VP of North American marketing and even I don't know the actual number."

"Because you don't need to," Franz snaps.

"That's probably true, but you don't think you're going to get that question after Santa visits Antonne Tucker? Because you will, Franz. And if you don't tell the media, they'll grab their shovels and will dig the information up. Whether they squeeze it out of a government bureaucrat or someone on our board of directors is irrelevant. They *will* get the information. I know this company makes billions, but they will get the actual number. The profits are obscene, and I can't wait to see you justify them to a world that will demand better."

"If we provide Hemoexgen free of charge for one kid, we have to do it for everyone. It sets a dangerous precedent."

Malcolm hated that defense when teachers used it in elementary and middle school. He hates it just as much now.

"Nobody is saying you should just give Antonne the medication, although it'd be the right thing to do at Christmas. What everyone is questioning is why it costs what it does. That's why so many people have donated to his cause. They see injustice in the price we are charging, and that's the last thing anyone wants at Christmas."

"Good. Then the family can use the donated money to pay our asking price."

"I'm sure they will," Malcolm moans, knowing that Franz and Klaus both missed the point. "The family is close to the PleaseHelpMe goal because of the generosity of strangers who stepped in when we didn't. That's going to be Heilung's legacy for the foreseeable future – that we put profit and greed over all else."

"What is your plan to change that? I'm assuming you have one. Any good marketing executive would, at least one who was sitting at his desk actually working on the problem."

Malcolm takes a deep breath and flexes his hands. "I certainly do, and I didn't need to be at my desk to develop it. I'm going to address the Tucker family directly and apologize on behalf of corporate leadership for not making the drug more affordable."

"No, you aren't!" the CEO and CMO scream in unison.

"I am. It's long overdue."

"It will be the last thing you do as an employee of Heilung," Klaus threatens.

"Sir, you entrusted me to work on this problem and have done everything you can to get in my way. I assume that's why you handed it to me to deal with instead of Franz. You know this won't end well, and you need a sacrificial lamb to appease the board of directors after the holidays. You made me the fall guy."

Every organization has behavioral patterns that become integrated into the culture. Some have a positive impact, while others do more harm than good. One of these patterns that causes the most worry in corporations is the "cover your ass" phenomenon. Casually called "CYA," the practice is driven by fear and a toxic work environment, undermining performance and often resulting in the premature departure of high-performing employees.

Most corporate workers walk a fine line between serving the organization and protecting themselves. In the executive and managerial ranks, a favorite tactic to shield themselves from criticism or exposure to negative attacks or consequences is to evade responsibility or deflect blame after something has gone awry. It's an almost understandable response to protect one's status, job, or reputation. For Klaus Eberhardt, it's all three. He's among the first to push his subordinates in the way of incoming fire. Malcolm is next in line to take bullets for him.

"I don't think I like your tone," Klaus says with a sneer.

"Really? My tone is what's bothering you?"

"No, what's bothering me is that I gave one of my executives a task to deal with this public affairs crisis and expected you to deal with it. You failed."

Leadership is an art. Good leaders know that wielding power comes with shouldering the responsibility for decisions that impact those around them. It's a learned trait that doesn't come naturally to most people. Too many bad leaders follow their natural inclination to pass the buck to someone else instead of bearing the consequences.

Klaus Eberhardt is one of those bad leaders. He will rarely pass on an opportunity to delegate critical decisions. It provides him two benefits – the ability to step in and take credit when things go well and to scapegoat when they don't. If Malcolm had somehow managed to extract the Heilung brand from this negative news cycle, Klaus would take the credit for putting the right man in charge. Since that hasn't happened, he has the person he can blame lined up squarely in his crosshairs.

"My failings are your failings. Without any means to sway public opinion, any effort was doomed to fail. You knew that."

"I resent that implication! This was *your* responsibility!"

"I don't have a magic wand to make something like this disappear. Nobody does. Once it goes viral and the mainstream media latches on, options are limited. I gave you sound advice on how to turn this to our benefit, and you have rejected all of it. So, I'm taking matters into my own hands and doing it my way – the way it should have been done from the beginning. I'm going to talk to the Tuckers."

"Then you're going to find yourself fired."

"Fine. You're going to fire me no matter what, so I'll speak to the family as a *former* employee. We're heading to St. Louis now. If you want to stop me from talking to them, you had better tackle me as I walk through the doors of that hospital. Nothing short of that is going to stop me."

Malcolm ends the call with a punch of his finger. He takes a deep breath and looks down to see Braylen staring up at him with concern on his face. In the chair on the other side of the plane, Janelle has the same look.

"Are you going to get in trouble, Daddy?"

He squats to look his son in the eyes. "Of all the lessons I can teach you, the most important is that it takes courage to do the right thing."

Malcolm walks his son over to the seat next to Janelle and buckles him in. She sets the clock he received from Jacopo Bartolini on his lap, and he becomes fixated on watching its face. His wife offers Malcolm a sympathetic look. She knows that conversation was likely career-ending. He can only hope it was the right thing to do as he stares at the mantel clock in his son's lap. Only time will tell.

Chapter Fifty-Eight

WYATT HUFFMAN

Morning has come too soon in this quiet, peaceful desert camp that is seemingly in the middle of nowhere. The countless nights of tossing and turning over the past few months gave way to stillness. Is it contentment? Stowe fell asleep in his arms. They slept so soundly that Wyatt woke in the same position they fell asleep in.

Nothing happened between them, not that he expected something to. Cuddling with an ex-girlfriend is much different than engaging in other activities. Spending the night close together is awkward enough, but the pre-breakup comfort with each other has seemingly returned. He is content to lie here and enjoy that.

The knock on the door ruins the moment. Stowe stirs, but it's Wyatt who hops out of bed to answer it. This isn't the kind of place that has room service, so he's curious who's outside their tent at this early hour.

"Good morning. I'm sorry to do this, but I need you to pack and grab a quick breakfast," their driver says after Wyatt swings the door open and wipes the sleep from his eyes. "We need to get going."

"This early?" Stowe asks from the bed.

"Yeah. I have to get you back to Marrakech. Santa wants to depart for St. Louis as soon as possible."

Wyatt does some mental calculations. "Won't it take a day to drive back there?"

"Longer for me. The two of you have other arrangements that were made for you."

"What arrangements?"

"You'll see."

The driver walks away, and Stowe begrudgingly climbs out of bed. They each take a quick shower, pack what little clothing they have, and make their way to the big tent where breakfast is being served. They say goodbye to their eternally grateful host and slam down a couple of cups of coffee before walking over to the black Suburban that looks very out of place in Morocco.

"No camel this time?" Stowe asks the driver as he double-checks to ensure their two small bags are in the SUV.

"Camels are fun, but the Suburban is much faster for where we are going. We're on a strict schedule."

He's not going to spill, despite Wyatt's attempts at extracting that information. Whatever surprise he has planned is going to be just that – a surprise. They load up in the SUV and begin heading northeast. It's abundantly clear that they are not going back over the mountains, at least not through the pass they took to get here.

There is a small passenger terminal at the airport, but the driver doesn't stop there. Instead, he steers toward a hangar with a helicopter parked out front. Normally, that wouldn't raise suspicions, but a pilot is walking around the bird as he conducts a preflight inspection. The corner of Wyatt's mouth curls. Their chariot awaits.

"You have got to be kidding me," Stowe moans. "Santa arranged this?"

"I'm sure he had help," the driver admits. "My instructions came from a chippy woman who spelled out every detail."

"Aurielle," Wyatt says, smiling at Stowe.

"She didn't tell me her name. You'll depart in fifteen minutes. I'll wait to ensure you get off the ground and then I need to start my trek back. Good luck. I'll be watching what happens in Missouri."

Apparently, so will the rest of the world. Wyatt maintained cell service most of the way to the camp and managed to fight the nausea as he stayed caught up on the news. Other than admiring the scenery, there wasn't much else to do. Half the world is following this adventure, and many more than half of the Americans in the United States are.

"Why is Santa suddenly in a rush to get to St. Louis now?" Stowe asks.

Wyatt has had no time to put any thought into that. He rubs his chin. "Maybe the final pieces are in place."

"What pieces? What changed since we got here?"

He shrugs. "Your guess is as good as mine."

The pair is escorted onto the red and white Airbus H125 helicopter and strapped in. The pilot gives them headsets to wear and begins the procedure to fire up the engine and start the blades turning. It's comfortable in the back with room for four. Wyatt is guessing that this bird is usually used for sightseeing tours out of Marrakech.

"Have you ever been on a helicopter before?" Wyatt asks.

"It's a first for me. You?"

"Once. One of my father's friends flew an AH-64 Apache attack helicopter during the first Gulf War. He kept his license and would take people up in a civilian bird from time to time. It was a long time ago."

"How old were you?"

"I'm not sure…six or seven."

"You know, if Santa arranged this last night, he put it together fast."

"I doubt that's the case. Most likely, it was either before we arrived in Morocco or just after landing. We should ask the pilot if he has a red envelope."

Stowe smiles. "What do you think this is all about, Wyatt? Vienna, Florence, now Morocco? What is Santa Claus cooking up?"

"I'm not sure," Wyatt says, his voice growing louder to be heard over the volume of the engine and the beating rotors, "but it has everything to do with Antonne Tucker. I can tell you one thing, though – something big is about to happen."

"Why do you say that?" Stowe asks, not feeling the need to yell since she has a microphone a centimeter from her lips.

"Because it would be a shame to do all this planning and have this great adventure finish in an anti-climactic ending."

Chapter Fifty-Nine

COMMUNICATIONS DIRECTOR
MACKENZIE WALSH

Journalists research, write, and report news and information to the public. At least, that's what their historical role has been. The media format has changed dramatically over the years, morphing from print to radio to television to online. With that change came a different way to view themselves.

Researching stories through interviews and public records has often given way to speculation in the name of timeliness. Clear, accurate, and well-crafted stories were sacrificed in the need to be first. Editing and fact-checking have taken a back seat in the rush to break a story. The need to compete in the marketplace creates stress for journalists, and they have changed because of it.

While still harboring a natural inclination to ask questions and seek information to uncover hidden stories, many reporters have eschewed their commitment to ethical journalism. Honesty and fairness are a thing of the past. Few of them are ever held accountable for the stories they write, even when proven to be factually inaccurate.

Nobody embodies that more than Keith Meadows. Once Stowe and Wyatt arrived by helicopter from wherever they were, Santa Sleigh One departed Morocco, ascended through the clouds, and pointed west. That freed everyone to move around the cabin. That doesn't mean she's used to seeing anyone from the press corps this far forward.

"They let you out of the back of the plane?" MacKenzie asks.

"I could get used to this," he responds.

"Don't," she says with a half-smile.

Whoever designed the layout of Air Force One is a genius. Whether it was through political maneuvering or divine intervention, the engineers put the president's suite and office in the nose and second deck of the plane while placing the seats for the press in the tail. Outside of strapping them to the bottom of the fuselage or sticking them in the cargo hold, they could not have put any more physical distance between the media and the leader of the free world.

The fact that Keith Meadows is allowed to eat in the dining area of the plane near the front is a testament to the relaxed rules the flight crew is following without the president on board. There is no massive Secret Service detail to enforce separation. The press still doesn't have unfettered access to Santa Claus, but they are getting more freedom of movement than they are used to.

"Where's your story about the government colluding with Santa Claus?" MacKenzie asks as she pours herself a cup of coffee. "I expected to have been reading it already."

"It's a work in progress," he admits.

"What are you waiting for? I would hate to think my not providing you with a quote is holding up the works."

MacKenzie can't suppress a smile. Of all the reasons not to publish, failing to get a quote from the White House ranks near the bottom of the list. In many cases, saying that there wasn't a comment makes the story feel more legitimate and creates the sense that the government has something to hide.

"The hook that will get everyone to read my story."

"Ah, the fact that Santa Claus is traveling the world and spreading cheer isn't big enough for you?"

"It is for my colleagues, but not for me. There's more to this, and we both know it. Fortunately, I think I found what it is."

"Oh, yeah? Enlighten me."

Keith dabs his mouth with a white linen napkin and leans back in his chair. He's enjoying this moment far too much.

"Tell me something, MacKenzie. Is the government trying to force a private company to give away a very expensive drug?"

"We have no power to do that."

Her response was too quick and too automatic. That's a red flag for reporters.

"Well, *legally*, you don't."

"What are you implying?"

"I'm not implying anything. I'm asking a question."

MacKenzie stares at him for a long moment. "No, we are not forcing Heilung to provide the Tucker family with anything."

"Are you sure? I know they were *big* campaign contributors to the president."

This is why Americans hate journalists. They like to insinuate malfeasance without actually asking a direct question. He's implying that there may be a "quid pro quo," a Latin phrase meaning "something for something." There is nothing dirtier in politics. In a government of the people, by the people, and for the people, situations where a party provides something of value in exchange for a favor are viewed as despicable. It's how many voters view campaign contributions – money is exchanged for access and, in some cases, favorable legislation or executive actions.

"There is no quid pro quo, I promise you."

"You're sure?"

"Yes. Why wouldn't I be?"

Keith presses his lips together before speaking. "Because you've been here and not in the West Wing. You aren't privy to arrangements Marco Ramirez may or may not be making."

"If he was making arrangements, he would tell me," she says, sounding more defensive than intended.

"I would hope so, but that's not always how things work in Washington."

"Keith, if you're going to make an accusation, just make it."

He smiles. It's the wry one he uses when he thinks he knows something that someone in power doesn't. The grin isn't what concerns MacKenzie. What's bothering her is that he may be right.

"Not now. Maybe when the time is right."

He winks at her as he leaves the dining area and turns toward the rear of the aircraft. Part of her is tempted to contact Marco to see if he knows what Keith is digging for. She passes on the thought, knowing that the White House chief of staff isn't going to want to hear a question like that. MacKenzie knows she will need to be ready for the moment when Keith makes his move. Or, in a best-case scenario, he's bluffing and has nothing of substance after this fishing expedition.

Chapter Sixty

STOWE BESSETTE

The media is infuriating. Local reporters may or may not be that bad, but the national media, at least in Washington, are jackals. Everything is a conspiracy or scandal in their eyes. Nothing is pure in its intentions. Even a trip involving Santa Claus must have a political angle in their minds. Maybe, at some level, it does, but most people aren't following along on the journey because the president or his plane is involved. It's Christmas, and everyone wants a feel-good, heart-warming story. It's as simple as that.

Stowe could use a stiff drink or, at a minimum, a cup of Santa's hot cocoa after hearing most of MacKenzie's conversation with Keith Meadows. There was a brief thought of intervening, but it wasn't warranted this time. The White House communications director can take care of herself, and Stowe is better off not giving the veteran correspondent another reason to come after her.

She moves out of the hallway next to the dining room and walks through the aircraft before spotting Janelle staring blankly at the darkness out the window. Her son is curled up next to her under a blanket with the presidential seal on it. Malcolm is nowhere in sight.

"Do you mind if I sit?" she asks Janelle in a soft voice as she passes the seats she and her son chose for this flight.

"No, please, go ahead." Janelle checks on Braylen, who is dead asleep next to her. He doesn't even stir.

"I won't bother him, will I?"

"Are you kidding? Braylen could sleep through a bombing run once he dozes off. He's always been a heavy sleeper. I guess that's why he has so much energy during the day."

"That must be nice. Where's your husband?"

Janelle nods toward the front of the plane. "Talking to Santa. I'm betting it's an interesting conversation."

She probably has no idea just how interesting. Whatever Santa is up to, Stowe is betting that conversation is a key piece to the puzzle.

"Most talks with Santa are. I was in the back with MacKenzie. I think a member of the media may have just figured out who your husband works for."

"Are you sure?" Janelle asks, lowering her eyes.

"No. He didn't come out and say it plainly, but there was knowledge behind the questions he asked MacKenzie."

Janelle scowls. "And you're wondering why I didn't tell you."

"No. First, it's not my business. Second, I saw Malcolm's botched interview a couple of days ago and recognized him in Florence. Third, I'm not at all surprised."

"Why not?"

Stowe presses her lips together, figuring out how to say this without sounding crazy. "Because Santa Claus is involved."

Janelle cocks her head. "Are you saying that you think Santa knew who my husband was even when we met in Vienna without my telling him?"

"I'm saying that it's a little convenient that he finds the wife of a Heilung executive shopping in a city we were visiting when the boy we're ultimately going to see in St. Louis needs a drug from that company."

"Is that what the media is going to say?"

Stowe shrugs. "I don't know. Probably."

Janelle fidgets in her seat. The conversation is making her uncomfortable. The Chapmans haven't advertised who Malcolm works for, although Stowe doubts they knew it would remain a secret. The interview he gave was aired by most major media outlets. That means she thinks Stowe is here to leverage the information somehow.

"What do you need me to do?"

"Nothing. I'm not here to talk about who your husband works for or why the three of you are on this plane."

"Okay…then why did you stop to talk to me?" Janelle asks, her eyes narrowing.

"To talk about second chances. I know things aren't good between you and your husband, and I put together some of the story. I thought you might want to talk about it to someone with a sympathetic ear."

Janelle nods. "Things between Malcolm and me…well, you're right – they haven't been good for a while. He's always been focused and driven. Hell, that's why I fell in love with him. No matter how busy he was, he always found time for Braden and me. Somewhere along the line, that focus shifted to his job. This damn promotion…he wants it so badly. He hadn't even realized the toll it took on the rest of us."

"I understand."

"Do you? Because saying it out loud…I sound high-maintenance, which I'm not."

Janelle doesn't strike her as the type of woman who needs to have everything done for her. She is well put together, but nothing she's wearing has a designer label. She is strong, independent, and confident in how she carries herself. From all evidence, Janelle is a doting mother and not an attention seeker. Maybe she is emotionally needy, and maybe she isn't. Stowe doesn't live with her and can't know that, but she doesn't come across that way.

"Are you willing to fight for your marriage?"

"Of course!"

"Then you're better than I am, Janelle. I didn't fight for Wyatt when we hit a rough patch. I got into an argument with him last summer and said some pretty vile things. Untrue things. Until this trip, we hadn't even spoken."

"MacKenzie told me."

"I should have known better. When Wyatt and I were searching for the perfect Santa to testify in front of the subcommittee, we ran into some real beauties along the way. We called them Sauced Santa, Jaded Santa, Streaker Santa, and Tax Evasion Santa."

Janelle chuckles. "Interesting names."

"They were interesting characters. One was an alcoholic with a string of DWIs, one took his clothes off and went streaking at a college football game, and one hated children and was in it for the money."

"That's three. What about the fourth…tax evasion?"

"Yeah, he tried to claim that he was Santa to avoid paying property taxes to the city he lived in," Stowe says, getting a genuine laugh from Janelle. "It's good for a laugh now, but it wasn't funny at the time. Our journey finally took us to Finland, where we met…I'm sure you know the rest of the story."

"And the moral of this story is…?"

"We met a lot of duds before finding the right guy. You're mad at Malcolm, just like I was at Wyatt. But how many duds did we go through to find those two men? My last boyfriend cheated on me. I know in my heart that Wyatt would never do that. I don't know Malcolm at all, but he jumped on a plane and flew to Italy, hoping he could find you and Braylen. That's worth something. Don't let him go out of anger. Fight for him harder than I did for Wyatt. You don't want to live with the regret if you don't."

"Thank you, Stowe. I will. May I offer a piece of advice in return?"

"Of course."

Janelle leans closer to her. "Wyatt is here. I don't think second chances only apply to Malcolm and me."

Stowe nods in appreciation. "I hope you're right."

Chapter Sixty-One

SVP MALCOLM CHAPMAN

Malcolm wasn't raised Catholic, but he imagines this is what being in a confessional is like. Santa isn't a priest, but he's wise and admired, much like priests once were. This St. Nick is easy to talk to, which is a little surprising. Kids have a fascination with and even a fear of him, but who could know he would be an effective therapist for an adult?

The conversation, as easy as it has been, has avoided one topic. It's a touchy one that could spoil everything. That doesn't mean it shouldn't be addressed. The news could spoil this entire journey and upend whatever St. Nick is trying to accomplish.

"I have a confession to make, Santa," Malcolm says, staring at his hands to avoid eye contact.

"It's okay. I know who you work for."

"That's…uh…wow. How did you know?"

Santa laughs and sips his hot cocoa. It's not the hearty "ho, ho, ho" that Malcolm expected, but one with an amused tone. He shouldn't have bothered asking the question.

"Right. You're Santa Claus. Okay…who I work for could cause problems for you and what you're trying to do."

"How so?"

"I'm the guy in charge of defending the cost of a drug that's…."

"Outrageous?"

"Yes. Yes, it is."

It's an admission that Malcolm would never make to anyone except Janelle. He gets paid to toe the corporate line, and Klaus Eberhardt doesn't think there is anything outrageous about it. He pays Malcolm to convince others of that.

"You don't agree with the price?"

"I don't make those decisions at Heilung."

"I understand. I'm asking you as Malcolm Chapman and not the senior vice president of North American marketing at Heilung Pharma."

Malcolm shifts his weight in his chair. There are two reasons – Santa used his full title, meaning he wasn't bluffing when he said he knew who Malcolm was. The second reason is more personal – he isn't used to giving *his* opinion, only what the company pays him to say.

"It's more complicated than people think it is. Do I believe that insulin should cost as much as it does? No. It's not a cutting-edge medication and should be more affordable for the millions of people living with diabetes. This isn't the same thing.

Therapies for very rare illnesses, like the one Antonne Tucker has, cost millions of dollars to develop. Millions. The company needs to recoup those costs, or there won't be any research into life-saving drugs."

Santa nods. "Multiple millions of dollars per dose?"

"It's a lot. An obscene amount. It's also why the CEO won't permit me to give the drug to Antonne."

"I know, Malcolm. That's why I'm not asking you to."

When the elf summoned Malcolm to the president's office to meet Santa, he half expected to hear a pitch to provide Antonne the drug. Then he convinced himself that nobody on this plane, other than his wife, knew who he was. It was bound to come out sooner or later, but there has been no indication that anyone has a clue. That's what makes Santa's response so shocking. He *did* know who Malcolm works for and still isn't asking him for the drug.

"Truthfully, I wouldn't set the price that high, but I'm in marketing, not accounting. Is that what you want me to tell people? Is that why you invited Janelle, Braylen, and now me to come along?"

"No," Santa says, closing his eyes and shaking his head.

"Then why did you?"

"Why did you come down from Germany?"

Answering a question with an unrelated question is a marketing technique. Malcolm is tempted to point that out, but the man is Santa Claus. It'd be considered rude.

"Janelle decided to return to the United States because my job was taking up all my time. She probably told you that…or you knew it already. I promised to spend more time around Christmas with them, and then the world found out about Antonne Tucker."

"And because of that, you haven't been able to," Santa says, getting a nod from Malcolm. "And what about now? Shouldn't you be working?"

"The CEO thinks so. He laid into me pretty good at the airport. I still got on the plane because I thought it was more important that I was here for Janelle and Bray. I told him off right before we took off from Marrakech. I'm not sure I'm still employed there."

"You're choosing your family over your job?"

A pained look flashes across Malcolm's face. "I was desperately trying to hold onto both…now, I've made my decision."

Santa nods. "Your son is precious, Malcolm. He has a unique understanding of time for someone his age."

"Yeah, I know. It's pretty amazing. It must come from Janelle's side because it doesn't come from mine."

Malcolm doubts it comes from there, either. Punctuality is a foreign concept in her family. They are completely indifferent to the concept of time. It's why their wedding started a half hour late.

"Time, at least how we interpret it, is a zero-sum game. A gain is balanced by a loss. Time devoted to one activity must be taken from another. There is no possible way to be in two places at once."

"And you think I need to choose between my job and my family?"

Santa takes a long sip of his cocoa. "You've already made the choice by your own admission, Malcolm. You only need to come to terms with it."

Malcolm hangs his head again. That's easier said than done.

"I have spent my whole life trying to climb the corporate ladder. Obstacles, constraints, perception…none of that was going to get in my way. I've always wanted a big job with a lot of responsibility so I can provide for my family."

"And now you feel like you're losing them because the responsibility you seek costs you something that's very important to them…your *time*."

"I know I'm losing them," Malcolm says, his tone remorseful and filled with regret. "That's why I needed to find Janelle. It's why I'm here. I'm only afraid that it may be too late to fix things."

"Family is a cornerstone of human society. Janelle has always supported you because she loves you. You are here because your wife asked if you could join us. If she didn't think your marriage was worth saving, would she have?"

"She may have done it for Braylen."

It was a reflexive answer. Janelle is an amazing mother and would do almost anything for their son. It doesn't mean she's a pushover when it comes to rules, but she is ever-vigilant about taking care of his emotional needs. That's what much of their current turmoil is about. His son needs him to be present in his life, and Malcolm hasn't been there since they arrived in Germany.

"There are worse reasons to do something than for a child. But do you believe that in your heart? You are the captain of your life, Malcolm. You make the decisions that affect your future. Now that you are at a crossroads, you get to determine your path."

Malcolm finishes his cocoa just as the elf returns to the office. He stands, knowing his time with Santa is up.

"Thank you. For the cocoa, the invite to accompany you…for everything."

"You're very welcome, Malcolm. Know in your heart that things will work out as they should."

It's sage advice, but it could as easily be wishful thinking. Malcolm can only hope for a Christmas miracle to make everything right. Fortunately, he may be in the right place for one.

Chapter Sixty-Two

WYATT HUFFMAN

Cliff is an interesting guy. He didn't talk much about MacKenzie other than the scant details about what happened to their relationship. Instead, he focused on the future and what lay ahead of him.

His time in Morocco opened his eyes to the plight of the rest of the world, much like what Santa managed to do in that village deep in the Atlas Mountains. As Americans, we genuinely forget how fortunate we are. While many people struggle with the basics of life, like shelter, clean water, and food, we complain about our Internet speeds being too slow.

Despite having far less than those living in countries in the West, what these people do have is an unrivaled sense of community. Cliff is starting a non-profit that helps get people the basic necessities they need most. He isn't out to save the world, but he does want to make it easier for people to survive in it. They have some generous donors who have helped them with startup money. Now, he needs to fundraise and begin operations to prove their worth.

Aurielle swings by and interrupts their conversation. She says that Santa wants to see Wyatt and asks him to accompany her. He excuses himself and dutifully follows her to the president's office aboard the aircraft.

"Welcome, Wyatt," he says from behind the desk. "Come in, please."

"No hot cocoa? It's the stuff dreams are made of."

Aurielle laughs. It's actually more of a giggle.

"Thank you! We're too close to landing, I'm afraid. I promise I'll make it up to you someday."

With that pledge, she leaves, closing the door behind her.

"Aurielle has to be the nicest woman I have ever met. How long has she been with you?"

"A very long time. Please, take a seat," Santa says with a smile, gesturing at the chair Wyatt eases himself down in. "Things are bound to get crazy after we land. I wanted to talk to you before we do."

"About Stowe?" Wyatt asks, getting a grin in return. "You said you weren't trying to get us back together."

"I said no such thing," Santa says, waving his hand. "I said in Italy that I cannot force two hearts together. I told you and Stowe in Finland that you are still writing your story. So, speaking of which, how's that story going?"

Now, it's Wyatt's turn to grin. "Santa knows."

He slaps his knee. "Yes, he does."

"Why are you so invested in us, Santa? There are millions of other people in the world. Why are you playing matchmaker with the two of us?"

"Because you found me. Do you remember walking into my office last year?"

Wyatt nods. "Like it was yesterday."

"You were both filled with so much Christmas spirit. You couldn't stand that I was under attack in your country. The idea of banning public depictions of Santa Claus was unconscionable. So, you and Stowe put your differences aside and focused on the one thing you knew you agreed on."

"It turns out it was about the only thing," Wyatt mumbles.

"Was it? You've always been a good judge of character, Wyatt. Would you have even considered dating Stowe if you didn't share more with her than just a love of Christmas? Would you have bothered having a conversation with her in your barn when she came to see you if you still didn't feel something for her?"

"How did…?" Wyatt grimaces, forcing himself not to ask how Santa knew that. "That was Ellie's doing. She kinda…."

"Blackmailed you. I know. Nobody wants to be labeled as having an STD," Santa says, causing Wyatt's mouth to hang open. "Your sister grew up with two stubborn older brothers. She learned how to manipulate you at a very early age. Fortunately, Ellie is a remarkable woman who only uses her powers for good. Well, usually."

"I don't suppose I can bribe you to put coal in her stocking this year."

Santa laughs. "It doesn't work that way."

"You're right. Things with Stowe are good right now, but what happens when Christmas is over? What happens if something pulls us apart again?"

Santa leans forward. "That's the nature of all relationships, Wyatt. You learned the lesson about politics interfering with love long ago. After Jessie, you swore to not let it happen again. But Stowe has different demons. She needed to learn that lesson for herself."

"Has she?"

Santa grins. "You tell me."

"I hope so, but I just don't know. I'm sure that Santa does."

The pilot comes over the intercom and announces their initial descent into St. Louis. He didn't realize they did that on the president's plane. Maybe they normally don't, but this is no ordinary passenger.

Santa retrieves a red envelope from his pocket after the pilot finishes. "I'm going to give this to you now, but you must promise not to open it with Stowe until the end of the day."

"Another assignment?" It was an innocent question, but all Wyatt gets is a warm smile and another twinkle in Santa's eye. "Okay, I won't."

"Excellent. Now, let's get ready to fulfill a Christmas wish and maybe, just maybe, make some magic happen in the process."

Chapter Sixty-Three

COMMUNICATIONS DIRECTOR
MACKENZIE WALSH

The amount of media present at the edge of the tarmac is almost unprecedented. MacKenzie has been involved in politics for more than a decade. She has been an avid follower of it since she was in grade school. While kids her age were playing video games or surfing the Internet, she was watching cable news. Never before has she seen this level of coverage. Even the presidential inauguration wasn't this well-covered.

MacKenzie coordinated an order of disembarkation from Santa Sleigh One to make the most of the event visuals. Once the rolling stairs were positioned and the door opened, the media left the aircraft first with instructions to load up in the vehicles and head over to the children's hospital. There will be local and state coverage already on-site, along with some additional national outlets. There is no reason for them to hang around when the time is best served setting up shop at the hospital. The press pool will round out the reporters inside to cover the meeting with Antonne.

Lambert-St. Louis International Airport is not huge, but it isn't small, either. There is plenty of room for a press gallery filled with cameras and journalists as well as onlookers who brought their children to catch a glimpse of the iconic figure. This is not the typical line of people waiting for a picture at some campy, colorful plywood recreation of Santa's workshop. There is real excitement here. And energy.

The staff is the next to depart the plane. Malcolm and his wife lead the way, followed by Wyatt and Stowe. Cliff follows them, and MacKenzie trails him as they descend the stairs. The Air Force personnel will remain with the plane, as per protocol. All of them crowd near the door to wish Santa luck.

They make their way over to the next group of vehicles that arrive. Transportation is coordinated through the Government Services Administration, an independent agency tasked with managing and supporting the basic functioning of the federal government. They are a centralized procurement hub for necessities, handle property management, and perform various administrative services, including transportation. In this case, they placed at MacKenzie's disposal a fleet of shiny black Suburbans and other large SUVs.

Only Santa is left on the plane with Aurielle. He was instructed to wait about five minutes before emerging at the top of the stairs. This is designed to be a pageant, not a typical arrival. The anticipation from the eager crowd is palpable. The president wanted a show, so that's what he's getting.

MacKenzie leans against the vehicle's door and checks her phone. There still isn't a call from Marco. He has hounded her on every other stop of this journey, so why would today be any different? It might have something to do with her telling him off. She's beginning to wonder if she still has a job, but that's still a problem for when she gets back to the capital. This needs to wrap up first.

"It will be fine, Mac," Wyatt says after walking over to her and taking a position to her right.

"I know."

"Then stop fretting about why your boss isn't interrogating you. We made it here, so enjoy the moment."

"I won't relax until this is over and I'm back in Washington," MacKenzie admits.

"Then you're going to miss the best part of the experience," Stowe piles on. "Let Santa do his thing. He has a plan, and it's better if you accept that and roll with it. The current is too strong, and you aren't a salmon."

"Old habits die hard with MacKenzie," Cliff muses as he assumes a spot on her left side. "This woman was born to swim upriver."

"You're not going to drag out some old dating story to embarrass me, are you?"

"I could. There are hundreds of them." His smile is the only thing saving him from a salvo of verbal abuse from a woman who communicates for a living.

The crowd erupts with a roar when Santa emerges carrying a large sack over his shoulder. He's dressed in red and white, looking more like the traditional Santa Claus in this country. He's still thinner, and his beard is straight, so he isn't trying to completely look the part. His coat looks more like a robe, much like the one he wore in Italy.

The cheering is almost deafening, even in the open space of a major airport. Kids jump up and down. Even the media looks like they are having fun covering this. Santa makes a grand wave from the top of the stairs before he and Aurielle walk down them.

"The man knows how to make an entrance."

"He slides down chimneys once a year," Stowe says, standing next to Wyatt. "That should go without saying."

MacKenzie frowns. "Are those toys he's carrying? He didn't have those when we left Finland. Where did he get them from?"

Wyatt shrugs. "He's Santa Claus, so probably from his workshop."

"Wyatt, there is no Santa," MacKenzie argues.

Stowe cocks her head around him. "MacKenzie, after everything you've seen on this trip, do you really still believe that?"

She turns to her old flame, who is stifling his laughter. He shrugs. "Don't look at me. I'm already a believer."

Santa devotes a few minutes to posing for pictures with the children. Time is getting short, and Santa climbs into his vehicle before MacKenzie needs to say something to move this along. The rest of the team loads up in the convoy, and the drivers pull off the airport grounds for the fourteen-mile trip southeast to downtown St. Louis.

The city is situated along the western bank of the Mississippi River, directly across from Illinois, and has a population of approximately three hundred thousand people. The greater St. Louis metro area is considerably larger, home to nearly three million residents.

Founded in the mid-1700s by French fur traders, St. Louis played a crucial role in the country's westward expansion. That's where it got its nickname, "Gateway to the West," and the origin of its iconic landmark, the Gateway Arch.

"You're not as nervous as I expected you to be," Cliff says, studying MacKenzie's face from beside her in the back seat.

"What's going to happen is going to happen. I did my job and got Santa here. Whatever happens next is outside of my control."

"Who are you, and what did you do with MacKenzie Walsh?" he says with a laugh.

"Are you saying I'm a control freak?"

"No, but you used to be."

That's the problem with exes – they know more about you than you want them to. Cliff is right in that she tends to be controlling. It's what makes her good at her job. But nobody likes being labeled a "control freak," regardless of whether it is a fact. One of Cliff's best attributes was his ability to balance her out when she became overbearing. She misses that.

"I was told by a guy that I should learn to enjoy the journey. I'm embracing that advice."

Cliff stares down at his hands. "Are you still with him?"

"Are you asking because you're curious or because you're interested?"

"Both." The answer was quick and honest.

"I was never with him. He's traveling with the love of his life in the car behind us. Wyatt said that right before you walked up to us on the tarmac. He got that advice from Santa Claus last year."

"Ah. Wyatt and the hearings. That's interesting."

"How so?"

Cliff turns to face her with a mischievous grin. "I thought you said there is no Santa."

"I forgot how annoying it was to argue with you," MacKenzie says with a smile.

"I always prided myself on bringing out the best in you. Then I realized that you never really needed me to do that."

She takes his hand and turns to look out her window. "That's where you're wrong. I needed it more than you think I did."

Chapter Sixty-Four

STOWE BESSETTE

The fanfare here is bordering on the ridiculous. What started as a small crowd in a Vienna Christmas market grew exponentially in Italy. While the trip to Morocco attracted more curiosity than anything else, it was widely followed by people around the world. Now that they are in the United States, Stowe has a better appreciation of the effects of the trip. There were thousands of people at the airport. There are easily a few thousand outside the Gateway Children's Wellness Center.

A phalanx of St. Louis police officers keeps the entrance to the building clear. At least none of them are in riot gear, although she suspects there is a team close by just in case. Events draw protesters who want to use the media coverage to draw attention to their cause du jour.

Santa doesn't stop for pictures this time. He leads the way into the hospital foyer, which is every bit jammed with people as the outside. The foyer isn't a small room but a massive, welcoming space laden with cartoon murals, children's artwork, and even a play area. People are standing four deep along the walls, with breaks in the crowd only for the reception desk and access to the elevator bank.

There are a lot of kids here. If Santa thought the toys in his sack would be enough, he's mistaken. In front of them is Antonne Tucker, sitting in a wheelchair with his sister standing alongside and their parents behind them. Some of the staff – likely the ones charged with his care – flank the family on both sides.

A wall of reporters and camera crews has formed in a dedicated space against the windows. They are positioned to capture every part of this big moment from the perfect angle. Cameras are tracking Santa's every step as he walks up to the stricken boy, who gawks at him through eyes large with awe. After days of anticipation, the climax of this story is finally here. Antonne Tucker, inflicted with the Christmas disease, is about to get his Christmas wish.

"Hello, Antonne. How are you feeling?"

"Okay," he says quietly. "Thank you for coming, Santa."

St. Nick closes his eyes, places his hand over his heart, and bows slightly. "It is my honor."

"This is my sister, Alaya."

"It is very nice to meet you, Alaya," Santa says, extending his white-gloved hand to shake hers.

The young girl isn't as impressed as her brother. She gazes at him apprehensively. "You don't look like pictures of Santa. Your costume is wrong, and your beard isn't curly."

"Alaya! Where are your manners?" her mother scolds her.

Santa laughs. "It's okay. People around the world picture me differently. In your country, I'm a fat man with a white beard dressed in a red suit with white fur trim and a thick black belt. In Great Britain, I wear a red or green robe. In Belgium and the Netherlands, I am Sinterklaas and wear bishop's attire when I arrive on a white horse. In Russia, I am Grandfather Frost, and they depict me as tall and slender. Personally, I like the idea of buff Santa Claus, but nobody else does."

Santa makes a show of flexing, and all the children laugh. Even the adults get a kick out of it. Stowe turns to look at Wyatt, who has his eyes closed and is shaking his head, clearly amused.

"See? I told you he was real," Antonne says, nudging his sister.

She folds her arms across her chest. "He could be dressed up like Santa to fool us."

"You have always had a suspicious mind, Alaya. Like the time Antonne told you he put your doll in the dresser drawer, but you knew he was trying to trick you. So, you called your mother to get it, and she screamed when she saw the rubber snake."

Alaya's eyes grow wide. His words are effortless, and his demeanor is reassuring. She is probably still thinking this could be a trick, but Santa has a way of disarming people. Stowe learned that lesson a year ago.

"Or the time when he called you outside so he could hit you with water balloons, and you came out with a shield to protect yourself."

"How do you know that?" Alaya asks.

"Santa knows."

Stowe smiles. There has never been more evidence of that than on this trip. He does know. Santa or not, the man is special. That is undeniable at this point. Even the skeptical Alaya seems to accept that.

"He's mean to me."

Santa nods. "He plays tricks on you because he loves you. You are twins, and you will forever be bonded because of that."

"Except he's sick."

The adults in the room practically melt into puddles. Women dab at the corners of their eyes. Nurses, caring but conditioned after years or decades of dealing with raw emotion, cover their hearts with their hands or wear sad looks on their faces. Even the men in the room are getting misty-eyed.

"I know."

"Can you help him?"

Santa gets down on a knee so he can look her in the eyes. "There are some Christmas wishes that even I cannot grant."

"Why not?"

"I am not divine. I do not control life and death any more than I control the sunrise and sunset. I can only help the way people live their lives, teaching them to experience joy and inspire kindness. Do you understand?"

Alaya doesn't speak. She lowers her eyes to the floor. Even if she understands, it's not the answer she wants to hear. Nobody in this room wants to hear it. They may not expect Santa to be a miracle worker, but they haven't given up hope.

"I want my brother to get better."

"I know you do. And there are a lot of people who are trying to help you because they have been inspired to be kind. Isn't that right, Mr. Tucker?"

Chapter Sixty-Five

SVP MALCOLM CHAPMAN

The timing is so perfect that it feels staged. Maybe it was, but it would be an impressive feat for anyone to pull off, even the White House. Marvin's phone chimes, and he reaches into his pocket and scans the incoming text message. He breaks out in a smile so wide that it'd be impossible to build a bridge across.

"That generosity is because of you, Santa. Your journey helped us so much. I just got a notification from our PleaseHelpMe fundraiser. We just surpassed the goal of three and a half million dollars. We raised the money for the medication that Antonne needs!"

The room breaks into rapturous applause. Doctors and nurses exchange hugs and high-fives. Alaya hugs her brother tightly as her parents embrace behind them. Even the reporters are fist-bumping each other. The mood is celebratory, and everyone turns to Santa when it quiets down.

"What do you say to that, Mr. Chapman?" a reporter calls out from the legion of media arranged in front of the windows. His words echo in the cavernous foyer.

Keith Meadows is a prominent journalist working in the nation's capital. He's known as a pit bull, although his targets are more political than corporate in nature. Until this trip, Malcolm only knew him by reputation and had never met him in person.

The journalists look at each other and shrug. They have no idea what this interruption is about, but they're paying attention. His timing was superb, at least for someone waiting to drop a bomb until it had the most impact. He's probably known that piece of information for a while – if not on the tarmac in Italy, then definitely during their stay in Morocco.

"I'm not sure if you all know this, but Mr. Chapman is the senior vice president of North American marketing for Heilung Pharma. Isn't that right?"

Malcolm straightens. "I am."

The answer was quick and confident. The worst thing that anyone can do is get caught in a lie that's easy to prove. It erases any credibility a person has in an instant. So, the admission is a no-brainer, and now dozens of pairs of accusatory eyes are glaring at him from around the room. Joy, kindness, and the celebration over welcome news have given way to anger and the hostility of a modern lynch mob.

"Is that why you're here? To collect a check for your expensive drug?" Keith presses.

Malcolm looks at his spouse and then down at his son, who is still clutching the golden clock Jacopo gave him in Italy.

"No. I'm here because my beautiful wife, Janelle, and my son, Braylen, met Santa in Vienna and accompanied him to Italy. They were coming home because I was too busy to spend Christmas with them like I promised. I was at work, laboring to convince all of you that Heilung Pharma is not the Scrooge you think it is. That the executives aren't just motivated by revenues and profits."

"You failed," Keith barks, twisting the metaphorical knife a little deeper.

"I know. Miserably. If being on this trip taught me anything, it's the value of family. My son taught me kindness when he handed an old man suffering a great loss a clock that was a gift from Santa. I then watched him deliver soccer balls to kids in a foreign land whose families had lost everything. If we could only all find it in our hearts to be that generous. So, maybe it's time to—"

"Malcolm? What are you doing?"

Klaus Eberhardt, draped in a wool overcoat and scarf, strides into the foyer like a Roman Caesar returning to the Senate fresh from his latest conquest. His jaw is tight, and his face is hard with determination. None of that is what spooks Malcolm most. It's the flashes of anger in his eyes. He made this trip because he feared Malcolm would seize this moment, and he was right. The soon-to-be former senior VP of North American marketing is counting on the CEO not realizing the one good card Malcolm has left to play in his hand.

"Oh, good, you're here, sir. I didn't think you would make it in time to share the news."

The comment throws Klaus off. He expected a weak defense or for Malcolm to crawl back into his shell like a meek turtle. Neither happened, and the CEO glances at the massive crowd of reporters whose eyes and cameras are trained on him.

"For the last week, people have challenged the cost of the drug," Malcolm continues, addressing the doctors, nurses, and especially the Tucker family. "I understand why, and so does our chief executive officer. It's very expensive, but despite reports to the contrary, that price isn't due to profiteering. Research and development on this cost us tens of millions, and it will be very difficult, if not impossible, to recoup that.

"However, what good is spending time, money, and research on medicines that nobody can afford? So, Heilung's CEO, Klaus Eberhardt, who was gracious in agreeing to travel here while I share this news, has authorized me to donate the dose of Hemoexgen to the Tucker family free of charge."

The foyer erupts in thunderous applause. The offer was as unexpected as the news about the fundraiser, and now everyone is getting the happy ending they wanted this story to have – all except Klaus, who looks like he's about to have a stroke.

"There is one condition, I'm afraid," Malcolm says, moving to stand in front of the Tuckers as the clapping dies down. "We're asking you to pay it forward, Antonne. We're all touched by the generosity of those around the world who helped fund your PleaseHelpMe plea. Three and a half million is an incredible sum of money, especially in tough economic times. Klaus and I are asking you to donate that money to a charitable trust we will set up in your name so that it can be used to defray the costs of the drug for other people who are sick. Would you be willing to do that?"

Antonne looks at his parents. "Can we?"

"I think that's a marvelous idea," his mother says.

"I agree," Marvin Tucker adds. "Thank you, Mr. Chapman."

"Don't thank me," Malcolm says, shaking the man's hand. "This is the brainchild of Mr. Eberhardt. I understand it's hard to believe, considering what has been said about us this week, but Heilung is dedicated to healing people. That's what the word means in German. We are all hoping we can grow the money in this trust to help with affordability while we continue having the funds to research life-saving drugs like Hemoexgen."

The room breaks into enthusiastic applause. It's the feel-good story that the world not only wanted but needed. Antonne getting the medicine he needs because of the charity of people around the globe is a great story, but being able to use that for others is the icing on the cake. Santa nods at him, and for a brief second, Malcolm swears he can see a twinkle in the old man's eye.

Chapter Sixty-Six

COMMUNICATIONS DIRECTOR
MACKENZIE WALSH

There are three types of lies in the world: lies, damned lies, and statistics. Statistically, there is a much greater chance of Klaus Eberhardt being a tyrant made to shine in a single moment than him being a decent human being. Not that it matters. Malcolm got what he wanted, and that's Heilung donating the treatment Antonne needs while creating a fund to help defer the cost for others who find themselves in this predicament. It was a master class in how politics actually works and an impressive feat to accomplish by someone not in the political realm.

The lie is the one Malcolm told that Heilung always planned to give away a dose of their three-and-a-half-million-dollar medication to the Tucker family. There is no way that's true. MacKenzie saw the way Klaus Eberhardt entered the hospital. That wasn't a man who had any interest in charity. He was there to throttle his senior vice president of marketing.

That leads to the damned lie. America and, by extension, the world will think that the CEO is responsible for this Christmas miracle. In less than five minutes, Malcolm Chapman changed his cantankerous boss from a pariah into a hero. It's an impressive feat. If he doesn't remain employed by Heilung when this day is over, some company is going to be thrilled to land his services.

This is all very clear to her. MacKenzie has been in the political game long enough to recognize the facts behind the fiction. Politics is built on a foundation of deceit and spin. Facts are made to suit agendas and smear political opposition. She knows a ruse when she sees one. In this case, she hopes it never sees the light of day. The story is too good as it is to be spoiled with unvarnished truth. Antonne will get his medicine. Others will benefit from the money raised. Everyone gets to spend this Christmas a little happier.

Maybe that was the point. A lot had to come together just the way it happened for St. Nick to pull this off. People can agree to disagree as to whether he is really Santa Claus, but she has become a believer.

Santa turns to the cameras. He has the attention of the assembled media and every pair of eyes in this hospital foyer. He didn't say much to the press during their journey. The expectation of what Santa will say when talking to the world is palpable.

"Thank you all for going on this journey with me. I know many of you followed along during my visits to Austria, Italy, and Morocco. You all knew, or at least hoped, that I would end up here, and you have my heartfelt appreciation for your patience. It was a necessary journey – not just for me, but for all of us to take together."

MacKenzie closes her eyes and enjoys the warm wave of understanding that washes over her. Now she gets it. Santa wasn't taking a taxpayer-funded vacation – he was building interest. By the time they left Morocco, hundreds of millions of people around the world were part of their journey. They were tuning in to see the joy he was bringing to people. It was a means to an end.

Whether it was meeting Janelle and Braylen in Vienna, giving an old man a new lease on life outside Florence, or providing soccer balls to kids in a devastated part of Morocco, he kindled warmth in people's hearts. In that way, he has done more for the world than any politician or leader could ever hope to.

"Christmas magic isn't something I make – it's created by all of us. Because of the generosity of so many, not only would Antonne have received the medicine he needs to live a normal life, but others will now benefit from the fund that will be set up in his name. It's a feel-good story, but why should it end there?

"We live in a difficult time. There is so much division – here and around the world. We have arrived at a place in time where we let our differences define who we are. Whether it is skin color, gender, culture, political or religious differences, we have grown apart. We have been pulled apart. We have been pushed apart.

"It wasn't always like that. Christmas used to be when those divisions took a back seat. Even on a World War I battlefield, soldiers took a brief respite from killing each other to celebrate the holiday before returning to their trenches to once again engage in desperate acts of warfare. Christmas is a season when the world is just a little happier…and people are just a little nicer to each other. At least, it used to be.

"As I tried to illustrate last year, that feeling has changed, and not for the better. Christmas has become a burden for too many who don't want to buy gifts, attend parties, or spend time with their families. The Christmas spirit has become secondary to the expectations we place on ourselves to celebrate the holiday."

MacKenzie glances at Cliff, who is hanging on Santa's every word. She doesn't celebrate Christmas at all because of what happened six years ago. Of all the pain that day caused, losing her love ranks first. Losing her Christmas spirit is a close second.

"It shouldn't be that way. Last year, I wanted to convey a message that the true way to celebrate the holiday lies in each of us – you only need to recognize it within yourself. The spirit of the holiday is waiting for people willing to recognize and embrace it over the self-inflicted stress we bring on ourselves.

"This year, I wanted you all to experience the magic that can happen when you all work together. What happened here was nothing short of a miracle. So many of you helped fund a treatment for a boy none of you knew. Those without means still came together and hoped for a happy ending to the story.

"My presence here is not only about showing Alaya that I exist. It's about proving that the Christmas spirit still lives within all of us. It is about bringing a global community together to help a complete stranger. In the process, you not only fulfilled a Christmas wish, you created a Christmas miracle. That is the magic of the season."

There it is. MacKenzie smiles after hearing the moral of this story. She almost feels bad about pushing Santa to come here more quickly than he planned. It turns out that Wyatt and Stowe were one hundred percent right – the journey was as important as the destination.

"We are all citizens of Earth. Despite our different cultures, religions, languages, and political divisions, we are united in our common humanity. And while everyone may not celebrate December 25th as Christ's birthday, we can all relate and embrace the spirit of what that date means – love, forgiveness, and joy. I hope I was able to bring that to you this holiday season. More importantly, I hope you recognize that you were the ones who delivered it."

The applause is as enthusiastic as it is deafening. MacKenzie can only imagine what people are saying at home. At her core, she is a politico. It's the lens through which she views the world. If there is anything that can be said about Santa Claus, it's that he's an inspiring figure who would make a great politician on the campaign trail.

Chapter Sixty-Seven

STOWE BESSETTE

Politicians and the people who work for them have a love-hate relationship with the media. The art of governing is about how to best allocate limited resources to meet nearly unlimited needs, but politics is influencing and manipulating the governing process to fit an agenda. Much of that relies on messaging, and news outlets are one of the best conduits for getting that message out to the voters. That makes journalists a necessary evil. Unfortunately, Stowe has always considered many of them just plain evil.

That's probably not fair. The average reporter is just trying to earn a living under the stressful circumstances their demanding editors put them in. Then, there is Keith Meadows. He's a special case because it's pure ambition that drives him, not some unrelenting passion for the truth. He wants to be a big name, and today's outburst during a touching moment was designed to be another rung on that ladder.

"Well, that didn't turn out the way you wanted it to, now, did it?" Stowe asks, cornering him off to the side of the media area.

"What makes you say that?" he asks, looking up.

"Keith, I may only be a low-level staffer on Capitol Hill, but that doesn't mean I'm an idiot. You knew who Malcolm Chapman worked for, probably since Morocco."

"I figured it out the night we were in Marrakech. I would have known sooner if my newsroom was paying attention. Idiots."

That's the other reason Stowe doesn't like Keith Meadows. He's smug, and nobody likes people who have an elevated sense of self-worth and arrogance. That, and he has a punchable face.

"And you sat on that information until you found the perfect time to strike."

Keith shrugs. "That's how the game is played, Miss Bessette."

"Why?"

"Excuse me?"

"Why is it played that way?"

"Okay, you're apparently serious about this…Malcolm Chapman and Heilung were always going to be the villains in this story. That's the way it began with that local news report and how it was determined to end. You must have recognized that."

"That's funny because I thought a rare illness afflicting a young boy was the true antagonist in this saga."

"Ah, of course. Except people can't relate to abstract. Cancer is bad. A sick child is bad. We can all agree on that, but how do you blame an illness? How do you channel anger into something that people can do nothing about? We live in a binary world — one that has to have good guys and bad guys. I needed a bad guy."

"And you think it's your job as a reporter to tell people which is which?"

Keith scoffs. "Absolutely."

"That may be the most arrogant thing I have ever heard," Stowe says, tensing up while trying to tamp down the impulse to spit on him.

"I didn't make the rules," he says with an indifferent shrug. "People stopped thinking for themselves long ago. Someone needs to fill that vacuum. It can be the politicians who nobody trusts, or it can be us."

Stowe wants to ask if there is a third option. Not all politicians are corrupt, uncaring egomaniacs. Angela certainly isn't one. Neither is Wyatt's old boss, John Knutson. They are honest people who want to be good representatives in a system they deeply believe in.

As for journalists, she supposes some out there want to fairly and accurately report the news. By the law of large numbers, a few men and women must take their responsibility to inform the public very seriously. But the people didn't elect them. What gives them the right to choose for everyone?

"Gee, I can't imagine why public faith in the news media is at an all-time low."

"I didn't join this occupation because I wanted to win a popularity contest."

"No, you do it because you want to be influential."

"Everyone has their ambitions, Miss Bessette. Don't be jealous."

That may be the most honest thing she has ever heard Keith say. "Jealousy isn't what I would call it. So, what now? Are you going to write an article taking credit for Heilung's change of heart when all you really did was step on a beautiful moment?"

Keith cocks his head. "It's telling that you think that's what I did — that I almost ruined some grand plan. Nothing about that trip was planned. The White House is good, and MacKenzie is world-class, but neither could have pulled this off. And I saw the look on the CEO's face when he arrived. I would bet my salary that Klaus Eberhardt didn't authorize Malcolm Chapman to give away anything. First, from what I've learned, it's out of character. Second, he looked like he ate bad sushi after Malcolm made the announcement."

"So?"

"There's a story there. If people want to believe the ridiculous narrative that other media outlets are spinning, then that's their prerogative. I'm going to get to the truth of the matter one way or another. It's what I do."

It's not what he does. He wants to create a scandal. Keith needs intrigue to get clicks and justify advertising rates for his newspaper. And he will. There's little Stowe can say here to change that. Shaming him certainly isn't going to work.

"Then I wish you luck. You might get a few dozen people to read whatever ridiculous article you peck out on your laptop."

"Okay, I get that you disapprove, Miss Bessette. So, why don't you give me an answer to a question that I can put in my article? You've been at the center of this from the beginning. You've traveled to Austria, Italy, Morocco, and now Missouri. What made Heilung change their mind about providing a dose of Hemoexgen to Antonne Tucker?"

Stowe smiles. There is one thing in the world that defeats smug arrogance. It's the combination of contentment and happiness. There is one answer to that question, and it's the only one the world needs to hear.

"Christmas magic."

Chapter Sixty-Eight

SVP MALCOLM CHAPMAN

The feel-good moment of the announcement wasn't destined to last. The joy in the room is shared by everybody except the cantankerous head of Heilung Pharma. He is forcing a smile for the people coming up to thank him, as he knows that cameras are still pointed in his direction. That's the public face he's wearing. Malcolm knows the CEO is a boiling cauldron of anger on the inside.

Some of it has to do with the lost revenue. Another part is having to explain this to the board of directors. Both of those take a back seat to the real issue at hand: Klaus is a control freak who gave orders that were explicitly ignored in the most public of ways. One of his executives disobeyed him, and that cannot be tolerated, regardless of the result.

"A word with you, please," Klaus says, guiding him away from the prying eyes of reporters and their cameras. "Do you know what you've done here today?"

Malcolm smiles, further enraging the chief executive officer. "Yes. What we should have done all along."

Klaus sticks his index finger in Malcolm's face. "I explicitly told you that we weren't giving that drug away for free!"

"We didn't."

"What do you mean?"

Why does he have to explain this? Did he not go to some fancy business school and read case studies on marketing and public perception? Executives are supposed to understand these kinds of things, even when in the throes of a temper tantrum.

"We gave the drug away for a mountain of good publicity and a rise in corporate prestige that will rival the Apollo Program."

"And you think that matters to the board? To our bottom line? To me?"

Those are the types of queries that powerful people lob at underlings to gain compliance. A week ago, Malcolm would have shrunk at the tone of those questions. That was a week ago. Now, it's an opportunity to speak truth to power because a reality check is what Klaus Eberhardt needs more than anything.

"Sir, I'm not sure if Franz ever explained this to you, but marketing isn't just about creating advertisements to sell products. It's about explaining to people what a company *values*. What do we value at Heilung, sir? I always thought it was the health of our customers. We make products that heal bodies and restore families. By giving away that dose of Hemoexgen, that's what millions of people saw today."

"At a tremendous financial cost."

"You're looking at this from a pure accounting perspective. That's a mistake. Three and a half million dollars couldn't buy the free airtime and positive mentions Heilung is going to get from this. It can't buy the feeling that people will get hearing our name, knowing that we did the right thing for a child in the middle of America during Christmas. People want to buy products from companies they feel good about, and they feel very good about us right now."

It's also the right thing to do, but Malcolm doesn't bother mentioning that. If Klaus cared about doing what was best, this would have been settled long ago.

"Unless they have no choice but to buy our drug. Hemoexgen is the only drug of its type available."

"And what about the countless drugs that aren't? How many of our products have competitors making the same thing, and what is our market share for those drugs and treatments? Who do you think the people will want to support after watching what happened today on the news or online? You're about to see a surge in sales across the board. The dollars that come tumbling in will more than cover the cost of one donated dose of a drug. And so long as you stay on message, that goodwill will last a very long time."

Janelle and Braylen join Malcolm, indicating that this private conversation just became a family affair. He stares down at his son, who is still clutching the gold clock he got from Jacopo in Florence. His wife isn't quite glaring at the head of Heilung, but her eyes aren't conveying Christmas wishes of peace and joy, either.

Klaus seems oblivious to Malcolm's family arriving at his side. The CEO is running calculations in his head. It's a new line of thought for him, and he slowly nods several times when he finally gets it. Better late to the party than never arriving. He looks at Braylen and Janelle before staring at his senior vice president.

"You mean 'we.' I'm going to need a good man running things from headquarters. Franz Brunner has been a good chief marketing officer. What you may not know is that he's retiring next year. We didn't announce it because we wanted to search for his replacement without the candidates knowing what was at stake. That's the promotion you just auditioned for, Malcolm, and I think you just proved that you earned it. I want you to be the next CMO of Heilung Pharma. You won't have any problem with board approval, assuming you are correct in forecasting our sales numbers."

Klaus extends his hand, and Malcolm shakes it. It's the promotion that Malcolm has wanted since he graduated high school two decades ago. In college, his studies were always geared toward achieving that goal. All seemed lost until this moment.

"Thank you, sir," Malcolm says with a smile. "I appreciate the opportunity. But I meant what I said as you arrived here today. If the past week taught me anything, it's the value of family. You have a lot of dedicated people at Heilung who are willing to give everything they have for the company. Unfortunately, I'm not one of them. My family needs to come first."

"What are you saying?" Klaus asks, cocking his head.

"I'm resigning as SVP of North American marketing effective January 1st."

"I…I don't understand. You came to Germany hoping to get a promotion. I'm offering you on a silver platter the biggest one you will ever earn. Are you really willing to pass up the opportunity to be the CMO of a major multinational corporation?"

Malcolm wraps his arm around his son. "Yes, I am."

"I'm…disappointed. It's a shocking lack of judgment."

"Maybe. Do you know who doesn't have a lack of judgment? Karoline. She's a fantastic member of my team, and I think she would be a great CMO. Have her work with Franz when you return to Germany. She's young and still has a lot to learn, but I have no doubt she'll make you proud. You'll see what I mean."

"Your decision is final?"

Malcolm glances at Janelle, who is staring at him with shocked eyes. "It's final. I will be back to collect my things and move back to the U.S. at the beginning of the new year. Have a Merry Christmas, sir."

"Very well. You, too."

The CEO strides to the exit with the same angry gait he entered with, and Malcolm wraps his arms around Janelle. She hugs him harder than she has in years. Neither is in a rush to let go as Braylen stares up at them.

"Well, I hope you don't mind your husband being unemployed for a while," he says when they finally part.

She takes his face in her hands. "Malcolm, you just passed up the opportunity of a lifetime. You're sacrificing your career."

"No, I learned that my career wasn't worth the sacrifices I was making for it. You and Braylen are what matters most to me. I'm only sorry that it took me so long to recognize that. I thought providing for my family meant being successful and making a lot of money. I thought climbing to the top of the corporate ladder solved our problems.

"It didn't – it added to them. Providing for your family means meeting their emotional needs, too. I have to be *with* my family to do that. I can't do that while chained to a desk at work."

"I don't want you to regret this, honey."

"I don't want to regret not doing it. You have always supported me. You didn't demand that I make this decision. You left the choice to me, and now I've made it."

She looks like she wants to cry. Malcolm lowers his head and kisses her. It's the start of a new chapter. He has no income now, so they will need to rely on their savings until he can find something new. That should be terrifying, but at least they will face those challenges together as a family.

Chapter Sixty-Nine

WYATT HUFFMAN

Wyatt overheard more of the conversation than he should have. Sure, there is no real expectation of privacy in a hospital foyer, but it still wasn't meant for others to hear. That's why Klaus Eberhardt pulled Malcolm away. It's also why Wyatt positioned himself within earshot. Something inside pushed him to eavesdrop on their conversation. Now, he's glad he did.

The CEO of Heilung is the villain Wyatt thought the man would be in this story – a cross between Gordon Gekko from *Wall Street* and Scrooge McDuck with his giant cartoon vault full of money. He may not be a complete tyrant, but his focus on the bottom line undoubtedly makes him a cold-blooded and ruthless businessman. Malcolm is a good man, too good to be the cutthroat executive Klaus would want in that position. Accepting the offer to become chief marketing officer would have been setting himself up for failure. The right choice was made. Malcolm may have gotten the promotion he covets, but it would have cost him everything – his family, his happiness, and even part of his soul.

It's not the happy ending Wyatt wanted. In choosing his family over his job, the man is now unemployed. Sometimes, things happen that way. The best path forward is the tortured one that comes at a steep price. Or does it?

"That man is insufferable," Stowe says, walking over to Wyatt with a sour puss on her face.

"Which man?"

"Keith Meadows. He's a real piece of work."

"Yeah. I don't miss working with the…."

Wyatt's voice trails off, and Stowe waves her hand in front of his eyes to regain his attention. "What's wrong?"

"Malcolm just quit his job."

"Ah, that's what that was about. I thought I caught a glimpse of the Heilung CEO storming out of the hospital like an angry boy taking his bat and ball and going home."

"Yeah, there was some drama. Klaus offered him a promotion to chief marketing officer for the whole company instead of just North America. Malcolm politely declined and resigned."

"Wow. Janelle must be thrilled. I spoke to her on the plane for a bit. His not being home enough to spend time with Braylen was the most contentious part of their marriage."

"Except he's unemployed now."

"For how long? After this, he'll find something else in a snap."

"Yeah…and I think we can help that along," Wyatt says, scanning the crowd still milling around the foyer.

"What do you have in mind?" Stowe asks, trying to figure out who he is looking for.

"I'm going to play Santa and see if I can make some Christmas magic of my own. Do me a favor? Find MacKenzie and keep her close by."

"Sure. Why?" Stowe asks.

"Because I'm starting to understand the point of this whole journey."

Stowe cocks her head. "That makes one of us. Are you going to clue me in?"

"After. We need to put this in motion before everyone leaves."

Stowe says something, but Wyatt doesn't hear her. He is locked on to Cliff, who struck up a conversation with a pair of doctors at the far end of the foyer. This has become a personal mission now. Wyatt walks over with a purpose and taps Cliff on the arm to get his attention.

"I'm sorry to interrupt. Will you excuse us, please?" Wyatt asks, encouraging Cliff to follow him before stopping a few steps away. "Sorry for that. This is important."

"No problem, Wyatt. This was a hell of a thing that just happened. It's a real Christmas miracle. What's on your mind?"

"The hope that you can help me perform another one."

The request causes Cliff to recoil slightly with his eyebrows raised. "Uh, sure, if I can."

"The company you are starting up here in the States – the one you were telling me about on the plane. How close is it to being operational?"

"We're planning on starting some operations in the new year. We have some key roles we still need to fill before we can really start rolling."

Wyatt nods slowly. "I don't suppose one of them is public relations."

Cliff sighs. "That's the biggest hole right now. There are a lot of qualified candidates, but they are all stuffy corporate types who don't get what we're trying to do. This is a different monster. We need someone with heart and can't seem to find the right person for the job."

"I may have the person you're looking for if you're interested in having an impromptu interview on very short notice."

"It'd be stupid of me not to vet anyone at this point," Cliff admits, his eyes lighting up. "Who do you have in mind?"

Chapter Seventy

FORMER SVP MALCOLM CHAPMAN

It will take Malcolm a while to get comfortable with what just happened. He's at peace with the decision, but he has never been out of work for an extended period. He isn't relishing that prospect now. Climbing the ladder meant having a firm grasp on the next rung before moving skyward.

It's going to mean making some difficult financial decisions. The move back to the U.S. will be expensive. They will need to find a new place to live, buy furniture…everything that comes with picking up and establishing a home base in a new community.

At least he and Janelle will be doing it together. That's the most important part. If there is any part of this he is comfortable with, it's the reason he made that decision. In the nick of time, Malcolm discovered the need to put his family first.

"Are you getting ready to leave?" Wyatt says after walking over with the State Department guy they met in Morocco.

"Yeah, our work here is done," Malcolm says, looking at his wife and son. "It's time to find a hotel and get a good night's sleep before booking a flight home. We've decided to spend Christmas in the U.S. with our families."

"That's awesome! I'm happy for the three of you. Where is home?" Wyatt asks as Stowe and MacKenzie join their little gaggle.

"Northern Virginia," Janelle says.

Wyatt smiles. "That's what I thought."

Malcolm and Janelle exchange looks. Malcolm beats her to the punch. "I'm sorry, I don't understand."

"Do you remember Cliff Sutton?"

"Of course. You were on the plane with us."

"I was stationed with the State Department in Morocco," he confirms. "Now, I'm starting a new chapter in my life. I have teamed up with a few others in a startup company that operates much like a franchise to bring important services like water purification and agricultural processing to the developing world. It will create local jobs by leveraging the skills and work ethics of indigenous people in a non-exploitive way, allowing them to earn a living while staying closer to their families. It's not a purely profit-driven enterprise, so they will keep much of what they earn and the small percentage we take will be used for paying our employees and helping with future expansion."

"That sounds amazing," Malcolm says.

"We wish you the best of luck on that endeavor," Janelle adds.

"Thank you. The thing is, we are having problems finding the right man to run our public relations team. A little birdie told me that you might be available."

Malcolm can't hide the surprised look on his face. "As it turns out, I am."

"Good to hear. In that case, I'm hoping you'll consider the position."

Wyatt is smirking as Malcolm presses his lips together. He can feel Janelle tighten the grip on his arm in excitement. Maybe he won't be unemployed for long after all.

"Um…I might…where is it located?"

"McLean, Virginia."

MacKenzie's eyes grow wide as she gasps from a few feet away. "You're moving to Virginia?"

"Surprise," Cliff sings out as he turns to look at her.

"I don't know what to say," Malcolm stammers.

"Well, I'm a little partial, but I'm hoping you'll say yes. The salary isn't astronomical, and you'll need to put a small, dedicated team together, but it's pretty much a nine-to-five job outside of the occasional fundraiser."

"Do spouses get to go to the fundraisers?" Janelle asks.

"We're founding this company to be all about family and community. People are its mission, and that starts with treating our own right. Besides, I've always thought it was better to retain good people than constantly try to replace them. So, family involvement is highly encouraged, especially at fundraisers. This isn't a non-profit, nor will people see a sizable return on their investments. Without the tax breaks or promise of an insane ROI, it will be challenging work."

"Sounds like it."

"If you need to take some time to talk it over—"

"Yes, I'm very interested in accepting the position," Malcolm says, getting a supportive nod from Janelle.

"Excellent. I can arrange for you to meet the other executives after the holidays. I'm sure they aren't going to have any objections to welcoming you aboard, especially after what we just witnessed here today. We'll present a formal offer, and if it's to your liking, you can start as soon as the ink dries on the acceptance."

"Thank you, Cliff."

"No, thank you, Malcolm," he says as the two men shake hands. "I'm looking forward to having someone of your caliber on the team."

MacKenzie pulls Cliff away by the arm, likely wanting to know why he didn't tell her he was relocating to Virginia. Stowe and Wyatt retreat into the foyer to give them some space.

Malcolm is left believing in Christmas miracles. Ten minutes ago, he passed on a job he would have given almost anything to have after realizing it wasn't worth almost anything he already does. Now, a new chapter may be beginning with a company that is looking to make a difference in the world.

"Are you certain you're okay with this?" Malcolm asks his wife, taking her two hands in his.

"Are you?"

"I think it's an exciting opportunity. I can't remember the last time I worked anything resembling normal hours."

That's the downside that people don't consider when they start moaning about the number of zeroes at the end of executive salaries. Yes, their earnings can be excessive, but everyone in the top ranks of any company puts in a lot of hours. That applies to small businesses as well. A restaurant owner is practically married to their eatery and spends more time there than at home. With great power comes great responsibility, or so was said in *Spider-Man*.

"Me neither. You know, it's not the high-powered Fortune 500 job you wanted."

"No. It's better. One of the reasons I joined Heilung is that I wanted to help people. As it turns out, I was only helping the company pad its bottom line. This sounds like perfect work for me. And the best part is that I get to share it with you and Braylen."

Malcolm turns to hug his son. The only problem is he's not standing there anymore.

Chapter Seventy-One

COMMUNICATIONS DIRECTOR
MACKENZIE WALSH

She's not angry. Well, maybe a little. MacKenzie works in a world where information is the coin of the realm. Cliff has revealed himself as a hoarder of it. Not once on the trip in the car back to Marrakech did he mention moving to Virginia. Not a "Hey, we're going to be living in the same state" or a "How's the housing market in the D.C. metro area?" There was nothing to indicate that he was coming to live a stone's throw from her, and that is important news.

He was the one who got away. The fork in the road. The path not taken, and whatever other cliches MacKenzie's future biographer can conjure to explain what happened after that Christmas Day six years ago. Running into Cliff in Morocco has all the makings of a Greek tragedy. She reconnects with her true love an ocean away, knowing a second chance is still out of reach. Instead, she finds out in the most nonchalant way that it isn't.

Part of her is pissed about that, and the other part…it's oddly happy and optimistic. MacKenzie isn't sure what side of her Jekyll and Hyde persona he's seeing right now.

"Were you planning on telling me?" MacKenzie asks after pulling Cliff away.

"Telling you what?"

"That you're basing your new company in Northern Virginia?"

He shrugs. "I didn't think it was relevant."

"Are you *serious*?"

Cliff cocks his head. He isn't being coy or purposely deceitful. From the confused look on his face, MacKenzie can tell he isn't playing games with her. He legitimately doesn't know why she thinks it's important. Are all men this dense?

"Yeah, I'm serious. Just because we have a past doesn't automatically mean we have a future, Mac. In fact, I would put a truckload of money on us *not* having one. You made your choice six years ago."

"And have spent the time since wondering if I did the right thing," she fires back with urgency in her voice.

"MacKenzie, you work for the president of the United States. It'd be tough convincing people that you made the wrong choice. You have a great career."

"I do. I'm not denying that, but don't think for a moment that I haven't asked myself if it was worth the price. I loved you, Cliff. You were my world."

It's taken her a long time to say those words. It's something she should have said six years ago. She was blinded by her ambition to be a major player in national politics. She didn't want anything to distract her from realizing that dream. The problem is, as she learned later, that it wasn't necessarily an all-or-nothing option. Who's to say that she couldn't have had both?

"So much so that you declined my proposal and never called after."

MacKenzie closes her eyes and purses her lips. "I hurt you that day. I know I did. You were humiliated, and I had no idea if you ever wanted to talk to me again after that."

"And instead of finding out, you just ignored the problem. Or worse, left it to me to decide what to do."

"Yeah. I took the easy way out."

Mackenzie can't look at him. She doesn't want to see his eyes. If this is a chance to undo a mistake, she doesn't want to blow it.

"I didn't think you would admit that," Cliff says, his voice even and devoid of anger.

"One of the benefits of having a good therapist."

"Mac, it's been a hell of a day, and I really don't want to rehash the past. What do you want from me? Do you even know?"

She nods slowly, lifting her eyes to meet his. "I do. A second chance."

"I wouldn't even know where to start with that," he admits after a surprised look.

"From the beginning," she says, extending her hand. "My name is MacKenzie Walsh. I'm in my early thirties, never married, although I had a very serious relationship with a man I was madly in love with until life got in the way. I work long hours in a sometimes-thankless government job, but I'm ready for a meaningful relationship with the right person."

He takes her hand. "Okay. I admire your honesty. I'm Cliff Sutton. I am a soon-to-be former government lackey who worked for the State Department. Now, I'm teaming up with some good people to start a company that will try to make the world a little better place. I was also madly in love with a woman who I have spent years thinking chose her career over me, so I'm a little gun-shy about diving into something serious."

"I understand. The thing about baggage is sooner or later, you need to set it down. Are you open to having coffee sometime? Maybe we can both start putting our pasts behind us."

"I don't know," Cliff says, rubbing the back of his neck theatrically. "I have to be in Virginia pretty early tomorrow."

"That's funny," MacKenzie says in a tone that foreshadows her revelation. "I happen to have a private jet heading in that direction."

"Oh, a private jet? How fancy! Is it one of those small, Gulfstream types?"

"No, it's a *touch* bigger and features plenty of legroom. My job comes with the occasional perk."

"Well, I think I would be crazy not to agree to that," Cliff says, taking her hand in his. "You know, Miss Walsh, I haven't spent Christmas in the U.S. in a long time. Any suggestions on how I should spend it?"

"I am probably the wrong person to ask…Christmas hasn't been my thing for the last six years. Here's an idea, if you're up for it: Maybe it's something we can think about together. Maybe we can start by buying and decorating a tree with some carols on in the background."

Cliff smiles broadly. "I'd like that."

Chapter Seventy-Two

WYATT HUFFMAN

There are precious few reasons for Montana cattle ranchers to ever be philosophical. They are men of action. Tasks are drafted, plans are made, and then they are executed. There is no reason to muse about life or the order of the universe when there are animals to feed, a ranch to run, and a family to tend to. With those demands, who has time to reflect on the musings of what life is really about?

That's what Wyatt finds himself doing as he leans against the reception counter and stares out at the scene in the foyer. It's more than just a cataloging of the voyage that led him here. He's having an ah-ha moment that would only be complete with a cartoon light bulb over his head.

This journey with Santa never felt random. It appeared that way to almost everyone else, but there was a master plan behind it that included more than delivering Christmas wishes written in gold ink on red cards. It was more than Santa quietly arranging romantic escapades for him and Stowe. They were all pieces to a puzzle that Wyatt finally put together.

Santa could have gone anywhere from Finland. He chose Vienna, and not just because it's a great city filled with Christmas spirit and countless amazing markets. Santa chose Vienna and Karlsplatz because Janelle and Braylen Chapman were there. He didn't extend a random mother and child an invitation to travel with him. He needed them to come to the United States with him.

After gifting Braylen the clock, his mother couldn't say no. And how many kids today have an infatuation with analog clocks? It's not a common thing, so what are the odds that the next stop would eventually lead them to the bedside of a depressed widower in Italy who happened to have a room full of them? There is no way that's a coincidence.

Braylen's excitement breathed new life into a man who had given up the will to live. That story alone would be enough to warm hearts for years to come. With all the media coverage of his son handing the man his cherished clock from Santa, there is no way Malcolm wouldn't see that. What father wouldn't race to Italy to find out what is going on? With an executive from Heilung joining the trip, the stage was set. Of course, there was one more piece.

Wyatt thought that Morocco was all about MacKenzie. She was miserable up until the point when she met Cliff on the tarmac in Marrakech. Reintroducing an old flame into her life sounds like something Santa would do, but it's more than that. The man happens to be returning to the United States to form a startup in Malcolm and Janelle's home city – a new company that just happens to need marketing expertise. The odds of that are…incalculable.

Did Santa know that Malcolm would resign his position after this? Is there any way he could have known that? He may be able to see whether children are naughty or nice, but that doesn't mean he can see the future. Does it? Is there any way to know?

But there is no Santa Claus. It's a myth derived from a saint who has long since departed this Earth. No man can travel the world in a sleigh propelled by flying reindeer. No vehicle ever devised could carry the number of gifts he delivers. And since when can anyone safely slide down a chimney, assuming that a house even has one? It's preposterous for anyone other than a small child to believe.

Yet, here we are. Maybe Santa Claus does exist, just not in the way that people think he does. Every country has its own myths about him, and they may be equally wrong. Could it be that the truth is far simpler than that?

Wyatt witnessed a series of Christmas miracles today. A young boy got the medication he needed, and countless more will be helped because of the generosity of hundreds of thousands of others. Malcolm Chapman has a new job that will allow him to keep his family together. MacKenzie has a second chance at love with the one who got away. And he and Stowe are getting their chance, too.

It's all too perfect to be random. It's three-dimensional chess on a global scale designed to do one thing – rekindle the Christmas spirit of an entire planet. And, from the looks on the faces of the people in this children's hospital, he succeeded again.

Chapter Seventy-Three

STOWE BESSETTE

Nobody likes hospitals. If you are a patient at one, with the possible exception of childbirth, it's not because something good is happening. Children's hospitals are even more depressing. Facilities like the Gateway Children's Wellness Center are equipped and staffed to provide medical care to meet the unique needs of infants, children, and adolescents.

This hospital has departments ranging from pediatric oncology to cardiology, neurology, and orthopedics. It's not unlike St. Jude Children's Research Hospital in Memphis, only smaller and slightly less focused on researching pediatric diseases than treating them. Many of the kids in the foyer watching Santa and interacting with him afterward are cancer patients.

One of them comes up to Stowe. She's eight or nine years old, is clutching a white stuffed bear against her warm flannel clothes, and has no hair at all. Not even eyebrows. Chemotherapy may be life-saving, but it does have a nasty effect on the body.

"You're very pretty," she says, her voice soft and innocent.

Stowe squats to look at her at eye level. "Thank you, sweetie. So are you. What's your name?"

"Cynthia," she sings out. "My mommy named me after her best friend. She died a long time ago."

"That's a very pretty name. I'm Stowe. I'm named after a majestic mountain in Vermont."

"You have nice hair," Cynthia says, running her fingers through Stowe's black locks before rubbing her bald head. "I don't have hair anymore."

Stowe feels very ill-equipped to deal with this. She doesn't have children of her own or even nieces or nephews to dote on. Knowing the pain of losing parents is one thing, but how can she relate to a child who is fighting for her life before even having the chance to live it?

"What's your bear's name?"

"Marshmallow."

"Ohh, I like that name."

"He's my best friend," Cynthia says, holding the bear so Stowe can see its face. "He thinks I'm pretty."

Stowe slightly frowns until she sees Wyatt looking pensive near the reception desk. She points him out to Cynthia.

"Do you see that boy over there? He's handsome, isn't he?" she asks, getting a nod from the young girl. "He's my boyfriend. I almost lost him not long ago."

"Why?"

It wasn't a probing question someone asks to be nosy or one with an accusatory tone that sounds like she's questioning Stowe's sanity. That was how Mandy framed the question when she learned of the breakup last August. No, this was the innocent question out of the mouth of a curious child.

"Because I was mad at him and said some really mean things to him last summer."

"Why were you mad at him?"

That's a good question that Stowe has barely been able to answer herself. What was so important in that moment seems so small and petty now. It's hard to believe she was willing to give up on a man like Wyatt for something so inconsequential.

"Because I thought something we didn't agree on mattered more than it does."

"Are you better now?"

She stares at Wyatt, who is still leaning against the counter. "I hope so. Cynthia, what's on the outside isn't what makes someone beautiful. It's what's on the inside. Marshmallow doesn't love you because of how you look – he loves you because you take care of him. Someday, you're going to meet a boy who loves you for who you are. It doesn't matter what your hair looks like. He will see that you are beautiful in here," she says, touching her lightly on the heart.

"Really?"

"I guarantee it. That boy won't be perfect. You may even get really angry at him from time to time. But don't push him away like I almost did. When you find your one true love, hang onto him with both hands and never let go."

Cynthia beams from ear to ear before giving Stowe the biggest, most sincere hug she has ever received. She has to fight back her tears. Stowe is pulling for this kid. She's pulling for all of them.

A nurse escorts Cynthia to the elevator. She waves to the young girl as the door closes, and she gets one in return. For as long as she can remember, Stowe has always wanted to work in Washington. The government touches everyone's lives, and she wanted to be a part of that.

It's not all it's cracked up to be. Stowe has learned a lot, and one of those things is that she will never make an iota of difference in people's lives that the doctors, nurses, and staff of this hospital do. This is ground zero. This is where the differences are actually made – on the front line of life, not the marble halls of the Capitol Building. Maybe it's time to rethink her career choice.

Chapter Seventy-Four

FORMER SVP MALCOLM CHAPMAN

Harambe was a seventeen-year-old western lowland gorilla who made his home at the Cincinnati Zoo. In 2016, he was shot and killed after grabbing and dragging away a three-year-old boy who climbed into the enclosure and fell into the water. Fearing for the child's life, zoo officials made the controversial decision to shoot the gorilla.

The killing sparked outrage at the zoo and began an intense social media discussion about animal rights, parental responsibility in supervising their children, and safety protocols at the enclosure. They were all appropriate conversations to have in the wake of a tragedy. Then, the memes took over.

They began by mourning the gorilla and quickly morphed into humorously attributing various global events and mishaps to Harambe's "curse." Nothing escaped the memes' clutches, from political upheaval around the globe to sports losses to celebrity deaths. Malcolm studied the phenomenon because it was an interesting case study in internet culture. Harambe became a symbol of tumultuous events in the years that followed, showcasing how modern Internet culture can turn real-life events into viral phenomena. This may be its latest example.

That's the marketing side. What Malcolm learned through that example, and fatherhood in general, is that you can't take your eyes off your child for even a few seconds. It doesn't matter whether you are on a trip to the zoo or standing in the foyer of a Midwestern children's hospital. Unfortunately, that's what he's done, and Braylen wandered off and disappeared during his inattentiveness.

"Janelle? Where's Bray?

"He's right…oh, crap!" his wife exclaims, noticing that Braylen is no longer standing next to them. Panic sweeps across her face. At least they don't need to worry about him falling into a gorilla enclosure.

The Chapmans search the main foyer with their eyes and relax when they spot their son in the middle. He is walking toward the Tucker family, who look like they are getting ready to return to Antonne's room upstairs. Malcolm stops Janelle from rushing forward to collect Bray. He wants to see what happens next.

"Hi. I'm Braylen," they overhear him say.

"I'm Antonne. This is my twin sister, Alaya."

Malcolm can see that she is very protective of her twin brother. She clings to his shoulder, looking like a bouncer ready to pounce at a nightclub. Sibling rivalries are a thing, but not in this case. Not with these two.

"I want you to have this," Braylen says, setting the golden clock in his lap.

"That's so pretty!" Alaya shrieks.

Antonne traces his finger along the top of the clock and around its face. "Thank you. Is this the one Santa gave you?"

"No," Braylen says, shaking his head. "It wanted to be with its friends in Italy. Jacopo gave me this one because he said it wanted to come here. It's special."

"Why is it special?" Alaya asks.

"Jacopo said it's magic."

The girl shakes her head vigorously. "There's no such thing as a magic clock, silly!"

"You also said there was no such thing as Santa Claus," Antonne fires back at his twin. His sister frowns, unable to argue against that point.

"Jacopo said whoever owns this clock will understand the value of time and be filled with the desire to make the most of it."

"I'm sick," Antonne admits, lowering his eyes.

Malcolm presses his lips together. He isn't sure if Braylen understands what that means. This isn't a case of the sniffles. What Antonne has is life-threatening, and even with the Hemoexgen treatment, he will still need to be very careful.

"I know. I think you have a lot of time ahead of you. This clock will show you that."

Alaya hugs Braylen. Malcolm and Janelle's hearts melt. He slips his arm around his wife, and she rests her head on his arm. There is nothing purer than the innocence of children. Marvin nods in appreciation as his wife covers her heart with her hands and mouths, "Thank you."

Malcolm knows he's not perfect – far from it. No father is, but if this interaction has taught him anything, it's that he and Janelle are doing something right raising their son. Braylen says goodbye to the Tuckers and hugs his parents, who greet him fifteen feet away.

"Thank you for coming here with us, Daddy."

"I wouldn't want to be anywhere else. I'm very proud of you, Bray."

"He needed the clock more than I do. I already know the value of time."

Malcolm always thought his son's infatuation was strange. He can see a young boy liking superheroes or military action figures. He could even understand chemistry sets or bicycles. But clocks? Now he gets it. His son may be brighter and more worldly than Malcolm will ever be.

Janelle bends forward. "Well, Braylen, since you keep giving away your gifts, what do you want for Christmas?"

"Nothing. I'm saving my wish for next year. I already told Santa."

"What did you wish for?" Malcolm asks.

"A baby sister," he says, turning back to the family as his mother straightens. "Someone like Alaya."

Malcolm takes his wife's hands and looks at her with a devilish grin. "I think we should get to work on that right away."

Chapter Seventy-Five

COMMUNICATIONS DIRECTOR
MACKENZIE WALSH

MacKenzie slipped away when Cliff began his talk with Malcolm. She wanted to experience firsthand the joy Santa brings. Finding a spot away from the crowd in the center of the foyer, she watches him interact with the children, all of whom are in awe. He distributes gifts and poses for pictures. He has made this a memorable Christmas for all of them.

The media is pining to interview him. The rules about it are strict, and most of the reporters seem to be following them. But they are circling the area near the windows like vultures, just waiting for the green light. Normally, MacKenzie would try to steer Santa over to them to give the reporters what they want. Not this time. She has her own business with St. Nick.

As the final children get their gifts and pictures, she strides over to him and patiently waits for him to notice her standing there. It doesn't take long.

"MacKenzie! I trust that this turned out the way you hoped it would."

"In more ways than one," she says with a toothy smile. "Thank you for that."

"You know, I was very sad about your losing your Christmas spirit after what happened with the proposal. I know you used to love the season."

"I did. It was…there was so much hurt. Even Christmas decorations brought back bad memories."

"Life can be that way sometimes," Santa says with a nod. "I have always believed that the best way to overcome bad memories is to forge good ones. We can let our pasts destroy us, or we can push forward with those lessons learned and create something…magical."

Santa glances at Cliff, who is engaged in a warm conversation with a pediatric doctor. It's a none-too-subtle indication of what he's referring to. She didn't know her ex was in Morocco. Somehow, Santa did. He must have.

"How did you plan this?"

"What makes you think I did?"

"Because I know I didn't. I also know that there is no way this could have happened randomly. Nothing comes together this perfectly."

"MacKenzie, the size of the universe stretches the limits of human understanding. The observable universe contains an estimated two trillion galaxies and many trillions of stars and planets. There is only one Earth — a place where liquid water can exist on the surface. We have a stable climate, an atmosphere rich in nitrogen and oxygen, an ozone layer, and a magnetic field that protects life from harmful solar radiation. Sometimes, things do come together perfectly."

"There could be many Earths in our universe, and I might still believe the spirit of your analogy if it wasn't for the story you told me at the Karlsplatz Christmas Market in Vienna. You talked about the myth of Santa being created to get *adults* to do the right thing by bringing families into the fold."

"I did say that, yes."

"That's what you did here with the Chapmans, Santa. You can't tell me it wasn't part of your plan."

Santa grasps his hands behind his back and rocks on the balls of his feet. "What you should be thinking about, my dear MacKenzie, is what you plan to say to Marco when he calls."

"He's not talking to me right now. What makes you think—?"

Her phone rings in her pocket. MacKenzie fishes it out to see the caller ID is from the White House. Santa flashes her a knowing grin before walking away. How he knew the call was coming is another mystery for another time.

"Hello?"

"All right, let me get this out of the way first because it's going to taste nasty coming out of my mouth. You were right, I was wrong, and I'm sorry for ever having doubted you."

The White House chief of staff isn't a man known for his contrition. He works in the cauldron of national politics, where a simple apology can ripple through the sands of time. In all the years MacKenzie has known Marco Ramirez, she has never heard the word "sorry" escape his lips, even once in public or in private.

"Apology accepted." There's a long pause on the line. Too long. "Hello? Marco?"

"That's it? I expected you to spend the next few minutes rubbing my face in it like I'm a puppy who just had an accident on the living room carpet."

"Merry Christmas."

"Okay, that's the last thing I expected MacKenzie Walsh to ever say."

"A lot of things have changed over the past week, Marco. A lot of things."

"I can't wait to hear all about it. Other than offering a groveling apology, I did call to let you know that the president would like his plane back. See you in the office tomorrow?"

Cliff finishes his conversation with one of the doctors and walks over to MacKenzie. The way he looks at her…it almost stops her heart. She doesn't know if this feeling is going to last. There is no way to instantly discern if he is the same man she fell in love with long ago. They have both changed since he took a knee that Christmas. The question is whether they can rediscover the reasons they fell in love. There is only one way to find out.

"Actually, I'm going to take the holidays off. I haven't had a vacation since the president began his campaign, and there isn't anything going on that my staff can't handle."

"Okay…what are you going to do?"

She looks up at Cliff. "Make up for lost time. Merry Christmas, Marco."

"And a very Merry Christmas to you, MacKenzie."

Chapter Seventy-Six

STOWE BESSETTE

The show is over. Doctors and nurses slowly begin returning to their duties. Some reporters are still hanging around, hoping to get an interview or quote from Santa. It likely isn't going to happen. Unlike politicians on Capitol Hill, he doesn't run to the cameras every chance he gets.

Santa is finishing up a conversation with MacKenzie, who should be eternally grateful for the way this turned out. Despite the naysayers complaining about the tax dollars spent or her worrying that St. Nick was using them for an all-expense-paid sightseeing trip, it's the feel-good story of the year or maybe the decade. Stowe didn't think anything could trump what happened last Christmas.

This is the last opportunity to get some answers. She signals to Wyatt, who just finished talking with the Tucker family. He follows her over to Santa, who leads them to a corridor that exits into the parking garage. It's about the only part of the foyer that offers any privacy. He turns to face them.

"Uh, oh. This feels like an ambush."

"It's not an ambush," Stowe assures him, "but I…we…do want to talk to you about something."

"Ah, yes, of course. You want to know why I requested you and Wyatt to come along on this trip with me."

Stowe and Wyatt exchange a glance. "It's been on our minds."

Santa smiles. "The answer is simple: This trip is all about granting Christmas wishes."

"I haven't made a Christmas wish this year."

"You're right," Santa says, clasping his hands together. "And I'm still waiting to hear it. But you did make one a few years ago that I haven't been able to grant until now."

Stowe shakes her head slowly. "I don't understand."

"My dearest Stowe, when you found out about Bobby's infidelity, it was the darkest time in your life. Your grandparents were very supportive, but you still felt very alone. That Christmas, you made a wish to find someone dependable who would never do that to you.

"And Wyatt, your first love will always be Jessie, and you made a wish that you could find a true love like her who wouldn't let political perspectives get in the way of your relationship. Then you found each other."

"But they did get in the way, Santa," he argues.

"Did they?" he says, placing a hand on their shoulders. "It was a stressful summer. You had an argument. But was it the argument that drove you apart, or was it your own underlying fears about each other? Stowe, you thought Wyatt was going to turn into another Bobby and lashed out. Wyatt, her lashing out over a political dispute made you think she was turning into another Jessie."

The pair lowers their eyes. Facts are difficult to refute, but truth can be elusive. It's a fact that both of them were wounded following those relationships. The truth is that they hadn't fully gotten over the hurt when they first met.

It's why Stowe was so hostile to Wyatt. It was nothing he did. He reminded her of Bobby, and she resented that until she got to know him better. Wyatt was more open, but his break-up with Jessie wasn't as recent or raw. Nonetheless, both of them needed to reconcile with the past, and neither knew how. That was the real tragedy of what happened in August. It took meeting Santa Claus a second time to figure that out.

"So, you were determined to get us back together?"

"No, as I told you in my office, I don't do that kind of thing."

"Really?" Stowe asks. "A romantic carriage ride in Vienna, wine at a Tuscan villa, and a sunset camel trek through sand dunes before staring at the stars in a brilliant night sky? You gave us those assignments for a reason."

"Okay, yes, I am guilty of giving you opportunities to work through your problems while helping me grant some Christmas wishes to deserving people. It was a win-win. You love each other very much. As much as you tried to bury your feelings after you split, neither of you could."

"How could you know that?"

There's that twinkle in his eye again. "Santa knows."

"I'm sorry to interrupt, Santa," Aurielle says, pulling on his sleeve. "We really need to get back. Christmas Eve will be here before you know it."

Santa nods. "My duties await me back home. Stowe, Wyatt, it has been wonderful seeing you again. You must come to visit me again in Finland."

"We will."

There's a commotion as the sound of pounding feet and urgent shouts announces a swarm of reporters charging around the corner into the corridor. They all have press passes dangling around their necks, but she doesn't recognize any of them from her time working for Angela Pratt. If they are Washington beat reporters, they are junior ones.

"Where's Santa?" one of them asks.

"He's right...."

Wyatt turns to find both Santa and Aurielle gone. He checks down the passage that leads to the parking garage, and they aren't in it. They didn't head for the main entrance, either. For the second time in two years, Santa has disappeared into thin air.

"He went back home," Wyatt says, unable to fight the smile marching across his lips. "There is a lot to do between now and Christmas."

"We can catch him at the airport," one of the reporters says to another before they lead the herd to the doors. From the camaraderie and the Midwestern accents, they are definitely from local, not national, news outlets. It makes sense that they would want to make this a bigger story.

"Do you want to tell them?" Stowe asks, watching them hustle out of the corridor and turn toward the hospital's entrance.

"Nah. Why spoil the mystery? It will give them all something to write about for the next three months."

Chapter Seventy-Seven

WYATT HUFFMAN

There is nothing more to be done here. Santa is gone, and the children have begun retreating to their rooms. The press corps has dispersed, either content with the video they captured or on a fruitless mission to catch up to Santa. Some doctors, nurses, and administrative staff are still milling around before they return to their duties.

This afternoon was the climax of the kind of story authors and screenwriters dream about. Everyone gets their happy ending. Well, almost everyone. Sometimes, it's when two people need to say goodbye.

"So, mission accomplished," Stowe muses as they return to the far side of the hospital's foyer.

"Something like that."

She looks down. "I suppose you'll be heading back to Montana for the holidays."

Wyatt inhales and presses his lips together, surveying the room behind them. "I could, but then I'll have to face Ellie, and I'm just not ready to hear her say, 'I told you so' five thousand times. So…Nana and PopPop offered me a standing invitation to visit whenever I wanted. I was thinking of taking them up on it…assuming it's okay with their granddaughter."

Stowe's head pops up, and she stares at him through surprised eyes. "You want to spend Christmas with us?"

"I want to spend Christmas with *you*."

"I would love that, but won't your family be mad?"

It was a chance Wyatt needed to take because he wasn't ready to say goodbye. Those were the words he was hoping to hear. Everything between the two of them is new again, and he wasn't sure if the offer to spend the holiday with her would be warmly received.

"Christmas at the Huffman ranch lasts until New Year's Eve. I can be a few days late, especially since I was hoping you would come with me this time."

Stowe smiles brightly before a serious look overtakes her face. "Are you going to put me on a horse?"

"Actually, I was thinking about having my father purchase some camels. You looked so cute riding one."

Stowe smacks him in the chest. "I'm serious!"

"That depends — are you going to put me on skis?"

She laughs. "You know, your sister threatened to kill me and make it look like a skiing accident if I broke your heart again."

Santa may be the mastermind behind their finding each other again, but Ellie sounds like she gets an assist. His sister has always been protective of him and even his older brother in a mother-hen sort of way. That sounds like a threat she would issue.

"She'd do it, too," Wyatt confirms.

Wyatt pulls Stowe closer and is about to kiss her when MacKenzie barks their names from ten feet away. The moment passes as both of them turn to see her crossing the floor. Of all the lousy timing….

"I'm glad I caught you guys before you left," MacKenzie says as Cliff comes alongside her. "I just wanted to thank both of you…for everything. I know I didn't always make things easy on you, but words can't describe how much I appreciate what you've done – everything with Santa turned out…well, perfectly. You were right – you need to enjoy the journey as much as the destination."

MacKenzie steals a glance at Cliff, who smiles in return.

"This may be the first time I've ever seen your teeth," Wyatt muses. "You have a nice smile, Mac. I hope you have reason to use it more often."

"I hope so, too. This might be the first Christmas I've enjoyed in a long time," she confesses. "All right. What are you waiting for? Get on with it."

"What do you mean?"

MacKenzie points up at the sprig of mistletoe hanging above them in the doorway. There is already a history between Stowe and him where that weed is concerned. He lowers his head just as she grabs Wyatt by his coat and kisses him. It was the same slow, nice, firm, yet still tenuous kiss they shared in her nana's kitchen.

"I thought you hated mistletoe," Wyatt says when their lips finally part.

"I did, and then I realized it matters who you're standing under it with."

"That's more like it," MacKenzie says. "You two take care."

Cliff finds her hand and holds it as they leave the hospital. It's a year of seconds. Malcolm and Janelle get a second chance at their marriage, Mac and Cliff get a second chance at love, and Antonne gets a second chance at life. Stowe and Wyatt even got to share a second adventure with Santa. He wonders what a second chance will do for them.

"They actually make a cute couple. All's well that ends well," Wyatt says, frowning.

"That's true…so why do you look so sad?" Stowe asks.

"I'm not sad. I'm just figuring out how we're going to beat this next Christmas."

"I like the way you think. I guess we'll have to figure something out for the third installment. What is that in your pocket?"

"Oh! I almost forgot," Wyatt says, retrieving the sealed red envelope. "It's a card that Santa gave to me on Santa Sleigh One before we landed. He said to open it at the end of the day. I think it's our final assignment."

Stowe checks her watch. It's getting close to four p.m. For the nine-to-five office crowd, there is still an hour left in the workday. But this isn't a typical job, and government hours are never that static.

"I think it's close enough. See what it says."

Wyatt slides his finger to defeat the glue and pulls out the card. He reads it and laughs. After showing it to Stowe, she lets out a giggle of her own. She gives him a kiss and rests her head against his arm as they stare at the words written in gold lettering:

Live happily ever after.

Sequels are hard to write. I'm pretty certain I've mentioned that before. An author or screenwriter can rarely capture the magic of the first book or movie in the series. I loved the concept of this story, and I hope you enjoyed it, too. It is a little less Hallmark-y than the previous novel, but the messages are equally important.

This story afforded me the opportunity to write about some things that are important to me. The first is time. I began to understand long ago how important it is. I believe in a work-life balance. On September 11, 2001, I realized that a lot of people went to work that day with every expectation to return home. They didn't. Life is short, and each of us should live it to the fullest. Make every day count because tomorrow is promised to no one.

The second is children's cancer. I spent only a chapter on it with Stowe and Cynthia, but Antonne was originally going to be afflicted with that dreaded disease until I uncovered one named after the season and thought it was a better fit. I haven't been touched by this personally like so many families are, but I believe that children are precious, and my heart aches for them having to struggle to survive at such a tender age.

A good friend of mine works closely with a charity in Connecticut called Circle of Care. They provide emotional and financial assistance to children and families beginning on the day a parent hears the gut-wrenching diagnosis. They are there to support them through treatment and beyond with programs that meet the unique and challenging needs of pediatric cancer treatment. It is a fantastic organization filled with wonderful people, and I am happy to support their efforts.

Some of my latest novels, including *Banning Santa* and *The Dancing Life*, have involved a lot of traveling. Being able to leave the United States and experience cultures around the world is inspiring. I loved Iceland and Finland, and that's why they were featured in the first book of this series. Vienna, Florence, and Marrakech are firmly listed in the top ten cities I visited with my wife, and we had some great adventures in each of them.

On our trip to Vienna, which was not at Christmas, unfortunately, we went on a carriage ride much as it was described by Wyatt and Stowe. I have been to Machiavelli's estate outside of Florence and seen his desk. As a political science minor in my undergrad studies, I had a reaction to it similar to theirs. I don't subscribe to Machiavelli's tactics, but many still do. He was a fascinating character to study.

We've also been to Marrakech, Casablanca, and Merzouga. Morocco is an amazing place, and I highly recommend it to anyone who likes traveling. We drove over the Atlas Mountains on a three-day tour. The drive is every bit as nauseating as it was described, and the south side of the range is the worst part. The highlight was a ninety-minute camel ride over the Erg Chebbi dunes to a desert camp, much like the one Stowe and Wyatt took. The icing on the cake was that my wife got the "crazy camel."

I know these camps need to be licensed, but how it was done in the book is more fiction than fact. The rest was based on my experiences there. The dinner was amazing, and they did play music around a campfire. Our view of the stars ended up being masked by the brightest full moon I have ever seen. And yes, the tent is comfortable, and the mattress is…well, very firm.

Lastly is the importance of family. That closeness has eroded in American society over the decades. Whether it is with your spouse and children or your parents and extended family, don't let life get in the way of spending time with them.

The Santa Trilogy is meant to be a reminder of what should be important during the holiday season. Please take the lessons to heart. There is one more story left to tell.

Acknowledgments

I like to think the holidays are special. Whether you celebrate Christmas or not, thank you for spending some of your precious time reading _Delivering Santa_. I hope this novel warmed your heart and brought you some Christmas spirit. You have my undying gratitude for your support. And yes, I am writing this with a twinkle in my eye. I wish all of you a fantastic holiday season!

We are told not to judge a book by its cover, but everyone does. A huge thanks goes to Dave at JD&J Design for "delivering" a fantastic design. This trilogy is very cross-genre, and these stories aren't easy to reflect on a cover.

Mike Waitz of Sticks and Stones Editing is my go-to source for correcting my grammatical mistakes and consistency issues. He also likes pointing out the variations of names I use because I can't settle on one. I think I corrected all the Braylans to Braylen before submitting the manuscript this time. (I was informed after writing this that I missed three.) I appreciate your diligence in making this novel the best it could be.

To all my friends and family, you are the ones who round out this crazy life I have. I cannot express my gratitude for all your love and support.

My wife will say I saved the best for last, and that's her. I suppose that's true. Merry Christmas, my love, and you can pull all the decorations down to put up this year. Yes, we both know that isn't going to happen. Thank you for…well, being you.

Merry Christmas, everyone!

THE CHRISTMAS MAGIC CONTINUES. . .

Santa has gone missing from his Arctic Circle village.
People fear that his increased notoriety has opened him up to a
despicable attack against him and Christmas. Others think he
has had enough and is on vacation. Now, the world will turn to
Stowe and Wyatt to deliver one more Christmas miracle by…

Finding Santa

2025

About the Author

Mikael Carlson is the award-winning author of *The iCandidate* and the Michael Bennit Series of political dramas. He also wrote the Tierra Campos Series, Watchtower Thrillers, The Dancing Trilogy, and the dystopian America, Inc. Saga. *Delivering Santa* is his nineteenth novel.

A retired veteran of the Rhode Island Army National Guard and United States Army, he deployed twice to support military operations during the Global War on Terror. Mikael has served in the field artillery, infantry, and in support of special operations units during his active-duty career at Fort Bragg and in the Army National Guard.

A proud U.S. Army paratrooper, he conducted over fifty airborne operations following the completion of jump school at Fort Benning in 1998 and trained with the militaries of countless foreign nations. He never jumped out of Santa's sleigh, though. That aircraft would have been a great addition to his jump log.

Academically, Mikael earned a Master of Arts in American History and graduated with a B.S. in International Business from Marist College in 1996.

He was raised in New Milford, Connecticut, lives nearby Danbury, and always tries to stay on the nice list.

9 781944 972448